L. F.

D1219745

A Garland Series

Foundations of the Novel

Representative Early

Eighteenth-Century Fiction

A collection of 100 rare titles
reprinted in photo-facsimile in 71 volumes

Foundations of the Novel

compiled and edited by

Michael F. Shugrue

Secretary for English for the M.L.A.

with New Introductions for each volume by

Michael Shugrue, *City College of C.U.N.Y.*
Malcolm J. Bosse, *City College of C.U.N.Y.*
William Graves, *N.Y. Institute of Technology*
Josephine Grieder, *Rutgers University, Newark*

Hypolitus Earl of Douglas

by

Marie Catherine,
comtesse d'Aulnoy

The Island of Content

Anonymous

with a new introduction
for the Garland Edition by
Josephine Grieder

Garland Publishing, Inc., New York & London

1973

ALBRIGHT COLLEGE LIBRARY

The new introduction for the

Garland *Foundations of the Novel* Edition

is Copyright © 1973, by

Garland Publishing, Inc., New York & London

All Rights Reserved

Library of Congress Cataloging in Publication Data

Aulnoy, Marie Catherine (Jumelle de Berneville)
     comtesse d', d. 1705.
     Hypolitus Earl of Douglas.

     (Foundations of the novel)
     Facsim. reprints.
     Original t.p. of the 1st work reads: Hypolitus
Earl of Douglas. Containing some Memoirs of the Court
of Scotland; with the secret history of Mack-beth King
of Scotland. To which is added, The amours of Count
Schlick, Chancellor to the Emperor Sigismund, and a
young lady of quality: by Aeneas Sylvius, poet laureat,
and secretary to the same Emperor, afterwards Pope
Pious the Second. London, Printed for Ja. Woodward,
in St. Christopher's Churchyard in Threadneedle Street,
1708. Translation of Histoire d'Hypolite, comte de
Duglas.
     Original t.p. of the 2d work reads: The island of
content; or, A new paradise discover'd. In a letter
from Dr. Merryman of the same country, to Dr. Dullman
of Great Britain, by the author of The pleasures of a
single life. London, Printed: and sold by J. Baker,
at the Black Boy in Pater-Noster-Row. 1709.
     I. The pleasures of a single life, Author of.
II. Title. III. Title: The island of content.
IV. Series.
PZ3.A924Hy2 [PQ1711.A85]   843'.4   76-170516
ISBN 0-8240-0524-4 ·

Printed in the United States of America

843.4
A924h

148339

Introduction

In 1707 and 1708, the English reading public was virtually deluged by translations of the works of Mme d'Aulnoy. During the first year, the four-volume Diverting Works of the Countess D'Anois, *which included her memoirs, Spanish novels, letters, and fairy tales, the* Memoirs of the Court of England, *and* The History of the Earl of Warwick *were published. During the second,* The Secret Memoirs of the Duke and Dutchess of O::::, *as well as the novel here reprinted,* Hypolitus Earl of Douglas, *were issued. That the translations were not unacceptable literary fare is proved by the fact that all were soon reprinted at least once, and the* Diverting Works *had at least five editions between 1715 and 1737.*[1]

Remarkably little is known about Mme d'Aulnoy.[2] *The date of her birth appears to have been 1650; at sixteen she married either a count or a baron, much older than she; she was connected by birth to at least one lady of wit and charm at the French court. During the time of Charles II's marriage to Marie-Louise d'Orléans, she made a stay in Spain, accompanying her mother, who was entrusted with certain secret state negotiations. She died in 1705, leaving four daughters. Such a paucity of biographical information is all the more astonishing when one considers that her literary reputation in France was considerable and that it in fact*

5

earned her brief mention in the Dictionaries *of both Moreri and Bayle, the latter listing her works with the comment, "Ce sont autant de petits romans qui se sont fait lire."* [3]

This English translation, Hypolitus Earl of Douglas, *comes from the* Histoire d'Hypolite, comte de Duglas, *which first appeared in 1690 and up to 1864 was actually reprinted at least twenty-eight times. The reader who has inspected the title page should be disabused, however; neither the* Memoirs of the Court of Scotland *nor* The Amours of Count Schlick *is contained herein (the publisher issued them separately), and neither is by Mme d'Aulnoy anyway.*

In order to appreciate the merits and the faults of Mme d'Aulnoy's novel, it is necessary to situate it in its literary context. Henri Coulet, in his excellent study of the early French novel, points out that during the latter half of the seventeenth century, the novel as a "history" — best typified by Mme de Lafayette's La Princesse de Clèves — *supplanted the previously popular heroical romance.* [4] *This* roman-histoire *was characterized by a new effort to be more real, if not realistic: the time of its occurrence was relatively recent; the characters were not fabulous kings and warriors but private citizens (though always noble); the narration, linear and chronological, avoided abrupt temporal digressions; events and circumstances stayed within the probable; the heart and its sentiments formed the focus of interest; and the style, while dramatic, was not bombastic. About 1690, however, as Coulet qualifies, the novel tended to revert*

INTRODUCTION

to certain of the traits of the baroque heroical romance, particularly to the use of coincidence and exotic locales; but it did not lose the diction, decency, and dignity of the roman-histoire. *Hypolitus is an example of this hybrid form.*

Typically, for instance, Mme d'Aulnoy, even before she begins her real story, carefully establishes her historical context. Thus, she describes the meeting between Henry VIII and François I on the Field of the Cloth of Gold; she mentions Wolsey's machinations and describes Anne Boleyn's character; and she attributes the flight of the heroine's father to the persecution of Catholics after Henry VIII's divorce. Other historical details, like the political situation in the Mediterranean and the difficulties with pirates, are added as they contribute plausibility and color to the story.

There are, indeed, mind-boggling coincidences and improbabilities in the novel. How extraordinary that Hypolitus should capture a Turk who turns out to be none other than Julia's father, long believed dead; or that the hero should lodge in exactly the same room of the Calais inn where Julia scrawled her plaintive message on the window with a diamond; or that Lucilia, with whom Julia is staying in Italy, should never have heard the rumor of her friend's death, though her entire family in England knows of it. And most extraordinary of all, that final scene, in which the disguised Julia is brought to trial by her unknown husband Bedford and judged by her unrecognized lover and her father. Yet justification of such phenomena must be made on the

7

grounds of suspense and drama; and if the modern reader will willingly suspend disbelief, he will be that much more entertained.

Yet, other obstacles are probable rather than coincidental, caused as they are by some specific motivation on the part of the character involved. The anguished love of the young Hypolitus and Julia is promptly legitimized by the knowledge that they are not brother and sister; but Hypolitus' parents had been bound to secrecy by Julia's mother not to reveal her birth until she was of age. Julia's suspicions of her lover's inconstancy and her reluctant marriage to Bedford result from Lord and Lady Douglas' deliberate meddling with her private correspondence. Even the widespread rumor of her death in the convent is not improbable; the abbess is terrified at her own folly and the likely consequences of Bedford's anger should he learn of his wife's disappearance.

Julia herself is responsible for many of her own difficulties, for she is caught, as she well knows — and this self-knowledge makes her the best-drawn character in the novel — between her passionate love for Hypolitus and her obligations to duty and to virtue. Thus, unaware of her true identity, she bids farewell to Hypolitus before entering a nunnery: "severe Vertue, rigorous Duty, tender Passions, who have infused into my Heart such Sentiments as I ought and must disown, accept of this Sacrifice I make you, of all my Passions and Liberty, I am going to Bury my self for all the remainder of my Days; will not this be sufficient, to free

8

me from all sorts of Reproaches?" (p. 27). When she has married Bedford, she is harassed by "these desires of discharging ones Duty, and the violence of tearing from ones Heart an Inclination which now is become Criminal" (pp. 103-104). But she staunchly upholds her vows, disagreeable as they are. Visiting in secret the wounded Hypolitus, she declares this is her last farewell: "we must, Hypolitus, we must submit to this cruel necessity my Duty imposes upon us: Death shall always be more preferable with me, than a shameful Life" (p. 141). Nor will she think of leaving the convent in which Bedford has imprisoned her unless she directly receives a letter from her father annulling the marriage.

Justice must indeed be done to Julia's strength of character as she wrestles with love and duty, for love is presented as an all-consuming force that for good or evil determines one's destiny. Hypolitus, separated from Julia, looks as though "he had lately had some violent and long Disease; and truly can there be a more violent one than Love? Or can there be a more dangerous one? Because we are not sensible of the Danger at the Beginning of a Tender Passion, everything appears pleasing . . . the Poison slips insensibly into our Heart, and is the more dangerous, because we take it with delight; all our Senses conspire against us, and are as it were our Murderers" (p. 111). Nor does love benevolently protect the lovers against mishap: "their satisfaction was too great to last much longer, Fortune envious of the sweet enjoyments of Love, would needs disturb their Felicity" (p. 58). But as it scourges and torments its victims, it

9

also absolves them of guilt. Bedford, whose passion for Julia has driven him to so much cruelty, is at last pardoned and pitied by her, rather than scorned as the villain he has indeed been. The importunate old senator Alberti, on discovering that Julia loves Hypolitus, is "so far overwhelm'd with Love, Anger, Jealousie and Pain" (p. 234) that he dies, not an object of ridicule but of compassion.

How is one to judge Hypolitus Earl of Douglas *as a novel? The force that Mme d'Aulnoy attributes to love prevents, obviously, all character development, for rather than being an emotion which unfolds itself with those nuances that deserve examination, it is a passion that swiftly seizes and never dissipates until ended by death or consummation.[5] What one is obliged to admire or deprecate, therefore, is the skill with which the authoress contrives a plot which submits love to all possible trials, which offers the maximum opportunity for the display of sentiments – tenderness, despair, fortitude – and which at last accords to the lovers the reward they have so earnestly sought. Surely Mme d'Aulnoy has contrived such a plot; it is up to the reader to judge whether its effects justify its contrivance.*

A word should be said about the short work bound with Hypolitus. The Island of Content: or, A New Paradise Discover'd *is, of course, a utopia, and its mysterious author, Dr. Merryman, has like many utopian writers two goals in view: to propose an ideal society; and, by contrast, to condemn the evils of the*

10

existing one.[6] *The good doctor considers his description not only opportune but necessary, given England's present situation (one recalls the exhausting war with France and the bitter in-fighting between Whigs and Tories for political control in 1709), and he sends it to Dr. Dullman, "that you may be the better sensible how far the Pleasures of Peace and Dulcitude of Harmony, exceed the noisy Surprizes of uncertain War, and the grinning Malice of domestick Discord" (p. 3).*

A temperate climate and an abundance of natural wealth — plentiful potatoes, no lack of vines, and enormous spiders whose luxuriant webs clothe the populace — are of no small assistance in freeing the people of the island from the necessity of drudgery and the fear of poverty. Thus liberated, the citizens can attend to more pleasant pursuits, like decent conversation and seemly amusement. They also exist on a footing of perfect equality, the women enjoying the same prerogatives as the men; and when distinction is given, it is based on personal merit rather than family connections.

This utopia is not without religion and government; and it is to be suspected that Dr. Merryman is inspired by Tory principles when he describes their stable and centralized nature. "We are unanimous in our Devotion, have but little Preaching and that orthodox" (p. 20), he notes. The people hold to "one entire Opinion, which, without Scruple, is universal among us" (p. 21); they belong to the Church of Peace and call themselves the Brethren of Content. The clergymen are pious and

*learned; no "Apes, Monkeys, and Baboons" (p. 23)
mock the priesthood by imitating them. As to the
government, the country has prospered under a benevo-
lent hereditary monarchy, established by the initial
settlers of the island "because they had too lately
observ'd, [that] the miserable Confusions from whence
they had withdrawn, were all undisputably owing to the
Pride, Folly, and Madness of a stubborn, hot-headed
Senate, who pretended to have Share in the Government" (p. 25). The first king's name was, significantly,
Philodespot; and as each monarch has carefully followed
his principles, governing with wisdom and concern for
the common good and avoiding all attachment to
flatterers or ambitious upstarts, so the people have
always responded with loyalty and affection.*

*Unlike more subtle writers of utopias, Dr. Merryman
does not let the reader draw his own conclusions about
contemporary conditions from this ideal society. His
frequent initial phrase, "We have no," explicitly reminds
Dr. Dullman of the abuses and evils in his own country.
His charges are numerous and most frequently leveled at
the government, which deliberately corrupts the people
for its own ends. "We are a sober Nation, only for want
of a large Excise to make it the Interest of our
Government to connive at Drunkenness" (p. 7), he
boasts, and because the island has no brewers, "our
capital Cities are never govern'd by Lord Mayors and
Aldermen" (p. 8). Unlike the strict English laws which,
by forbidding Sunday amusement, drive the citizens to
taverns and coffee houses, their laws permit innocent*

12

INTRODUCTION

diversions after church, for "we think it but reasonable to tollerate what's harmless, since our Government gains nothing by the Sins and Vices of the People" (p. 18). Nor does he spare the British judicial system. The Island of Content has but one blindfolded judge before whom each citizen pleads his own cause; "we have no such Things as old musty Customs, Precedents, or ancient intricate Rules, lock'd up in a barbarous obsolete Language, to puzzle Justice, delay Judgment, and make Right a Difficulty" (p. 14).

But the decency, moderation, and unanimity of the islanders furnish the greatest contrast to the English, and in the longest passage of direct condemnation Dr. Merryman declares that in his homeland "we have no obscene Discourses, that begin with Bawdy, run into Blasphemy, and end with Religion; no wrangling about Government, or Disputes upon Matters which none of us understand; no factious Cabals, to propagate Sedition, or undermine the Church; no quarrelling about our Sanctity, to give our Adversary, the Devil the better End of the Staff; no politick Projects, to sell our Country's Welfare to the Avarice of our Superiours; no sinister Inventions, to make nineteen Parts of our Kingdom mere Slaves to the twentieth; no Party-Divisions, to occasion our Fools to contend about Shadows, whilst we lose our Substance. In short," he concludes with pride, "we are an amicable People, who, together and apart, study our King's Ease, the publick Safety, and our own Happiness" (p. 20).

How is such utopian harmony achieved on the Island

INTRODUCTION

of Content? "We suffer no Learning above Writing and Reading, to be taught among us; by which Means we preserve our Peace, prevent the Growth of Blockheads, and defend our ancient Constitution from all manner of Innovations" (p. 14). As with many utopias, it would appear that Dr. Merryman's island has bought its tranquillity at a dear price. But then, as one remembers the fantasies concerning climate and nature, perhaps the positive aspects of the island are to be considered as only so many chimeras; and what should remain prominent in the reader's mind is the doctor's condemnation of contemporary English society.

Josephine Grieder

NOTES

[1] *Bibliographical details on these English translations may be found in William Harlin McBurney's* A Check List of English Prose Fiction, 1700-1739 *(Cambridge, Mass.: Harvard University Press, 1960), pp. 12-16.*

[2] *The only biographical information about her comes from bits and snippets in literary biographical dictionaries; no extensive study of her life and works has been made, as far as I could determine. Even her name presents difficulties. The Library of Congress identifies her as Aulnoy, Marie Catherine Jumelle de Berneville, comtesse d'; the Bibliothèque Nationale records her as Aulnoy, Marie-Catherine Le Jumel de Barneville, baronne d'. The eighteenth-century English public knew her as Mme D'Anois, Dunois, D'Aunoy, and D'Aulnoy.*

[3] *Her literary reputation, in France and in England, rested chiefly upon her skillful fairy stories, little inferior to those of Perrault. The interpolated story "The Isle of Felicity" in* Hypolitus *was evidently an early attempt at the genre. Critics were less kind to her other works, finding them too distressing a mélange of fact and fiction.*

14

INTRODUCTION

[4] Le Roman jusqu'à la Révolution *(Paris: Armand Colin, 1967), pp. 208-215 and 286-291.*

[5] *Actually Leander, when he first meets Hypolitus, can speak off-handedly of women because he has never been in love; but when he once sees Lucilia, he too succumbs to passion's power.*

[6] *Exactly who is hiding behind "Dr. Merryman" is almost impossible to determine.* Howard W. Troyer, *in* Ned Ward of Grubstreet *(Cambridge, Mass.: Harvard University Press, 1946), refutes the idea of Ward's authorship. The Brithish Museum catalog attributes the pseudonym to Henry Playford. But the title page of this work specifically states that it is* "By the Author of *the Pleasures of a single Life," i.e., "the Pleasures of a Single Life, or, the Miseries of Matrimony," a poetical diatribe published by Hills in 1709 – and this work is listed by the BM as anonymous. To further confuse things, the catalog card for the poem in the New York Public Library enigmatically says that the Philadelphia 1763 edition attributes the work to Sir John Dillon. Dr. Merryman seems to have preserved his anonymity as successfully as Junius.*

Hypolitus Earl of Douglas

by

Marie Catherine,
comtesse d'Aulnoy

Bibliographical note:
This facsimile has been made from a copy in the Beinecke Library of Yale University (Hfc39 48jb)

HYPOLITUS Earl of *Douglas.*

Containing some

MEMOIRS

OF THE

Court of *SCOTLAND*;

WITH THE

Secret HISTORY

O F

MACK-BETH King of *Scotland.*

To which is added,

The AMOURS of Count *SCHLICK,*
Chancellor to the Emperor *Sigifmund,*
and a young Lady of Quality: By
Æneas Sylvius, Poet Laureat, and Secretary to the same Emperor, afterwards Pope *Pious the Second.*

LONDON:

Printed for *Ja. Woodward,* in St. *Christopher's Church-*
yard in *Threadneedle-street,* 1708.

THE
Epiftle Dedicatory
TO
Sir *CHARLES DUNCOMB* Knight, and Alderman of the City of *LONDON.*

SIR,

I Know it is no common Method, to chufe a Patron out of the City; but then it is as uncommon to find Men of fuch Generous Principles, as Sir CHARLES DUNCOMB's there; who in his Encouragement of Letters, has in more, than one Inftance difcover'd a larger Soul, than any of the Other End of the Town Patrons, however exalted in Title and Dignity. It has always been the Fate of the Sons of Art to ftand in need of the Protection and Help of the Great and the Wealthy againft that grinding Want, which their neglect of the ufual ways of

thriving

The Epiſtle Dedicatory.

thriving naturally threw them into. But brib'd *by a fooliſh, and very falacious Hope, the Mo-dern Authors have ſacrific'd to Idols, that* had Eyes and ſee not, and Ears and hear not: *Titular Deities, that had not Senſe or Gratitude enough to reward the Flattery, they were fond of; The Incenſe was grateful to them, but they had not Soul enough to be at the tri-fling Expence. Their Pride, tho' obvious and inſolent, being grounded on meer Vanity, and empty Title, or full Baggs, never cou'd exert it ſelf into a* Generous *or noble Action. Thus have I known a* Piper *receive Three Hundred Guineas for a Preſent, when the dignify'd Man of Let-ters has been put off with a Complement, for a Book worth all the* Pipers *in* Chriſtendom.

'Tis true, *there is no Vice, nor Folly that cannot boaſt a particular Intereſt in theſe Gen-tlemen, on thoſe they are ridiculouſly Profuſe, but none of them*

Were ever ſo expenſive yet,
To keep a Creature meerly for its Wit.

As the Ingenious Mr. Prior *ſays of one of the Patrons of the* Court End *of the Town, that was in the formoſt Claſſe of Wit : But for Arts, for the Support and Encouragement of Men of Science and Learning, they know nothing of it.*

In *ſo many Ages ſince Learning made a Figure in the World, we find not above Two Courtiers intereſting themſelves in their Protection :* Me-cenas *and* Richelieu *are the only Names of*
Figure

The Epiftle Dedicatory.

Figure that have known the true Reafons of Po-
lity in the flourishing of thofe Arts, which more
immediately polifh'd and refin'd the Manners of
the People. A trifling Prefent is the Extent
of the Bounty of our Contemporary Patrons,
which they give not to the Merit of the Performance, but to the Favour and Intereft of the
Author, with himfelf, or his Friends or Acquaintance. They ufe Poets and Authors like
Common Whores, juft pay them the Mercenary
Price of the Proftitution of their Pen, and as
foon as the fordid Pleafure is over, ne'er think
more on them.

While Arts and Sciences are thus neglected
by thofe, whom great Titles and great Intereft
qualify for Patrons ; and while the Fidlers
Fingers, and Dancers Heels, have more Power
with, and Favour from the Great Ones, than
the Poets Heads; it is but natural for the
Children of Providence, to feek a Soil more
grateful to the Tillers Care, where their
Art and Induftry will not be loft, but meet a
Produce equal to their Merits and Endeavours.
But where is that fortunate Climate ? Where,
in fo degenerate an Age, are Men of fuch
Generous and Public Spirited Principles to be
found ? Tho' the Anfwer may feem a Paradox,
yet I dare affirm, with that Boldnefs which Truth
will warrant, that it is in the City, among the
Gentlemen that Trade : For among them I have
known Men of Generous Spirits, not fou'r'd by
Age or Avarice, over-weening Pride, or fubtil
Ignorance ; but animated with Souls more Ca-
pacious

The Epiſtle Dedicatory.

pacious of true Glory, than the Vanity of Titles can inſpire.

There is no Station deſerves our Praiſe ſo
much, or our Court, as that of the TRADE,
which is a perpetual Benefactor to our Country.
For who but the Traders bring in the Nerve of
War, and Foundation of Power, MONEY?
by which we now make ſo glorious a Figure in
the World ; they ſet the Poor to Work, and
circulate the Coin round the Nation, like
Vital Blood, to give it Life and Vigour in all its
Parts. Alfred, one of our greateſt and wiſeſt
Kings, for this Reaſon made a Law, That
e'ery Merchant, whoſe Ships paſt the Seas but
Thrice, ſhou'd be equal to a Thane or Baron of
a Town ; which was indeed to give Titular
Dignities to real Merit, and Public Service.

It has been objected, —— How can the City,
which is the Scene of Avarice and Buſineſs,
where every one is employ'd in raiſing or encreaſing his Fortune, and diving into the Miſteries
of Stock-jobbing, &c. have any Leaſure or Soul
to mind the Politer Studies ; and having by
Conſequence no Acquaintance with them, how
ſhou'd they encourage their Profeſſors? The
ſame Queſtions may juſtly be put to the other
End of the Town, Avarice, and the making
or encreaſing Fortunes ; but theſe in the City
are of leſs Extent, leſs Prejudice, and leſs In-
veteracy: The one gets Riches by encreaſing the
Public Wealth ; the other by decreaſing of it.
Next, let the Idolators of Titles ſhew me ever
a Greſham or Sutton among them. Every
Part

The Epiftle Dedicatory.

Part about the City has lafting Monuments of Public Provifions for the Unfortunate ; and Grefham's Lectures were, in the Defign, more for the advancing Learning, and fpreading Knowledge, than ever yet was done by our Titulado's for Five Hundred Years.

If Grefham's *Example will not be fuffic*'*ent, let us go to Antiquity, and there we fhall find* Athens, *a City as bufy, and as much devoted to Trade as any in the World, which yet was the greateft Nurfery of Arts : For* Athens *had her Mifers, Money-Broakers, Ufurers and the like in Abundance, as is evident from* Ariftophanes, Menander, *&c. yet this bufy, trading, avaritious City, did more for the Encouragement of Arts, and brought them to a greater Perfection, than all the Monarchs and Titular Noblemen of all other Nations put together, ev'n more than* Rome *it felf under all the Indulgence of* Auguftus. Athens *indeed was the Emporium of Arts, as well as Trade ; and Merchants, Tradefmen, Philofophers, Poets, Painters, Sculptors, Mathematicians, &c. contributed an equal fhare to that Glory, which has fo long outliv'd the City it felf.*

If we come to the Revival of Arts, we find it in a trading City ; For Florence, *in the Time of, and infpir'd by the great Trader* Lorenzo di Medici, *made the neareft Approaches to the Glory of* Athens *of any, when it gave us* Michael Angelo, *and divers others in all* Arts *and* Sciences, *little inferiour to the Ancients.*

Thus,

The Epiftle Dedicatory.

Thus, Sir, I have, from Reafon and Example, made it out, That Trade, and the Encouragement of Arts, are fo far from being incompatible, that I have fhew'n Arts never to have been more flourifhing, than in Trading Cities. Why they fhou'd not therefore be fo in London *I can fee no Reafon, while Sir* CHARLES DUNCOMB *is alive to promote fo Noble an End, and fo Glorious for the City.*

I cou'd here, Sir, Inftance the feveral Acts of your Generofity, and thofe Benefits you defign'd, had you not been prevented by the Folly of fome, and Ingratitude of others ; but refolving to prefent you with an Epiftle quite contrary to thofe that are addrefs'd to the Gentlemen of the other End of the Town, I fhall delay what I have to fay on that Head to a fitter Opportunity, when I can't be fufpected of facrificing more to my own Hopes, than your Merit.

I fhall therefore only offer my felf, and my Book to your Protection : If this can contribute to the Diverfion of your leafure Hours, I have the chief Aim of my Wifhes, Who am,

S I R,

Your moft humble Servant.

THE

THE
HISTORY
OF
Hypolitus E. of *Douglass.*

Nder the Reign of *Henry* VII. King of *England,* *George de Neville* Earl of *Burgen,* had the misfortune to be suspected of having had a hand in the Conspiracy of *Edmund Profe:* He was taken up and Committed to the *Tower*; but being found Innocent, was discharged out of his Prison. Being sensible of his Innocence, and how ill he had deserv'd so harsh a Treatment, he might, without in in the least imparing his Honour, have quitted the King's Service, and was enclin'd to pass the remainder of his days in Tranquility in *France*, but wanting a plausible pretext to encompass that end for himself, he resolved nevertheless to have *Roger* Earl of *Warwick,* his Brother's Son, educated in that Kingdom, he being made his Guardian by the said Earl lately deceased.

'Twas not long before a favourable opportunity of sending him thither offering it self, he thought fit to delay his Resolution. *Henry* VIII. by this time being mounted on the Throne of *England,*

B   had

had a Sifter named *Mary,* a Lady of an exqüifite
Beauty, and defired in Marriage by feveral Soveraign Princes ; but King *Henry,* not defirous to fee
her Married, had refufed their Propofals, till the
Duke of *Longueville* being taken Prifoner by *Henry*
in the Battel of *Efperias,* he propofed to the *Eng-
lijh* Court a Marriage betwixt the Princefs *Mary,*
and King *Lewis* XII. of *France.*

The King of *England* received his Propofition
with fingular marks of Satisfaction ; and the *French*
King Charm'd with the Portraiture of this lovely
Princefs, immediately fent the General of *Norman-
dy* into *England,* who concluded both the Marriage
and a Peace in fourteen Days, and conducted the
Princefs to *Bologne.*

Before her departure from *London,* the Earl of
Burgen prevail'd with her to take along with her
the Earl of *Warwick* in the Quality of one of her
Pages of Honour, who, notwithftanding he was then
not above Eleven years old, was much refpected at
that Court. The *French* King fent the Duke of
Angouleme to receive the Princefs and to marry her
by Proxy ; and this great Lord, who was a very
compleat and handfom Perfon, difcharged his Commiffion with fo much Gallantry and Politenefs, that
the young Princefs was Charm'd with his Perfon,
and fecretly bemoan'd her Fate, in that Heaven
had not been pleafed to beftow fo aimiable a Perfon
upon her for a Husband. He on the other hand
began to be fo far fenfible of the effects of her
Beauty and Charms, that he foon found the fame
flame to break out in his Breaft, which already
burnt in hers ; and he would certainly have pufh'd
on his Paffion and amorous Adventure to a higher
pitch, had it not bin for the prudent advice of
Mr. *Duprat :* This Gentleman try'd all means to
diffwade him from it upon the motives of Intereft
and Prudence ; but finding the Duke not to give
ear

ear to them, (being two far gone to be recall'd
by his Perfwafions) he difclofed to him the fecret
Correfpondence betwixt this new Queen and the
Earl of *Suffolk*, and that was fufficient to cure him
of his Paffion.

The King met the Queen at *Abeville*, where
the Nuptials were celebrated with the utmoft
Magnificence ; but the King died in fix years after
his return to *Paris*, at his Pallace of *Tournelles*.
The Queen Relict declaring fhe was not big with
Child, and the Duke of *Angouleme* being Pro-
claim'd King under the name of *Francis*, She with
his confent married the Earl of *Suffolk*, and foon
after return'd into *England*.

The Earl of *Warwick* remain'd in *France* at his
Uncles defire, where the King admitted him into
his Court, in the fame quality he had ferved in to
Queen *Mary*, and he attended that King in his
Journey , when the two Kings of *England* and
France were to have an Interview betwixt *Ardres*
and *Guines*. They were without all contradiction
the two moft Accomplifh'd and moft Gallant Princes in the World, and their Court being the moft
magnificent that could well be feen, they fpent
feveral days in Courfes and Turnements in honour
of the Ladies; and there being a vaft Concourfe
of People of the greateft Quality there, to par-
take and be Eye-witneffes of the Interview and
the Diverfions of thefe two great Monarchs, the
Plain betwixt *Ardres* and *Guines*, got the Name of
The Plain of the Golden Cloath.

Amongft a great number of other Ladies there
prefent, the Countefs *de Lorge* had the fatisfaction
to fee her Daughter *Madamoifelle de Montgomery*
admired and extoll'd above all the other Ladies
that affifted at thefe folemnities. The Earl of
Warwick, who was then not above fifteen years of
Age, was charm'd to fuch a degree with this very
Lady,

Lady, that he thought he fhould have died for
Grief, when the Earl of *Burgen* told him, That
the King had ordred him to recondu&t him back
into *England*, and that he was going to return the
King of *France* thanks for the many Favours he
had bin pleafed to fhew him.   Not daring to dif-
obey King *Henry's* Order, or his Uncle's pleafure,
with the greateft diffatisfaction imaginable he faw
himfelf under a neceffity of following the intentions of his fuperiors, without fo much as declaring his Paffion to her who was the caufe of it:
Thus he embarqued for *England*, but carried a-
long with him fo violent and tender an impref-
fion of the Charms of *Madamoifelle Montgomery*,
that he bid adieu to all Delights and Pleafures,
fince the time he had left her behind him.

Thefe two Great Princes parted fo well fatif-
fied with one another, that nothing was talk'd of
in all places but their infeparable Union, and with
what magnificence they had appear'd at this Interview.   Among the *Englifh* Lords the Duke of
Buckingham had outdone all the reft in fplendour,
but Cardinal *Woolfey*, the King's Favourite, underftanding that that Duke, before his departure
from *London*, had fpoken againft the King's Journey as ufelefs and too chargeable to the Publick,
he refolved to take this opportunity to procure
his Ruin, out of a motive of felf Intereft, which
he found means to effe&t : For no fooner was the
King come back out of *France*, but he told the
King the Duke had confpired againft his Perfon
and Government, whereupon King *Henry* ordred
him to come to Court to juftify his Condu&t, but
was no fooner come, than he faw himfelf and
the Earl of *Burgen* his Son-in-Law committed to
Prifon ; and the Cardinal had the fatisfaction to
fee his Head cut off upon a Scaffold, and the Earl
of *Burgen* was not difcharged till after feveral
Months

Months Imprifonment, and with the lofs of his
Eftate.

The£e violent Proceedings foon put the Earl in
mind, to fend the Earl of *Warwick* once more into
France, dreading the King's violent Temper, or
rather his blind Inclinations for the Cardinal: He
took the liberty to Write a Letter to King *Francis*,
defiring him to continue to honour his Nephew
with his Protection, which being granted him by
that King with all the teftimonies of affection
that could be, the young Earl, whofe Heart was
ftill intirely devoted to *Madamoifelle Montgomery*,
was tranfported with joy to meet her again at
Court, fhe being then Maid of Honour to the
Queen. All his applications were to her, he made
his Court to no body but to her, his perfeverance
flattered him, not without fome reafon, with
hopes of a tender return from that lovely Lady.

About that time Cardinal *Woolfey*, who bare a
fecret grudge to the Emperour, put all his wits
at work, to bring about a Marriage betwixt his
Mafter and Princefs *Margret* of *France*, but Love
overpower'd, if not quite overturn'd his Defign;
for the King of *England* fell defperately in Love
with Mrs. *Anna Bouleign*, Daughter to the Cheva-
lier *Rochford*. This young Lady attended Queen
Mary, when fhe was Married to King *Lewis* XII.
into *France*, in the Quality of Maid of Honour,
and after her return thence, her exquifite Beauty
join'd to a refined Wit, and fupported by a great
fhare of Cunning, captivated King *Henry* to that
degree, that he was not able to live without her;
and took no other delight than how to pleafe her;
fo that her conftant refufals of granting him that
Favour he fo much defired, made him refolve to
marry her. He omitted nothing he thought might
engage the Pope to diffolve his Marriage with
Queen *Catharine*, but finding him to perfift im-

movable in granting ſo unjuſt a demand, he was
ſo exaſperated thereat, that from that time he
reſolved upon the ruin of the Catholick Religion
in *England.*

King *Henry* went to *Bologne,* where being met
by King *Francis* I. and his Children, they there
gave one another freſh aſſurances of a moſt ſincere
Friendſhip. The trué motive of this Interview
was, that the King of *England* intended to make
his Complaints againſt the Pope to King *Francis* I.
in Perſor, hoping to prevail with him, to oblige
the Pope by their joynt Intereſt, to call a general
Council.

In the mean time the Earl of *Warwick* had, by
his own Merits and conſtant Addreſſes to *Mada-
moiſelle Montgomery,* who had now no other dependance but on the Queen (her Mother the
Countcſs *de Lorge* being dead) prevail'd ſo far
upon her, that ſhe conſented he ſhould ask her
in Marriage from the King and Queen, he being
now of Age, and independant from his Relations.
This being a very advantageous Match for him,
all his Friends ſhared his ſatisfaĉtion with him,
and having without much difficulty obtained from
their Majeſty's a preſent he valued above every
thing elſe, the Marriage was conſummated at
Calais with the utmoſt magnificence and entire ſatisfaĉtion of all Parties ; both Kings heap'd their
Favours upon this Illuſtrious Couple, who went
along with King *Henry* into *England:* The obſtacles that Prince met with in his Love for *Anna
Bouleign,* ſerving only to encreaſe his flame, he
Married her, and had her Crown'd at *Weſtminſter:*
But the Pope darting his Thunderbolt at him upon that account, he declared himſelf the ſupream
head of the Catholick Church, and perſecuted
thoſe that oppoſed it, without any diſtinĉtion of
Sex and Quality, not excepting even thoſe who
had

had bin his moſt intimate and faithful Friends before; nay, he carried his Reſentment ſo far, as
not to ſpare the Reliques; for he cauſed that of
S. *Thomas* of *Canterbury* to be burn'd among the
reſt. *Edward de Neville Courtray*, Marqueſs of
Exeter, and one of Cardinal *Poole*'s Brothers, animated with a juſt Zeal, repreſented to the King
the wrongs he did to the Church; but they paid
with their Heads for their Councel. The Earl of
Warwick being a near Kinſman to *Edward Neville*,
he was accuſed of having uttered ſome diſreſpect-
ful expreſſions; ſo that to avoid a ſhameful Death,
he was, notwithſtanding his Innocence, forced to
leave the Kingdom. The reſt of that Family dreading more the loſs of their Lives and their Eſtates,
than of their Souls and Honour, comply'd with
the Kings Commands, and prov'd the moſt violent Enemies that could be to the Earl of *Warwick*,
whoſe Eſtate was Confiſcated: But what moſt
ſenſibly touch'd him in all his Misfortunes was, to
ſee himſelf neceſſitated to leave behind him one
of the handſomeſt and moſt virtuous Wives in the
World; and a Daughter named *Julia*, not then
above two years old. Having recommended this
young Infant to his diſconſolated Lady, as the only Pledge of their Conjugal Loves, he told her,
He was reſolved to go to Venice, *That the Pope, the
Emperor and the* Venetians *being entred into a League
againſt* Solyman *the* Turkiſh *Emperor, 'twas there he
intended to gain Honour or elſe a glorious Death.*

The Counteſs of *Warwick* was ready to expire
for Grief at the intended departure of her Spouſe;
ſhe would not make uſe of the Power ſhe had over
him, to diſſwade him againſt it, becauſe the
hazard he muſt dayly be expos'd to if he ſtay'd in
England, appear'd moſt dreadful to her; beſides
being ſenſible that he had nothing to hope for in
his native Country, and being then of an Age,

which

which incites great Hearts to brave Actions : Her Virtue and Courage got the Afcendant over her Love.

He took Shipping, and in a little time got to *Venice* without any finifter Accident; and being received by their General *Capello* with all the marks of particular efteem (becaufe the Houfe of *Warwick* was very well known to him) he embark'd aboard him, in order to joyn the Pope's and *Spanifh* Gallies off of *Corfu*. It being refolved in a Council of War to attack the *Turks*, thefe were fo much furprized at the fight of the Confederate Fleet, that they did not know whether they had beft to fight or not, till the brave *Barbaroffa*, refolved to repair his difgrace in his Retreat from *Corfu*, advanced with his Squadron againft the Confederates.

The *Venetian* General *Capello* leading the Van, no fooner faw the *Turks* come in fight of him, but ftimulated by a noble Emulation, engaged the *Turks* fo furioufly, that they were forced to retire; and the Prince *Doria* feeing the advantage the *Venetians* had got over the Enemy, advanced with his Squadron ; but when every one thought he was ready to Engage, he gave the Signal to Retreat to *Cape Cal.*

All the other Admirals and Generals vex'd to the Heart at this unexpected difappointment, could not forbear to break out into violent Expreffions, and by this time the Wind beginning to flacken, the *Turks*, who perceived the Diforder in the Confederate Fleet, came out of the Gulph of *Prevefa* offering Battel to the Chriftians, who durft not venture upon an Engagement ; their Commanders being vex'd to the Soul, to fee fo fair an opportunity of vanquifhing the *Turks* out of their Hands. Above all the reft, *Capello* and the *Venetian* Patriarch *Grimaki*, animated with Shame and

and Anger, went aboard Prince *Doria*, urging him not to suffer that favourable opportunity Fortune presented to them to be snatch'd out of their Hands. *Come, Come, my Lord,* said the Brave *Venetian, Let us go where Honour calls us, let us Engage an Enemy half Beaten already, witness their flight, I only stay for your Orders to Engage :* At the same time the whole Fleet resounding with the joyful acclamations of the Soldiers and Seamen, who cried out, *A Battel, a Battel, Victory, Victory. Doria* almost confounded with Shame, ordred his Squadron to Advance towards the Enemy; but soon Retreated a second time, when every thing seem'd to have a fair prospect of Succefs.

In the mean time *Dragat Rais,* a famous *Turkish* Corfair, intercepted and engag'd two *Venetian* Gallies, left behind at a good distance from the rest; in one of which, as ill fortune would have it, was the Earl of *Warwick :* He perform'd such Actions as amazed the Christians, and terrified the *Turks* ; never did a Man make a braver Resistance; but was at last overcome by the great Numbers of the Enemy. Some of the *Venetians,* who saved themselves by swimming, having given notice of his Death to the Admirals and Generals, they, as well as every body else that knew him, were most sensibly afflicted at his Fate. Ill News commonly flys faster than good, and the Countefs of *Warwick,* who was in continual Pains for her beloved Spoufe, never neglecting any Opportunity of hearing of him, she soon was inform'd of the Lofs she had suffer'd.

The Virtuous Lady, now no more Miftrefs of her Paffion, found her felf so far over-whelm'd with Pain and Grief, that she soon perceiv'd her last Hour not to be far off; and her Inclinations being now altogether averse to the World, after such a Misfortune, there was nothing affected her

but

but that fhe was now to leave her dear *Julia.*
This lovely Infant, which was not much above
Two Years old, did already in its tender Infancy
give the moft promifing Hopes that could be expected: Her afflicted Mother holding her in her
Arms, and bathing her Face with her Tears, *O my
dear* Julia *! faid fhe, O my dear Child ! What will
be thy Deftiny? Who will be a Father to thee ? Who
will be inftead of thy Mother ? Thy Father is no more,
and thy Mother is at the point of Death. Alas ! I
muft leave thee, and that at a time when thou wilt
ftand much in need of me ; but I don't doubt, but that
Providence will take care to preferve thee againft all
Dangers thou beeft likely to be expos'd to, and 'tis to
her I deliver thee up.* At thefe Words, with her
Eyes lifted up towards Heaven, fhe implor'd its
Protection for this innocent Babe.

Whilft fhe was labouring under this heavy
Affliction, my Lord *Douglafs* and his Lady came to
give her a Vifit in the Country, where fhe had bin
ever fince fhe receiv'd the News of her Lord's
Death : They were both Perfons of fingular
Merit, and the beft Friends her late Husband and
fhe had in the World. The Houfe of *Montgomery*
being alfo nearly related to that of *Douglafs,* which
is one of the moft illuftrious Families of *Scotland* ;
but upon fome Difguft my Lord had left that
Kingdom, and fettled in *England,* where he
Married Madam *Bedford,* a very deferving Lady,
and both were at that time in great Efteem with
the King.

At firft fight of the Countefs of *Warwick,* they
were fo much afflicted at the doleful Condition
they found her in (being almoft reduc'd to the
laft extremity) that for fome time neither of
them was able to fpeak for Sighing, Sobs and
Tears, till at laft my Lord forcing himfelf to
fpeak, told her whatever he could think might
con-

conduce, if not to comfort her, at leaft to allay her Grief. She then laying her Hand to her Heart and fetching a deep Sigh, broke out into fuch doleful Complaints, as would have touch'd the moft unconcern'd Perfon in the World. ' Oh Sir, ' *faid fhe,* here it lies, my Recovery is impoflible, ' let us not lofe, I beg you, that little time I have ' left in this miferable Condition. It feems, Madam, ' *faid fhe, turning towards the Countefs of* Douglafs, ' as if GOD had brought you hither on purpofe ' to be aiding towards my Tranquility. I have ' one favour to beg of you, which if you grant ' me, I fhall dye without regret ; and I know you ' both to be of fo generous a Temper, and of fuch ' good Inclinations, that I dare promife my felf ' you will not refufe it. No certainly, Madam, ' *faid they,* you may be affur'd of us, and be ' fatisfied, that we fhall think nothing too much ' for your fatisfaction ; then pray difclofe your ' Mind, with an entire Confidence that you will be ' obey'd in whatever you fhall defire from us. Alas ! ' continu'd fhe, how is it poflible for me to make ' you fenfible of my acknowledgment, if you, ' according to my requeft and my hopes, will take ' this dear Infant of mine, and make it your own ; ' this poor Child is a going to lofe all in lofing ' me ; fhe will fall into her Uncles Hands, who, ' to carry favour at Court, will have her educated ' in the New Religion : I know you to be true ' zealous Catholicks, and therefore without re- ' flecting upon the Friendfhip you always bore to ' my Spoufe, and whereof you have given me fuch ' fignal Affurances juft now, this Confideration ' alone, of feeing her brought up in our own Re- ' ligion, makes me hope you will be very careful ' to conceal her true Extraction, and to fuffer her ' to go for one of your own Children : I have the ' Honour to be related to you, I confider that you

being

'being not born the King's Subject, you are not
' so easily expofed to his Violences, and therefore
' are the only Perfon into whofe Hands I can put
' this Treafure without fear of lofing it.

The Earl of *Douglafs* told her all that could be
expected from a generous Man, a near Relation,
and a true Friend : And the Countefs protefted to
her, that the little *Julia* fhould have a place in her
Heart, equal to what *Hypolitus* and *Lucilia* her
own Children had ; and that, if fhe made any
difference betwixt them, it fhould be to the advantage of *Julia.* 'I want Words fuitable to exprefs
' the Sentiments of my Heart, *return'd the Countefs*
' *of* Warwick ; for, what is it I am able to fay,
' that bears the leaft Proportion to fo infinite an
' Obligation! I accept, in behalf of my dear Child,
' the kind offers you make me, Madam, and I will
' deliver up to you fome Jewels I have,that they may
' ferve her in cafe of Neceffity. At the fame time I beg
' you to believe,that in putting 'em into your Hands,
' I miftruft not your Generofity, I am entirely fatis-
' fy'd, that in this regard, as well as in refpect to her
' Education, you will do every thing for her ; but
' fince I have 'em in my Power it won'd be a piece of
' injuftice not to let her enjoy what is her own.

She had no fooner fpoken thefe Words, but
taking a fmall Trunk from under her Bed, fhe deliver'd it to them with the Jewels in it, to the
Value of Six Thoufand *Guineas.* ' Here, *faid fhe*,
' this is all I have left out of a vaft Eftate, 'tis a
' flender Portion, *continu'd fhe*, for a young Woman
' of her Quality, and who perhaps will have a
' Heart fuitable to her Birth ; but as true Felicity
' is in Virtue, I hope fhe will never want Riches,
' Madam, being educated by you. For the reft,
' when fhe comes to an Age fit to keep a Secret,
' tell her, I conjure you, whofe Daughter fhe is,
' fhew her her Father's and my Picture, (which I
                                                    give

' give you) make her fenfible how tender we were
' of her, and, Madam, engage her to pay the
' fame Duty to our Memories, fhe would queftion-
' lefs have pay'd to our felves, had it not pleas'd
' God to take us away from her.

Having finifh'd thefe Words fhe embraced the
Child over and over, and then opening her Arms
to the Countefs of *Douglafs*, fhe bid them, all overwhelm'd with Tears, her laft Farewel. ' 'Tis time
' for you to go, *faid fhe*, *with a feeble Voice*, 'twill
' be late before you get to *London*, and tho' it be a
' great Comfort to me to fee you, 'tis time we
' fhould part ; I find my Strength to fail me, and
' am willing to beftow the fmall remainder, in
' making Preparations for my long Journey.

My Lord and my Lady*Douglafs* were fo far overwhelm'd with Grief, that they could do nothing
but fhed Tears, without being able to utter one
Word, or to leave her ; But when they were juft
ready to go, this dying Lady, who had always an
extraordinary prefence of Mind, told him, ' There
' was one thing more that much difturb'd her, that
' was, How fhe fhould fend her little Daughter to
' them, unknown to her Domefticks, who if they
' fhould know where fhe was, would perhaps give
' notice thereof to little *Julia's* Uncle. So, after
having paus'd a while, fhe caft her Eyes upon her
Chaplain, who being a Man capable of keeping a
Secret, fhe told them, ' She would leave that Part
' to his Care ; and that with the Affiftance of her
' Nurfe, who was a good Catholick, and in whom
' fhe could confide, it fhould be given out that
' fhe died fuddenly.

Every thing being thus concerted betwixt them,
they took their Farewel of this virtuous Lady ;
Grieved to the verySoul to be oblig'd to leave her
in fo weak a Condition, they once more told her
whatever they judg'd might fettle her Mind on

ac-

account of her dear Child, and for fear their affiduity might create fome Sufpition among her
Domefticks, they durft not fend very often to
know how fhe did; But in Five Days after they
receiv'd a Letter from the Chaplain notifying her
Death, and the Place whither he had privately
convey'd the Child. The Countefs of *Douglafs*
took it to her own Houfe, unperceiv'd to any of
her Family, becaufe fhe had a Daughter much of
the fame Age with *Julia*, which being at Nurfe in
the Country died not long before. When they
brought her into her Mother's Apartment (for fo
now we muft call my Lady *Douglafs*) *Hypolitus*
happned to be there, being then about Seven Years
old, and one of the faireft and wittieft Children
in the World ; he was mightily taken with his
little Sifter *Julia*, fo that *Lucilia*, who was then
Four Years old, was nothing to him in Comparifon of the youngeft ; he could fcarce ever be without her, and even in that tender Age, when
Nature acts without controul, his Inclinations
for her were fo ftrong, that all his care and affi-
duities were confin'd to *Julia*.

It muft be confefs'd fhe was charming to the
higheft Degree, and that to this Day never was a
Woman feen more accomplifh'd either in Body or
Mind. When fhe was fcarce Twelve Years of age
fhe might already pafs for the Wonder of her
Time : She was tall, attended with a noble Air,
yet full of Modefty and Sweetnefs, fhe had large
Black Eyes, which caft fuch a Luftre, that it was
not an eafie matter to look at them without being
ftruck to the Heart : She had a little Mouth, red
Lips, a glorious fet of Teeth : Her Complexion
was exceeding fair and bright, intermixt with
the moft lively red that can be conceiv'd ; and her
fair curl'd Hairs were no fmall addition to the reft
of her Charms. Moft *Englifh* Ladies have very
hand-

handfome Legs, Necks and Cheft ; in this point alfo *Julia* furpafs'd her Country Women : She walk'd fo finely, fhe danc'd with fo good a grace, fhe fung fo charmingly, that fhe gain'd the Hearts and Admiration of all that beheld her. *Hypolitus* was no lefs accomplifh'd in his Kind than *Julia* was in hers : His Shape, Head, Features, his Air, his noble Fiercenefs, his Deportment, his Cunning, his Wit, his Complaifance, all thefe, I fay Nature had beftow'd upon him with fo profufe a Hand, that no body that faw him could leave him, without retaining fome Inclinations for him. *Lucilia* had a great fhare of Wit and Pleafantnefs, and exceeded moft others fo far in Beauty, that fhe was fcarce inferior to any but her Sifter ; for both *Hypolitus* and fhe believ'd her to be their Sifter, and they liv'd as fuch in a perfect Union. But at laft *Hypolitus* began to be very Melancholy, and *Julia* very Penfive, they always lov'd to be together, and would always look for one another, and at meeting figh and fay little ; they would fpend whole Hours in cafting languifhing Looks at one another, and whilft they were indulging themfelves in this innocent Pleafure, they would fometimes colour, caft their Eyes to the Ground, and fall in a deep ftudy.

All this while the Day feem'd too fhort to them, to fatisfy their defire of feeing one another ; and at parting they were really fenfible, that all their fatisfaction really centred in being together. *Lucilia*, who was of a very pleafing Temper, would often banter them about it : ' Brother, *faid* ' *fhe to* Hypolitus, you love my Sifter better than ' me, I being the eldeft can't but be jealous of it ; ' but after all, I can't blame you for doing her ' juftice, and tho I love you entirely, yet it feems ' to me, as if fhe ftill lov'd you more than I do. ' Don't believe her Brother, *faid* Julia *blufhing*, we

' love

'love you both alike. And why dear Sifter,
· *reply'd* Hypolitus, why fhould you envy me the
' Pleafure to hear you fay that you love me? *Julia*
being netled at thefe Words, faid no more, but
fell into her former Penfivenefs. *Hypolitus* look'd
furpriz'd and full of Veneration ; and *Lucilia*, who
look'd at them with fome amazement, knew not
what to think of the matter.

One Day when the Earl of *Douglafs* hapned to
be with his Family at *Buckingham*, where he had
a fine Seat, it hapned that *Julia* with her Brother and Sifter, was walking on the fide of a Lake
or ftanding Water, in the midft whereof being
an artificial Ifle, fhe had a mind to go thither, to fee the Swans that ufed to build their
Nefts in or near that Ifle : She no fooner had
fpoken of it, but away runs *Hypolitus* to a place at
fome diftance thence, where he faw a fmall Boat
tied with a Rope to a Tree ; having loofened the
Cord, into the Boat he gets and Rows to his
Sifters, who immediately went into it ; but having
no Skill in managing the Boat, they got in among
the Bullrufhes, and the young Ladies diftracted
with fear, throwing themfelves both on one fide
overturn'd the Boat, fo that they were in great
danger of being drown'd ; *Lucilia* was fav'd by a
ftrange good Fortune ; and as for *Hypolitus*, he
might have got off well enough, had he bin by
himfelf ; but we always think our felves in danger,
if what we love is fo ; this made him think more
of his dear *Julia* than of himfelf ; his dexterity
and ftrength was fo far improv'd by his Tendernefs for *Julia*, that having got hold of her
Clothes, he would not let go his hold, till he
pulled her out of the Water to the Ifland, they
being not far off. But 'tis impoffible to exprefs
his Diftraction, when he faw her Eyes fhut, and
her Cheeks cover'd with a deadly Palenefs, with-
out

out either Senfe or Motion ; and it being natural
to imagine moft readily what we dread moft, he
thought no otherwife than that fhe had bin dead.
Oh ! Unfortunate I, cry'd he, *I am the Caufe of my
Sifters Death, fhe funk to the Bottom before I came to
her Affiftance* ; Julia, *my dear* Julia, *what will become of me ?* At thefe Words he clofed her in his
Arms, and laying his Lips to hers was ready to
expire there for grief ; but the natural heat of
his Sighs, and the Deluge of Tears, wherewith
he bathed her Face, foon revived her from a
Swoon, which ow'd its caufe to nothing but
fear.

She no fooner open'd her Eyes, but fixing them
on *Hypolitus,* who himfelf had fcarce recover'd his
right fenfes, *What makes you fo much concern'd,*
faid fhe, *dear Brother ? What makes you think me
worthy of your Concern to fuch a degree, when I my
felf fhould fcarce think my Life worth repining after ?
Oh ! dear Sifter,* reply'd he, Embracing her, *never
talk to me of parting, were you fenfible of what I felt
within me you would pity me.*

She was juft going to return an anfwer, when
they faw a Boat juft near them ; which my Lord
Douglas had fent to fetch them out of the Ifle :
For by good fortune he hapned to walk that way
when this Accident befel them ; and had he not
taken immediate care for *Lucilia,* fhe had infallibly bin drown'd : For tho' her Brother lov'd her
dearly, he was fo bufy about *Julia,* that he not fo
much as thought of *Lucilia.*

When they were got home, my Lord and my
Lady *Douglas* gave them a fharp Reprimand, becaufe they had thus expofed themfelves to need-
lefs danger ; But *Lucilia* reflecting upon the Danger fhe had fo lately efcaped, and her Brother's
indifferency to her, *Truly Hypolitus,* faid fhe, *it
feems I alone are to run all hazards, for when ever my*

C *Sifter*

Sifter is with us, fhe *is affur'd of your Care, but as for my felf I don't know what to expect.* Thefe words not only nettled the Brother and Sifter, but alfo ferved to open my Lord and my Lady *Douglas's* Eyes in reference to *Hypolitus's* Conduct upon this occafion, which afforded them fomewhat of vexation, having for a confiderable time paft, taken a refolution to marry *Hypolitus* with a Grand-daughter of *Guilefpie,* Lord High Chamberlain of *Scotland,* and Earl of *Argyle,* fhe was Heirefs to a vaft Eftate, and educated at *Edinborrough;* and then being befides this near Relations, my Lord *Douglas* was for fending *Hypolitus* into *Scotland* to his Miftrefs to gain her favour and approbation, intending at the fame time to make a Match betwixt *Julia* and the Earl of *Bedford,* who being of the fame Family with my Lady *Douglas,* was extreamly in Love with this young and lovely Lady.

My Lord and my Lady *Douglas* difcourfing the matter together, *What,* faid they, *is it poffible* Hypolitus *fhould love* Julia *otherwife than as a Brother does a Sifter !* and recalling to mind feveral paffages, which they had fcarce taken notice of before, they agreed that the Countefs of *Douglas* fhould talk to *Julia* about it, as if it were by accident. One Morning hapning to come into her Daughter's Bed-Chamber, fhe found *Hypolitus* upon his Knees at the Bed-fide of *Julia,* fhe being as yet in Bed ; *You are very early,* faid my Lady *Douglas* to her Son, with an angry tone, *you had better fpend your time in learning thofe things 'tis requifite you fhould know, than be continually in your Sifters Bed-chamber.* Hypolitus went away full of Grief, and my Lady afterward addrefling her felf to her Daughters, told them, *That, tho' it was their Duty to have a tendernefs for their Brother, and that fhe commanded them fo to do, by all the power fhe had*
over

over them, that neverthelefs now they were beyond the
age of Infancy, fhe thought not fit they fhould continue
the fame familiarity as before ; That, tho' fhe wifh'd
they might always live in a perfect good underftanding,
yet this did not hinder, but that they might act with
Circumfpection. Lucilia told her, *She was ready to*
obey, but *Lucilia* Blufh'd and fcarce durft lift up
her Eyes: And this Reprimand proved fuch an
addition to her former Melancholy, that whatever care fhe took to conceal it, it was eafily to
be perceived.

She fpent part of her day in the Clofet, and
towards the Evening, looking out of the Window, fhe faw the Earl of *Bedford* coming into the
Court ; His prefence was at all times difagreable
to her, but efpecially at this time , She thought
it would be infupportable to her : This
made her go down into the Garden, which being
very fpacious, with a fmall Wood at one end of
it, fhe retired thither, intending to keep herfelf
private for fome time , in a very fine Grotto,
adorn'd with artificial Rocks and Waterworks,
and Green Turfs. 'Twas here that the fair *Julia*
did abandon herfelf entirely to her Melancholy
Thoughts, when *Hypolitus* drawn thither by his
Spleen, which rendred him uncapable of enjoying
the Company of feveral Perfons of Quality who
were come to pay his Father a Vifit, feated himfelf in the fame Grotto (without feeing his Sifter)
leaning his Head againft one of the Rocks, from
whence arofe a large Spring, which divided it felf
into many fmall branches : He remain'd for fome
time immoeable like one in a Trance; but at laft
all on a fudden, Julia, *my dear* Julia, cry'd he, *fince*
the Paffion I have for you is a prohibited Paffion, fince
in adoring you I commit a Crime, and that it is eafier
for me to ceafe to Live, than to ceafe to Love you, I
am refolved to die, and to die Innocent, by a flame

I

I am not able to extinguish. At thefe words, drawing his Sword, he turn'd the point thereof towards his Breaft, when *Julia* almoft quite out of
her Senfes, fetching a great cry, ' Alas ! Brother
' faid fhe, throwing her felf in his Arms and ftop-
' ping his Hand, What is it that drives you thus
' to Defpair? Can any thing be more dreadful
' than the Refolution you have taken ? *Hypolitus*
quite amazed at the fight of her felf, threw himfelf at her Feet, without faying one word, till at
laft breaking filence, ' Sifter, faid he, I am no
' more Mafter now of my Secret, becaufe you
' have heard it from my own Mouth; but the
' only thing that aftonifhes me is, that, knowing
' the true Caufe of my Defpair, you fhould have
' fo much Compaffion, as to defire I fhould live:
' I don't, dear *Julia*, deferve your Pity, and tho'
' my Crime be not voluntary, and that I have
' neglected nothing which I thought might regu-
' late my Paffion and reduce it into its due Bounds,
' that fatal Planet under which I am born, oppo-
' fes it felf againft it with all its might, fo that
' finding my Misfortune unavoidable, I was going
' to feek for a Remedy another way, juft when
' you ftopt me. Alas ! reply'd *Julia*, Alas Bro-
' ther, That Planet you complain of, has proved
' no lefs malignant to me than it has to you;
' know then our Misfortunes are the fame, *Hypo-*
' *litus* I Love you, and I love you too much, you
' being my Brother ; I am willing to make this
' ingenuous confeffion unto you, to deferve your
' Compaffion, as well as you have mine, being re-
' folved never to fee you any more. Yes Brother,
' I am refolved to go into *France* into a Nunnery,
' where I will hide both my Shame and Vexation
' from all the World : Nay, I had even taken a
' refolution you fhould have known nothing of it
' your felf; But how is it poffible for me to fee
                                                    ' you

' you in this Condition, without affording you
' this Confolation ? *Hypolitus* was fo tranfported
at what he heard his dear *Julia* tell him, that he
was not able to fpeak. He remained all this
while at her Feet, and at laft fixing his Eyes on
her with a fearful Countenance, ' I can't, faid he,
' oppofe fo generous a Refolution, tho' it will be
' the greateft Affliction to me in the World to
' lofe you for ever, and fee you fhut up in a
' Nunnery. My Heart finds a certain Comfort in
' this Confideration, That you are not to be
' Married to the Earl of *Bedford*. Oh! faid fhe,
' wou'd you I fhould Marry another Man? Alas
' Sifter, reply'd he, don't urge me to tell you my
' fentiments upon that head, but reft affured,
' that on my fide I will never alter my Condi-
' tion; and that fince we muft part, I will lead fo
' fad and fo deplorable a Life, as will foon put an
' end to my Days.

Julia return'd no anfwer but by Sighs, and
both burfting out into Tears, ' Brother, faid fhe,
' with a tender look, 'tis refolved I fhall fee you
' no more, let us hide our Misfortunes from all
' the World, and if poffible even from our own
' knowledge. She had no fooner faid thefe
Words, but fhe left the Grotto without daring to
look upon *Hypolitus*, and he faw her depart without daring to ftop her.

In the Condition fhe was then in, fhe thought it
beft not to appear in the Countefs of *Douglas*'s
Chamber till pretty late, knowing the Earl of
Bedford would be there, it being an additional
trouble to her, to meet with a Lover who was
indifferent to her; and he finding no opportunity
to fpeak to her, went away again the fame Evening.

Julia had a very ill Night of it, being quite
diftracted with the Thoughts of the odnefs of

their

their Fate ; *Good God,* said she, crying most bitterly; *What is it my Brother and I have done at so young
an Age as ours is, to deserve so severe a Chastisement?*
At last arising out of her Bed very early, (which
she might very well do, having not shut her Eyes
all that Night) She dress'd herself very neatly,
and knowing my Lady *Douglas* to be in her Closet, she went thither, and in a trembling posture
threw herself at her Feet: My Lady surprized at
this action, *What do you want* Julia, said she, very
tenderly ? *And what makes you to appear in this
posture. I see you before me?* Madam, reply'd she,
'*tis the desire I have to crave a favour of you, which I
beg you not to refuse me: I am now fifteen years of
Age, and being your youngest Daughter don't expect
any considerable Fortune ; I don't find my self inclined to Marriage, but rather to a Religious Life;
so that, Madam, if the desire I have of going into*
France *is not displeasing to you, I conjure you to consent to it, and that either you or my Father would conduct me to a Nunnery.* Daughter, said the Countess with a tender Air, *have you seriously considered
of what you are going to do ? I should be very sorry to
see you make a false step of this kind ; you are so very
young, that you ought to take some longer time before
you resolve upon a matter of such Consequence.* Julia
persisting in her request, told her with a great
deal of resolution, *She had well weighed the matter,
and hoped she should never repent of it :* So Madam
Douglas promised, *she would do her utmost with her
Husband, to make him give his Consent.*

Accordingly she went immediately into the
Earls Apartment ; *I was always scrupulous,* said
she, *to believe that* Hypolitus *and* Julia *loved one
another, poor Child she has quite another thing in her
Head, she has a mind to embrace a Religious Life,
and I came in on purpose to consult with you, what
is best to be done on this occasion, for she desires that*
                                            either

either *you or I should carry her into* France *in the Nunnery.* I don't see, *said my Lord* Douglas, *how we can refuse her this satisfaction; but if she goes, it will fall to your Lot, Madam, to Conduct her her thither: However I think it requisite,* added he, *that above all things we let her know (according to her Mothers last request) who she is, and have the thing confirm'd to her by the same Chaplain, who was entrusted to deliver her to us.* My Lady *Douglas* approved her Lord's advice, and having perceived some uneasiness in *Julia,* she sent for her into her Chamber, and told her, *Dear Child, your Father and I wish nothing more than your satisfaction; He grants that you desired, and I am to conduct you my self, tho' it is not without a singular affliction, to have you at such a distance for ever.* Julia return'd Thanks with all imaginable Tenderness, and so left the Countesses Apartment.

She was no sooner come back into her own Chamber, but *Lucilia* told her, *That* Hypolitus *waited for her coming in his Closet; he is so much altered,* added she, *that I am much troubled to see him: Dear Sister, you are his Confident, pray do all you can to Comfort him, for he seems to me to be full of affliction.* Julia, not a little disturb'd at what had pass'd betwixt her Mother and her self, but much more at what *Lucilia* told her, went straitways to his Closet. Here she found *Hypolitus* lying upon his Couch, his Face cover'd with his Handkerchief; At her coming in he would have raised himself, but for want of strength fell down again upon the Couch. *Julia* drew nearer, and squeezing one of his Hands betwixt hers, look'd upon him for some time with Tears in her Eyes: After a long silence, 'Brother, said she to him, the ' Condition I see you in afflicts me to the highest ' degree, Am I not sufficiently miserable already, ' that you should add new afflictions to those I

C 4 　　　　　'am

148339

ALBRIGHT COLLEGE LIBRARY

'I am ready to fink under before ? You are re-
'folv'd to die *Hypolitus,* and I would have you live.
'I require of you in the name of . . . . 'Oh!
'Dear Sifter, faid he interrupting her, Don't
'make ufe of that Power you have over me, to
'engage me preferve this miferable Life, rather
'confider, That I am going to lofe you, that it
'is not in my Power to oppofe it, that I fhall ne-
'ver fee you any more ; nay, that I muft not as
'much as endeavour to fee you : Set before your
'Eyes the difmal Confequences of this Adventure,
'and let me dye without delay, this being the on-
'ly Remedy againft that Evil I fuffer, I can ei-
'ther find or wifh for. Dear Brother, reply'd
'*Julia,* Reafon will put you in mind of your Du-
'ty; you will forget me when you fee me no more.
Hypolitus turning his Head another way, withdrew his Hand, which *Julia* ftill held faft, without anfwering her one word.

She look'd ftedfaftly upon him for fome time;
but perceiving he would not fpeak, *Now Brother,*
faid fhe, *It feems as if you were quite feparate, you
won't as much as talk to me* ; *Do you think me unworthy of your Compaffion, and that I don't put a
great Violence upon my Inclination, in what I am
going about to do?* He return'd no anfwer, and
would not as much as open his Eyes to look at her.
You are then refolv'd to die, my *Dear* Hypolitus, faid
fhe, *Well let us die together, I am not againft it* ; *but
you muft make great hafte, if you intend to die before me.*
Oh! Sifter, cry'd he with a deep Sigh, *Permit me
to be the only Victim to be offered at this Sacrifice* ;
*take my word for it, you have over-done your Duty al-
ready* ; *Live, Live,* my *Lovely* Julia, *what fhould
make you die? And why will you die Barbarous Man?*
reply'd fhe angerly, *Is it not your obftinacy that
makes you die?* *Hypolitus,* now not able to bear
her Reproaches, threw himfelf at her Feet, and
taking

taking hold of her fair Hands, kifs'd them moft Tenderly; *Be fatisfy'd Dear Sifter,* faid he, *I am refolv'd to obey you, and to follow blindly your advice, and to convince you of the Truth thereof, I will take immediately fome Nourifhment, becaufe I intended to procure my Death, by abftaining from all manner of fuftenance, but now will abfolutely fubmit to your Commands.* Julia called to her Sifter to fetch fomething to eat for their Brother, fhe being not in a condition to be feen by any body.

She told *Hypolitus,* what had paffed betwixt Madam *Douglas* and her felf, that fhe had promifed to Conduct her into *France,* and was making preparations accordingly for their journey. *Hypolitus* eat a little, which threw him into a violent Feaver the fame Night. *Julia* was as much concern'd thereat as you may imagine, and in this fad Condition, did not fail to fee and attend him, with great affiduity, and her Eyes were more Eloquent than her Lips, to difcover to *Hypolitus* what fhare fhe bore in his Illnefs: But that, which at another time, would have afforded him no fmall matter of Confolation, ferv'd at this time only to augment his Affliction, and he would willingly have preferr'd *Julia's* Averfion to her Tendernefs; and this vertuous young Lady entertained the fame Thoughts concerning him.

It being foon noifed abroad that fhe intended to be a Nun, even thofe that had no peculiar regard to her, rejected her Fate, and it was the wonder of the whole Town, that fo accomplifh'd a Lady, both in body and mind, fhould fhut her felf up in a Nunnery, for the whole remainder of her Life; But among the reft, the Earl of *Bedford* was the moft concern'd at this refolution: He went to the Earl of *Douglas,* who

was

was by this time return'd to *London*, and told him, 'That he had so violent and so pure a Paſ-'ſion for *Julia*, that if he would but beſtow her 'Perſon upon him, he would not look for any 'thing further, both his Eſtate and Fortune being 'ſufficient to make *Julia* happy ; That all his de-'ſires were Centred in her, that he adored her, 'and that if all hopes were taken from him to 'enjoy her, he ſhould be the moſt unfortunate Man 'on Earth. My Lord return'd his Complement with all imaginable Civilities ; but withal, told him, 'That he could not without blaming him-'ſelf, take away from his Daughter, the Liber-'ty of making her own Choice, of what Con-'dition of Life ſhe was inclined to embrace; 'That 'twas true, 'twas ſuch a one as he had a 'great Averſion to, and that nevertheleſs he thought 'he ought not to oppoſe her Intentions, and that, 'to ſhew him the Eſteem and Regard he had to his 'Perſon and Family, (Madam *Douglas* being of the 'ſame name) if he could ſettle his Affection up-'on *Lucilia* his eldeſt Daughter, who would have 'a much better Portion, he would give her him 'with all his Heart. The Earl of *Bedford*, re-turn'd his Thanks as well as his preſent Condi-tion would permit him ; and ſo returned home full of Affliction.

Thus things were carry'd on, whilſt my Lady *Douglas* was buſied in buying ſuch things as ſhe thought neceſſary for *Julia*; which done, *ſhe told her*, 'twas now time to take leave of her Friends, becauſe ſhe intended to ſet out for *France* within two days. At this news, that Courage which was ſo Natural to this young Lady, began to fail her: She run up to her Brother's Chamber, overwhelm'd with a flood of Tears; He being ſtill in Bed, ſhe bid the Servant that attended him, to withdraw, and then Seated her ſelf upon his Bed, and look-

ing

ing upon him with a very Melancholy Countenance, I am now come at laſt, *ſaid ſhe, Dear Brother,* I am come at laſt to bid you farewel for ever. Oh! what dreadful words! Farewel for ever. Is it poſſible it ſhould be ſo? She could ſay no more, the repeated Sighs and Sobs intercepting the uſe and ſound of her Voice. *Hypolitus,* with his Arms acroſs, and his Eyes lifted up to Heaven, *reply'd with a low and almoſt unintelligible interrupted Voice,* My Dear *Julia,* is this the day on which I am going to loſe you? Is this dreadful Moment come at laſt, and I dare not as much as to diſſwade you from what will render this Life of mine unfortunate and deplorable? Nay, I will ever endeavour to hide from you, if it is poſſible, what a miſerable Condition you leave me in, for fear your Compaſſion ſhould get the Victory of your Reſolution and Courage. We muſt, we muſt part Siſter, *added he,* Fate will have it ſo. Oh! *Julia, Julia,* why was I your Brother? At theſe words, he turned away to conceal his Tears, which he ſhed in abundance: But *Julia* deſiring him to look at her, Don't envy me, *ſaid ſhe,* dear *Hypolitus,* this only Comfort I have left, Let me be an Eye-witneſs of all your Pains, 'tis impoſſible it ſhould encreaſe mine, but it may eaſe them. And you, *continued ſhe,* ſevere Vertue, rigorous Duty, tender Paſſions, who have infuſed into my Heart ſuch Sentiments as I ought and muſt diſown, accept of this Sacrifice I make you, of all my Paſſions and Liberty, I am going to Bury my ſelf for all the remainder of my Days; will not this be ſufficient, to free me from all ſorts of Reproaches? She was then going to ariſe, but her Strength failing, and a deadly Paleneſs overſpreading her Face, ſhe fell backward into an Elbow-Chair, and thereby reduced *Hypolitus* in-

to

to the moſt pitiful State that can be imagined. However, ſhe ſoon recover'd her ſelf, and fixing her Eyes on her Brother, who was half dead himſelf, Farewel my Dear *Hypolitus*, *ſaid ſhe to him*, I have loved you too well, both for yours and my own Repoſe. Farewel Dear Siſter, *ſaid he embracing her*, *and Bathing her Cheeks with his Tears*, you leave me the moſt unfortunate, and moſt afflicted of all Men living, I have no hopes of Relief, but in a ſpeedy Death. So *Julia* left him, and retiring into her Chamber, threw her ſelf upon the Bed.

Oh! What a diſmal Night was this for the Siſter and Brother! What abundance of Tears! What Numberleſs Sighs! What a doleful Parting and violent Separation! But they muſt ſubmit to the Laws of Duty, and two ſuch great and fair Souls could not but accompliſh them. *Julia* quite tired out with ſighing and crying, ſlumbred a little towards Morning, when *Elizabeth*, her waiting Woman came to tell her, that my Lady *Douglas* wanted to ſpeak with her. She got up immediately, and going into my Lady's Cloſet, found her there with the Earl of *Douglas* and a Clergy-man. My Lady bid her to ſhut the Door, and ordering her to ſit down near her, My dear Child, *ſaid ſhe*, we are going to tell thee ſomething, which will not a little ſurprize you.

'You believe your ſelf to be our Daughter, and 'in reſpect of the Love and Tenderneſs we bare 'you, you are not miſtaken in it; But we muſt 'now diſcloſe to you a ſecret that highly con- 'cerns you, You are only a Relation of ours by 'your Mother's ſide, who was of the Family of '*Montgomery*; Look, here is her Picture, *conti- 'nued ſhe*, and this is that of your Illuſtrious Fa- 'ther, *Roger* Earl of *Warwick*, Son to the Earl

of

' of *Salisbury*; look here are to the vallue of betwixt
' 6000 and 7000 *l.* Sterling, Jewels, this vertuous
' Lady were put into our hands for your use; and
' Mr. *Eratua*, who was her Chaplain when she dy'd,
' him you see here before you, is the person whom
' she intrusted to deliver you up into our hands. 'Tis
' now Thirteen years ago, when the King having
' introduced certain Innovations in point of Re-
' ligion to please *Anna Boullain* whom he lov'd ;
' he afterwards made her dye upon the Scaffold,
' such was his fickle and inconstant Temper, even
' in relation to those things that had been once the
' deareſt to him.

   ' The Earl of *Warwick* your Father, a good zea-
' lous *Catholick*, saw himself involved in the mis-
' fortunes of one of his neareſt Kinsmen of the
' same name, who loſt his Life on a Scaffold ; not
' to fall under the same fate he retired to *Venice*,
' and went a Volenteer along with the *Venetian*
' Generaliſſimo *Capello* to *Corfu*, and thence to the
' *Gulph* where the *Turkiſh* Fleet then had their Sta-
' tion. The Famous *Dragut Rais*, who had ren-
' dred himself so redoubtable by his many Pyracies,
' engaging two *Venetians* Gallies, took them ; but
' not till the Earl of *Warwick*, after a moſt noble
' defence, was ſlain and cut to pieces : Your Mother
' quite overwhelm'd with grief at the loſs of your
' Father, being soon reduc'd to the laſt extremi-
' ty of her Life, and fearing that, under the
' preſent moſt deplorable circumſtances of her
' Family, you would fall into the hands of your
' neareſt Relations, and that by their Authority
' they would have you Educated in the new Re-
' ligion they had embrac'd themſelves, she en-
' truſted us with this precious Pledge, and we
' may juſtly ſay, That were you our own Daughter
' we could not love you more than we do: Keep
' this secret my dear Child, *continu'd ſhe*, (for I nei-
                                    ' ther

' ther can nor ought to call you otherwife than fo)
' don't impart it to any Body ; you fee how un-
' der this prefent young King *Edward* this new
' Religion increafes dayly ; you fee they act not
' conformably to the laft Will of King *Henry* VIII.
' in behalf of the *Catholicks*; you fee that the
' Duke of *Somerfet* (who by the Rank he bears of
' being the King's Uncle, and Protector of the
' Kingdom, is in great Authority) protects pub-
' lickly the *Lutherens*; that he infufes the fame
' Principles into the King, and that on that ac-
' count the *Catholicks* are in more danger here
' than ever; all this obliges you by that love you
' ought to have for your felf, to conceal your ex-
' traction ; but at the fame time to pay due Ho-
' nours to the memory of thofe Perfons who
' brought you into this World.

Julia troubled, confounded and tranfported
with joy (tho' fhe did all fhe could to conceal it)
arifing and throwing her felf at the Countefles Feet
moft tenderly kifs'd her hands, Madam *faid fhe*,
' The obligations I owe you are the more valuable
' becaufe I am not actually your Daughter ; had I
' that Honour, it would feem as if nature had in-
' cenc'd you to give me that noble Education you
' have beftow'd upon me ; but as the cafe now
' ftands, it is all owing to your own Generofity :
' At the fame time I lofe all I have to lofe in lo-
' fing the honour of being yours, you will be no
' more my Mother, and I know not were to meet
' with another. God forbid, *faid my Lord* Douglas,
' *interrupting her*, you fhould be no more my Daugh-
' ter, you fhall always be fo my dear *Julia*, *conti-*
' *nu'd he*, and you muft look upon ours as your
' own Father's houfe as long as you live. *Julia*
return'd her hearty thanks for this frefh Demonftration of their Friendfhip, in the moft tender
and engaging Expreffions fhe could ; and the old
Chaplain

Chaplain repeated and confirm'd to her as his Verbal Teſtimony, every thing my Lord and my Lady *Douglas* had told her before; and that with Tears in his Eyes, becauſe he fancy'd he ſaw in the Perſon of *Julia* the lively Picture of the Counteſs of *Warwick* her Mother; and to ſpeak the truth, their was ſo perfect a reſemblance betwixt both their Features, that when this beautiful young Lady caſt her Eyes upon her Mother's Picture which my Lady *Douglas* gave to her, ſhe really believed for ſome time it was drawn for her without her knowledge.

My Lord *Douglas* deſired her to take the Jewels into her own Cuſtody, and when ſhe refus'd to take them, and begg'd they would keep them for her, *he told her*, 'That they belong'd to her, and 'that therefore it was but reaſonable ſhe ſhould 'have them; but, *added he*, dear Child,that will be 'but for a ſmall time, becauſe to morrow you go to '*France* to take a Nuns Habit, which has not the 'leaſt reſemblance to ſuch magnificent Ornaments. She bluſh'd, and left them without anſwering one word.

She no ſooner was got into her Cloſet, but finding her ſelf alone, and at full liberty to abandon her ſelf of her joy,ſhe thought ſhe ſhould never have out-liv'd it; ' What, *cry'd ſhe*, am I not *Hypolitus*'s 'Siſter? Heaven has wrought a Miracle for my 'deliverance, without which I muſt have bin 'all my days the moſt unfortunate Woman on 'Earth. What would become of me had they 'kept this ſecret but a little longer? My Vows 'and the Auſtere life of a Nunnery would have 'robb'd me of all my hopes of ſeeing our Fate 'United: Alas! What makes me tarry ſo long? 'Why am I not before this time in his Chamber? 'Am I not now Miſtreſs of a thing that ſo nearly 'concerns him, and I loſe time in not telling it
'him?

' him ? So fhe went towards his Chamber, her
Eyes fparkling with joy, with an Air fo lively and
pleafing, that thofe that had feen her but two
hours before,would fcarce have known her now. She
defired *Lucilia* to go along with her to *Hypolitus's*
Chamber, whom they found fo dejeƈted and fo
deeply afflicƈed with his Melancholly Thoughts
and his Feaver, that he had fcarce power to fpeak.
They ask'd him how he did ? He told them in a
languifhing tone, he was very ill. And obferving,
not without fome furprize mix'd with Vexation,
Julia in fo gay and brisk a humour, which fhe was
not able to conceal at that time ; 'And as for you
' Sifter, *faid he*, one need not ask you how you do,
' 'tis enough to fee you, and you never appear'd
' to me fo well fatisfied in your life. I never had fo
' much reafon, *faid fhe fmiling*. How ! *cry'd he*, you
' are going to leave us, and you are overjoy'd at
' it ; pray at leaft have fo much complaifance as
' to keep within the rules of Decency, and don't
' infult over *Lucilia* and I becaufe we are forry
' for your departure, which, alas, being near at
' hand, will foon rid you of your pain ; Don t you
' know that to morrow is the fatal day we muft
' lofe you ?
   Lucilia perceiving her to return no anfwer, but
to make a fign to her Brother, went to the Window, which fhe opened, and whilft fhe was looking
out of it, afforded them an entire freedom of
entertaining one another. Then *Julia* fixing her
Eyes on *Hypolitus*, who was quite confounded to
fee her fo contented, ' What good news have I
' to tell you, *faid fhe*, 'tis fuch *Hypolitus* as you will
' fcarce be able to believe, you will imagine it to
' be a Fiƈion. I will believe every thing you tell
' me, faid he, *interrupting her with fomewhat of im-*
' *patience* ; But dear Sifter what can you tell me
' that fhould be fo pleafing to me, my misfortunes
                                                    ' are

' are paſt a cure; and ſuppoſing I ſhould not be
' your Siſter, would not that go a great way in
' procuring you that ſatisfaction you now deſpair
' off? He return'd no anſwer; but only lifted up
' his Eyes to Heaven, as if he would ſay, that no
' ſuch thing could enter into his Thoughts.

Then *Julia* continuing, I blame my ſelf, *ſaid ſhe*,
for ſuffering you to languiſh ſo long, after having
told you, that I knew ſomething that might afford
you ſome Conſolation. Dear *Hypolitus*, be aſſured
you are not my Brother, nor am I your Siſter,
She then told him all ſhe had underſtood concerning her Birth, ſhew'd him the Earl of *Warwick*
and the Counteſs her Mothers Pictures, together
with the Jewels. Every thing that can be conceived, falls far ſhort from what this Lover
felt at that moment: He was ſo far tranſported
with Joy as to loſe the uſe of his Tongue; his
Eyes, which were fix'd on *Julia*'s, ſometimes by
their ſprightlineſs, ſometimes by their languiſhment, diſcovered the different paſſions and agitations of his Soul: He took hold of one of her
Hands, which he kiſs'd with ſo much tranſport, as if
he would never have parted with it. He continued
for a conſiderable time in the ſurprize, till at laſt
recovering himſelf, like one revived from the
dead, O God! charming *Julia*, ſaid he, Don't you
only flatter my Pain? Is it poſſible what you tell
me ſhould be ſo? Nay, it was not to be imagined
that ſuch fair Eyes as yours ſhould kindle a flame
that is Criminal; what a pleaſure is it, to abandon ones ſelf to all the tranſports, to all the agitations of Mind, the ſtrongeſt and moſt reſpect-
ful Paſſion in the World is able to inſpire? But
pray take your ſhare in my Felicity, my lovely
Miſtreſs; pray tell me, Are not you well pleaſed
with it? Ah! dear *Hypolitus*, Can you queſtion it?
ſaid ſhe interrupting him, You are too well acquaint-

D   ed

ed with my moſt ſecret Thoughts, not to be ſenſible what effect this unexpected Miracle may produce in my Heart; But can't I but confeſs to you,
That my Joy is not without ſome alay of Fear,
you are for a conſiderable time paſt deſign'd for
my Lady *Argyle*, I have no great Fortune, and
you will find that after we have eſcaped theſe
dreadful Rocks at Sea, we ſhall ſuffer Shipwreck in
the Port it ſelf.

No, Madam, *replied* Hypolitus, *kiſſing her Hand*,
no, I will not miſtruſt my good Fortune, after ſhe
has done ſo much for me, every thing will be eaſie
for her for the future; provided my dear *Julia* you
act in concert with her. In the mean while Brother, *ſaid ſhe*, (for I will not wean my ſelf from
calling you ſo) what muſt I do to put a ſtop to
that fatal Journey which is fix'd for to morrow?
Conſider every thing is ready, and what a *nonplus* I am likely to be put to. You muſt, dear
Julia, fain your ſelf Sick, and tell them, 'tis the
effect of your ſurprize at ſo ſingular an Event
wherein you are ſo nearly concern'd: 'Twill not
be very hard for me, *ſaid ſhe*, to make them believe for ſome few days that I am ill, but healthy
Countenance will ſoon betray the Cheat, there is
a very apparent difference betwixt one that labours under real Sufferings, and one that only fains
himſelf ſo to do. Dear Siſter, *reply'd* Hypolitus,
Let us make a beginning with this, and afterwards we will conſider what is farther to be done.

Having ſaid theſe words, *Lucilia* drew near ;
I think, *ſaid ſhe*, you will at leaſt think your ſelf
oblig'd to me for my complaiſance? I hope, *added
ſhe, with a pleaſing ſmile*, you do not think I took
delight for theſe two Hours paſt to look at the
Birds, truly I am too good natur'd: Oh! *Lucilia*, *Lucilia*, ſaid *Julia*, *embracing her*, if I knew
you could keep a ſecret, how pleaſed ſhould I
                                                          be

be to repay your Goodnefs, with making you my Confident. If I could keep a fecret, *reply'd* Lucilia *fmiling*, you make very bold with your Elder Sifter, pray a little more refpect *Julia*, or elfe I will defire Juftice from my Brother. Your Judge is fure to give it againft you, *reply'd* Hypolitus, ftretching out his Hands, 'tis not in my Power to be againft *Julia*. And who then fhall ftand up for me, *added* Lucilia? I will for you againft my felf, *faid* Julia: I am already blaming my felf for having call'd your fecrecy in queftion, and for the future, I will have none but what you fhall know off. She then related to her every thing fhe had told her dear *Hypolitus* before, and being a young Lady of great Prefence of Mind, fhe judg'd rightly it would be very beneficial to them, to bring over *Lucilia* into their Intereft. She then receiv'd upon this occafion, the moft convincing Proofs of her Friendfhip; for, after the firft furprize, occafioned by fo unexpected a piece of news, was over, and that fhe had leifure to confider, how for the future fhe was no more to be *Julia*'s Sifter, fhe fell a crying moft bitterly: Alafs! *faid fhe to her*, now you know that we don't belong to one another, I have all the reafon to fear you will withdraw your Heart from me, and fix it on fome body elfe, which may better deferve it than I. I know not dear Sifter, *reply'd* Julia, *interrupting and embracing her*, where I fhould meet with fuch a Friend as you fpeak off; and I believe I might look for fuch a one in vain; then don't think me fo frail, as to be Guilty of fuch a change; you fhall always be dear to me my tender *Lucilia*, and I give you the moft convincing Proofs of it, that is in my Power to give; But I think it is time for us to retire, for fear of a furprize. you know what a dark Leffon we had once on that account.

They left the Amorous *Hypolitus* to his own Thoughts, being like one Enchanted and Transported with Joy ; His *Feaver* which ow'd its Cause to nothing else but the disturbance of his mind, left him on a sudden, and in spite of all his weakness, he left his Bed at the same time *Julia* took hers. The better to Counterfeit this Sick Woman, she had all the Windows of her Chambers darkned, and she engaged *Lucilia* to assist her in perswading my Lord and my Lady *Douglas*, that she was really ill, which they soon believed. The Physitians finding no Symptoms of a *Feaver*, and there being no signs of illness in her Countenance, they were not a little puzled what to prescribe her ; She complain'd of a violent *Head-ach*, and would cry out sometimes for Pain. *Lucilia* told them, 'Twas most at Nights, and that her Sister did not shut an Eye all Night long. So no body suspecting the Truth thereof, the Physitians order'd her to change the Air, which was done accordingly, and they carry'd her to *Buckingham*.

Whilst she was there, *Hypolitus* was made sensible of a certain Pleasure he never had tasted before, I mean, he now had the opportunity of giving vent to the most tender and most violent Passion a Heart ever was possestt with : He lost not a minute, but always was with his Mistress ; and no body imagining otherwise, than that she was really Sick, and every body wishing for her speedy recovery, nothing was omitted that could contribute towards her Diverfion. This offer'd abundance of Liberty to *Hypolitus*, and facilitated his free access to her at every hour of the day.

Neither my Lord and my Lady *Douglas*, in the least concern'd thereat, being fully perswaded she had not altred her Resolution, but that she would pursue it as soon as the recovery of her Health would

would permit her to go into *France*. The Earl of
Bedford, in the mean time flattering himself, that
by his continual Addresses, he might prevail upon
this fair Lady to alter her resolution, made her
frequent Visits at *Buckingham*, not omitting any
thing on his part, which he thought might be
requisite to touch her Heart with Compassion;
though at the same time, she always receiv'd
him with so much indifferency, as might well
make him lose all hopes of Success. Notwithstanding all this, his repeated Addresses could
not but cause some uneasiness in the Amorous
Hypolitus, so that he could no longer forbear to
discover it to *Julia*, one day as she was taking a
solitary Walk in a small Adjacent Wood. Having
for some time spoken in general terms of this
Lover, I know, *added he*, he adores you, he
carries your Fetters, and every body knows he does
so. I can't be an Eye-witness of it, without
much vexation. Ah! If you could be sensible how
dear he pays for this Honour, *said* Julia *to him
smiling*, you would have nothing but Compassion
for him; for I give him such an Entertainment,
as will make him not relish very long his importunate Perseverance.

Whilst they were thus diverting themselves in
discourse, they came to the Grotto; and *Julia*
being somewhat tired with walking, they went in
there to rest themselves. The Countess of *Douglas*
hapned to be at the same time in the Grotto, to
consider of some additional Embellishments she
had made there; but perceiving her two Children coming that way at some distance, and
willing to overhear their Discourse, the better
to satisfy her Curiosity and Jealousy concerning
the pretended Sickness of *Julia*, and the fear she
lay under lest *Hypolitus* should prove an obstacle to
her intended Departure for *France*, she slipt im-

mediately

mediately into a defart place, which being between two Creeks, made a kind of a Niche.

Julia having feated her felf, *Hypolitus* threw himfelf at her Feet; I can't fee you, *faid fhe*, in fo uneafie a Pofture, and fo made him fit down by her. Ah! have you forgot me, *faid he*, my charming Miftrefs, that this is the fame place where you faved my Life; and ought I not to fhew you my Acknowledgment at your Feet? Alas! *Hypolitus, faid fhe*, why will you recal to my mind that Melancholly Day? I fhall always remember it, and I ought to do fo much more than you dear *Julia, faid he, interrupting her*, for that day you call Melancholly to you, proved very Charming to me, being the fame day when I underftood from your own Mouth, that you were not infenfible of my Paffion; were it poffible for me to tell you, what a Comfort this Confeffion produced in my Soul, at the very extremity of my Defpair, whilft I ftill thought my felf to be your Brother, and that I could not reap any benefit from that Tendernefs, on which depended the Prefervation of my Life, you would then be more fully convinced of my Paffion. Ah! my dear *Hypolitus, faid fhe with a languifh-ing look*, be fatisfy'd with thofe Sentiments I have for you, they are fuch as I could wifh them to be lefs violent; but my Heart will not hearken to the advice of Reafon. and I dread fometimes the difmal Confequences of your Tendernefs. If your Friends, who defign you for your Coufin, fhould get notice thereof, without doubt they wou'd fend me far enough off; and 'tis poffible *Hypolitus*, 'tis poffible, alas! your *Julia* might never fee you again. Don't difturb the Sweetnefs of my prefent Satisfaction, *faid he interrupting her*, with your difmal Predictions, Madam, and reft affur'd, I will rather ceafe to live, than ceafe to be yours; no Power on Earth fhall be able to alter my refolution.

I am

I am fufficiently convinced of your Conftancy, as not in the leaft to doubt of what you tell me, *reply'd* Julia ; but after all, fuppofing they fhould force me to go into *France*, and there to embrace a Religious Life, what muft we do then ? Venture at all, *reply'd* Hypolitus *abruptly*, Venture all Madam ; for rather than fubmit to fuch a Conftraint, I would carry things to the laft extremity : How ! do you think I will fee you to be made a Sacrifice to the Misfortunes of your Family, and under pretence, that Fortune has deny'd you her Favours, when Heaven has heap'd them upon you, and made you the moft adorable Perfon in the World ? Under this Pretence, fay I, fhould they force you to embrace a Life that is contrary to your Inclinations and my Repofe ? However, *said he*, and fo arifing in the utmoft fury from his Seat, and walking towards the other fide of the Grotto, he efpies Madam *Douglas* ; and *Julia* feeing her as well as he, they remain'd as immovable, as if they had been two Statues.

My Lady *Douglas* feeing 'twas in vain to conceal her felf any longer, came forth out of that fatal place, and looking upon both with Eyes fparkling with Anger , I never thought, *said fhe to* Julia, that a Young Woman fo well born as you are, would difpofe of her Heart without the Approbation of thofe to whom fhe belongs; And, as for you, *Hypolitus*, you I fay, who knew our Intentions concerning your Marriage, you are very Infolent in daring to enter into an Engagement with *Julia*, at a time when we were upon the point of concluding a Marriage with my Lady *Argyle* and you ; and fo fhe went abruptly out of the Grotto without faying one word more.

Who is able to defcribe the deplorable condition thefe two Lovers faw themfelves reduc'd to ? Certainly nothing could exceed their Trouble and

Grief: *Hypolitus* drawing near *Julia*, she dropt
as it were into his Arms; What will become of
us *Hypolitus*, *said she*, What a dreadful Storm is
hanging over our Heads? Every thing I foresee is
enough to confound and render me quite inconsolable; Alas! Why did they undeceive me? O-
therwise I had bin in a Nunnery in *France* by this
time. What makes you regret this your Destiny my
Dear Lady, *said he, interrupting her?* Our Misfortunes appear greater to you than really they are;
a reasonable share of Constancy will clear our way,
and deliver us from those persecutions they prepare for us. *Hypolitus, said she*, I shall neither
want Courage nor Constancy; but my Duty is
still dearer to me than my Love, and you may be
certain that when the first speaks, the last must o-
bey. Oh! what do I ask of you my dear *Julia*,
continu'd he, that is contrary to your Duty? Was
there ever a Passion more pure or full of respect
than mine? Don't therefore disturb your self with
vain Notions, at the time we stand in need of all
our Passion and Strength to support the War they
are going to make upon us.

He then kiss'd *Julia*'s Hands, and by his Rap-
tures and the motions of his Heart, sufficiently
discover'd the true state of his Soul. It was already very late, Lovers soon forget themselves when
they are together, and the hours of Love are very
ry short: At last our two Lovers parted, but not
without giving all the mutual assurances that could
be, that they wou'd Love one another till Death.

Julia intended to shut her self up in her Closet,
there to ruminate upon the odness of their adventure, and upon the future deportment towards
my Lady *Douglas*; but it was not long before one
of her Maids came to desire her to come down
stairs to her Mother, who wanted to speak with
her. Poor Lady, she went down Trembling, and
with

with such paleness in her Countenance, that one
wou'd have believed she was going to recieve Sen-
tence of Death ; and when she came into my Lord
and my Lady's Apartment, she found them so far
chang'd in their looks from what they us'd to appear to her, that she was quite startled thereat. You
deviate so far, *said my Lady* Douglas *to her*, from the
opinion I had conceiv'd of your tenderness, that I
can't at this time give you the name of my Child :
How ! *Julia*, after you had bin receiv'd and treated by us like our own Child, can you have so little gratitude in you, as to endeavour the Ruine
of *Hypolitus*'s Fortune, and to make his Heart Rebellious against his Duty to us? You have rais'd in
him a Passion you know must be displeasing to us ;
you Cajole us with the hopes of your going into a
Nunnery, whilst at the same time, you take quite
a contrary measure as what is becoming *Julia*, of
those Dispositions so full of Sincerity and Dutiful-
ness we have infused into you. Are you not still
the same you always us'd to appear to us?

The fair *Julia* was touch'd to the quick at the
Countesses reproaches ; she was so Nice in what
we call Duty and Sincerity, that she thought it
the highest piece of Injustice that cou'd be done
her, to be charg'd with want thereof : She
Blush'd both for Shame and Spite to have so severe
a Reprimand given her. She kept her Eyes fix'd
upon the Ground for some time, but at last turning them upon the Countess, she return'd her an
Answer, containing an equal mixture of Modesty
and of a noble Haughtiness : I dare assure you
Madam, *said she*, I am not Ungrateful, and the
Obligations I owe you, shall never be razed either
out of any Remembrance or my Heart ; I am willing
to own to you at the same time, that I betray'd
my self by my tender Sentiments for *Hypolitus* ;
I thought I loved him no otherwise than a Brother,
and

and 'tis in vain to deny it, fince you know it already: This Friendfhip fhould never have made any further progrefs in my Heart than I would have wifh'd it fhould, had I bin Miftrefs of it; but I was not fenfible of my Misfortune till it was too late, and paft cure. *Hypolitus* his cafe was as defperate as mine; he protefted to me in terms fo violent and fo convincing, that his Life depended on me; that my frailty feconded by certain particular motives that engag'd me in his behalf, I had not power to deny him fome acknowledgments; and what encourag'd me in fhewing this Indulgence both to him and to my felf, was, that I thought my felf not altogether unworthy of the Honour of being your Relation. 'Tis true Madam, my Fortune is but moderate, but that don't always make the repofe and happinefs of our Life; I have heard fay, That the Union of Hearts is a moft neceffary ingredient in Marriage, which is not to ceafe till Death; I have the Honour to be related to you, as well as my Lady *Argyle* whom you defign for *Hypolitus*, and —— fo that Madam, *faid the Earl of* Douglas *interrupting her*, you thought it enough for my Son to love you, and you to love him, you thought that your fatisfaction and ours muft be the fame; but you have flatter'd your felf too far, and that for the future you may take fuch meafures as will be neceffary for your Repofe; I now declare to you, that you muft either chufe to go into *France* in a Nunnery, or Marry the Earl of *Bedford*, there is no *Medium* to be chofen betwixt thefe two; confider what you think moft convenient for your felf, and let us know your Refolution to Morrow.

Julia quite diftracted at fo rough a treatment, went out of the Room ftrait to *Hypolitus*'s Chamber, where fhe fell in to a Swoon like one half Dead. *Lucilia* came to give her all the neceffary affiftance, but

but as for poor *Hypolitus*, he was so full of Affliction, that he stood no less in need of aid than his
dear Mistress: But after some time, being recover'd out of her Swoon, she told them every thing
that pass'd in her Coverfation with my Lord and
my Lady.

'Twas at this time they began to set before
their Eyes all the Misfortunes they foresaw were
intended for them : Was I too happy, just *Heaven, cry'd Hypolitus ?* Was I too happy, to see all
my hopes thus overturn'd at once ? But *continu'd
he,* What is it I say my dear Lady ? If you are
not against me, who is able to seperate our Hearts ?
Believe me *Hypolitus, said she with a tender look,* 'tis
Death alone can part us ; I am resolv'd to venture at All,and I promise you I will never alter my
Sentiments ; not that I am insensible of what
I am likely to suffer ; but all my pains will be welcome to me, so long as they can contribute any
thing towards preserving for you your *Julia.*
This faithful Lover touch'd to the Heart with
Love and Acknowledgment, told her every thing
that may be call'd tender and engaging upon such
an occasion as this ; But they were both of them
put to the greatest Nonplus that could be, what
answer *Julia* was to give to Morrow to my Lord
and my Lady *Douglas* ; at last they resolved,
she was to desire a longer time to consider of the
matter, or else to be carry'd into *France* ; and if
they did consent to the last, then *Hypolitus* was to
go thither also to see *Julia,* but that she should
flatly reject the proposed match with the Earl of
Bedford in such Terms, as might for ever after
free her from any importunities upon that score.

Whilst they were thus framing their Projects,
my Lord and my Lady *Douglas* were consulting
with themselves what course they had best to take to
be diliver'd of the fear they lay under of seeing
their

their Son involv'd in too deep a Paſſion for *Julia*.
If we carry her into *France*, ſaid they, he will
doubtleſs go and find her out there, Love never
wants ingenuity, and *Hypolitus* has Wit enough to
find out a way to meet with her; we can't make
her a Nun againſt her will, ſo that the beſt expedient will be to ſend *Hypolitus* out of the way into
forreign Cauntries; perhaps he will forget *Julia*
when he ſees her no more, and perhaps ſhe may
alſo change her mind, and the Earl of *Bedford's*
Conſtancy may at laſt prevail with her to marry
him.

Having taken this Reſolution which they thought
moſt ſuitable to their preſent Intentions, they
ſent word to *Julia* by her dear *Lucilia*, that they
gave her ſome longer time to think of the
matter. This News reviv'd in her ſome ſmall
glimpſe of hopes, that my Lord *Douglas* intended
to make them both happy; ſhe communicated her
thoughts to her Lover, but he was not ſo eaſie to
flatter himſelf as ſhe. Oh! dear Lady, *ſaid he to
her*, I only am too well acquainted with the Character of thoſe that oppoſe our ſatisfaction, they
will not ſuffer us to live long at eaſe; my Soul is
diſturb'd, and I know not what it is that foretells
me our Tranquility will be of no long Continuance. At theſe words *Julia* burſt out into
Tears, and *Hypolitus* did the like; It was not long
before theſe Troubles they labour'd in, produc'd
ſuch a change in their Countenance, that my Lord
and my Lady *Douglas* fearing they wou'd both fall
into ſome dangerous Diſtemper, thought fit to
haſten *Hypolitus's* departure; for this purpoſe they
got ſecretly an Equipage in readineſs, which being
very ſplended, they hoped he would be well pleaſed
to ſee himſelf thus ſumptuouſly equipp'd, that he
might appear with the more Luſtre in forreign
Courts. Things being in this forwardneſs, my Lord and
my

my Lady fent one day to fpeak with him : My Son,
faid my Lord, had we no other regard but to our
one fatisfaction, 'tis certain it wou'd be much more
pleafing to us to keep you near us than at a Confiderable diftance ; but you are now of an Age,
when it will feem undecent for you to ftay at home ;
and therefore it will be requifite for you to go and
fee other Countries, to Fafhion your felf, to Accomplifh your Deportment, and render your
Converfation more Polite. We don't queftion but
that you are overjoy'd to find us inclin'd to fecond
your laudable Intentions of feeing the World ; you
fhall firft of all go into *France*, from thence to *Italy*,
afterward into *Germany*, and fo return home by
the way of the *Netherlands*, and within Three
years time we hope to fee you again with much
joy and fatisfaction. *Hypolitus* was full of diftraction at this propofal, every word was like a Dagger to him that was ftruck at his Heart, he was
under the greateft perplexity what to do ; fometimes he was for fpeaking out boldly, and telling
them of his Paffion for *Julia*, tho' they were acquainted with it already, and that nothing on Earth fhould
part them and that ; if they wou'd fend him a-
broad, they muft firft fecure him in the poffeffion
of his Miftrefs ; but foon changing his mind,
he began to confider that this would ferve only
to bring frefh Perfecutions upon this fair Lady,
and that perhaps they would carry her where he
fhould never hear any Tidings of her : To be
fhort, 'tis impoffible to exprefs the oppofite and
various Agitations of his Soul. My Lord and my
Lady were not altogether infenfible of it, by the
uneafinefs and irrefolution they obferv'd in him ;
but they thought it beft to diffemble, and to take
no notice of what they knew caus'd his inquietude ;
fo they told him they would have him go along
with Monfieur *de Bois Dauphin* (the then *French*
Abaffador

Ambaffador in *England*) into *France*, who being his intimate Friend, he could not meet with a better conveniency than this ; but that he being ready to leave *England* in two days time, he had nothing elfe to do but to beftow it in taking his leave of his Friends. *Hypolitus* concealing his Trouble as much as poffible he could, told them coldly, he would obey ; but that fo fodain a Departure was more like an Exilement than a voluntary Travelling ; and fo he withdrew.

He intended to have gone ftraitways to *Julia*'s Apartment, to give her an account of what had pafs'd ; but he confidered, it would be requifite above all other things, to fpeak with the deareft of all his Friends, in order to take his Meafures with him : So on Horfeback he Mounted to the Earl of *Suffex* Houfe in *London*, not queftioning but that upon this occafion he would prove as generous a Friend to him, as he had done feveral other times. Underftanding he was in the Park, he went thither, and met him in Company of the Earl of *Northumberland*, and of the Son of the Earl of *Northumberland*; after the firft Civilities, he took two or three turns with them, and took the firft opportunity to tell the Earl with a low voice, he had fomething of Confequence to import to him.

The Earl of *Suffolk* foon parted from his Friends, telling them he would foon come to them again ; but turning towards *Hypolitus*, you have oblig'd me very much, *faid he*, in giving me an opportunity of leaving their Converfation, which was not very pleafing to me fince it was upon State Affairs, they intending to engage me in the intereft of the Princefs *Jane*, who tho' fhe be very Young and Handfome, and Niece to our King *Henry* VIII. yet I can't but think the Princefs *Mary*, (wherein the Crown is to defcend into the Female Line) the

lawful

lawful Heirefs of this Kingdom. He was going
on in the fame difcourfe without obferving that his
Friends hearkned to it not without much difturbance and inquietude, till coming into a folitary
Walk, We are now at full liberty faid the Earl to
Hypolitus, *embracing him*, fpeak my dear Friend,
and don't delay to tell me wherein it is I can ferve
you. You may do me a great deal of Service,
faid he, in the Condition I am reduc'd to thro' the
harfh Treatment of my Father; I know not where
to look for aid but from fo true a Friend as you
are : My dear Earl, *continu'd he*, I am almoft
defperate ; I am to go into *France* with *Bois Dauphin*, the *French* Minifter, who is recall'd by his
Mafter; I am to leave *Julia*, the fame *Julia* whom
I adore, and who is the only Enjoyment of my
Life; you are fo well acquainted with my Sentiments, that I need not infift upon that point any
further at prefent ; but let come of it what will,
I am refolved to pretend only that I am a going,
but will fend my Servant to your Country Seat (if
you approve of it) and will my felf lie conceal'd
there, to take all opportunities as poffible I can of
feeing my Miftrefs.

All that is in my Power, *faid the Earl*, is at your
difpofal, as much as if it were your own ; but
give me leave to tell you, 'twill be a hard task to
deceive the Earl of *Douglas* for any confiderable
time. Were it but for one Day reply'd the Amorous *Hypolitus*, it will be very delightful to me,
fince it fhall be fpent in feeing of *Julia*. But tell
me whether you will oblige me in it ? Whether I
will oblige you, *cry'd the Earl*, truly this is a dif-
obliging queftion, and I hoped you knew me much
better than I find you do. *Hypolitus* embracing
him, ask'd his Pardon, and having return'd him
thanks for his kindnefs, he was for going away as
faft as he could, being very impatient to return to
his

his dear Miſtreſs ; but the Earl wou'd needs go
along with him part of the way. Whilſt they
were upon the Road, alas ! *ſaid he,* If an abſence
of ſome hours is ſo troubleſome to me, what
would become of me if it were for Years ? 'Twould
be impoſſible for me to live long without her, I
ſhould dye infallibly for Grief. So ſoon as they
came in ſight of my Lord *Douglas*'s Seat they
parted, and *Hypolitus* ſoon after ſaw *Julia* looking
out of a Window, and making a ſign to come to
her ; he made all the haſte he could, And from
whence come you Brother, *ſaid ſhe to him* ? What !
after ſo long Conference with my Lord and my
Lady, you Mount an Horſe back without giving
me an account of what diſcourſe paſs'd betwixt
you ? Oh *!* Brother, is it thus you Love me ! Me-
thinks had I bin in your place, I ſhould not have
done ſo.

Tho' *Hypolitus* knew himſelf not in the wrong,
and that he might eaſily juſtify his Conduct, nevertheleſs *Julia*'s Anger had ſuch an influence upon
him, that her Reproaches rendred him quite
Speechleſs ; but after having recover'd his Senſes,
he told her, with an Air full of Reſpect, My
Lovely *Julia*, ought not I to complain of your
ſurmizes ? How is it poſſible you ſhould thus ſuſpect
my Heart, and that upon ſo ſlight an occaſion ?
Certainly you are not ſufficiently ſenſible of my
Paſſion, thus to accuſe me. *Julia* had too much
Tenderneſs for him, to ſuffer him to continue long
under that inquietude, whereof ſhe was the cauſe ;
I muſt confeſs, *ſaid ſhe,* I am in the wrong to give
you this trouble; we are Unfortunate enough already without my being injurious to create us
new Pains. Come let us make Peace my dear Lady, *reply'd* Hypolitus, *kiſſing her Hand,* I agree
with you, that our Misfortunes are ſufficiently
great without any addition of our own ; my Father

ther will have me leave you, he intends to fend me into *France*, but I have taken fuch meafures as not to go out of *England*; the only thing we have to do now, is to confert meafures how we may fee one another.

He then gave her an account of what Refolu. tion he had taken with the Earl of *Suffex*, and after feveral deliberations, how they might now and then fpeak to one another in Private, they defired *Lucilia* to come becaufe they conceal'd nothing from her; Come dear Sifter, *faid* Julia *to her*, come to our aid, your mind is much more free from Troubles than ours, and you will therefore fooner think of a good expedient than we, and they told her what they were confulting about; *Lucilia* was filent for fome time, but foon after told them, fhe knew a pair of back-ftairs leading out of their Apartment into one of the darkeft Walks of the Garden, at the end whereof, juft at the extreamity of the Wildernefs there was a little Door looking into the Field ; that they muft get a Key to it, and that fhe would go down thefe private ftairs in the Evening unperceived by any body to open it and let *Hypolitus* in. Nothing could be better contriv'd, *cry'd he* ; 'Tis true *faid* Julia, but what name will you give to this Contrivance? I am not your Sifter, and if you let him in at Night, this will be like an Affignation, and I think there ought a better Decorum to be obferv'd in our Interview. Are your Circumftances fuch, *reply'd* Lucilia, as to infift with the utmoft nicety upon fuch matters? Tho' my Brother is not your Brother, yet is he to be your Spoufe ; I engage I will never leave you alone whilft your Interview lafts, tho' in fo doing, I run the rifque of expofing my felf to my Father and my Mothers Anger : I will willingly do it, to give you the utmoft Demonftrations of my Friend-

E   fhip.

ſhip. And as for me, my Charming Lady, *ſaid*
Hypolitus, me, ſays I, who ſtay in *England* for no
other reaſon than to have the opportunity of ſeeing you now and then in this place, What muſt
become of me, if you will not conſent to it ? I had
as good go into *France*, Is that your meaning *Julia ?* You have a mind to Baniſh me ? You are too
well acquainted with what Power you have over
me to engage me ; however conſider unto what
danger we are going to expoſe our ſelves to, the
very thought of it makes me dread it moſt cru-
elly. They did all they could to remove her fear,
and the ſame Evening *Hypolitus* took a pattern of
the Key in Wax, which he ſent immediately to
the Earl of *Suſſex* by his *Valet du Chambre*, in order to have another made after it, which he intended to deliver to *Julia* before his pretended departure.

This being done accordingly, and the Day appointed for *Hypolitus*'s departure come, my Lord
would needs Conduct him to *London*, intending
to ſee him Aboard the Yatch ; but contented himſelf to ſee him in his Barge with his Attendants
and Embraſing him with all the marks of Tenderneſs at parting, he return'd well ſatisfy'd to ſee
his Son take his leave of him, without the leaſt
Reluctancy.

Hypolitus coming Aboard the Yatch, found
Monſieur *de Bois Dauphin* to be there before him,
and knowing him to be his Truſty Friend, he took
him aſide, and told him, That ſince ſome irreſiſti-
ble reaſons oblig'd him to ſtay in *England*, he
would open his whole heart to him, that he conjur'd him to take Compaſſion of his preſent Condition, and that he hoped the Confidence he put
in him, would produce an effect ſuitable to what
he expected from his goodneſs, and diſcerning
by his Countenance and Actions a favourable diſpoſition

pofition in him to ferve him, he told him his intention was to engage my Lord and my Lady
Douglas into a belief of his being fick at *Diep*, becaufe if they fhould pretend he lay ill at *Paris*,
his Father wou'd wonder he fhould hear no Ty-
dings of him by the *Englifh* Minifter, and fome o-
ther Gentlemen of that Nation, refiding at the
French. Court : But that if he would write to
my Lord *Douglas* to that purpofe, and deliver it to
him, he wou'd make ufe of it in due time ; that
laft of all he was oblig'd to confefs to him, That
the prefervation of his Life depended upon his
goodnefs in granting his requeft. I underftand
you, *faid Monfieur* de Bois Dauphin *fmiling*, you
are in Love my Lord, and you would have me in
order to favour your Paffion, expofe my felf to
my Lord your Father's Indignation ; But be that
as it will, I have been Young as you are now, and
I find a certain Inclination within me, rather to
efpoufe yours, than your Father's Caufe : Come,
I will write immediately juft as you will have me.
Hypolitus overjoy'd at his Courtefy, return'd him
all imaginable thanks for fo fignal a piece of Service, and having received his Letter from his
hands, wherein he told his Father, That his Son
was forc'd to ftay behind at *Diep* by reafon of his
Illnefs; He took leave of him, and got into one
of the Ships Boats (becaufe he had fent back his
Father's Barge immediately) and fo was carry'd to
London where he Landed at the *Tower* Wharff,
the Earl of *Suffex* expecting his return there in
his Coach ; and had brought along with him a
Gentleman in whom he could confide, with fome
Horfes who was to conduct his Friend and his Servants to his Country Seat, where they did not
Arrive till pretty late, it being requifite they
fhou'd come at fuch a time, when no body might
fee and take notice of *Hypolitus*, who's thoughts

being altogether with *Julia*, began to bemoan his Fate, becaufe he could not be in the fame Houfe with her.

I ufed to talk to her every moment, *faid he to the Earl of* Suffex, *who ftaid that Night with him in the Country,* I had the freedom to come into her Chamber Forty times a Day, and in fpite of all my Lady's Cautions, we found out ways and means to fee one another almoft every hour in the Day ; but at prefent we are a great many Miles diftance, which tho' it may feem no great matter to indifferent Perfons, I find it too much for one that Loves: Add to this, what continual precautions I fhall be oblig'd to take at our meetings, what fears of being difcover'd I fhall be expofed to, and of a Thoufand unlucky Accidents a Man can neither avoid nor forefee, and which too often will break all our meafures at one ftroak. You are very Amorous, *faid the Earl, interrupting him with a fmile,* thefe falfe Alarms which thus difcompofe you without any real occafion, being the effects of a moft violent Paffion : Pray do but confider, *continu'd he,* is it not much better to be here than to be at Sea in a Yatch, which perhaps, at this very hour being under full Sail with a fair Gail towards the Coaft of *France,* would foon carry you at a greater diftance from your belov'd Miftrefs ? Don't you think it a happinefs to find your Attendants fo pliable in obeying your orders, and even that fame Gentleman, who, by reafon of his Age, and his ftation of being appointed by the Earl of *Douglas* for your Governor, had the moft occafion to be furpriz'd at your return, and to ask you the reafon of it, was the firft who gave a good example to the reft ; I proteft to you, I wonder at your good Fortune, and find no reafon to pity you, fince *Julia* is contented you fhould come and fee her, this being in my Opinion a moft effential Demonftration of her Friendfhip.   Perhaps,

Perhaps, *reply'd* Hypolitus, *with some impatience*, I am in the wrong not to be fatisfy'd with my good Fortune ; but Alas! my dear Earl, were you fenfible what a violent Paffion is, you would foon be of my Opinion; but you act the Coquet with the fair Sex, you tell a Thoufand pretty things to every Lady you meet with, and never Love any of them : I have often wondred, nay, have bin Angry at it. My dear *Hypolitus*, *faid the Earl interrupting him*, you fancy the true felicity of Life to confift in Loving beyond all meafure, but I am of a quite contrary Sentiment : I would have a Man appear Gallant among the Ladies, I would have him alfo make his Addreffes to them, in order to merit fome of their favours; but I would not have him engag'd fo far as to difturb his own Tranquility, or to make him neglect either his Duty or his Fortune. *Cæfar* was Amorous in time of Peace, but indifferent to Ladies in time of War : Every Kingdom or Province he came into afforded him a new Miftrefs, and thus Love in Great Men ought not to go beyond an Amufement; but after all I would not have a Man be without it, becaufe we owe moft of our Politenefs to the Converfation of Ladies, fince it by degrees fmooths our Temper and takes away its roughnefs, for it muft be confefs'd that they are moft refin'd in Converfation; notwithftanding all this, I ftill am of Opinion that nothing is more dangerous than thofe violent frenzical Paffions, which diffenable us to think of any thing befides how to adore our Miftreffes A Man under thefe Circumftances foon grows troublefome to all the World, nay, even to himfelf; he is unfit for Civil Society, he cry's, he fighs, always difturb'd, and very often jealous and peevifh : You pay dearly for a happy Moment, which is preceded and follow'd by a Thoufand others that difturb your reft. For

E 3 God

God fake, *cry'd* Hypolitus, *interrupting him*, your
Criticifin is too fevere, and your Palate out of tafte,
two or three fuch Interlocutions wou'd make me
your irreconcilable Enemy, and I am not able to
tell you what a Paffion you have put me into,
whilft you was framing your procefs againft the
True Lover. The Earl of *Suffex* burft out a Laughing, and told him, He would vex him no more,
provided he would not contradict him in his way
of loving after his own fancy.

It being day-break before they finifh'd their
difcourfe, they did not rife out of their Bed till it
was pretty late; *Hypolitus* defired the Earl to go to
Buckingham Houfe, in order to fettle matters with
Julia and *Lucilia*, to let him in at the back Gate
near the little Wood. He willingly accepted
of the Commiffion, and my Lord and my Lady
Douglas having a great efteem for him, they
were both overjoy'd to fee him: You come in a
lucky time, *faid my Lady* Douglas *to the Earl*, to
give me fome Confolation on account of the departure of my Son, which much afflicts me. You
are the occafion of it your felf Madam, *faid he to
her*, fince it was your will it fhould be fo, and in
your power to have kept him near you, if you had
thought it convenient. I take you Sir, *faid fhe*, to
reproach me with fuffering him to leave us; but in
truth, tho' his abfence caufes me abundance of
pain, I fee not how we could do otherwife than let
him go Abroad; Tendernefs muft give way fometimes to Intereft, I hope we may fee him again
with fatisfaction within thefe Three Years. *Lucilia* and *Julia* were in the Room whilft they talk'd
thus, and the Earl of *Bedford* coming in foon after, the Earl of *Suffex* entertain'd *Lucilia*, becaufe the Earl of *Bedford* had feated himfelf next
Julia. Every thing being regulated betwixt *Lucilia* and him, concerning the Nocturnal Interview,
he took his leave and return'd to *Hypolitus.*   It

It was judged moſt expedient they ſhould go thither in a Diſguiſe, for fear of being known and diſcover'd upon the Road, which they did accordingly, hiding their Hairs under their Bonnets, and ſo they ſet out on their Journey about Ten a Clock : It happen'd to be a very fine Night, and very ſtill and quiet, they took no more than a *Valet du Chambre* along with them, who was to take care of their Horſes : They came to the little back Gate, which being open, they entred into the Garden, and the two Siſters, who were not far off, hearing the noiſe, immediately came to meet them.

Hypolitus and *Julia* felt at this meeting all that can be ſuppoſed to proceed from a violent Paſſion, their Converſation run for ſome time upon General matters, but ſoon after they parted Companies, tho' neither of them went out of the ſame Walk : *Hypolitus* leading his Miſtreſs by the Hand, as the Earl of *Suſſex* did *Lucilia*. Thanks to Heaven, dear *Hypolitus*, *ſaid ſhe to him*, our abſence has not bin very long, and you are come back in ſpite of all the precautions they have taken to ſeperate us. Were my Paſſion for you, my dear *Julia*, ſaid he, leſs violent than it is, perhaps I might have found it difficult to ſurmount ſo many Obſtacles ; but my Love is too ſtrong, and too ingenuous to be check'd by all the Obſticles they can put in my way. You were ſcarce gone, *continued ſhe*, but your Mother talk'd to me in private, and with ſuch demonſtrations of Friendſhip as almoſt ſurprized me, conſidering how matters ſtood betwixt us ; told me, She had reaſon to believe I intended not to embrace a Religious Life, and that therefore ſhe was oblig'd to adviſe me, as the beſt Friend and Relation I had in the World, to give a favourable Ear to the Earl of *Bedford*'s Addreſſes ; who was a Man of Honour, of Quality, and of a

E 4   GREAT

Great Eftate ; and that once for all, I muft bid
farewell to all thoughts of a Maraiage betwixt you
and I; that fhe could not but frankly tell me,
That it was I that was the only caufe of your abfence, and that neither my Lord nor fhe would
ever confent to your return till I was Marry'd.
And what anfwer pray did you give them, my dear
Lady, *faid* Hypolitus, *with fome impatience?* I told
her, *continued fhe,* That as for the Earl of *Bedford,*
I begg'd of her never to mention any more to me,
fince nothing in the World could have a greater
Averfion againft him than I had ; and, that fince
fhe had fix'd your abfence for three Years, I might,
not without reafon, promife my felf fhe would allow me fome more time to confider of the matter, fince all the Repofe of my Life depended on
it.

She could not refufe me fo reafonable a requeft,
and the Earl of *Bedford* coming at the fame time
when the Earl of *Suffex* was here, he began to renew
his Addreffes, till at laft I told him, That his perfeverance had quite tired my Patience ; that hitherto I had confidered him as one that was indifferent to me ; but that the cafe was alter'd now,
and that I could not look upon him now, but with
an invincible Averfion; and that, if he had a mind to
make me Unfortunate, he might continue to make
his Addreffes to me.   How Madam, *cry'd he,* And
will you enjoyn me not to fee you ? Yes, reply'd I,
I moft earneftly require you would let me be at reft.
Oh ! Madam, *continu'd he,* you reduce me to defpair, Will you envy me the only Felicity I have
left in the World ? I Love, nay, I Adore you, and
what will become of me if I fhould not fee you ?
You muft endeavour to cure your felf, faid I, of a
Paffion which is only troublefome to me, and
which makes you fuffer in vain : Having fpoken
thefe words I left him ; but could at the fame
time

time fee all the marks of defpair in his Eyes. Ah! My dear Lady, how happy am I, and how much am I indebted to you for this Sacrifice, *said* Hypolitus *to her?* It does not deferve the name of a Sacrifice, *reply'd* Julia, I am very well pleas'd when I have an opportunity of treating him at that fcurvy rate; fo that you are not oblig'd to me upon that fcore.

Thus having entertain'd one another for a confiderable time, and given one another a Thoufand reciprocal Affurances and Oaths of an everlafting Fidelity, they agreed to fee one another as often as poffibly they could, for which purpofe a *Valet du Chambre* of the Earl of *Suffex* was to walk every Day, once, at leaft, through the Garden (for fear of being taken notice off if he fhou'd come fo often into the Houfe) and whenever he found a Flower pot with Flowers ftanding in a certain Window of *Julia's* Apartment, this was to ferve as a Signal for *Hypolitus* to come the next following Night to the back Gate near the Wood. Every thing being thus concerted they parted, but with fo much regret, that had it not bin for the Earl of *Suffex* and *Lucilia* who urged them fo to do, they had ftaid together till day light.

In the mean time *Hypolitus* had taken care to have Monfieur *de Bois Dauphin*'s Letter delivered to the Earl of *Douglas* by an unknown hand; The news of the Illnefs of his beloved Son caufed no fmall trouble and vexation in the whole Family, but efpecially to the Earl; and the Son writ from time to time Letters to the Father, as if they had bin dated at *Diep:* Sometimes he would tell him he was on the mending hand, and at another time, that he was worfe again, according as he judg'd it beft for his purpofe, whilft he enjoy'd the fatisfaction unknown to every body, of frequently feeing his Miftrefs. They continu'd in this happy
State

State for above two Months, without the leaſt
ſiniſter Accident or Obſtacle; but their ſatisfaction was too great to laſt much longer, Fortune envious of the ſweet enjoyments of Love,
would needs diſturb their Felicity.

The Earl of *Bedford* touch'd to the very Heart
with Grief at what *Julia* had told him when he
made her the laſt Viſit, had taken a Reſolution
never to ſee her again, and if poſſible not ſo much
as to think of her any more ; He upbraided himſelf, he kept more Company than he us'd to do,
nay, he wiſh'd he might meet with ſome Lady or
other, whoſe Perfections might efface out of
his Heart *Julia's* Charms; but theſe were ſo far
beyond all thoſe he ſaw or knew, that when he
began to compare them to *Julia*, they appear'd
diſpiſeable in his Eyes, and ſerv'd only to encreaſe
his Love for her ; at laſt his Paſſion Augmented to
ſuch a degree, that he began to have recourſe to
violent Remedies, and reſolved to carry off *Julia*
by force. I am ſure, *ſaid he to one of his Friends*,
my Lord *Douglas* will be very glad of the match,
becauſe his Lady is deſcended of my Family, and
he himſelf has offer'd me his Eldeſt Daughter in
Marriage; perhaps he is unwilling to conſtrain
Julia to Marry me, but when I once have got her
in my Power, I am apt to believe he will be ſo far
from being my Enemy, that he will contribute as
much as in him lies to make me happy.

To put his Deſign in execution with all poſſible
expedition, he pitch'd upon my Lord *Douglas's*
Gardiner, who had formerly lived with him, and
knowing him to be a Covetous and Daring Fellow,
he look'd upon him as a fit Inſtrument to aſſiſt him
in the carrying off of this young Lady : He ſent
for him, gave him a good Summ of Money, and
promiſed him more, if he would be aiding in
bringing his deſign about. 'Twill be an eaſie matter

ter for you to compaſs it, ſaid this Fellow to him,
I have the Key of the little back Gate at the farther end of the Garden, and I can conduct you
through a dark Walk to a little pair of back
Stairs, leading up directly into *Julia's* Apartment; I am ſure that Door is very ſeldom lock'd,
becauſe I us'd to go up in the Evening to carry
her ſome Flowers and Fruits; ſo you may eaſily
carry her off, without making the leaſt noiſe in
the Family.

The Earl ſeeing every thing ready to favour his
Deſign, appointed a certain Day for its Execution,
he went accordingly, attended only by two Gentlemen, his faithful Friends, about Eleven a Clock
at Night, and finding the back Door open, left
one of the Gentlemen at a ſmall diſtance thence
with the Horſes, whilſt he and the other entred
the Garden without making the leaſt noiſe. As
ill fortune would have it, this hapned juſt upon
one of theſe Evenings when a Meeting had been
appointed betwixt *Luſilia*, *Julia*, *Hypolitus* and
the Earl of *Suſſex*; and the two firſt, as they were
going to let them in, eſpied two Men by the light
of the Moon, but the Walk leading thither being
pretty Dark and thick of Trees, they could not
diſcern whether they were the ſame Perſons they
look'd for; as theſe on the other hand ſeeing two
Women coming that way were for ſhunning them
and concealing themſelves: What makes you ſhew
ſo little concern for young *Julia*, my dear *Hypolitus*,
ſaid ſhe, to the Earl of *Bedford?* You don't make haſt
to meet me! nay, it ſeems as if you were inclined
to ſhun me, what means this coolneſs? Theſe o-
bliging Reproaches were ſufficient to make the
Earl know his Miſtreſſes Voice, who was almoſt
diſtracted that theſe tender expreſſions were not
intended for him; however overjoy'd to meet
with her in the Garden, he anſwered her not one
word

word for fear of difcovering himfelf; but making
a fign to the Gentleman that was along with him,
to take afide *Lucilia*, and keep her from making
a noife, he himfelf at once laid hold on *Julia*,
and being a lufty ftrong Perfon, he carry'd her, in
fpite of all the refiftance fhe could make, to the
foremention'd back Gate, juft when *Hypolitus* and
the Earl of *Suffex* came into the Garden ; and it
being a very clear Moonlight-Night, and the Earl
of *Bedford* not far from thence, they perceived at
firft fight every thing that pafs'd.   Who is able to
exprefs the fury of *Hypolitus*! Love and Anger
foon made him draw his Sword, and the Earl of
Bedford letting go his hold did the fame, and the
Gentleman that came along with him was glad to
quit *Lucilia :* They were all four brave, and animated by a juft refentment againft one another.
Poor *Julia* and *Lucilia* were put to the greateft
nonplus that could be, what refolution to take ; for
if they call'd for help, *Hypolitus* muft of neceffity
be difcover'd ; if they did not, they feared his deftruction.

In the mean while the Gardiner fearing, not
without reafon, that the clafhing of the Swords
might be heard in the Family, he went thither
himfelf, and having told the Earl of *Douglas* of it,
he haftned into the Garden in Perfon, juft as his
Son was running the Earl of *Bedford* through the
Body, which made him drop in an inftant. *Hypolitus*
hearing a noife of feveral more Perfons coming
that way, told the Earl it was time to fecure their
Retreat; but they found the little Gate lock'd up,
and all the Earls Family running that way ; fo into the Gardners Lodge they get, were they baricado'd up the Door, whilft my Lord *Douglas* pofted
his Servants round about it to prevent their making their efcape, little thinking it had bin his Son
and the Earl of *Suffex* that were come thither in
                                    Difguife.

Difguife. He order'd the Earl of *Bedford* to be carry'd into the Houfe, and for fear, in cafe he fhould happen to dye, his Death might be laid at his door, he fent for a Conftable ; This Night Magiftrate with his Attendants came well arm'd after their manner at Day break, juft when *Hypolitus* and the Earl of *Suffex* had bin opening their way with their Swords thro' thofe that guarded the Lodge, and had infallibly made their efcape, becaufe they drove my Lord's Servants before them, like as two Young Lions would have done a parcel of Curs, had they not been Surrounded by the Conftable and his Affiftance, who crying out they fhould Knock them down, and rather Kill them than fuffer them to get off, they thought it better to Surrender themfelves, than to expofe their Lives at fuch vaft odds.

Julia and *Lucilia* were fitting all this while under a Tree, almoft half dead with fear and vexation, which was fuch as is paft expreffing it ; but when they faw them carry'd Prifoners to the Houfe, they follow'd them at fome fmall diftance, fo as not to lofe fight of them. The Countefs of *Douglas*, big with expectation to fee them, as they were brought into the Dining-room ordred their Bonnets to be taken of (which conceal'd their Hair, and in fome meafure hid their Faces ;) but fhe no fooner difcover'd *Hypolitus*, but fetching a great cry, juft Heaven, *faid fhe*, 'tis my Son, and fo fell into a deep Swoon. My Lord *Douglas*, who had not taken notice hitherto of what had hapned, turning that way, was not a little furpriz'd to find his Son Prifoner in his own Houfe, when he thought him to be Sick at *Diep :* He was not able to fpeak for fome time, but at laft recollecting himfelf, and looking upon him with Eyes fparkling with Anger, Is it poffible that what I fay be true, Is it you *Hypolitus ?* What is
your

your meaning by all this? At a time when I suppo-
fed you to be in *France*, I find you Difguis'd in
my own Houfe with Sword in Hand, and under
the misfortune of having Wounded a Gentleman
who was our real Friend, one who bares the
fame name as your Mother does, and who is a
Perfon both of a great Eftate and Intereft? What
do you think will be the end of this? For my Part
I think you fo unworthy of my Protection, that
I am fully refolv'd to leave you abfolutely to the
feverity of the Law.

Julia, who till now had remain'd in one Corner
of the Room, being now no longer Miftrefs of her
pain and fear, Oh! Father, *cry'd fhe*, throwing
her felf at his Feet, and crying moft bitterly, no
body deferves to be punifh'd but my felf, becaufe *Hypolitus* was oblig'd to fight the Earl of
Bedford in my Defence; and had it not bin for him,
he had carry'd me away, he held me in his Arms
and was hurrying me away by force, and in a
moft rude and barbarous manner: Difcharge all
your Anger upon me, continued fhe, fpare your
own Blood, and rather be profufe of mine.
Withdraw *Julia*, faid the Earl, endeavouring to
hide part of his Refentment, I find there is more
in the bottom of it than I could wifh for; go
along with your Sifter to your Chamber, and
don't ftir thence without my Order.

The unfortunate *Julia*, as fhe was going to her
Confinement, caft a Melancholly, but very amorous look at her Lover; who, foon fenfible of
the effects thereof, ftop'd her: He, I fay, who
had not as much as fpoken one Word in his own
behalf, would not be wanting in taking his dear
Miftreffes part: Sir, what has *Julia* done, faid he
to his Father, you punifh her for my faults? what
is it fhe has committed to deferve fo ill a Treatment
at your Hands? Hold your Tongue Young Confidence,

dence, *said my Lord*, don't exasperate me more, and so he parted with them.

The Earl of *Suffex* who was a Spectator of this whole Scene, was ready to run Distracted at this unlucky Accident, and my Lady *Douglas* no sooner was recover'd out of her Swoon, but she addrefs'd her self to him : Sir, *said she*, you are a very dangerous Friend, you have shew'd too much Complaisance for my Sons frailties; you fee alas! to what extremities we are reduc'd to; can there be a more deplorable cafe than ours? I think *Hypolitus*'s cafe, *reply'd the Earl, with a great deal of Refolution*, is much more worthy of Compaffion, you are too rigorous in exacting fo strict an Obedience, and to fend him away at a time, when you knew he was fo violently in Love. 'Twas done said the Countefs, *interrupting him*, to cure him of this Paffion ; we were in hopes that abfence would produce the fame effect as it does in moft Men; and I believe, had my Son not found you fo much difpofed to ferve him, he had gone for *France*, and don't doubt but would have forgot *Julia* by this time.

Whilft they were thus difputing the matter, in comes the Surgeon who had drefs'd the Earl of *Bedford*'s Wounds, and told them, he had no lefs than three ; but that one appear'd to them to be mortal. The Conftable underftanding this, required my Lord *Douglas* to deliver up his Son to him, in order to have him examin'd and committed to *Newgate* ; but my Lord found means to engage the next Juftice of Peace to take Bail for his Son's Appearance to the Value of 2000 Pounds Sterling : My Lord and my Lady *Douglas*, the Earl of *Suffex* would have withdrawn with the reft, becaufe they had conceived a fingular Averfion againft him, but this Generous Friend did as if he did not perceive it, and diffembling his

Refentment

Refentment at this time, told them frankly he would run the fame Fate with *Hypolitus* ; that he refolv'd not to leave him, and that if he were to be ruin'd, he would bare his fhare in his Deftruction : So they were lock'd up in one Apartment, and *Julia* and *Lucilia* were as narrowly Confin'd in theirs.

Matters being thus regulated at Home, My Lord and my Lady *Douglas* went ftraitway to *London*, and immediately waited on the Countefs *Dowager* of *Bedford*: She was not unacquainted with her Son's Paffion for *Julia*, and had given her Confent that he might feek her in Marriage, but knew nothing of the laft Nights Adventure ; fhe was no lefs afflicted at the danger fhe underftood he was in, than at the odnefs of the misfortune he had brought upon himfelf. You may perhaps Madam, *faid my Lord to her,* create us abundance of Trouble, but in the end it will fall heavieft upon your felf ; for when it fhall be proved at his Tryal, that the Earl was attempting to carry off *Julia* by force, and that her Brother to refcue her was forc'd to fight him, and gave him his Wound on that account, all the blame will be laid at your Son's Door ; therefore I would have you confider whether you will be fatisfy'd with the offer I intend to make you, that is, I will condefcend fo far as to fend *Hypolitus* Abroad for Three Years, that he may be no Eye fore to you ; and in cafe the Earl of *Bedford* recovers of his Wounds, and that his Paffion for *Julia* is ftill the fame as 'twas before, I will do all that is in my Power to make her Marry him.

My Lady *Bedford* told them, She would refolve upon nothing in a cafe of this nature without the advice of her neareft Friends and Relations, who, upon this difmal news reparing to her Houfe, and being confulted withal concerning my Lord *Douglas's las*'s Propofition, they willingly agreed to it, telling my Lady, fhe could defire no more, and that they wondred my Lord would confent to his Son's departure out of *England*; but they were altogether Strangers to thofe fecret motives that induced him to make this Offer. Every thing being fetled betwixt them, the Earl of *Douglas* went immediately in his Barge to *Gravefend*, (being inform'd that a Veffel lay there ready to fail for *Leghorn*) with a refolution to fend away *Hypolitus* aboard her, not doubting but that the *Italian* Beauties would foon make him forget *England*, and what he had left behind him there; He agreed with the Captain for the Price of his Tranfportation, and being told by him, that he was ready, and ftaid only for a fair Wind, and therefore much queftion'd whether he fhould have time enough to fend for his Paffenger out of the Country, My Lord told him, he would bring his Son to *London*, to be ready to embark as foon as opportunity fhould prefent.

'Tis impoffible to reprefent the deplorable ftate *Hypolitus* was reduc'd to, he fear'd every thing in behalf of *Julia*, and did not in the leaft doubt, but that his Father was feeking means for their feparation; thefe fad Reflections would certainly have thrown him into Defpair, had not that Courage which was natural to him, triumph'd over all his Misfortunes; he could not prevail fo far upon any of thofe that were fet to guard him, to connive at his Efcape, but he found it no great difficulty to learn by them every thing that paſs d; for looking upon him in fome meafure as their Mafter, and having a fingular kindnefs for him, they told him what his Father had bin doing at *London*; fo that being fully convinced that this *Gravefend* Voyage would produce but little good for him, he ask'd the *Valet du Chambre*, that con-

F   ftantly

ftantly attended him, Whether he would oblige him fo far as to deliver a Letter to *Julia*, and bring her Anfwer to him? The young Fellow paufed a while, but at laft, thinking there could be no great hurt betwixt a Brother and Sifters Correfpondence, he promifed to do it; and as for *Hypolitus* he run no hazard in the Cafe, fince his Parents were not unacquainted with his Paffion for *Julia*, unto whom he writ thefe following Lines:

IS it poffible, my Lovely Julia, *that the fame Houfe where firft of all I felt the powerful effects of your Eyes, where I fo often have tafted the pleafure of entertaining you, we fhould at prefent be fo far remote from enjoying that Felicity? I being the only Caufe of your Sufferings, the Torments I feel had before this put an end to my Life, were it not that Love protects and fupports me againft my Defpair. But, alas! what can I hope for from this Love? I am upon the point of lofing you, in fpite of all my endeavours againft it. What Terrors, Good God, don't I feel within me? Alas! they are going to hurry me away from the place you are in? The very Thought of this Separation touches me fo to the quick, that nothing but your own Heart is capable of judging what a condition I am reduc'd to. If in the very depth of this Abyfs of Miferies, I have fome glimpfes of light left me, that may afford me fome Comfort, 'tis the hopes I have conceived, that you will prove for ever Faithful and Conftant to me. Is it poffible,* Julia, *you fhould prove treacherous to a Man who thinks every thing in the World below you, and who will never believe any thing worthy to be compar'd to you? I am free to tell you, that I think it unneceffary to Vow you my everlafting Conftancy by new Oaths, you being too well aequainted with my Heart, and what power you have over it. No, my* Julia, *no, I fhall always be the fame, 'twon't be in my power to ceafe to*
                                        adore

adore you, and in spite of all the Rage and Malice our Enemies are able to contrive to cause me new Vexations and Torments, my Passion shall always be as constant as ever it was. Write to me, dear Lady, don't leave me in this deplorable State, unto which I am reduced, you being the Soveraign Mistress of my Destiny, and the only Object of all my Desires and Wishes.

The Fair *Julia* having received this Letter, was a long time reading of it, because she was scarce able to see the Characters of her dear *Hypolitus*, by reason of the abundance of Tears that covered her fair Eyes and Cheeks; *Lucilia* had much to do to Comfort her a little, tho' she almost stood as much in need of it as her self, my Lord and my Lady *Douglas* being highly incensed against her, because they believed her to be a Confederate in the Intrigues betwixt *Julia* and *Hypolitus*; She urged her to send an Answer to her Brother, she did all she could to stop the Torrent of her Tears; but tho' she did all she could to refrain her Passion, the Letter she writ was quite bathed with her Tears before she could finish it, and was as follows:

A Las! are you at the point of being seperated from me, my dear Hypolitus? *And must I see you no more? Who can possibly comprehend my Pain, and the miserable state I am reduc'd to? Alas! Is it possible that Innocent Tenderness we conceiv'd for one another, even before we were sensible of it, or in a condition to resist it, should thus raise the Anger of Heaven against us? What Torrents of Misfortunes! How is it possible for us to stop them? I have not only lost all my Enjoyment and Repose, but even Reason it self; 'tis not in my Power to resolve to see you leave me, and yet notwithstanding all the Torments that oppress us, I must see you to depart. Let us then my dear Lover,*

F 2   *endeavour*

endeavour to Tryumph over our Misfortunes by our Con-
ftancy ; You promife to remain always faithful to me,
and in whofe Power is it then to render us unfaithful to
one another ? Nothing in this World, nay, not Death
it felf; your Conftancy fhall Tryumph over our Mif-
fortunes, we fhall fee one another again dear Hypolitus, *and Love will be the reward of our Sufferings.*

These tender and engaging affurances given by
the fair *Julia* to her *Hypolitus*, could never have
come at a more proper time, when he ftood in
need of all his Refolutions to fupport his drooping
Heart againft thofe violences my Lord *Douglas* was
at that very time preparing for him ; for within a
few Hours after, he fent for him and the Earl of
Suffex, and likewife for *Julia* and *Lucilia*, and in the
prefence of his Lady, after a few moments filence,
began thus to harangue his Son: I did not, *Hypolitus*, fend for you now hither, to load you with Reproaches, fuch as you have too much deferved ;
you have withdrawn your felf from that fubmiffion
you owe unto us; you have deceived us by ficti-
tious Letters ; you have blindly follow'd the firft
motions of your Heart, and *Julia* bares her fhare
in that Difobedience you have fhew'd us: But reft
affured, and I call Heavens to witnefs to what I am
going to declare to you, That we will never confent to your Marriage with her. Had your Conduct bin otherwife than it has bin, fomething perhaps might have bin expected from our Complaifance; but now it is become fo odious to us, that
rather than to give our approbation of fuch a
Match, there is nothing we would not undertake
both againft you and her ; for tho' fhe is not really
our Daughter, fhe has fo much dependance on us,
that it is in our power either to make her whole
Life happy or miferable; therefore be advis'd,
and recal your Heart within the bounds of its
                                                    Duty

Duty, refolve to take a Voyage to *Florence*, where
to your good Fortune you will meet with fome
Friends, who in your Perfon will give me infallible Demonftrations of their affection ; you will
be look'd upon with a good Eye by the Illuftrious
Houfe of the *de Medices* ; and to make you acquainted with the true caufe thereof, I will tell
you, That above Forty Years ago, being a Tra-
veller in *Italy*, juft as you are going to be now,
Fortune furnifh'd me with an opportunity of doing
a confiderable piece of fervice to the Cardinal *de
Medicis*, who was afterwards made Pope, and
known under the Name of *Leo* X.

He being then the Popes Legate in the Army of
the League, was taken Prifoner at the Battle of
Ravenna, and by *Gafton de Frixy*, order'd to be
fent into *France :* He was fo feufibly afflicted at
his Misfortune, that all his Thoughts were employ'd how to make his efcape, but met with fuch
Obfticles as rendred all his Efforts impracticable,
till at laft a Gentleman of his Bed-Chamber, who
attended him, found means to engage the brave
Zaeti into his Intereft. I hapned to be with *Zaeti*
when this Gentleman propofed the Cardinal's deliverance to him, and *Zaeti* defiring me to go along
with him upon a certain fecret enterprize, we
came to the Banks of the *Po* juft as the Cardinal
was ready to pafs that River in a Ferry-boat ; to
be fhort, we beat the Convoy and refcu'd the
Cardinal, whom we carry'd in Difguife to the
Caftle of *Barnaby Melifpine* ; here I took leave of
him with my Friend *Zaeti*, and the Cardinal affured us of his acknowledgment in the moft obliging Terms that could be; and I muft confefs,
that fince his Elevation to the Papal Chair, which
hapned about a Year after, he gave me fufficient
reafon, (upon divers occafions) to believe that
he was not forgetful of what I had done for him.

　　　　　　　　　　Thus

Thus you fee Son, you may expect a favourable
reception from Duke *Cofmus*, unto whom you
fhall be introduc'd by the Senetor *Alberto*, defcended from one of the moft illuftrious Houfes of *Florence*, my moft intimate Friend ; for tho' I am
much older than he, our friendfhip is never a jot
the lefs : He has bin twice in *England* and *Scotland*,
and I can affure you, he is a Perfon of fuch vaft
merits, that I fhall not be in the leaft uneafie, after
I hear you are with him, and I will take care you
fhall want nothing there that may be either neceffary or pleafing to you ; not that we are willing
to part with you, but that according to a late A-
greement made with my Lady *Bedford*, I am under a neceffity to fend you out of *England* on account of the Quarrel betwixt you and her Son, who
is not beyond all danger of his Life ; if you don't
go, or return into *England* before the three years are
expired, I will be the firft that will get you feiz'd,
and perhaps the mortifications of a naufeous Prifon
will prove more prevailing Arguments with you
than all our Remonftances. Son, your Liberty is
in your own hands, but we can't enjoy any till
you are gone out of *England* ; if my Lord *Suffex*,
who has bin fo faithful in ferving you of late,
will fpeak to you as a real Friend, he will certainly advife you to obey us, and, that your dear *Julia*
may do the fame with the lefs conftraint, we will
leave you together to bid her farewel.

At thefe words he went out of the Room without ftaying for an Anfwer, being follow'd by my
Lady *Douglas* in an inftant. Our Lovers then
drawing nearer to one another, whilft the Earl
entertain'd *Lucilia*, *Hypolitus* threw himfelf at
Julia's Feet, kifs'd her Hand, not being able to exprefs his Grief but by his Looks and Sighs ; a
fort of Language which proving very intelligible and endearing to *Julia*, fhe broke filence firft ;
Don't

Don't be quite difmaid, *faid fhe,* my dear and too
Unfortunate *Hypolitus,* if our Misfortunes are
great, our mutual Tendernefs is ftill greater ;
one Moment may caufe a great alteration in our
Deftiny ; You are going at a great diftance from
me, 'tis a neceffity I don't fee we are able to avoid,
and therefore muft fubmit to it with Patience ;
and 'tis impoffible for thofe that feperate our Bodies, to fnatch from our Hearts thofe Engagements
that have united them ; our abfence is to laft
Three Years, perhaps before they are at and End,
Heaven will take pity of us. Oh ! *Julia, Julia,*
cry'd he, You put no fmall conftraint upon your
felf, in hopes to fupport my drooping Spirits ;
you would comfort me with hopes full of Uncertainty, at a time when I am going to lofe, without
Reprieve, the only thing that is dear to me in this
World : I ufed to fee you, dear Lady, and now I
muft fee you no more, what a Fatality is this ? Can
you refolve to ftay behind in this detefted place,
were you meet with fo much ill Treatment ? Is
not that alone fufficient to caufe in me a Mortal
inquietude where-ever I go ? You are too Ingenuous in Tormenting your felf, *Hypolitus, faid* Julia,
I fhall be the fame here I fhould be in any other
place ; for my whole mind being taken up with
you, I fhall look upon all other objects with fo
much indifferency, as to make me infenfible both
of the good and ill Treatment I am likely to
meet with. And will you not let me hear of you,
my *Julia, faid he?* I could wifh, *reply'd fhe,* you
could hear as often as I could wifh ; you might be
fure you would never want that fatisfaction. But
how fhall we do to write to one another ? *Lucilia*
and the Earl of *Suffex* were not fo deeply engag'd
in difcourfe, but that they took notice fometimes
of our two Lovers ; over-hearing thefe laft words,
drew nearer, and told them, They fhould leave

that part to *their* Care, and that they would manage it well enough betwixt them; That they had nothing to do but to direct their Letters to the Earl, who was to deliver them to *Lucilia*. That cruel Moment which was to seperate these two Lovers being now at hand, *Julia* took out of her Bosom a Bracelet set with Diamonds, on which hung a small Picture, representing two Hearts pierced thro' with one Dart, made of her own Hair, with this Motto underneath: *They are joyn'd for ever.*

Keep this Present, *said she*, my dear *Hypolitus*, you are the only Man that knows the value of it. He was Transported with joy at this favour he durst scarce have ask'd; he kiss'd this dear Pledge of his lovely Mistress with all the Transports of Love that can be imagined, and then Embracing, once bid farewel to one another; but with such Agonies and Distraction of mind, that the Earl of *Suffex* and *Lucilia* were not able to forbear to mix their Tears and Sighs with those of the two Lovers. At that very instant the Earl of *Douglas* and his Lady coming into the Room, ordred *Hypolitus* to follow them out, whereat he appear'd so surpriz'd as if he had never expected any such thing; he turn'd his Eyes upon *Julia*, who kept hers fix d on the Ground to hide her Tears. *Lucilia* and the Earl, observing *Hypolitus* unresolved what to do, took him under the Arms and so led him down stairs; he embrac'd his Sister with all the marks of Tenderness, and told her several times, That the best and the only proof she could give him of her Friendship was, to devote all her cares to be servicable to *Julia*; and to him, in speaking to her at all times in his behalf.

So he departed, and *Julia* was left at full Liberty to give vent to her Moans, Sighs, and Sobs; 'twas in vain for *Lucilia*, to endeavour to afford
her

her fome Confolation ; For, fo foon as *Hypolitus*
was got out of fight, fhe threw her felf upon the
Ground, and leaning her Head in *Lucilia*'s Lap,
fhe exprefs'd her felf in Terms fo full of Tendernefs and Paffion, as would have allay'd in fome meafure *Hypolitus*'s Grief, had he bin near enough to
hear it. He on the other hand abandon'd himfelf
no lefs to this tormenting Thought than fhe, keeping a moft profound filence, without fo much as
uttering one word, till coming Aboard the Veffel,
he was to take leave of his belov'd Generous
Friend the Earl of *Suffex*. The Wounds of his
Heart beginning to bleed afrefh at this Seperation, I
am then Condemn'd to lofe All my dear Friend, *faid
he, embracing him* ; We muft part, I thought after
what I had left behind in *Buckinghamfhire*, I could
not be fenfible of any other lofs, fince that firft
ftroak would make me infenfible of all the reft ;
but confidering the condition I find my felf in at
this Moment, I am apt to believe, that Love even
in its moft exalted degree, is not incompatible
with Friendfhip ; preferve me yours my Lord,
pray do that juftice to thefe Sentiments I have for
you : He was not able to fay any more, and the
Earl was fo highly afflicted at this difmal parting,
that he could fay not one word, but Embraced
him with fuch extraordinary marks of affection
and with Tears in his Eyes, in my Lord and my
Lady's prefence, that, notwithftanding all their
anger on account of having fupported *Hypolitus*
his Caufe, they could not but be very well pleas'd
thereat. As for *Hypolitus*, he was himfelf again
expos'd to the trouble of his Father's and Mother's
Leffons and Advice ; but being vext to the Heart
at their rigorous proceedings, he would not put
fo much of conftraint upon himfelf as to hide his
Sentiments, but broke out into fuch mournful
complaints, as would have touch'd any body's
Heart

Heart but that of his Fathers. They had taken
care also to provide him new Servants, being not
very well satisfy'd with those that had remain'd at
the Earl of *Suffex*'s House in the Country. *Hypolitus* rewarded their Fidelity with some Mony, defiring his Father to take care of them, which he
promis'd to do, by taking some into his own Service, and recommending the rest to some of his
Friends.

My Lord and my Lady *Douglas* return'd in their
Barge towards *London*, and took the Earl of
Suffex along with them, to take away all hopes
from *Hypolitus* of returning a second time : Before
they were got quite out of fight, the Wind chop-
ping about, they saw the Veffel hoift their Sails,
and after a difcharge of some Cannon, to make
the beft of his way to purfue his Voyage for *Italy.*
Hypolitus remain'd upon Deck as long as he could
fee the *Englifh* Shoar, fending forth a Thousand
Sighs towards that part of the Country where a-
bout he judg'd his dear *Julia* might be ; He wifh'd
a Thousand times, that by some violent Tempeft
they might be forced back into one of the *Englifh*
Harbors : And it was not many Days after they
had loft fight of the *Englifh* Coaft, that they were
overtaken by so violent a Storm, as put them in the
utmoft danger of being loft, all the Hands they
had a Board being not fufficient to manage the
Ship ; for the Mafts came by the Board, the Cables
broke, and the Sails were fhatter'd to pieces, the
Veffel being fometimes covered with Mountains of
Water, which foon wou'd raife her up to the
Clouds, and immediately afterwards feem to
fwallow her up in the Depths of the Sea; every
one dreading his approaching fate, they fent forth
moft Lamentable crys to Heaven, looking with
doleful Countinances upon thofe fhelves on which
they fear'd the Veffel would be ftav'd to pieces.

Hypolitus

Hypolitus was the only Perfon there, who appear'd more Courageous than all thofe that had for a long time bin accuftom'd to the Danger of the Seas; he feem'd undifturb'd, expecting Death with an unfhaken refolution; nay, he wifh'd for it fome times, as the only Remedy that was likely to rid him of his Pain; notwithftanding which, fuch was his prefence of Mind, that he gave Orders in every thing that fell within his Knowledge.

At laft this terrible Tempeft ceafed, the Sky began to be Serene, no Thunder or Lightning to be heard or feen any longer, the Storm was fucceeded by a Calm, and the Sea became fo fmooth as if the Wind were quite Banifh'd from the Sea. All Hands were now employ'd in repairing the damage the Veffel had received during the Tempeft, and they had much ado to finifh the'r Work before they were threatned with another Danger, by the fo much celebrated and redoubted Pirate, *Dragut Rais :* He no fooner got fight of the *Englifh* Ship, but he prepared for an Engagement, the *Englifhman* refufing to Strike at the Sign given him by the Pirate. 'Twas at this time that *Hypolitus* laying afide all his Troubles, behaved himfelf like a Man of Action, encouraging the Captain and Seamen, not only by his Words, but alfo by his Example. After they had ply'd one another briskly for fome time with their Great Guns, the *Turk* Boarded the *Englifhman*, upon which occafion *Hypolitus* did wonders in his own Perfon, appearing every where where the Danger was greateft, carrying every thing before him where-ever he came: At laft he leap'd into the Enemy's Ship, follow'd only by a few of his Men; but the great Actions they perform'd aboard the *Turkifh* Veffel, put *Dragut Rais* into fuch a Fright, that he thought it his fafeft way to think of retreating, for fear of falling into his Enemy's Hands.

Hands. Accordingly he gave the neceſſary Orders for getting his Ship off clear from the *Engliſh-*
man, which he would have found a hard matter
to effect, had not *Hypolitus* at the ſame time perceived a *Turk* aboard his own Ship laying about
him moſt bravely, killing all that came in his way,
and making a Baricado of dead Carcaſſes to defend himſelf alone againſt all the reſt, ſo that
ſcarce any one durſt venture to come near him.
Seized with a noble Emulation to fight this brave
Enemy, *Hypolitus* got back again into the *Englifh*
Veſſel, and whilſt theſe two brave Men were engaged in a moſt furious Combat, the Pirate took
the opportunity of getting clear, and ſhearing off:
Nothing elſe could have parted theſe two valiant
Men, who were both wounded in ſeveral places, and
he who belonged to the *Turkiſh* Ship ſeeing himſelf
left behind alone, had no other way left him
than to ſurrender himſelf to *Hypolitus,* whom he
judged to be moſt worthy of that Honour. Uſe
me, ſaid he to him in *Englifh,* as I have always uſed
thoſe of your Nation, who hitherto have always
had reaſon to be ſatisfied with my Deportment
towards them. I hope, ſaid *Hypolitus* to him,
you ſhall likewiſe have no other reaſon than to
be ſatisfied with me ; and ſo he went to the Captain of the Ship, deſiring he might be treated
with peculiar reſpect, as a brave and valiant Man.
We owe every thing to your Valour ſaid the
Captain, and ſince without your aſſiſtance, we
ſhould ſcarce have come off with ſo much Honour
as we have done, the Perſon you intercede for is
at your abſolute diſpoſal ; the only thing I have
to deſire of you, being to take care of your ſelf,
and to have your Wounds look'd after without
delay. *Hypolitus* return'd him thanks for his Civilities and Care, and finding himſelf much weak-
ned, becauſe he had loſt abundance of Blood, he
                                                         was

was forced to lay himfelf to reft upon his Bed;
but he fcarce got thither, when remembring his
Prifoner, he ordred a Bed to be got ready for
him in his own Cabin, where he defired him to
lye down and let his Wounds be fearch'd. None
of them were found to be dangerous, and had
Hypolitus bin as fecure in all other refpects, his
Cure would have been both eafie and fhort; but
fo foon as he had no more Enemies to encounter,
he relapfed into his former Melancholy, and his
Prifoner heard him cry out in his Sleep for feveral
Nights fucceffively, Oh! *Julia, Julia,* in lofing
thee I have loft All; nothing can Comfort me for
your Abfence.

After this, it was no hard matter for *Muley*
(for that was the Valiant Prifoner's Name) to
guefs that *Hypolitus* was in Love, and overburthen'd with heavy Afflictions. *Muley* was of a
middle Age, exactly well fhap'd, and had moft
regular Features with a certain haughty and
noble, but moft engaging Air, and Politenefs in
his Converfation. I cant well conceive, faid *Hypolitus* to him one day, how a Perfon that makes
profeffion of Pirating fhould appear with fo Ho-
nourable a Character, fo agreeable, and fo far
different in his whole deportment from what may
be fuppofed to belong to the Life that you lead!
Muley fetching a deep figh, told him, that every
one was not at all times Mafter of his own Deftiny,
to chufe fuch as he could wifh; That he could not
but own, that God had not fent him into this
World to act the Pirate; but that he was com-
pell'd to embrace this Life by the Barbarous
ufage of *Dragut Rais.* This Anfwer raifed a more
than ordinary Curiofity in *Hypolitus,* I fay in the
fame *Hypolitus,* who ever fince he had bin forced
to leave his Miftrefs, had not fhewn the leaft concern for any thing; but now feeling within his

Breaft

Breaſt a certain Emotion which made him very
deſirous of being better acquainted with *Muley* ;
I know not who you are, ſaid he, but you appear
to me to be above what you ſeem to be ; if you
will diſcover your ſelf upon your Honour and
Faith, I ſhall take it as a ſingular Obligation, and
you may be fully aſſured both of my Secrecy and
of my Friendſhip. Your Duty obliges you to
both, ſaid *Muley*, embracing him ; for I dare
aſſure you, that I am one of your Father, the
Earl of *Douglas*'s beſt Friends : The firſt thing I
did, was to enquire after your Name, and it ſeems
to me next to a Miracle, I ſhould happen to fall into
your Hands. Whilſt he was a talking, *Hypolitus* had
leaſure to view him much better than he had done
before, and diſcovered in him a certain near reſemblance to his dear *Julia*, both in reſpect of his
Air and Features. Ah! I pray you don't envy
me any longer the ſatisfaction of knowing you,
ſaid he to him. You can ſcarce remember any thing
of me except my Name, *continu'd* Muley, and perhaps you may have heard your Parents talking of
my Misfortunes : I am the ſame Earl of *Warwick*,
who was ſuppos'd to be Slain in the *Venetian* Service Fourteen Years ago. At theſe words *Hypolitus* fetch'd a ſudden cry, and appear'd ſo far
Tranſported with Joy, that my Lord *Warwick*
(for it was actually he) could not but be ſurpriz'd
at his Deportment, nor gueſs at the reaſon thereof ; but their firſt ſurprize being over, *Hypolitus*
by thoſe extraordinary marks of Tenderneſs and
Reſpect, having ſoon convinc'd him that he had
ſuch Sentiments for his Perſon, as could not be
the product of a few Minutes Converſation, he
conjur'd him to give him a relation of his Adventures, aſſuring him, that no body in the World
could take a greater ſhare in them than himſelf.

I may

I may foon fatisfy your Curiofity, *faid he to him*,
I am a Catholick, you are not unacquainted with
my Family, I Married one of the moft Handfomeft
and moft Vertuous Women in the World ; but
Fortune envious of my happinefs, and the fatisfaction I enjoy'd in her, thought fit to part us ;
For *Edward Navelle* my near Kinfman being accus'd
of, and Condemn'd for High Treafon, had his
Head cut off ; and the King being inform'd that I
had let drop fome threatning words, I foon became the object of his Hatred, which oblig'd me,
to avoid the effects of his Vengeance, to quit my
dear Spoufe and the Kingdom alfo, leaving with
my Vertuous Wife one Daughter only, nam'd *Julia*,
which was then no more than Two Years old, and
very dear to us both. If at that very inftant the
Earl of *Warwick* had caft but an Eye upon *Hypolitus*, he might foon have difcover'd in his Countenance the various Agitations this name produc'd in
his Soul ; but his thoughts being taken up wholly
with his Relation, he continu'd thus : I went
to *Venice*, embark'd aboard the Fleet Commanded by their Chief General *Capello*, and being joyn'd
by the *Spanifh* and the Popes Gallies near *Corfo*,
we engag'd *Barbaroffa*, and the Galley I was in,
more than once attack'd that wherein was the
Famous *Corfaire Dragut Rais*, with good fuccefs on
our fide, but very unfortunate for him ; for I
flew *Zinkin Rais* his own Brother, whom he lov'd
as tenderly as his own Life : He Swore he wou'd
be reveng'd of me, and fucceeded in his Vow ; for
whilft we were hovering about the Gulph of *Arta*,
and the Prince *Doria* retreating with his Squadron
to the furprize of all the World, *Dragut Rais* animated with hatred againft me, took this opportunity of furrounding our Galley with his whole
Squadron ; I did all I could to defend my felf againft
fo many Enemies, and was feconded moft bravely
by

by another *Venetian* Galley ; but being quite over-power'd, drop't into the Sea cover'd all over with Wounds : *Dragut Rais* who faw it, Commanded me immediately to be taken up, not out of any kindnefs to my Perfon, but to fatisfy his revenge for the Death of his Brother, for he put me imme-diately in Chains.

Whatever promifes or propofals I could make to him for my Liberty, it avail'd nothing : I had continued in this miferable condition for above four Years, when we took an *Englifh* Veffel after a fmart Engagement ; the Misfortunes of my Country-men ferved only to revive in me the Thoughts of my own ; I afk'd them what news they brought from *England*, and whether they had heard nothing lately concerning the Countefs of *Warwick?* There hapned to be among the *Englifh* Prifoners, one whom fhe had taken into her Service fince I left *England*, and who had liv'd with her till fhe dy'd ; a doleful fatal Day to me, and which I can never call to mind without Tears. The Earl over-burthen'd with Grief, ftopt here for fome time, till at laft reaffuming the thread of his Difcourfe, and recovering his Spirits, almoft drooping at the remembrance of that Malancholly Hour, I underftood by him, *continu'd he*, that my Lady *Warwick* hearing the news of my being flain (which fhe believed to be too true) fhe was fo overwhelm'd with Grief, as to fink quite under it pafs'd all Recovery ; in fhort, fhe Dy'd in a few Days after. This fad Relation was follow'd by a-nother, *viz.* By that of the Death of my Daugh-ter, that Innocent Babe, that was fo dear to me, being the only thing after her Mother's Death that could incline me to live. 'Tis certain that this laft ftroak, quite crufh'd me almoft to nothing, fuch was my Affliction as to render me quite infenfible of all the hardfhips of my Captivity ; and that to

fuch

such a degree, that the *Corsair* was vex'd at it to the Heart, he renew'd his Threats continually, but these proved ineffectual upon me, because every thing was now become so indifferent as to me, even my Misfortunes themselves, that the best Comfort I had, was to see my self in Chains, shut up in a dark Hole as like in a Grave, which put me in hopes of my approaching Death. How often used I to blame my self, to have left my Wife and Daughter at such a distance from me ! If it had pleased God, *said I*, to have spared but one of these Two, it would have afforded me some Consolation ; but, alas ! all is lost to me ! And such is my Misfortune, that whilst I am debarr'd from being among the living, I can't as yet be number'd among the dead.

I will not abuse your Patience with a long recital of my Grief, it will suffice to tell you, that after a most doleful Captivity of Eight Years, *Dragut Rais* one day remembring me again (for I am sure he had forgot me) sent for me, and no sooner came I into the open Air, but I fell into a Swoon ; but soon recovering my self, Come, come, *said he*, *Warwick*, take courage, I have a great mind once more to put a Sword into thy Hand, provided thou wilt swear to me by what is most Sacred among you Christians, that thou wilt draw it for nobody but for me, and against all my Enemies without Exception ; If thou agreest to this Proposal, *continued he*, giving me his Hand, I will give thee my Word, thou shalt be as much respected here as my self ; nay, thou shalt Command and be obey'd here, and thou shalt have an equal Share in my Fortune ; and to give thee a convincing proof of it, thou shalt be call'd *Muley*, a Name I have in great Veneration, and wear the same Habit as I do, tho this be a thing scarce ever practised among the *Mahometans.* Thy offers

G   are

are not fufficient to tempt me, *faid I*, I difdain thy
Fortune and thy Command thou fets fo high a
Value upon, becaufe they are all below me ; but
if my Services are capable of purchafing me my
Liberty, tell me what time thou wilt appoint,
and I will befides this pay thee my Ranfon. It
fhall coft thee 6000 *Rixdollars*, *faid he to me*, after
Ten years are expir'd, during which thou fhalt
ferve me faithfully, and upon thofe Conditions
the Agreement is made. 'Twas this that obliged
me to fight againft you, I was engag'd upon Honour fo to do, and could in no ways avoid it, tho
my Wifhes were all that while for you, and Heaven
has bin pleas'd to hear them at laft ; *Dragut Rais*
has bin forc'd to leave us, and thereby my Captivity has bin leffen'd for feveral Years. I did not
think it convenient to difcover my felf, being
taken fighting againft the *Englifh* for the *Infidels* ;
but the good Opinion I had conceiv'd of you,
continu'd he, made me foon imagine you would
make as good Ufe of this Secret as I could wifh
for.

I think this a very happy Day to me, *faid* Hypolitus *to the Earl of* Warwick, on which you are pleas'd
to judge me worthy of being your Confident,
before you had any particular Knowledge of
me; this Teftimony of your Efteem I fhall be
careful not to mifufe, and after all, you could
not have entrufted your Secret with any other
Perfon in the World, who is able to repay you
this Obligation fo well as I can, by communi-
cating to you a piece of News, which will
prove no lefs acceptable than furprifing to you,
and which, Sir, very nearly concerns you. He
then gave him an exact and faithful Account
of every thing relating to *Julia* ; and tho he
did not think fit to tell him of his Paffion for
her, his moft paffionate manner of fpeaking concerning

cerning her, and the Defcription he gave of her, join'd to other Circumftances the Earl had taken notice of before, and now recall'd to his Remembrance, as his Sighs, his Moans in the Night time, his calling in his fleep upon *Julia* by her Name, eafily convinc'd him that he was moft paffionately in Love with her.

Nothing can be compar'd to his Surprize and Joy, when he heard that his Daughter was ftill alive ; and it was no fmall Satisfaction to him, to underftand that fhe was adopted in the Catholick Religion, and become a very accomplifh'd young Woman : His defire to fee her was fuch, that had there bin a Veffel to be found that would carry him to *London*, and had it bin in his power to appear there, he would have undertaken that Voyage immediately, with the greateft Pleafure imaginable. The next thing he ask'd, was, How Matters went in *England*, as well in point of Religion as the Government. *Hypolitus* told him, That not long ago *John Dudley*, Duke of *Northumberland*, had got the Title alfo of Earl of *Warwick* ; That he had accus'd *Edward Seymour*, the King's Uncle, and Protector of the Kingdom, of a Confpiracy to Affaffinate him, and for that purpofe was entred into a League with the Duke of *Sommerfet* ; That *Seymour* being unable to refift the Power of his Enemies, was put to Death, with his Lady and feveral other Perfons of note. That after this, the Duke of *Northumberland* being become abfolute Mafter of all, and procur'd a Match betwixt the Princefs *Jane*, King *Henry* the VIIIth's. Niece and his Son, and fet her up for Heirefs apparent of the Crown, That it was generally believed they had poifon'd King *Edward*, a very hopeful young Prince, in order to facilitate and anticipate this Succeffion ; upon whom they

had

had also prevail'd so far, as to conſtitute *Jane* his Succeſſor, and excluded the Princeſs *Mary* his Siſter from the Throne: But that the Legality of her juſt Pretenſions, prevailing above the King's laſt Will, ſhe now Reign'd in *England*, and was very zealous in re-eſtabliſhing the *Roman* Catholick Religion there; and that this was the true ſtate of the Kingdom, at the time of his departure from *London*.

After long and ſerious Deliberations upon what *Hypolitus* had told the Earl of *Warwick*, he thought it moſt expedient to go to *Venice*, in hopes to reap there the fruits of ſo long and painful a Captivity he had undergone for the Service of that Republick. He did not in the leaſt doubt, but that his Daughter was extreamly well at the Earl of *Duglas*'s, the generous care his Lady had taken for her hitherto, being a ſufficient Pledge of what ſhe was likely to do for the future; and little thinking that Matters ſtood in that Family as actually they did, he reſolved only to give them News of his being alive by Letters, whilſt he was to manage his Affairs at *Venice*. He imparted his Thoughts to *Hypolitus*, who was not ill pleaſed to underſtand that he intended not to go to *England* as yet. 'Tis poſſible, ſaid he to a Gentleman in whom he much confided (tho he was one of thoſe ſent along with him by his Father) that if my Lord *Warwick* were at *London*, they would be urgent with him to marry *Julia*, and in ſuch a Caſe it would prove a much more difficult Task for her to reſiſt her Father's Commands, than my Father's Arguments; ſo that, as long as I am abſent, 'tis beſt for me he ſhould be ſo to. Theſe Reaſons obliged him to confirm the Earl in the Reſolution he had taken; and from that time on they entred into the moſt ſtrict and moſt tender

engage-

engagements of Friendfhip that can be conceived, with this difference only, that *Hypolitus* had always fo much Refpect and Deference to the Earl, that it could not but feem moft furprizing, to all thofe that were unacquainted with the true Motions thereof. *Hypolitus* moft generoufly fhar'd his Money and every thing elfe with his Friend, and would have given him all, but that he would not accept of it ; thinking that in ferving the Father of his Dear *Julia*, he did her an acceptable piece of Service ; and he thought nothing in the World too much to oblige her.

His Inclinations and Defire of being ferviceable to my Lord *Warwick*, kept *Hypolitus* his Melancholy Thought as it were in fufpence, and the Satisfaction of fo agreeable a Companion prov'd a great allay to his Pain. They arriv'd without any further finifter Accident at *Leghorn:* Here the Captain of the Ship told *Hypolitus*, he would refign to him all his Intereft to the Prifoner, for he knew not that *Muley* was an *Englifh* Man. *Hypolitus* would not be behind with him in point of Generofity, but prefented him with a Jewel valued at 400 Piftoles, a piece his Mother had given him at parting. and told him, He hop'd to be one day in a Condition, to make him a better Prefent, to fhew his efteem for *Muley*, and his Acknowledgment for the Civilities they had both receiv'd at his hands.

No fooner were they landed at *Leghorn*, but *Hypolitus* preffed the Earl of *Warwick* to write to *Julia*, but there needed not much to engage the Earl to what he was fufficiently inclined too before ; he writ at the fame time to my Lord and my Lady *Douglas*, giving them an Account of what had befaln him, and returning his hearty Thanks and Acknowledgment for all thofe Favours they had heap'd upon *Julia*. *Hypolitus* enclofed a

Letter

Letter in the Earl's Packet for my Lord *Douglas*,
and fent a Packet of his own with feveral other
Letters, among which you may fuppofe, That to
his dear *Julia* was the firft in Rank and Moment,
the reft being for *Lucilia* and the Earl of *Suffex*, unto whom the Packet was directed, with advice,
That he expected their Anfwer at *Florence*, whither he was to go by his Father's abfolute Orders.
He had given a Letter to his Son to the Senator
Alberti, wherein he recommended his Son to his
utmoft Care, with all imaginable Expreffions of
Tendernefs. So the Earl of *Warwick* and *Hypolitus*, without making any ftay at *Leghorn*, *Lucca*
or *Pifa*, went directly to *Florence*, where they
continued to give one another all poffible Demonftrations of Efteem and Friendfhip.

Whilft thefe things pafs'd betwixt them in
Italy, the diftrefs'd *Julia* enjoy'd neither the leaft
Repofe nor Health in *England*; her Grief had
produc'd fuch an Alteration in her, that fhe was
fcarce to be known by her beft Friends : She
was fo far from appearing abroad in the World,
that fhe fcarce ever ftirr'd out of her Chamber.
If fhe had any tolerable Moments, it were thofe
fhe fpent with her dear *Lucilia*, or with the Earl
of *Suffex*, which was not very often, for fear of
creating frefh Sufpicions in my Lord *Douglas*,
which would have prov'd a means to be quite debarr'd of the Earl's Company.

As for the Earl of *Bedford*, he was for fome
time fo ill, that he was thought to be at Death's
Door : But fo foon as his Mother underftood that
he was in the leaft on the mending hand, and in a
Condition to be carry'd in a Litter, fhe would
not fuffer him to ftay any longer in the fame
Houfe where he had fought with *Hypolitus*, but
fent for him to *London :* However, before he left
Buckingham, he defir'd the Favour of my Lord
Douglas

Douglas, to bid Farewel to *Julia*, but could not obtain it, she persisting resolutely in her Refusal of seeing him, in spite of all the Intreaties of my Lord and my Lady; nay, she desir'd them to be conducted into *France* into a Nunnery, because she was now resolv'd to renounce the World for ever. But whatever she could tell them upon that point, they did not believe her to be real, and were so far from complying with her request, that not doubting, but, that if they consented to it,. *Hypolitus* would soon find her out in *France*, and that thereby all the Precautions they had taken of breaking their Correspondence would be frustrated; they put her off sometimes, under Pretence of their Tenderness to her, and sometimes by a full Denial, and gave her to understand, that she must either resolve to Marry now, or stay with them till she did.

So rigorous a Treatment could not but revive in her all the Pains she had felt before. I am then Prisoner, dear Sister, *said she to* Lucilia, they will not as much as allow me the Liberty to retire to some solitude, where I may at my own leasure reflect upon and abandon my self to my tormenting Thoughts: Here I am oblig'd to be constantly upon my guard to conceal my Pain; I am forc'd to see those whose Importunities serve only to encrease my Affliction; Alas! what am I refery'd for! All other Women are permitted to chuse what is now refused to me; nobody opposes a young Woman in her Intentions of embracing a religious Life, nay, they are often forc'd so to do, and I alone am so unfortunate as to be subjected to new Laws, and it seems as if those who cause my Sufferings took delight in seeing them. These different Thoughts so far prevail'd both over her Body and Mind, that, notwithstanding her natural sweet Disposition, she appear'd to be full

G 4　　　　　of

of Spleen and Vexation, tho' *Lucilia* did afford
her all the Confolation fhe could. This young
Lady being very difcreet and prudent, alledg'd
to her every thing that could be faid or thought
on to allay her Troubles, and was no lefs affidu-
ous in obliging her with any thing fhe thought
might ferve to give her fome Diverfion; but
without any confiderable fuccefs.

In the mean while *Hypolitus* being arriv'd at
Florence, met with a Reception from the Senator
Alberti, even beyond what my Lord *Douglas* could
have defir'd or hop'd for from fo generous a
Friend A few days after his arrival, he and the
Earl of *Warwick* were conducted by him to *Cajena*,
to a magnificent Summer-Seat, built by *Laurence
de Medicis*, where you may meet with every
thing that was thought rare and curious in thofe
Times. *Cofmus de Medicis*, the then reigning
Duke of *Florence*, who happen'd to keep his Court
there at that time, would fain have engag'd the
Earl of *Warwick* to ftay at *Florence*; and gave fo
favourable a Reception to *Hypolitus*, that he might
well have flatter'd himfelf with great Advantages
to be obtain'd there, had he bin in a Capacity to
employ his Thoughts upon any thing elfe but upon
his prefent troublefome State. Moft People
perceiv'd it, and *Hypolitus* finding himfelf not
in a Condition to hide it, defir'd *Seignior Alberti*
not to make any long ftay at Court.

At the fame time my Lord and my Lady *Douglas*
did, in the fo much defir'd abfence of their Son,
tafte the Sweats of an agreeable Tranquility, there
being nothing now left to interrupt it at this
time, unlefs it were the Apprehenfion they lay
under, of feeing themfelves difappointed in
thefe Meafures they had taken, of getting all
the Letters that 'fhould be writ betwixt them
into their Hands: For, when upon *Hypolitus* his
De-

Departure, his Father gave him Liberty to bid
Farewel to *Julia* ; 'twas not done so much with
an Intention to give some cause of Satisfaction to
him, as to find out what measures they would take
to maintain their Correspondence by Letters.
For this purpose they had placed one of the
Countesses Waiting-women, in a hollow part of
the Room, cover'd only with Tapestries, where
she could see and over-hear every thing that
pass'd betwixt them ; and it was by her means
they were inform'd, that all their Letters were
to be directed to the Earl of *Sussex* : So they resolv'd to intercept them, not questioning but this
might be done, provided they spar'd neither Pains
nor Charges. To encompass their Design, my
Lord *Douglas* corrupted one of the Post-Officers
with Money, who was to deliver to him all the
Letters that came from *Italy* to the Earl of *Sussex.*
On the other hand, he prevail'd with the *English*
Agent, or Chief Factor, at *Florence*, who was his
old Acquaintance, to secure for him, all the
Letters that should be directed to his Son : He
told him, that his Son being fallen in Love with
a young Woman who had no Fortune, he had sent
him away on purpose to cure him of that Passion ; and, that therefore he lay under a Necessity
of making use of all Stratagems that possibly
he could, to reduce him to Reason, and to his
Duty ; and that he conjur'd him to lend him a
helping hand, since *Hypolitus* his Fortune lay at
Stake.

The first Packet my Lord *Douglas* receiv'd from
Italy, was actually directed to him from *Leghorn*,
and in it the Earl of *Warwick* and *Hypolitus* his
Letters : He was not a little surpriz'd to understand that *Julia*'s Father was still alive, and he had
not the least reason to doubt of the Truth of it,
after the Letter he had writ him upon that subject.
He

He did not think it convenient to impart this good News to *Julia* ; She will, *said he to the Countess his Spouse*, make this a plausible Pretence to contradict us, when-ever we shall propose a Match to her ; she will say, she ought to stay till the return, or at least for the Consent of the Earl of *Warwick* ; and, since he himself tells us of the great Obligations he has to our Son, and that 'tis probable he may have discover'd to him his Passion for *Julia*, her Father is not likely to act contrary to the Interest of a Friend who is already so dear to him. Upon these Considerations, it was resolv'd not to let *Julia* know the least thing relating to the Earl of *Warwick* ; and that they might not omit any thing they thought requisite to thwart the Designs of these two Tender and Unfortunate Lovers, they got certain Letters forg'd, and directed to the Earl of *Sussex* (after having intercepted the true ones sent him from *Leghorn*) to *Lucilia*, and to *Julia*, in *Hypolitus* his Name. In these 'twas pretended he writ them Word, That having receiv'd a Wound in the Hand, in his late Voyage, he was oblig'd to make use of a Friend to write to them in his behalf. This was done to remove all suspicion, when they should see their Letters written by another Hand but *Hypolitus* his own ; and to play their Cards the better, that written to *Julia*, was conceiv'd in Terms full of Indifferency and Changing ; whereas those for *Lucilia*, and the Earl of *Sussex*, were extreamly Tender.

On the other hand, my Lord *Douglas* caus'd other Letters also to be forg'd, as if written by *Julia*, her Sister, and by the Earl, to *Hypolitus*, stil'd in such a manner as they judg'd most proper to perswade him they were written by them ; and to take away all manner of suspicion from him,

him, becaufe they were not written with their own
Hands, they let him know, that it was agreed
among them to difguife their Hand Writing, that
in cafe they fhou'd mifcary, it might not be known
from whom they came.

Then my Lord *Douglas* writ again to the *Englifh* Head Factor at *Florence*, to defire him to intercept thofe Letters that actually came from the
Earl of *Suffex*, and inftead thereof to deliver to
Hypolitus the Sufpicious ones ; to diftinguifh thefe
Letters, he fent him a Print of the Signet wherewith the Sufpitious Letters were to be Seal'd, conjuring him to fuffer none but thofe come to his
Sons Hands, and fend all the reft back to him. By
this means, feeing himfelf Mafter of all the fecret
Correfpondence betwixt *Julia* and her dear Lover,
he began now to hope to bring his defires about
according to the Scheme he had laid of them;
for according to his Directions, thefe Suppofitious
Letters by degrees appear'd more and more cold
on both fides ; *Julia* became inconfolable, alafs !
Sifter, *faid fhe to* Lucilia, your Brother Loves me
no more ; pray mind how indifferently he writes,
and he has mifs'd feveral Pofts without letting me
hear from him, and when he does, it feems as if
it were only out of Complaifance, and as if I were
forced to fnatch from him his Demonftrations and
Remembrance of our Friendfhip; 1 am fure what
he does is only for a Decorum's fake, his Heart
has no fhare in it : *Hypolitus* is chang'd Sifter, *continued fhe*, *Hypolitus* is chang'd ; at thefe words fhe
dropt from her Chair like one half Dead. *Lucilia* would willingly have fpoken in juftification of
her Brother, and maintain'd his Conftancy ; but
thinking her felf convinced of his Infidelity,
fhe was not a little difcompos'd at his Inconftancy.

Whilft

Whilft thefe lovely Perfons paft whole Nights under the moft fenfible Affliction that cou'd be, and in their Letters loaded the Unfortunate *Hypolitus* with a Thoufand Reproaches, his mind laboured under no lefs diftraction than theirs. Upon the departure of the Earl of *Warwick* for *Venice*, he had difclos'd to him his Paffion for *Julia*, without in the leaft difguifing the matter, and told him, how much my Lord *Douglas* was exafperated againft him on that account, and he had prevail'd at laft fo far upon the Earl, that he brought him over quite into his Intereft, and obtain'd from him a promife, That this fair Lady fhould be no bodies elfe but his. He did not fail to acquaint his belov'd Miftrefs with this agreeable piece of news, but to little purpofe, fince every thing was kept from her fight and knowledge, except what might ferve to encreafe her Grief; as *Hypolitus* on the other hand obferved that fhe writ to him, as if it were with fome conftraint and diffidence, which proved the conftant occafion of new difturbances in his Mind.

I told you before, that he was received with all Demonftration of efteem and friendfhip by the Senator *Alberti*; he had a Son much of the fame Age as *Hypolitus*, nam'd Signior *Leander*, a Perfon well Shap'd, Witty, Obliging, of a fweet Temper, and a pleafing and moft engaging Converfation: Thefe two Gentlemen foon difcovered in one another fuch a mutual difpofition to love one another, and their Tempers fuited fo exactly well, that at firft fight, by a certain effect of Sympathy, they contracted fo near and fo firm a Friendfhip, that in a very fmall time after, they had no Secret, nay, nor fcarce even a Thought but what they communicated to one another. 'Tis eafy to imagine that living in fo ftrict a Friendfhip, *Hypolitus* could not forbear to make him his Confident

of

of his Paſſion for *Julia*, and he took much delight
in talking of her, and in extolling the Charms,
and other great Qualities of his Miſtiſtreſs, that
it wanted but little, but that *Leander* had fallen
in love with her. Nothing in the World, *ſaid he*,
is comparable to her for Beauty, nothing more
Accompliſh'd than her Wit ; ſhe has a great Soul,
and an engaging Air, enough to enchant every
body that converſes with her. How happy are you,
Hypolitus, ſaid Leander, to be, myDear, belov'd by ſo
Accompliſh'd a Lady ! As for my ſelf, I have not
as yet taſted the pleaſure of a tender Love, I never met with any yet in my way but what were
Coquets, who are fond of many Lovers, without
loving or being cruel to any one. Thoſe are dangerous Women, *cry'd* Hypolitus, I lov'd *Julia* before I knew my ſelf, and I knew not what Love
was, when I felt my ſelf in Love with her ; ſo it
is not experience has made me a Lover, Oh! How
I ſhould dread ſuch a Woman as you ſpeak of, I
ſuppoſe them to be of ſo unreaſonable and unequal
Temper, that I can't but pity all thoſe that ſerve
them.

After they had ſpent ſome time in ſuch like diſ-
courſes, he ſhew'd him the Bracelet with *Julia's*
Hairs in it, he kiſs'd it a Thouſand times with all
the Tranſports of tenderneſs that can be imagined,
expeçting with the utmoſt impatience to have a
Letter from her fair Hands : But tho' he neglected no opportunity of having his Letters as ſoon
as they were delivered out, the *Engliſh* Factor
took ſuch effectual care to oblige my Lord *Dou-*
glas, that he had none but the ſuppoſitious Letters
inſtead of the others ; ſo that his Grief encreas'd
in proportion, as he obſerv'd in his Miſtreſſes Letters a certain coldneſs he thought he deſerved
leſs now than ever. Pray mind, *ſaid he, with a*
Melancholly Air to Leander, what effects abſence
　　　　　　　　　　　　　　　　　　is

is able to produce; the longer it is, the more ne-glect I obferve in *Julia*: Oh! cruel Abfence, *cry'd he*, thou haft robb'd me of my Miftreffes Heart.

Leander would willingly have perfwaded him to take a turn to *Rome*, and thence to *Venice*, and to ftay their for fome time: No, *faid* Hypolitus, no, I will not ftir out of *Florence*; for fince my Father's defire was to fend me out of *England*, I will at leaft ftay at *Florence*, becaufe it is nearer to it than any of the other two places you would have me go to; all the Beauties in the World I can look at with indifferency only, till fuch time I fee that again I love; and fince I can delight in nothing, fince I am infenfible to every thing, nothing can reach my Heart; all my Paffions being centred in that lovely young Lady. I can take no other impref-fions but what proceeds from a moft profound Grief: But tho' I Adore without intermiffion, you fee fhe kills me by her Indifferency. 'Tis that, *faid* Leander, which obliges me to find out fome means or other to engage you to conclude a Truce for fome time with this Splenatick Temper, which makes you fhun the Converfation of all the World. I can't conceal it any longer from you, That you are look'd upon at Court as if you were a *Barbarian*, every one asks me the reafon of it, and the Ladies efpecially fhew very much their diflike at your Deportment; pray at leaft be a lit-tle more Sociable. I neither can nor will be o-therwife than now I am, *anfwer'd* Hypolitus. Give me leave to Sigh, my dear *Leander*, give me leave to bemoan my Misfortunes at pleafure; don't ftraiten my Pain, alas! this is a Requeft few will be able to deny me.

A whole Year being thus pafs'd, my Lord and my Lady *Douglas* were extreamly pleas'd to fee their defigns to fucceed fo fortunately, that not the leaft difcovery thereof has bin made hitherto; but

but at the fame time they were convinc'd to their
no fmall grief and vexation, by thofe of their
Son's Letters, and by fuch of *Julia's* Letters as fell
into their hands, that abfence had made not the
leaft alteration in their Hearts; that their tendernefs continu'd ftill to be the fame; and that it was
evident by what they had writ to one another,
that even Death it felf fhould not make them
change their minds. My Lord having all the reafon in the World to fear that fome accident or o-
ther might overturn the frame of his Structure,
before he fhould be able to bring it to perfection,
went immediately to the Agent of *Florence* then
refiding at *London*, and having told him what
vexation he lay under on account of his Son's
Paffion, from which neither Time, nor his pofitive
Commands, had bin able to divert him hitherto;
he intreated him to lend him a helping hand in
bringing about a defign he had fram'd to bring
him to reafon. Finding him fufficiently enclining
to comply with his defires, they contriv'd certain
Letters, one as if written by *Hypolitus*, the other
by the *Englifh* head Factor at *Florence*, the third
by the Marquefs *de Neri*, and the fourth by the Senator *Alberti:* Thefe Letters contain'd in Subftance, That *Hypolitus* defired my Lords confent
to Marry Madam *Neri*, a young Lady of Quality,
whofe Houfe was Related to the moft Illuftrious
Families of *Italy*, and who being an Heirefs,
would be a vaft Fortune to him: They fent alfo
her Picture, which being not drawn after any O-
riginal, but meerly according to the Picture drawers fancy, he had made it a perfect pattern of
Beauty, fuch a one as no body coul'd look upon
without Admiration. The Senator *Alberti* in his
pretended Letter, pofitively told my Lord *Douglas*, That his Son was fo far Enamour'd with this
lovely Lady, That, if he refus'd his Confent to
Marry

Marry her, he would certainly dye for Grief. The *English* Agent added to this, That it would be a very advantageous Match. And the suppositious Marquess *de Neri*, sent a Complimental Letter to my Lord, telling him as it were *en Passant*, That *Hypolitus*'s Merits has made so deep an impression upon his Daughter, and that he had given her such undeniable Demonstrations of a most violent Passion for her, that he was no longer able to resist both their Prayers and Entreaties to acquaint him, that he should joyfully embrace the Honour of his Alliance, provided his might not be unacceptable to him.

Every thing being thus concerted, one Day when the Earl of *Sussex* was at Dinner with my Lord *Douglas*, in comes a Servant of the *Florentine* Agent, desiring to speak with my Lord; He told him that his Master might come at what hour he pleas'd, and that he would expect him all the remainder of the Day. Not long after, in he comes, and *Julia* who loved to be Solitary was going to withdraw, but this being a time wherein she was to have the chief part, the Countess told her with a low voice, that Decency required she and *Lucilia* should stay as long as she stay'd. After the first Compliments were pass'd, the Agent told my Lord he had something of Moment to communicate to him concerning *Hypolitus*; and my Lord told him he might tell it with all imaginable freedom, there being no body present but his Mother, Sister, and intimate Friends. Then the Agent, who acted his pare to the Life, offer'd the beforemention'd Letters, which my Lord *Douglas* read first with a low voice; but soon after told his Wife, so that every body there present might hear him, There is nothing that is a Secret in these Letters, *said he to his Lady*, pray mind what they write me; and then he read the Letters again aloud, and
opening

opening the Cafe wherein was the Picture of the pretended Madam *Neri*, feem'd furprized at her Beauty, as well as my Lady *Douglas*, whilft the Agent took care to extol her to the Sky, for a Thoufand other great Qualifications: At laft he intreated my Lord to give them a favourable anfwer, and not to retard the Felicity of two fuch Accomplifh'd and Paffionate Lovers. Good God! Who is able to defcribe that miferable ftate, unto which the Unfortunate *Julia* faw her felf reduc'd during this cruel Converfation; fhe refolved to put a conftraint upon her felf, and would fee her Rivals Picture; but fhe had no fooner caft her Eyes upon that fatal piece, which appear'd to her moft furprizing Beautiful, but fhe fell into a Swoon, without Senfe, Voice, Motion, or Pulfe, and Death feem'd to have fixt his guafhly look in her Face. Any body lefs prejudic'd than my Lord and my Lady were, would have bin touch'd with Compaffion at fo Melancholly a Spectacle; but they feem'd unconcern'd, and only ordred her to be carried into her Bed-chamber. *Lucilia* and the Earl of *Suffex* almoft drown'd in Tears, ftay'd with her; but for all the Help and Remedies they could give her, it was above four hours before fhe recovered fo far, as to judge whether fhe were Dead or a Live.

Then fhe juft open'd her Eyes, fixing them fteadfaft on *Lucilia* and the Earl, but faid not one Word, nor fhed one Tear; and foon after fhut them again, nor would fhe open them any more nor fpeak one word. Dear Sifter, *faid* Lucilia, *embracing her very tenderly*, perhaps your Evil is not paft cure, *Hypolitus* is not Marry'd as yet, and 'tis likely he will repent of his Inconftancy; If he fhould return to his Duty, would not you receive him again? And if he continues to be Ungrateful, will you facrifice your Life for an Ungrateful Perfon, and leave me in this defperate Condition I am in

H　　　　　　now?

now ? The Earl forgot not to joyn his Arguments
to the Entreaties of *Lucilia* ; but *Julia* would not as
much as make them underftand by a fign that fhe
took notice of what they faid, and it being very late,
the Earl went away without having the fatisfaction
of hearing her fpeak ; and *Lucilia* fpent the whole
Night with her in Tears and Lementations. The next
Day the Earl came again, and being told by *Lucilia*,
That fhe would take nothing at all, nay, that whatever fhe could tell or pray her, fhe would not as
much as open her Eyes, nor fpeak one Word; he went
immediately to fpeak with my Lord and my Lady,
thefe feem'd not in the leaft furpriz'd nor touch'd
with Compaffion at poor *Julia's* defperate Cafe ;
they only told him carelefly, That Hunger would
bring her to Eat, and that Lovers had generally but
a flender Appetite to Victuals. How! *cry'd the Earl of*
Suffex *in an Angry tone,* you don't only ruin a young
Lady, but alfo infult over her Misfortunes ; Can you
imagine but that fo unjuft a proceeding will not make
you blufh one time or other ? He continu'd to intermix moft bitter Complaints with his Reproaches, but
all in vain : So perceiving no good was to be done
with them, he went full of Affliction to *Julia's*
Chamber again.

Lucilia ceas'd not to make moft preffing inftances
to *Julia* to take fome Nourifhment, but to no purpofe ; however, at laft opening her Eyes, fhe told
them with a feeble voice, intermixt with Sighs and
Sobs, Dear Sifter, and you my Generous Friend,
faid fhe, Don't urge me any further to Eat, I am
highly oblig'd to you for all your Cares, and the Demonftrations you give me of your Tendernefs ; but
I hope foon to fee an end of this deplorable Life.
Oh ! Barbarous *Hypolitus, faid fhe,* Oh ! Barbarous
Man ! What have I done againft thee, to deferve fuch
cruel treatments at thy hands ? What is become of
all thy Oaths and Vows ? Thou loveft me no longer
faithlefs Man; and I am fo frail and foolifh as to afflict

flict my self at it. Having said these words, she spoke
no more, nor would take the least Nourishment,
tho' she was reduc'd to a very weak Condition, having taken not the least thing for two whole Days.
Lucilia and the Earl being sensible her design was to
Starve her self to Death, they thought it their
best way to touch her in her Conscience, knowing
her to be very Meek and Tender in that point ; so
they sent for her Father Confessor, and having dis-
cours'd him in private, left him alone with her. His
Authority proved more prevailing upon her, than
all the Tears of *Lucilia*, and all the Intreaties of the
Earl of *Sussex* were able to do before. *Julia* sub-
mitted her self to the Directions of him who had
always bin her Guide ; and he was no sooner gone,
but she spoke thus to her Sister and the Earl of *Sussex* ; Don't bear me no ill will, *said she to them*, because
I was so possitive in resisting what you desired of
me, it was not an affect of want of Friendship for
you, but of my despair only: They tell me I must not
shorten my own Days, and that I must be accounta-
ble for it to him who gave it me. Then I will Live,
continu'd she, with a deep Sigh, Then I will Live, the
most Unfortunate Person that ever was seen ; and
since I am under a necessity to Live, I would not
have the Ungrateful *Hypolitus* know all those troubles and grief he has occasion'd in me. Sister, *added
she*, if I dare hope that you Love me, give me this
proof of it, don't speak to your Brother concerning me ; or if it happen you can't avoid it, tell him,
I was not concern'd at his Infidelity ; That Indifferency has made me set aside all my Anger, and that
I scarce ever so much as nam'd him. Grant me this
favour, *said she, Addressing her self to the Earl*, don't
let him be acquainted with the pains I suffer for
him ; I make you my Confident, but don't reveal my
Secret. They promised to do as she desired them,
being overjoy'd to see her take some care for the
preservation of a Life which was very dear to them.

A

A confiderable time was fpent in bringing her to
the entire ufe of her Reafon, and *Lucilia* and the
Earl of *Suffex* in their Letters,writ fuch bloody Reproaches to *Hypolitus,* that fuppofing the matter of
Fact upon which they were founded to have bin fuch
as it appear'd to them, they muft needs have re-
minded and perhaps alfo recall'd him to his Duty :
But alas! None of thofe, no more than all the reft
they had written before,came to his hands. In the
mean while *Julia* wou'd fometimes flatter her felf in
the midft of her Defpair with the pleafing hopes,
That her Lover might repent and not confummate
the intended Marriage; fhe cou'd not forbear fometimes to tell *Lucilia,*Notwithftanding what *Hypolitus* has done againft me,*said fhe,*I am fenfible I fhou'd
be glad to pardon him, if he could return to his
Duty; but alas! when I confider thefe rare Qualifications of Madam *Neri,* I have all the reafon to
fear he will never be mine. At this Confideration,
fhe plung'd into an Abyfs of Pain and Torments ;
Lucilia on her fide,being refolved not to flatter her
with fuch uncertain hopes as will ferve only to revive her Paffion, and confequently to Torment her
in vain ; You muft forget *Hypolitus, said fhe,* dear
Sifter,you oughtto hate him,and notwithftandinghe
is myBrother, I am abfolutely againft him. Forget,
and to Hate him, *reply'd* Julia, Oh! Sifter, Do you
think me to be Miftrefs of my own Sentiments? A
Soul prepoffefs'd with a habit of Loving and being
Belov'd, and that contracted by a long procefs of
time, a fincere Heart engag'd in a Paffion without
difguife,is not in a condition to recover it felf at the
very Moment it finds it felf betray'd. Don't you
fee how Unfortunate I am, even after I was confirm'd to have loft this faithlefs Man? I muft own
to you, my Love for him is rather encreas'd, I am
very ingenious in contriving my own Torments, I
call to my mind every thing he has told me, every
thing he us'd to do before me,he is alwas prefent in
                                                    my

my fight, I difcover every Day new perfections in his Perfon, all which ferves only to increafe my Pain ; No, Dear Sifter, no, my cafe is deplorable beyond all comparifon, and 'tis impoffible for you to be fenfible of the Pains and Torments I fuffer.

The News moft of all dreaded by *Julia*, I mean that of *Hypolitus*'s pretended Marriage, being come at that juncture my Lord *Douglas* had contriv'd it fhou'd be known, this fatal ftroke once more revived in this fair Lady all her Difcontents and Troubles ; for tho' fhe expected to hear of it every Moment, yet fhe ftill flatter'd her felf with fome fmall glimpfe of hopes to the contrary: So that now feeing her Cafe to be fuch as to be paft all cure, fhe took a refolution of fhutting her felf up in a Nunnery, and there to linger away the remaining Days of her languifhing Life, when on a fudden, a certain motive of Honour and Pride overturn'd this whole defign. How, *faid fhe to* Lucilia, fhall I leave the World for this worthlefs Lover ? and fhall he have the fatisfaction of imagining, that it was Grief that made me take this refolution, becaufe I was not capable to difpence with the lofs of him ? No, I can't bear the very thoughts of it ; no, let it coft me what it will, I will make him believe at leaft, that I am contented and happy : And fince the Earl of *Bedford* continues to make his Addreffes, and with the fame Paffion Courts me to be his Spoufe, I will facrifice my Repofe to my Pride. I hope you are not in earneft, Sifter, cry'd *Lucilia*, How can you refolve to Marry a Man whom you Love not? Do you forefee the ill confequences that attends fuch a Match ? I fufficiently forefee them, *reply'd fhe, in a Melancholy Tone*, but I forefee alfo that this will prove a means to prevent your Brother's being acquainted with my Frailties and tender Inclinations for him ; he will then have reafon enough to believe that I chang'd as well as he ; nay, it wou'd be a kind of fatisfaction to me, if he was perfwaded that I did fo

firſt. All Lucilia's reaſons and entreaties to diſſwade
her from it, proved fruitleſs upon this occaſion, and
as the Counteſs of *Douglas* let ſlip no opportunity
of diving into *Julia*'s Sentiments, ſhe no ſooner underſtood her favourable diſpoſition for the Earl of
Bedford, but ſhe acquainted him with it; nor loſt they
one Moment to ſtrengthen *Julia* in her Reſolution.
Dear Daughter, *ſaid ſhe to her*, tho' your Inclinations are not much for the Perſon you have pitch'd
upon, you have ſo great a ſhare of Vertue, and he A-
dores you (if one may ſo term it) in ſo extraordinary a manner, that your Gratitude and Duty will
produce in his behalf, what your Tenderneſs would
engage to for another Man. *Julia* kept ſilence for a
while; but when ſhe was obliged to return an Anſwer, *ſhe ſaid, with a Melancholly Air*, That ſince ſhe
had reſolved upon this Match, ſhe hoped ſhe ſhould
not be wanting in her Duty. So great Preparations
were made for the Nuptials, and that fatal Day being come, *Julia* appear'd in a White Apparel, Bro-
cado'd all over with Silver, adorn'd with abundance
of Jewels, and her fair Hair curiouſly ty'd up in Locks
and Buckles; ſhe had never appear'd more Beautiful, and at the ſame time more Languiſhing ; ſhe
look'd ſomewhat Pale, but without being the leaſt
injurious to her Complexion; and her large Eyes
containing a certain Languiſhment by reaſon of her
Grief, ſeem'd rather to encreaſe than to Diminiſh
her Charms. The Earl of *Bedford* thought himſelf
the happieſt Man in the World, and coul'd ſcarce i-
magine how ſo unexpected a change could fall to his
Lot. He was not able to conceal the Tranſports of
his Mind; but neither his Tranſports, nor his Love,
nor his Conſtancy, were able to touch the lovely
Julia's Heart. She was Marry'd at *Buckingham*
Houſe, in the preſence of a Noble and Numerous
Aſſembly; every one took notice of her Melancholly, and ſome would ask her the cauſe of it ; but ſhe
ſcarce return'd any anſwer to any thing, whether
ſerious or otherwiſe.   The

The Earl of *Bedford* underſtood the ſame Day he was to be Marry'd to her, That *Julia* was the Earl of *Warwick*'s Daughter, My Lord and my Lady *Douglas* thinking it not convenient ſhe ſhould Marry the Earl in the Quality of being their Daughter; but he deſired the thing might be kept as a ſecret, and that he might paſs for her Father hereafter as he has done hitherto. The Earl, inſtead of bringing his new Spouſe to *London*, carry'd her into *Barkſhire*, where he had a Country Seat not inferiour in Magnificence to a Royal Palace, Art and Nature being joyn'd together to Accompliſh it; Its Situation being infinitely delightful, by reaſon of an adjacent Forreſt which furniſh'd it with the moſt Pleaſant Walks in the World, in the midſt of a Spacious Solitude: For tho' this Seat was not above Forty Miles diſtant from *London*, its Situations among the Woods, made it appear much more remote from that great City than actually it was, and tho' abundance of Gentlemen live in that Country, yet none had their Houſes within a ſmall diſtance from this Seat. This was the place whether the Unfortunate *Julia* was Conducted by her new Spouſe; ſhe deſired the Counteſs of *Douglas* to let the lovely *Lucilia* ſtay with her ſome time, which was ſoon granted. Alas! were it poſſible to repreſent to you the doleful ſtate of her Heart, you would afford certainly her ſome Compaſſion. I did not think, *ſaid ſhe to* Lucilia, that my Pain could poſſibly be encreaſed; I beleived that after what I had undergone, nothing cou'd augment my ſufferings; But how much do I find my ſelf deceiv'd? My Dear *Lucilia*, every Moment produces additional Torment to my Pains; this continual conſtraint I am forc'd to put upon my ſelf for a Husband I don't Love, theſe ſecret Reproaches I conſtantly feel within my ſelf, and theſe Remorſes, which are the conſequences of the tender remembrance of a Lover who is ſtill belov'd by me, theſe deſires of diſcharging ones Duty, and the violence of tearing

from ones Heart an Inclination which now is become
Criminal, all thefe Confiderations appear fo dreadful,
and caufe fuch heavy Afflictions to me, as makes me
apprehend fometimes they will reduce me to Defpair.
Whilft I was my own Miftrefs I had this comfort at
leaft, That I need not Blufh on account of my Paffion;
Juft Heaven, What a Martyrdom is this! How long
fhall I be thus Afflicted! At thefe words fhe Cry'd
bitterly; her Sifter mingling her Tears with hers,
would fain have afforded her fome Confolation; but
without Succefs.

The Earl of *Bedford* in the midft of all the pleafures he enjoy'd, could not but be fenfible that he was
not beloved by his Lady; For tho'Love be blind, it is
very quick fighted and difcerning in certain Refpects:
'Tis true, we are apt when we are in Love, fcarce to
make a real diftinction betwixt that which is the
effect only of Complaifance, and betwixt what proceeds from pure Inclination; we are very willing to
flatter and to deceive our felves: But after all, there is a
certain nice and delicious relifh which effects the Heart
from time to time with a mutual Paffion; but when only one of the two happens to Love, he muft expect
abundance of Turbulent Hours, and the Object belov'd, muft alfo bear her fhare in them. This was
the Cafe of the Earl of *Bedford*, who during thefe
Turbulent Minutes, thought of nothing fo much than
who could be the Perfon that robb'd him of his Lady's
Tendernefs, tho' at the fame time he new not where
to fix the matter, fhe being a Lady of fo much Prudence, of fo much Indifferency and Refervednefs to
all the World, that he had all the reafon in the World
to believe, that if fhe did not Love him, fhe did not
Love any thing elfe in the World; and tho' he cou'd
not but look upon it as a great Misfortune to know
himfelf not to be belov'd by his Wife, he thought
it neverthelefs none of the leaft Felicities, that her
Heart was not engaged another way. Time will
make me happy, *faid he, to one of his Intimate Friends,*
Julia is Infenfible to all the World now; but when
her loving Hour is come, I don't queftion but fhe
will do that in my behalf out of Inclination, what
now is purely the effect of her Duty and Virtue.

THE

THE
HISTORY
OF
Hypolitus E. of *Douglas.*

PART II.

THree whole Months were now expir'd, in which neither *Lucilia* nor the Earl of *Suſſex* had written to *Hypolitus*; they were ſo enrag'd againſt him by reaſon of his Inconſtancy, that they could not forgive him, and the Earl moſt of the two; for, tho' he never us'd to keep conſtant to one Miſtreſs, he was a Man of Honour, whoſe Maxim it was, That a Man who pretends to Honour, ſhou'd never break his Word; and this it was that made him ſo angry with his Friend.

My Lord *Douglas* having now gain'd his point, writ to the *Engliſh* Factor at *Florence*, that he return'd him Thanks for his aſſiduity in intercepting his Son's Letters, but that for the future he might let them take their due Courſe; but this afforded no matter of Comfort to *Hypolitus*, becauſe thoſe Perſons from whom he expected his Letters, thought

thought fit now to fend him none: This put him under ftrange Inquietudes, Forty times was he upon the point of refolving to go into *England* to fee his dear *Julia*, had not *Leander* made ufe of all the power he had over him, to divert him from it. One Evening, when his Spleen made him quite averfe to all Converfation, even of that of his intimate Friends, he walk'd out of the Town, following for fome time the Current of the River *Armis*, till turning off a little way, he got into a Wood of *Orange*, *Myrtle*, and *Pomegranate Trees*, he traced for fome time the Tract of the Highway, but at laft by feveral By-paths got into the moft remote part of the Wood. He finding himfelf at full Liberty, and without the leaft Conftraint, he began to figh, and to make the moft dreadful Reflections in the World, upon what could be the Caufe of his Miftreffes not writing to him, as alfo of his Sifter's and the Earl of *Suffex*, and that in fo long a time: He took a fix'd Refolution to leave *Florence* without delay, much about the fame time when his Valet, who knew he was under the greateft Vexation that could be, on account of his hearing no News from *England*, having now receiv'd fome Letters, went with all poffible hafte to find him out. 'Being told that his Mafter was feen to go into the Wood, he fearch'd all Corners thereof, till having found him out, he deliver'd him the Packet. *Hypolitus* fent him home again, and overjoy'd to fee the Earl of *Suffex*'s Hand, he open'd it haftily, and found in it thefe Lines.

THo' I had taken a Refolution not to write to you any more, yet I thought at laft, Three Months filence a time fufficiently long, to make you fenfible how highly I am concern'd at your Infidelity to the Fair Julia; and tho' all your Friends ought to be well

*satisfy'd in so advantagious a Marriage as yours is,
and that I am one of those, who is most sensibly
touch'd with every thing relating to you, I can nevertheless not forbear to own to you, that I can't be
overjoy'd at it, and that I could have wish'd you had
never changed your Passion. Poor young Lady, she
was troubled to the highest Degree when the* Florentine *Agent deliver'd your Letters to my Lord* Douglas,
*and with them the Picture of your New Mistress :
The Consequence of this Affair, did reduce her to the
very point of Death ; and she has since done something
out of meer spite, whereof I fear she will soon repent.
Tho' perhaps your concern may not be so great as it
used to be in this Case, nevertheless I believe you can't
but have some resentment against it, when you understand that she is marry'd to the Earl of* Bedford. ;
*this Sacrifice has bin attended with so many Tears,
that her Nuptial Day seem'd to be rather design'd
for a Funeral, than for a Feast. She is now in*
Barkshire, *the lovely* Lucilia *keeps her Company in
her solitude ; and whilst you wallow in Pleasures, in
the Place where you are, she feels a Thousand Torments where she is. Don't take it amiss, because I
did not write sooner, and because I write with so
much Indifferency, my dear* Hypolitus, *I was not
able to overcome my self upon that point ; and that
I might be yours again, as entirely as I was before,
it was requisite I should discover my Mind to you
with an unlimited freedom.*

Hypolitus read with the greatest surprize in the
World the beginning of this Letter, not knowing
what to make of it. His Marriage, his Inconstancy, and all these Reproaches, seem'd to be
nothing but Chimera's to him : But when he
came to that Passage, where the Earl told him,
that *Julia* was married to the Earl of *Bedford,*
he was like one Thunder-struck, he real'd down
                                                under

under a Tree, and was several times in mind, to run himself through with his own Sword, and so at once to put an End to his unfortunate Life, but that some small glimpses of Hopes stop'd his Hand : 'Tis no difficult matter for me, *said he*, to see what they aim at ; 'tis possible *Julia* has conceiv'd some jealousy, and to put me to the Tryal, she has pitch'd upon this Contrivance, to put me in fear of losing her, and to bring me back to my Duty, in case I had laid it aside. But these Thoughts continu'd not long, being succeeded by others, much more afflicting than those : How ! Is she married, *cry'd he ?* Is it possible I should be acquainted with this fatal News, without dying out of Despair ! *Julia,* adorable *Julia,* what is it I have done to you ! What could move you to suspect my Heart to be guilty of such a Treachery ! That Heart you have entirely link'd to yours by a Thousand endearing Engagements! Do you think it could have any other Disposition but for you? Alas! I am afraid you were inclin'd your self to be unfaithful to me, and 'tis this doubtless that has made you give ear to those Insinuations against me. He paus'd a while, and soon after repenting himself to have accus'd his Mistress, he ask'd her Pardon, no otherwise than if she had bin present, with Tears in his Eyes, and such moanful Expressions, as are scarce to be imagin'd ; threatning the utmost of his Revenge to him who had robb'd him of his Felicity, and to all those who had given a helping hand to play him such a Game. In this afflicted Condition he little minded what time of the Night it was, and tho' it was pretty late, he was not inclin'd to go as yet out of the Wood ; but sometimes would be leaning against a Tree, sometimes sitting upon the Ground, but without finding the least ease in this variety ; the violent Agitations of his Mind, his

Despair,

Defpair, Anger, all thefe Paffions tormented him
to fuch a degree, that he feem'd to be nearer
Death than living:

Signior *Leander*, with whom he was to fpend
that Evening, not a little difturb'd becaufe he did
not fee him, ask'd the fame Servant who had
carry'd the Packet of Letters to *Hypolitus*, where
his Mafter was? and being told he had left him
in the Wood, he was fomewhat furpriz'd and difcompos'd at his ftaying fo long there, (tho' indeed
the pleafantnefs of the Place, and of the Seafon,
might have invited any Body to ftay there fome
part of the Night) fo he went to look for him,
foon found him, and heard him fend forth moft
doleful Lamentations. This faithful Friend, fearing left fome finifter Accident was befaln, haftned
towards the Place where he heard his Voice, and
by the Light of the Moon faw him lye ftretch'd
along upon the Ground, like one without Senfe or
Motion. Oh! my dear *Hypolitus*, *cry'd he*, I doubt.
you are wounded? What, were you affailed by
Highway-Men, or fome other Villains? *Hypolitus*
looking at him with a fad Countenance, How
happy fhould I be, *faid he*, were I either wounded
or dead? My Misfortunes are of a much worfe
Nature, my dear *Leander*, I have loft every thing,
Great God, I have loft every thing. He faid no
more; the Earl of *Suffex*'s Letter lay juft by him.
Leander finding he could not get one Word from
him, in anfwer to thofe Queftions he ask'd him,
and not queftioning but that that fatal News
which had reduc'd him to fo deplorable a State,
was contain'd in this Letter, he took it up, and
by the brightnefs of the Moon-light read it.
Finding himfelf opprefs'd with Grief at the News
which he knew had caus'd his Friends Affliction,
he went at fome diftance from him, to give vent
to his Paffion; but foon after, returning to the

Place

Place where he had left him, found him to be
gone thence: For, *Hypolitus,* without thinking
on what he did, or without remembering that
Leander was far off, had left that Place, and was
walking in the Wood as fast as he could, without
knowing whether. *Leander* was much concern'd
thereat; he call'd him several times by his Name,
till at last he heard him sigh and speak to himself
so loud, that he could easily trace and overtake
him by his Voice : He took hold by his Arm, and
embracing him with all the most tender Demonstrations of a sincere Friend, told him every thing that
either Reason, Wit or Tenderness is able to inspire
into a Man upon such an Occasion as this. He
join'd with him in his Complaints, not thinking it
convenient to contradict him at once; but by degrees endeavour'd to allay his Pain, sometimes by
flattering him with Hopes ; sometimes by representing to him, that a great and generous Soul,
such as Nature had endow'd him with, ought not
to suffer it self to be so far to be over-burthen'd
with Afflictions, as not to be able to support it
self under the weight thereof; he conjur'd him by
every thing that was most dear to him, and in particular by the same *Julia,* who was the only Object both of his Love and Pain, to endeavour to
vanquish himself, left that might be attributed to
his want of Courage, which actually was the effect
of his Passion and of his Pain. He knew *Hypolitus* to be a Person of Honour, and that he hit him
in a Point, which he was not in a Condition to
contradict. He added, that since his Mistress had
shewn so much repugnancy to that Marriage, it was
an infallible Sign, that he was still Master of her
Heart ; and that his Misfortunes were not quite
past remedy, because he was still belov'd.

Thefe several Arguments produc'd this effect
upon *Hypolitus,* that he gave some respite to his
Sighs

Sighs and Sobs, and contented himfelf for this time to eafe his Mind by his Moans, which fome-times prove no fmall Confolation to an unfortunate Lover.

Day began to appear before *Leander* could prevail upon *Hypolitus* to go home along with him; for by his good Will he would have roav'd about in the Wood for ever, like a Mad Man. They were no fooner got home, but *Leander* caus'd him to be put into a Bed ; but would needs ftay along with him, knowing that his prefence might ftand him in great ftead at this time. 'Tis fcarce to be imagin'd, what a ftrange Alteration this Fatal News had made in *Hypolitus*, and that in a few Hours ; it was fuch, that any one that had feen him then, would have fworn he had lately had fome violent and long Difeafe ; and truly can there be a more violent one than Love ? Or can there be a more dangerous one ? Becaufe we are not fenfible of the Danger at the Beginning of a Tender Paffion, every thing appears pleafing ; every thing feems engaging ; the Poifon flips infenfibly into our Heart, and is the more dangerous, becaufe we take it with delight ; all our Senfes confpire againft us, and are as it were our Murderers.

A confiderable time was elapfed, before *Hypolitus* could take any fix'd Refolution, till after, having fram'd a Thoufand vain Projects, he at laft refolv'd to travel back to *London :* His Father's Anger, his Agreement with my Lady *Bedford* that he fhould not come into *England* within the fpace of Three Years, were not Motives ftrong enough to divert him from this Defign, and he was fo far from being concern'd thereat, that he thought it below himfelf, as much as to make the leaft Reflection upon it ; fo that, when Segnior *Leander* put him in mind of it, Oh ! thefe Treacherous People, *cry'd he,* fent me out of the way for no other End, than that they might
　　　　　　　　　　　　　　　　　with

with the more eafe do their worft to me. What
reafon have I to fear them now ? Juft Heavens!
there is no Danger fo great, but what I would encounter without fear ; my Misfortunes are come
to their utmoft Period ; my ill Fortune has poured
upon me all its Malignancy, and in that deplorable
State I am reduced to, I can fear nothing, unlefs it
fhould be the dread of living too long. *Leander*
feeing him fo refolute, refolved to go along with
him ; and as *Hypolitus*'s Grief rendred him incapable of taking care either of his own Perfon or of his
Affairs, he managed every thing with that earneftnefs and affiduity, as is becoming a True Friend
upon fuch like an Occafion : He told him, They
would pretend to go no further than to *Rome*, and
would take along with them each only one Servant,
whom they knew to be true to them. Accordingly
Leander ask'd his Father leave, to take this Journey
with *Hypolitus*, which he eafily obtained.

They both left *Florence* at the fame time, and
travell'd to *Bologne* ; but tarried there no longer
than juft to give a Vifit to Count *Bentivoglio*, an intimate Friend of the Senator *Alberti*, who had fent
him a Letter by *Leander* ; then paffing over the
Apennines, return'd privately through *Fierofola* to
Florence, and thence to *Leghorn:* But there being
no Ship in that Port, then ready to fail for *England*,
they hir'd a *Tartane*, which carried them with a fare
Wind to *Marfeilles*. They had fcarce bin there two
days when they embark'd for *England*; but *Hypolitus*,
before his Departure thence, had the fatisfaction to
receive a Letter from the Earl of *Warwick*, with
whom he had all along maintain'd a very ftrict Correfpondence, tho' they had not very often an Opportunity of writing to one another. The Earl of
Warwick was gone to *Venice*, with an Intention to
offer his Service to that Republick, but he foon
found that they enjoy'd the fweets of a perfect Peace
there ;

there ; this great and glorious City remaining an idle Spectator of all the Calamities *Europe* was then involv'd in. 'Twas about the same time, that *Cosmus de Medicis*, with the assistance of the Imperial Auxiliaries, besieged and took *Siena*, and that the *Venetians* had revenged themselves upon *Mustapha Biso* ; This so much celebrated *Corsair* entring the *Adriatick* Sea with his Squadron of light Ships, ravaged the Coast of *Dalmatia*, till being engaged and vanquish'd by General *Canalis*, he had his Head cut off on the Deck of his own Galley. After this Expedition, the *Venetians* directed all their Councils to the maintaining an exact Neutrality with their more powerful Neighbours : And the Earl of *Warwick*, whose Intention was to signalize himself in the Field, soon considering with himself that there was but little likelihood to succeed in his Design, in a Place which enjoy'd the fruits of a perfect Tranquility, understood, to his no small satisfaction, that great warlike Preparations were making in the *Isle of Maltha* against *Dragut Rais*, who, by *Soliman*'s Orders, was preparing to appear at Sea with 50 Gallies. And the Knights of that Island, became so jealous of these vast Preparations by Sea, left no Stone unturn'd to put themselves, not only in a state of Defence, but also to attack the Enemy. The Earl of *Warwick*, who had not as yet forgot the ill Treatment he had receiv'd at his Hands during his Captivity, was overjoy'd at this Opportunity of fighting for his Religion, to signalize himself in so good a Cause, and to revenge himself upon *Dragut Rais* ; so he desir'd *Alvisio Mocenigo*, the then Duke of *Venice*, to Honour him with his Recommendation to the *Great Master* of *Maltha*. The Duke was very ready to gratify the Earl of *Warwick* in his Request, to shew his own and the Republicks Acknowledgement of those Services he had done them : So he set sail for *Maltha*, where meeting

I

with

with a very agreeable Reception, he went aboard
the Commodore *Palette* ; and having perform'd e-
very thing that could be expected from the Valour
and Conduct of two such brave Men, and the Gallies being laid up again at *Maltha*, the Earl of *Warwick* return'd to *Venice*, and gave immediate notice
of his arrival there to *Hypolitus*, who had written
to him concerning *Julia's* Marriage, and into what
a deplorable Estate he had bin reduced too by this
terrible News. The Earl highly afflicted at the
Misery of his Friend, writ him, in answer to his,
That he was transacting some Matters of the greatest Consequence at *Venice*, which he soon hoped to
bring to a good issue, and that then he would make
all the haste he could for *England*, to snatch his
Daughter out of the Earl of *Bedford's* Arms, since
the Match could not stand good, being made without his Consent ; and that therefore he might rest
assured, that *Julia* should be nobodys but his. The
amorous *Hypolitus* being willing enough to flatter
himself with these pleasing Hopes, this gave some
present allay to his Pain, especially since Signior
Leander did not fail to put him frequently in mind,
that *Julia* having still a Father alive, and a Father
of such extraordinary Merits, and of no less Quality
than the Earl of *Warwick*, they would be glad to
restore her to him, so soon as he should demand her.

Our Two illustrious Travellers meeting with a
prosperous Gale, happily arrived in the Port of
London ; but *Hypolitus* bearing an Aversion to his
Father's House, would not as much as come in sight
of it, but went strait to the Earl of *Sussex* ; who at
first gave him but a cold Reception. Signior *Leander* seeing *Hypolitus* ready to run distracted, without being able to speak one Word in his own behalf, address'd himself to the Earl of *Sussex*, (tho
altogether unknown to him) discovering to him
the whole Truth of the matter, how treacherously
Hypo-

Hypolitus had bin dealt with ; how he had met accidentally with the Earl of *Warwick* at Sea ; and in
short,every thing he had understood from*Hypolitus*'s
own Mouth. The Earl then grieved to the Heart
at his Friend's Misfortune, threw himself about his
Neck,and clasping him close within his Arms, Oh !
my dear and most faithful Friend, *said he to him*,
What is it they tell me ? What shall we be able to
do, to remedy your Misfortune ? For you are not
married in *Italy*, and yet 'tis this false News has
occasion'd you the Loss of your Mistress. At these
Words *Hypolitus* reviving as it were out of his
Trance,and fetching a deep Sigh,Where is she, *said
he interrupting him ?* Where is she ? That Mistress
I still adore, in spite of all the Pain her too precipi-
tate Resolution has caused to me. She is still in
Barkshire, *reply'd the Earl of* Sussex, and the fair *Lucilia* stays with her : This young Lady is so generous
as to comfort her continually, and to bear Share in
all her Afflictions: I have bin told also, that she has
bin very dangerously ill, and that her Spouse is
mortally Jealous of her. The other day my Lord
Neville having invited me,with several other Persons
of Quality, to a Hunting Match at his Country-Seat
(which you know is not far distant from the Earl of
Bedford's;) I was very glad to embrace this Opportunity of staying for some days at a Place,where,by
reason of its Vicinity, I might visit *Julia* without any
manner of suspicion of a framed Design : The Earl
of *Bedford* being one of those that were invited to
this Match, I thought I would prepare him beforehand for that Visit ; but he told me, with much
coldness,tho in Terms full of Civility, that it would
be a great favour to him, but that he was scarce e-
ver at home. You have, *reply'd I*, a Lady at home,
who knows how to perform the Honour of the House
in your absence. He blush'd and seem'd discom-
pos'd at these Words ; but soon recollecting him-

self

self as well as he could. That Lady loves to be by her self, *said he*, and is very often out of order. This answer, inftead of checking me in my Defign, as the Earl fuppofed it would, produced a quite contrary Effect : for I refolved to run the hazard of a down-right Refufal.   Accordingly I went to his Houfe; but fuch effectual care was taken, that they were always ready with fome Excufe or other ; either that fhe was afleep, or that fhe was not very well ; fo that it was impoffible for me to fee her nor to fpeak to *Lucilia.*   Alas ! cry'd *Hypolitus,* and how is it poffible for me to fee her ! For me, who have wounded her Husband, and whom queftionlefs he hates more than any other Man in the Univerfe. I fee no Way for you to fee her, *reply'd the Earl,* unlefs it be under a Difguife.   They begun then to confider, by what Means to bring this Interview about ; but *Hypolitus's* Mind was too far over-burthened with Grief, to be able to reflect duly upon the matter: *Leander* being but newly come into *England,* was unacquainted with the Cuftoms and Manners of the Country ; fo that without the Earl of *Suffex's* affiftance, they might have thought long enough, and that to a very little purpofe.

A lucky Thought comes into my Head juft now, *faid he to them* ; My Opinion is, to get fomebody to buy fome Ribbonds, Gloves, Fans, and in fhort, all manner of other Toys, fuch as commonly are fold by your Hawkers and Pedlars in the Country ; with thefe you muft have 2 or 3 Boxes fix'd, every way like thofe the Pedlars make ufe of; and your Drefs being fuited to your pretended Profeffion, you may under this Difguife go to the Earl of *Bedford* s Houfe, and meet with an Opportunity of feeing *Julia,* without the leaft Sufpicion.   *Hypolitus* defired the Earl of *Suffex* to go and buy what Toys and other fmall Wares he thought moft convenient ; which being done, their Wares were put up in the Boxes, and
their

their Cloaths fitted to their Intentions; for *Leander*
being refolv'd to fhare his Friends Fortune and Adventure with him, would act the famePerfonas he did,
and tho he was unknown in *England*, yet thought fit
to difguife his nobleAir and Mien under this vulgar
Habit : But, as to *Hypolitus*'s being obliged to take
more efpecially care of himfelf, for fear of being difcover'd by the Earl of *Bedford*, he put a largePlaifter
upon one Eye, which covered part of his Face.

So they fet out towards night in their ownCloaths
attended only by two Servants, who carry'd their
Boxes and other Accoutrements.   A Thoufand melancholy Reflections, intermix'd with fome glimpfes
of Comfort, of Hope, and of Defpair, crouded into the amorous *Hypolitus*'s Head ; WhatDifpofition
am I likely to find my dear *Julia* in? *Leander*, faid he,
do you think fhe will look upon me with Compaffion? Do you think fhe will give a favourable Ear to
me ? Oh! the various Agitations of my Heart !
What an anxiety of mind! What a Paffion do I feel !
What will become of me at the firft fight of her ?
If her Husband fhould happen to be in the Room,
how fhall I be able to forbear him, and not revenge
my felf upon him, for all the Pains he has made me
fuffer ? They thus pafs'd their time away upon the
Road, till coming to the Place where they intended
to difguife themfelves, they did alight from their
Horfes, put on their Cloaths with their Boxes, and
for fear of any finifter Event, provided themfelves
each with a Pair of Pocket-Piftols, charged with
Balls, and then left their Two Servants with their
Horfes in the Wood.

Julia's Houfe was not far from thence, and *Hypolitus* having bin there before, they foon got thither,
and *Leander* undertook the Task of fpeaking and anfwering all the Queftions that fhould be ask'd him.
The firft Man they met with in the Court-yard
was the Earl of *Bedford* himfelf ; this fatal fight

I 3   made

made *Hypolitus* tremble for Anger ; fo that with much ado he could fcarce contain himfelf within due bounds. *Leander* accofted him in *Italian*, (a Language the Earl underftood perfectly well) and told him he had abundance of fine Toys and Rarities to fell : The Earl ordred them to be brought into a fpacious Room, where having taken a View of their Wares, he was fo well pleas'd with them, that he fent a Page immediately to defire his Lady and *Lucilia* to come down Stairs. They came in a few Minuets after, *Julia* leaning with one Hand up-on a Cane, and the other being fupported by *Lucilia*, like a fick Perfon ; befides, there appear'd a certain Palenefs in her Countenance, her Eyes full of Languifhment, and an Air full of Melancholy and Sadnefs : But, good God, notwithftanding all thefe difadvantages, *Hypolitus* thought her fo fur-prizingly handfome, that had he not bin leaning againft the Wall, he had certainly not bin in a con-dition to keep himfelf upright.

An Elbow-Chair being brought in for *Julia*, fhe over-look'd all the Rarities in a carelefs way, neither did fhe fhew the leaft Inclination of buying any thing, unlefs it were a piece of Miniature, repre-fenting *Love* feiz'd with a violent Difeafe, and *Reafon* ftanding near her and offering to her a Viol with Liquor ; but *Love* pufh'd it back with her Hands ; underneath were thefe Words : *Nothing can cure me.*

She could not forbear to fhew this little Picture to *Lucilia*, which *Hypolitus* (who narrowly watch'd every Action and Motion of hers) foon obferving, felt a ftrange Emotion in his Heart ; and percei-ving the Earl of *Bedford* very bufie in viewing what *Leander* fhew'd him, and fearing left *Julia* fhould withdraw before he could fpeak to her, he drew nearer, and pretending to look for fome extraordi-nary rare Things in his Box, he brought out among the

the reft, the fame Parapet and Picture *Julia* prefented to him, when they took leave of one another, upon his going for *Italy* ; he gave it into her
Hands, and without much difguiiing his Voice
(which was fufficiently changed already, by the
various Agitations he felt within himfelf,) Pray,
Madam, *faid he*, buy this Piece, which reprefents
Love, perhaps you never faw any thing fo fine in
your Life : She took it carelefly, but no fooner caft
her Eyes upon it, but fhe appear'd fo much furprized, that had her Husband but taken never fo little
notice of her at that inftant, he muft needs have
fufpected there was fome Miftery in the Cafe. After
having for fome time view'd, with much Attention,
the Hairs, the Colours, the Device, and the Hearts :
Where did you buy this Piece, *faid fhe to him with a
low Voice*, as not to be underftood by any body elfe
but by him ? *Leander* feeing his Friend engaged in
Difcourfe with his Miftrefs, took care to keep the
Earl of *Bedford* from over-hearing them : So that
Hypolitus finding himfelf fomewhat at liberty, *reply'd*,
You ask me, Madam, where I bought it ? But there
are certain things not to be purchafed for Money ;
I remember the time, which was the Happinefs of
my Life, when I adored a certain Lady, and fhe was
pleafed to accept of my Services ; but that time is
pafs'd and gone. Divine *Julia*, continu'd he, drawing nearer to her, as if he intended to fhew her the
excellency of the Workmanfhip of the Piece, that
time fo dear and charming to me, is now no more :
She fufpected my Conftancy, fhe believed me unfaithful, and I am come to proteft at her Feet, that
I never was fo. Thefe Words, which touch'd *Julia*
to the very Heart, foon putting her in Mind of her
dear *Hypolitus*, fhe fetch'd a deep Sigh, and leaning
her Head on one of her Hands, could not refrain
from fhedding fome Tears : It would be a great additional Misfortune to this Lady, *faid fhe to him*, if it
he

be true, that you are innocent upon that account.
Whilſt they were thus diſcourſing together, Signi-
or *Leander* ſhew'd the Earl of *Bedford* a moſt curious
Quadrant, and told him, that the better to obſerve
its exactneſs, they would make Trial of it upon the
Terraſs-walk that was without the great Room: So
that *Hypolitus* ſeeing nobody with *Julia* but her dear
Siſter, could not forbear throwing himſelf at *Julia's*
Feet, and taking hold of her Fair Hands, kiſs'd them
with ſuch a tranſport of Tenderneſs and Paſſion,
that it was thought he would never have ſtirr'd from
the place again. *Lucilia* was over-joy'd at her Brother's return, and *Julia* was not able to utter one
Word, being quite confounded with Joy, Fear, and
Pain ; neither had ſhe Courage enough to make a
more narrow Enquiry into the Truth of the matter,
(notwithſtanding ſhe felt within herſelf a great Eagerneſs of upbraiding him with his Infidelity) but
he was beforehand with her. My lovely Lady, ſaid
he to her, caſting a moſt Amorous Look at her, no,
I am not guilty ; thoſe Trayors that have deceiv'd
you with a ſuppoſitious Marriage, (a thing I never
as much as thought of) made this Contrivance on
purpoſe to render the remainder of my moſt doleful Life inſupportable to me: I am Faithful to you,
Julia, but you are not ſo to me. Don't encreaſe my
Pains, my dear *Hypolitus*, *ſaid ſhe to him ſobbing and
crying*, What I am convinced of to day, is a ſufficient Revenge to you, and a Puniſhment to me, for
having bin ſo unfortunate, as to ſuffer my ſelf to be
thus catch'd in the Snare. Tho' my Paſſion, and the
Reſpect I bear to you, will not ſuffer me to reproach
you, my dear *Julia*, I can't however but tell you, that
you were too haſty in conſummating that fatal Marriage, and that it ſeems to me, as if ſome other Reaſons, beſides your Anger, had had a great Share in
it ; For, what could make you ſo far neglectful of
your Duty, as not to ask your Father's Conſent, and
ſtay

ſtay for his Approbation? At theſe Words *Julia*
look'd upon him with Eyes full of Compaſſion, for
ſhe verily believed no otherwiſe than that he was
diſtracted: What do you tell me of myFather. *ſaid
ſhe*, whom, as far as I can remember, I never ſaw in
all myLife time? Alas! had he bin alive, I ſhould
not be ſo unfortunate as now I am. *Hypolitus*, by
thisAnſwer, ſoon underſtood, that my Lord *Douglas*
had intercepted and kept both the the Earl of *Warwick*'s and his Letters. You ought not to be ignorant any longer, my dear Lady, *continu'd he*, raiſing
himſelf from the Ground, for fear of being ſurprized, that that ſame Fortune which has bin ſo contrary to me in every thing elſe in myVoyage, would
however oblige me with one Favour that moſt
nearly concern'd me; I mean in that ſtrange Adventure of meeting with your illuſtrious Father at
Sea. He was a Slave to the Famous Corſair *Dragut
Rais*, the ſame againſt whom he fought in the *Venetian* Service, when he was ſuppos'd to be ſlain; I delivered him from his Captivity, and he acquainted
you with it in his Letters directed to you————
Here the Earl of *Bedford* came back into theRoom,
deeply engaged inDiſcourſe with*Leander*, concerning the Price he was to give him for the *Quadrant*;
for it being his buſineſs to keep him upon the Terraſs-
walk as long as he could had ſet ſo high aPrice upon
his Ware, that they were above a Quarter of an
Hour arguing the matter, before they could agree
about the Price; which they did at laſt, *Leander* being unwilling to carry theJeſt too far with theEarl.
Scarce were they got into the Room, where *Hypolitus* was entertaining*Julia*, but in comes theCounteſs
of *Neville*, who was actually *Julia*'s Aunt, without
knowing it; for ſhe was ignorant of her being the
Earl of *Warwick*'s Daughter; but ſhe had always
ſhew'd her as muchTenderneſs, as if ſhe had bin acquainted with the Secret of her Conſanguinity:
                                               Their

Their Seats were at no great diftance from one another in the Country, fo fhe came to invite her to
her Daughter's Wedding, who was to be married to
my Lord *Howard*, defcended from one of the moft
noble Families in *England*. Tho' I expect but little
Company there, *faid fhe to her*, I don't queftion but
we fhall be very merry. I muft frankly tell you,
Madam, moft obligingly, *reply'd* Julia, that unlefs it
be the Pleafure of feeing you and your dear Family
there, nothing will divert me ; for give me leave
to tell you, that I am fcarce recover'd of a very long Diftemper, which makes me ftill fo weak
and faint, that I am much afraid my prefence will
only prove troublefome to fo agreeable an Affembly. You may tell me what you think fit, *return'd
the Countefs of* Neville, but unlefs you are there the
Match fhall not be confummated ; we fhall not
enjoy our felves without you, and therefore am refolved to carry you immediately along with me to
my Houfe. My Lord *Howard* being a near Relation
of the Earl of *Bedford's*, he fo effectually join'd his
Entreaties with my Lady *Neville*, that *Julia*, not being able to refufe them, went immediately along
with the Countefs of *Neville*, without having the
leaft Opportunity of fpeaking with *Hypolitus*, or of
knowing where the Earl of *Warwick* now was ; fo
fhe, as well a *Lucilia*, contented themfelves for this
time, with telling the fuppos'd Pedlars, that they
fhould not fail to come again another time, becaufe
they intended to buy feveral Things of them they
lik'd. They took mutually their Leaves with the
moft tender and paffionate Looks that could be ;
and fo foon as the Ladies were got into their
Coaches, they likewife went their ways.

   Leander as well as *Hypolitus* walk'd along for fome
time, without fpeaking one Word, both their Minds
being quite taken up with their Thoughts, which
made them very penfive : At laft *Leander* addref-
                fing

fing himfelf to his Friend. You have, *faid he to him*, brought me to day to the Sight of Two of the handfomeft Ladies in the World ; I am of Opinion, 'tis impoffible for any one to behold them without Admiration : I look'd upon *Julia* as the Object of your Love, but *Lucilia*, the Charming *Lucilia*, is become the Object of mine ; But that you are her Brother, *continu'd he*, I fhould fear, left you fhould be my Rival : She has quite enchanted my Senfes, her whole Deportment, her engaging Air, her regular Features, her Shape, her goodly Mien, all thefe Perfections fhe is Miftrefs of beyond all other Women, have rais'd fuch an Amazement in my Soul, that I muft confefs to you, I never felt that for any other Perfon in the World, what I feel within my felf for her. *Hypolitus* overjoy'd to hear him, threw his Arms all on a fudden about his Neck ; I could find but one Fault in you, dear Friend, *faid he to him*, that was, your want of Love ; I fometimes relented my being in Love, unlefs you would be in Love as well as I ; it feem'd to me, as if what I told you, was not very intelligible to you, and as if my Pains did not effect you fufficiently, becaufe you had never felt any thing like it. I am overjoy'd to hear, you have at laft met with an Object, that is capable of touching your Heart, and it fhall not be my Fault, if my Sifter does not infpire into you a moft violent Paffion. But what do you think of the lovely *Julia?* Have I not fufficient reafon to dye for her? Did ever you fee any thing that comes near her for Beauty? For my part, I muft confefs, I am quite enchanted with it ; That Languifhment, that Sadnefs you obferve in all her Actions, only ferve to augment her Charms, and to render me the more unfortunate. Alas ! all thefe things taken together, ferve only to make me the more fenfible of my Lofs in her.

Their Converfation lafted till they came to the Wood, where they were to change again their
Cloaths ;

Cloaths ; but whilft their Two Servants were getting them ready, they on a fudden heard a great
Noife of Men and Horfes, who foon furrounded them.
They were not a little furprized, and had no reafon
to queftion, but that they aim'd at them, when
they faw fome with Swords drawn, others arm'd
with Guns and Piftols, approaching on all fides, and
(without fhewing their Authority) calling to them
to furrender. They were fenfible it would be in
vain to withftand fo great a Number; but being refolved not to fubmit tamely, they pull'd out their
Pocket Piftols, and wounded no lefs than Four, and
then clapping their Backs againft fome Trees, (to
avoid being furrounded) they fought it out moft
bravely, and were fuccefsfully feconded by their
Two Servants ; but at laft, finding the Number of
their Enemies encreafe, as their ftrength begun to
decay by degrees, and that they aim'd not at their
Lives, becaufe they call'd to them without intermiffion to furrender, they faw themfelves under a
Neceffity of doing fo. No fooner had they got them
into their Clutches, but, to revenge themfelves
and their Comerades, that were wounded, they tied
Hypolitus and *Leander*, and their Two Servants, Hand
and Feet, for fear they fhould either once more
fight againft them, or make their Efcape.

In this Condition they carry'd them before a
neighbouring Juftice of the Peace, upon whofe
Warrant they had feiz'd them ; tho (being mad and
in drink) they had not produc'd nor nam'd it : The
thing hapned thus, Juft as Signior *Leander* and
Hypolitus were changing their Cloaths in the Wood,
when they were going to the Earl of *Bedford's*
Houfe, fome Butchers happening to pafs by that
Way, and feeing them pull off their embroider'd
Coats, and inftead thereof to put on others of a
quite different make, and one clapping a Plaifter to
his Eye, they did not in the leaft queftion, but that
                                        thefe

thefe were the fame Highway-Men, who had of late committed many Robberies in that part of the Country. Several Conftables, with their Attendants, had bin abroad in Search after them, and were juft come back to the Juftice of the Peace's Houfe, when thefe Butchers came in, to give an account of what they had feen: There needed no more to fatisfy them that thefe were the Men they look'd for; and when after the return of *Leander* and *Hypolitus* from the Earl of *Bedford's* Houfe, they found them again bufied in changing their Cloaths, they thought themfelves fo certain that thefe were the Highway-men, that without any further Ceremony they fell upon them, feiz'd and carried them to the Juftice of the Peace's Houfe.

Whilft they were carried along, *Hypolitus* made the moft melancholy Reflections that can well be imagin'd, upon the oddnefs of this Adventure; not being able to conceive unto whom to attribute, or whom to blame for this Mifhap. Is this the Effect of my Father's Averfion, *faid he to himfelf?* Am I found out, and has fomebody or other difcover'd to him my return into *England!* Or perhaps, has my Lady *Bedford* and her Son taken the Advantage of my Father's Agreement with them! As he was under a great uncertainty as to his Enemies, fo he could not but be furpriz'd, what fhould make them to feize *Leander*, being vex'd to the Heart, he fhould prove the Occafion of his Friend's ill Treatment. They had taken care to part them, fo that they had not the Satisfaction of fpeaking to one another, and no fooner were they brought before the Juftice, but he examin'd them each apart; Guefs at their furprize, when he ask'd them, Whether they had not kill'd fuch and fuch Perfons and robb'd them? They difown'd the Fact, but you may believe, this would not difcharge them; fo far from that, that they were put, Hands and Feet tied, into a deep Cellar, the

Door

Door whereof was narrowly watch'd by a Conftable and his Attendants.

Being now at Liberty to fpeak, they told one another, every thing that can be thought tender and kind, or what can pcffibly be conceiv'd to proceed from a moft fincere Friendfhip upon fuch an Occafion as this. Be not difturb'd, my deareftFriend, *faid* Leander *to* Hypolitus, you fee the whole thing is no more than a Chimera, and that let the worft come to the worft, you need only difcover your felf, and they will be glad to fet us at Liberty. Would you have me not be difturb'd, *cry'd* Hypolitus? Oh! *Leander,* I fee you are far from being fully acquainted with the Sentiments I have for you, and with what may be theConfequence of this Mifchance : I fee you tied Hands and Feet like a Criminal, in a darkHole, upon the bareGround; you follow'd me into my own Country, after you had fhew'd me aThoufand Courtefies in yours : The firft place I bring you to is a Prifon, pray confider what Entertainment I give you in my Native Country? And would you have me remain infenfible at fuch aMisfortune? Yes, I would, *faid* Leander, *interrupting him,* I would not have you carry things to that Extremity of Tendernefs, and affure your felf that in bearing a fhare in your Misfortunes, I don't feel my own; befides, let me tell you myFriend, I am above fuch anAccident as this; a dark Hole, ill Treatment, thofe are things I value not in refpect to my felf, and were you thoroughly acquainted with the Sentiments of my Heart, this Mifhap would not give you the leaft Difturbance. I fhould be very unworthy of theGoodnefs you fhew me, my dear *Leander,* reply'd Hypolitus, where I not highly fenfible of it ; and not to conceal from you my further Inquietudes, pray confider, what will be the Confequence of it, if I am forc'd to tell my Name ; and if the Earl of *Bedford* fhould be inform'd of our Difguife and all its Circumftances,

what

what Conftructions do you think he will make of it? He will lay the blame at *Julia*'s Door, he is a violent Man and full of Jealoufy : Neither her Virtue nor her Innocence will be fufficient to remove his Jealoufy. What will be the End of this! Alas! 'tis I, that perhaps fhall prove the Inftrument of troubling her Tranquility for ever! Can there be any thing in the World beyond this, to reduce a Lover to the utmoft Defpair? Add to this, that in cafe the thing comes to my Father's Ears, he will think nothing too much for my Punifhment ; and, fo foon as I am difcharg'd by the Juftice, I muft expect to take up my Lodging in fome other Prifon, as he often has threatned me : So that at once I ruin *Julia* in refpect to her Husband, and lofe *Julia* in refpect to my felf. Truly, *reply'd* Leander, thefe are very cruel Extremities; and what is worfe, I fee not which way we fhall be able to avoid them. I have thought of fomething, *added Hypolitus*, you know thefe Juftices of the Peace are fometime covetous, I will try him that way, perhaps that may prove the beft at laft. *Leander* approv'd of his Thought ; and fo they paft away the Night, as well as they could, in this unfortunate Condition.

It was almoft Noon, when they came to take them out of the Cellar, to carry them up into the Juftice's Room. Inftead of examining them, as they thought he would have done, he ask'd them whether they had Courage enough to fight? They not being able to guefs at his Meaning in asking them that Queftion, *Hypolitus* told him, He ought to propofe that Queftion rather to thofe that came to affault them, than to them ; But, *continued he, fpeaking to him foftly*, if you will fet us at Liberty, you need only tell us your own Terms, you fhall have whatever you can defire. I am not to be brib'd, *faid the Juftice*, I will difcharge my Duty with Honour, and there being fo many People concern'd in this matter, you ought

to

to be made an Example to others. *Hypolitus* almoſt reduc'd to Deſpair to ſee his Project fail him, after ſeveral repeated Inſtances, to no purpoſe, at laſt reſolved to tell him his Name ; My requeſt of Diſcharging us, *ſaid he to him*, will not turn in the leaſt to your Prejudice, for I am willing to tell you my Name, and am ready to give you what Reward you pleaſe, provided you will keep the Secret, becauſe I have ſome weightyReaſons, to remain *incognito* here : I am *Hypolitus*, Son to the Earl of *Douglas*, and I am contented to ſtay with you, till I have made you actually ſuch a Preſent as you ſhall require. You are very bold, *reply'd the Juſtice, with an angry Countenance*, to dare to take upon you ſuch a Name before me, as if I did not know poſſitively, that the Perſon you mention is at preſent in *Italy*; and ſo out of the Room he went, ordering thoſe that guarded the Priſoners, to keep themſelves in readineſs to carry them away. 'Twas not long before the Juſtice put himſelf at the Head of theſe Guards, who had *Hypolitus* and *Leander* in the midſt of them ; they had not walk'd far, before they diſcover'd on the top of a Hill a very ſumptuous Structure, the Arches whereof being planted on both ſides with very fine Trees, affording a very agreeable Shade, and extended even from the Hill into the Plain ; they could perceive at a diſtance a great Concourſe of People, and as they came nearer, heard the pleaſing Sound of various Muſical Inſtruments. What does this mean, my dear *Hypolitus*, *ſaid* Leander ? Are we to be carried to this gloriousHouſe, where all the Pleaſures ſeem to have fix'd their Seat ; What Part are we likely to act in this Scene ? *Hypolitus* caſting a melancholy Look at him, I ſuppoſe, *ſaid he*, we ſhall only be Spectators of this Feaſt at a diſtance ; for I believe they intend to carry us to the next great Town, or perhaps to *London*.

Whilſt

Whilft they were thus difcourfing together, they faw a Perfon coming towards them, who appear'd to be a Perfon of Note, as well by his noble Air, as by his numerous Attendants. *Leander* ask'd his Friend, whether he knew him ? *No,* faid he, *but I believe him to be fomebody of this Country :* So he drawing nearer, the Juftice of the Peace alighted from his Horfe to pay his Refpects to him. ' My Lord, *faid he,* I am come on pur-
' pofe to beg your Pardon, and teftify my Unea-
' finefs at the Difappointment I am forced to give
' you. The two Prize-fighters that promifed to
' be at my Houfe yefterday, have fail'd of their
' Promife ; I ftaid for them till Noon, but they not
' appearing, I know not what to do. My Lord
told him with an angry Countenance, 'Had you
' not given me your word, I would have taken care
' to have fome others provided for me, and the
' Company that is at my Houfe, in full expectati-
' on of being entertain'd with this Divertifement,
' according to my Invitation ; What muft I do in
' this cafe ? My Lord, *reply'd he,* here I have
' brought along with me four fuppofed Highway-
' men, and fome of them being Foreigners, and no
' pofitive proof againft them, it will I believe prove
' no hard Task, either by fair or foul means, to
' make them fight together, provided they may
' be put in hopes of being difcharged. My Lord
told him, that if he would take the thing upon
himfelf, he would be contented ; and cafting his
Eyes upon them, was extreamly taken with the
goodly Mien and Air of *Leander* and *Hypolitus ;*
he told the Juftice thefe two might give fufficient
Diverfion to his Company, defiring him to make
what hafte he could, whilft he would go and
give order to make the neceffary Preparations
for the Combat ; and accordingly the Juftice

K   ordered

ordered his People to walk on as faft as they
could.

Leander being not fo well verfed in the *Englifh*
Tongue, as to underftand what they were contriving againft them; *Hypolitus* fetching a deep Sigh
told him, 'Oh! my dear *Leander*, what do you
' think they are preparing for us, the ftrangeft
' Cataftrophe that ever was feen; Good God, to
' what Misfortunes are we referved? They would
' have us fight againft one another. Pray explain
' your felf, *faid Signior* Leander, for I don't un-
' derftand your meaning. You know, *reply'd* Hy-
' politus, that the *Romans* ufed to divert the Peo-
' ple with Publick Spectacles, in thefe certain Cri-
' minals ufed fometimes to fight one another.
' This Cuftom was introduced into *England* when
' they made themfelves Mafters of this Ifland,
' and has been tranfmitted to our Times; with this
' difference however, that our Gladiators or Prize-
' fighters, devote themfelves voluntarily to this
' Trade: I fay devote themfelves, for there have
' been Examples of their having dy'd of their
' Wounds they received in thefe Combats, and I
' call that a Trade, which is made ufe of to get
' Money by it; they are commonly drefs'd only
' in a Shirt and a pair of Drawers, with a Scarfe
' about their middle, and a Bonnet on their Heads.
' Thus prepared, they make their Appearance in a
' place covered with Sand, upon a fpacious
' Theatre or Stage, with broad Swords but blunt
' at the Points, being intended only for cutting and
' flafhing, and promife the Spectators not to quit
' the Stage, till they draw Blood from one ano-
' ther two or three times. So to work they go,
' wound one another moft miferably, cut off a
' piece of the Skull or Shoulder, and don't fpare
' one another in the leaft at that time, tho' other-
' wife

' wife they are very good Friends, and go fnacks
' in the Money that is given. They have alfo a
' way of fighting with pointed Sticks almoft like
' fmall half Pikes, wherewith they prick one ano-
' ther's Eyes out; to be fhort, it is a moft terrible
' Sight, and thofe that are the Spectators of it, are
' no lefs to blame, than thofe that do it. This
' Tragedy, dear *Leander*, they intend we fhould
' act againft one another. I, my dear *Hypolitus*,
' to fight and to wound you, cry'd Leander, I will
' rather die on the Spot than do't.

They had juft finifh'd their Difcourfe, when
coming to the beforementioned fine Houfe, they
were conducted into a fpacious Room, without
being unty'd; fome Victuals was fet before them,
but they would eat none, which the Juftice (who
was an ill natur'd furly Fellow, and in thefe Times
of Trouble, prefumed he might ftretch his Authority beyond its due Bounds) being acquainted
with, he came to them, and told them, they had
beft to comply with what was defired of them;
that their Deliverance or Death was in his Hands,
as the cafe ftood, and that he fwore to them by all
that was holy and facred, that in cafe they would
not do what was propofed to them, they might
make no other account, than upon a certain Death,
and therefore he would advife them not to put it
to the Tryal. They requefted feveral times to fpeak
with the Mafter of the Houfe; but the Juftice, who
had obferved there was a ftrict Friendfhip betwixt
Hypolitus and his Friend, foon perceiving that
their intention was to beg of him, not to fuffer
them to fight againft one another, would not let
them fee any Body. Nothing can be comparable
to the Defperate Condition they faw themfelves
reduced to, the appointed Hour was come, and
the more refolute they appear'd in not complying

with the Juftice's Demands, the more he threatned them with Death and Deftruction. At laft
thefe two Friends dreading the Effects of an Ar-
bitrary Power, refolved, that as foon as they got
the Swords into their hands, inftead of employing
them againft one another, they would make ufe
of them to fell their Lives at the deareft rate they
could ; fo they took their Arms and appeared
within the Barriers where they were to fight.

Notice being given to all the Company there
prefent, that two Highwaymen, who had fought
fo defperately in the Wood before they were taken, were to fight, every one was very defirous to
fee the iffue of this Combat ; but no fooner were
they entred within the Barriers, but you might
have heard a confufed murmuring Noife among
the Spectators, every Body there looking upon
them with Admiration ; their Youth, their Beauty, their goodly Mien gain'd the Inclinations of
all that were prefent. There was not one Body
who could have the leaft knowledge of *Signior
Leander* ; but there were not a few who ftood almoft amazed, there fhould be fo great a Refemblance betwixt a Robber, fuch a one as they fuppofed *Hypolitus* to be, and my Lord *Douglas*'s Son:
were he not in *Italy*, faid they to one another,
who could believe otherwife, but it was himfelf
in Perfon ? Thefe two faithful Friends view'd
firft the whole Affembly with a noble and fierce
Countenance, and then caft their Eyes upon thofe
Wretches they were to engage; of thefe there
were thirty in number headed by the Conftable
and the Juftice of the Peace, who little imagined
there would be any danger in the cafe. Soon after
Hypolitus and *Leander* clofely embraced one another, imagining (as they had great reafon to do)
that they were to go to a certain Death ; but they
were

were too courageous to dread the Event ; and *Hy-*
politus had this particular satisfaction in this Misfortune, to think he should remain undiscover'd,
and that it would never be known, that he had
disguised himself, with an intention to see
Julia.

Pursuant to what was concerted betwixt them,
they leapt both together over the Rails, and running with Sword in hand towards the Justice, the
Constable and his Attendants placed along the
Barriers to guard them, they snatch'd their Swords
out of their Hands (because they would prove more
serviceable to them than those they had) and fighting like two enraged Lyons, you might have seen
them in an instant covered all over with Blood,
and wounded in several places ? *Julia* and *Lucilia*,
who were not present at this Spectacle, because
they being naturally of a sweet Disposition, took
no delight in so cruel a Divertisement, hearing an
extraordinary noise that way, and the Cries of the
Ladies, (some out of fear others out of pity) run
straightways to a spacious Terrass where the Spectators were placed, which had divers Marble Steps
leading into the Place where the Tumult was :
They cast their Eyes, tho' not without much Reluctancy upon the pretended Gladiators, whom at
first they could scarce distinguish in this Confusion from the rest : But alas! 'twas not long before
they discovered their dear *Hypolitus* and his Generous Friend : Guess what a fight what a stroak
this must be to them! What words are able to
express their Surprize, their Fear, their Affliction : Just Heavens! 'tis *Hypolitus*, 'tis him, cry'd
they both at once; so running headlong down the
Steps, made all the haste they could to secure
what they lov'd from so imminent a danger.
There was scarce any Body there but what was

ready

ready to espouse their Quarrel, every one follow'd
them with their Swords drawn.   They kept close
to their Lovers, and these seeing them come to
their Relief gathered new Strength and Courage,
so that Mr. *Justice* with his Guard seeing so many
Swords ready to be turn'd against them, were glad
to seek for their Safety in their Heels, leaving
these two Champions and dear Friends absolute
Masters of the Field of Battle; but their strength
hitherto supported by their Anger, now beginning to fail, *Hypolitus* almost drown'd in a
whole Rivulet of Blood, drop'd down half dead
at *Julia*'s Feet, and *Leander* drawing near to assist
his Friend, had the same Fate. *Julia* and *Lucilia*
at this most deplorable sight, being no more Mi-
stresses of themselves, *Julia* was altogether taken
up with her dearest Lover, whose Head leaning
upon her Knees, she held upright in her Arms,
bathing his Face with her Tears, breaking forth
into most passionate Moans and Lamentations, and
endeavouring to stop with one of her Hands the
Blood that gush'd out of one of his Wounds;
whilst *Lucilia* apply'd all her care to the assistance
of *Leander*; and this young lovely Lady, shew'd
already so particular a concern for the Preservation of this Stranger, as might well be supposed to
own its Origine to another Principle and Motive,
than to Generosity alone.   They were going to
carry *Hypolitus* into a Chamber, to dress his
Wounds, but he not considering before whom he
spoke, and casting a Languishing Look at *Julia*,
told her with the utmost Passion; ' Permit me,
' dear Mistriss of my Heart, to die in your Arms;
' this Death will be more agreeable and more hap-
' py to me than my Life: There were but few who
could hear these Words, and those that heard it,
look'd upon it as an effect of a Frenzy, which is
often

often the forerunner of approaching Death; but the Earl of *Bedford*, who was one of those that heard it, was struck with it as with a Thunderbolt; he knew *Julia* and *Hypolitus* to be no Brother and Sister; he knew that they were educated together, that it was he who had wounded him in the Garden, when he was attempting to carry off *Julia* by force; in one Moment every thing presented it self before his Eyes, which he had to fear, and these Surmizes were in his Mind changed into undeniable Realities : But so soon as he was told by the Justice of the Peace, that these two Gentlemen were taken disguised in Pedlars Habits, he had the curiosity to look into their Boxes, and there needed no more to convince him that there was a mutual Love betwixt *Julia* and *Hypolitus*, but he had so much Prudence, as to hide the Dart that had pierc'd him through the Heart.

Both these Loving Friends were carry'd into one Chamber, where their Wounds being search'd and dress'd immediately, were found to be much larger than dangerous. In the mean while *Julia* considering with her self, but too late, that her Spouse would be heartily vexed to see her so much concerned at *Hypolitus's* Misfortune, to repair in some measure this Fault, she desired *Lucilia* to tell her Brother, how she was obliged to act with much Circumspection, and not to see him unless it were in the Earl of *Bedford's* Presence ; that he himself might easily judge, what violence she put upon her own Inclinations, since she was so unfortunate as not to be able hitherto to efface out of her Heart the Impressions he had made there, and that she conjur'd him, to let her hear where her Father was.

K 4　　　　　My

My Lord *Nevil* was almoſt inconſolable, that
ſo unfortunate an Accident ſhould fall out in his
Houſe, bearing a moſt profound ReſpeCt to the
Earl of *Douglas*, and conſequently to his Son;
and being inform'd of the true Quality of *Leander*, he omitted nothing that might convince both
of them, of his uneaſineſs on that account, and of
the particular Eſteem he had for them. *Hypolitus*,
unto whom he addreſs'd himſelf in a moſt peculiar
manner, deſired him not to acquaint his Father
with what had happened, and told him frankly,
that it was his Love Paſſion that had haſten'd his
return out of *Italy* and made him diſguiſe himſelf in a Pedlar's Habit; that if his Family got to
know of it, it would prove the occaſion of great
Conteſts betwixt them and him, till he might
have time and opportunity of ſetling Matters upon a better Foot; and my Lord promiſed to do all
he deſired of him.

Several of the Company were mighty ſollici-
tous to know what could induce theſe two Gentlemen to diſguiſe themſelves thus, and there were
very few but what ſuppoſed there was a Love
Intrigue in the caſe, but they could not gueſs at
the Perſons concerned therein; for every Body believing *Julia* to be *Hypolitus* his Siſter, there was
not the leaſt room for any ſuſpicion upon her account, ſo that every Body gueſs'd according to his
Fancy, but no Body hit the Mark.

In the mean time the Juſtice of the Peace being
ſenſible how far he had abuſed his Authority, and
dreading the Revenge of thoſe he had ſo groſly
miſuſed, with the utmoſt Submiſſion beg'd *Julia*'s
and *Lucilia*'s Pardon, and that they would be ſo
generous as to intercede in his behalf with *Hypolitus* and *Leander*, which they promiſed to do, judging it moſt convenient, at this time, to ſacrifice their

Reſent.

Refentment to other more weighty Confiderations.

Lucilia frequently came into her Brother's
Chamber, becaufe *Julia*, as well as fhe, was impatient to hear, almoft every Minute, how he did,
he call'd her to him and faid, ' Why, dear Sifter,
' will you always come alone ? Does not the
' Lovely *Julia* think fit to come alfo fometimes to
' afford me fome Confolation under my prefent
' Affliction ? Were fhe to confult her own In-
' clinations only, *reply'd fhe*, you would have
' feen her oftner than me; but fhe is obliged to
' be fo much upon her Guard, that fhe dares not
' venture to fee you, unlefs it be when her Jea-
' lous Husband is prefent. She has enjoyn'd me
' to tell you fo, and to give you from her a thou-
' fand affurances of an eternal Friendfhip, and to
' defire you to let us know, in what place you
' parted with her Father, becaufe you were inter-
' rupted yefterday before you finifh'd yourRelation.
' Oh ! my dear *Lucilia*, *faid he interrupting her*,
' excufe me if I make the beft ufe of her Curiofity,
' pray tell her, the Amorous *Hypolitus* will tell
' no Body but her felf where the Earl of *War-
' wick* is; this will at ieaft engage her to come to
' fee me. 'After thefe words he paufed a while,
but foon reaffuming his former Difcourfe, ' Is it
' poffible, *faid he*, fhe can refufe me a Favour I
' ftand fo much in need of at this time. Dear
' Sifter, I conjure you, neglect nothing to make
' her grant me this Requeft ; I know not but that
' my Life may depend on it, or at leaft do you
' perfwade her as much as you can, that it does ;
' perhaps, that may prevail upon her to come.
Lucilia promis'd fhe would do all that lay in her
power, to engage *Julia* to give him a Vifit in his
Chamber.

The

The Aſſembly at my Lord *Howard*'s Wedding,
was ſo numerous, that being ſomewhat ſtraimed
for room, *Julia* and *Lucilia* lay together in one
Bed ; they went into their Chamber very early
that Night, and no ſooner were got into Bed and
their Maids gone, but finding themſelves at full
liberty to talk together, *Julia* fetching very deep
Sighs, intermingled with Sobs, and claſping *Lucilia* very cloſe in her Arms ; ' Oh! dear Siſter,
' *ſaid ſhe*, did ever any Body ſee ſuch a Series of
' odd Adventures as theſe ? Wonder with me at
' the fatality of my Stars; ſcarce had I got the
' fiſt Taſte of that Satisfaction of ſeeing again a
' Man who has remain'd always faithful to me, in
' ſpite of all the Reaſons I had given him to hate
' me, ſcarce had he acquainted me with the happy
' News of my Father's being alive, but this Feli-
' city is overturn'd by a thouſand ſiniſter Acci-
' dents. Here you ſee me at a Feaſt, where I had
' the Affliction to ſee him almoſt ſlain before my
' Face, and the ſingular concern 1 ſhew'd in his
' Preſervation, has proved a ſignal Prejudice to
' me with my Husband ; I could diſcern his Seri-
' ous Thoughts in his very Eyes and Countenance,
' in ſpite of all my Diſtraction, and the Pains he
' took to conceal them : I dare not flatter my ſelf
' any longer upon that Score, he is certainly con-
' vinced at this very Minute, that *Hypolitus* is
' dearer to me, than my own Life, and that he is
' the ſole Maſter of it : Add to this, that moſt
' cruel neceſſity I l'e under of not ſeeing him, and
' conſider, if you can —— You muſt overcome
' thoſe Niceties which thus diſturb you, dear Si-
' ſter, *ſaid* Lucilia *interrupting her*, my Brother's
' Life lies at ſtake, he has charged me to make
' you acquainted with it, and to conjure you in
' his behalf, by that Paſſion he has ſo inviolably
' pre-

'preferved for you, not to refuse him this on-
'ly Confolation he has left. Oh! dear Sifter,
'*cry'd* Julia, he has not rightly confidered of
'what he defires, if you could be fenfible of
'the Anguifh I am likely to feel within me,
'whilft I am with him, you would pity me,
'and not defire it; for, what I owe to my
'Duty, I am afraid will not agree fo well with
'my Sentiments for him, but that I may either
'be too favourable or too cruel to him: But
'Julia, *faid* Lucilia, if you don't go you will
'hear no further News concerning your Father;
'of your Father I fay, who being as it were re-
'covered from the dead, ought to be very dear
'to you. If you can be fo rigorous to poor *Hy-*
'*politus*, certainly your Curiofity to know what
'is become of the Earl of *Warwick*, will make
'you the more pliable; for my Brother protefts,
'*continued* Julia, he will tell it to no body but
'to your own felf. Alas! dear Sifter, *faid* Julia,
'you need not take fo much pains to perfwade
'me, my Heart declares for your Brother without
'it, it feconds your endeavours, and will prove
'too ftrong for my Reafon: O! how difficult is
'it to keep from feeing that which is dearer to
'one than one's own Life; how weak a Creature
'is a Woman upon fuch an Occafion as this, and
'how much in vain is it to ftruggle againft what
'one loves; muft I at laft make a frank Confef-
'fion to you, dear Sifter, I find my felf fuffici-
'ently inclined to follow your Counfel, provided
'you can find out a way to do it with fecrecy.
'Unlefs we go to him immediately, *faid* Lucilia,
'we may be in danger of being furprized; I
'left a Candle a burning on purpofe, and I have
'found out this very Evening a pair of priva e
'back Stairs which lead up to the upper end of
'the

' the Gallery, near our Chamber ; we may go
' that way if you pleafe, without making the
' leaft noife. What Sifter, *faid* Julia, *interrupt-*
' *ing her*, what, in the Night time, what if we
' fhould be difcovered ? That would fignify no-
' thing to the World, *faid* Lucilia, for all the
' World believes us both to be *Hypolitus's* Sifters.
' But the Earl of *Bedford* knows to the contrary,
' *faid* Julia *fighing*. You are too fearful, *an-*
' *fwered* Lucilia *fomewhat impatiently*, come,
' come, Sifter, let us go ; come, don't paufe a-
' ny longer upon the matter. *Julia* got out of
Bed trembling all over, and throwing a loofe
Gown about her, *Lucilia* took her by the Hand,
and conducted her to her Brother's Chamber. It
was by this time pretty late, but he had not fhut
Eyes as yet that Night : Hearing the Door to
make a noife, and feeing his beloved Miftrifs coming in, he was fo far tranfported with Joy, that
it had almoft coft him his Life; for all his Wounds
opening a frefh, he was covered with Blood, before he was fenfible of it himfelf. *Julia* feated
her felf near his Bed fide ; ' Dear *Hypolitus*, faid
fhe, with Tears in her Eyes (which fhe was not
able to retain, in fpite of all the Pains fhe took
to keep them back) ' you have this day been made
' fenfible by the excefs of my Grief, that the Un-
' fortunate *Julia* in changing her Condition, has
' not changed her Sentiments for you : Yes, my
' dear *Hypolitus*, I am willing to own it to you,
' you are at all times dearer to me than my own
' Life ; which I would willingly part with, to
' purchafe your Tranquillity ; I think of nothing
' but you, I lament you, and bemoan my felf,
' and I fhall always be inconfolable under my
' Misfortune; but fince'tis paft all Cure, we muft
' furmount it by Vertue : You fee I come to pay
' you

' you a Vifit, and it is in order to bid you my laft
' Farewel ; we muft, *Hypolitus*, we muft fubmit
' to this cruel neceffity my Duty impofes upon
' us: Death fhall always be more preferable with
' me, than a fhameful Life ; and were I the only
' Perfon now living in the World, I would act as
' if the whole Earth had their Eyes fix'd on me :
' Don't go about to fhake my Refolution, it
' would ferve only to augment my Pain. No,
' my dear *Julia, faid he to her*, no, I will not
' pretend to fhake it : I own my felf highly in-
' debted to you, becaufe you would foon free me
' from this Languifhing State ; you could not
' have pitch'd upon a more convenient time to
' put a fpeedy end to my Mifery. The weak
' Condition I am reduced to by my Wounds, and
' by what you have told me, will foon deliver
' you from an Unfortunate Lover, whom you
' would not have abandon'd as you have done,
' had you truly Lov'd him. I will not reproach
' you, Madam, you wifh for my Death, you
' have wifh'd for it long ago, and I do fo too, ha-
' ving more preffing Reafons for it than you.
He faid no more, *Julia* obferved him to turn
quite Pale, his Eyes half fhut, and his Silence
threw her into a Mortal Anguifh ; fhe call'd *Lucilia*, who was difcourfing with *Signior Leander*,
to his affiftance, who coming to *Hypolitus*'s Bed-
fide, found him fwiming in his own Blood : they
were fo furprized at the fight thereof, that at firft
they knew not what to fay unto him, but at laft
call'd for *Leander*. Tho' he was as yet very ill
himfelf, he got out of Bed and found means to
bind up his Wounds again. *Julia* was ready to
run diftracted, to find what difmal Effects her rigorous Proceedings had produced in her Lover,
fhe took him by the Hand and bathing it with her

Tears,

Tears, 'You did miſtake my Words, *ſaid ſhe*, and
' ſince there can be no medium betwixt your ſee-
' ing me and your Death, we will chuſe the firſt,
' my dear *Hypolitus*, becauſe the loſs of your
' Life would be beyond all other things to me.
At theſe words he was going to kiſs *Julia's* Hand,
but ſhe would not ſuffer him, 'I muſt own to
' you, *ſaid ſhe*, that every thing appears extraor-
' dinary to me, and that the leaſt Favour I ſhould
' grant you, would ſeem a Crime to me. Dear
' *Hypolitus*, reconcile your Paſſion with my Du-
' ty, and then I ſhall reſt contented. That won't
' be ſo difficult a thing as you imagine, Fair *Ju-*
' *lia, ſaid he,* you have a Father alive, you have
' been Marry'd without his Approbation, he did
' not give his Conſent to your Marriage ; if you
' doubt it, I have a Letter he writ me on that
' Subject, will convince you of it. He then deſired *Lucilia* to aſſiſt him in opening a ſmall *Spa-*
niſh-Leather Caſe, that was faſtned to his Arm,
and with it the formentioned Letter of the Earl
of *Warwick*, which he gave *Julia* to read, where-
by ſhe was fully convinced of the Truth of
what he had told her.' ' 'Tis certain, *added he,*
' he will ſnatch you from the Arms of that Un-
' worthy Raviſher; ſo that, Madam, if you
' pleaſe, 'tis ſtill in your Power to make me hap-
' py. *Julia* was not a little nettled, and under
no ſmall uncertainty what anſwer to make, tho'
her Inclinations ſufficiently told her what to ſay;
ſhe thought, that being once Married, ſhe was
obliged to ſtay with her Husband, that ſhe had
no force put upon her, when ſhe Married him; ſhe
conſidered what the World would ſay of her,
and theſe Conſiderations made her to delay her
Anſwer. *Hypolitus* ſoon perceiving her Irreſolu-
tion, 'I am undone, Madam, *cry'd he,* all that
                                        ' Ten-

' Tenderneſs you had for me is gone, you are un-
' reſolved to teſtify your Satisfaction in a matter
' which ought to be yours, were you not altered
' from what you uſed to be. Alas! *Hypolitus,*
' *reply'd ſhe,* I am not changed, you deal unjuſtly
' with me, let me ſee my Father, and I will obey
' him in every thing he ſhall command me, pro-
' vided it be not againſt my Conſcience and my
' Reputation; you are no leſs dear to me than
' my Life. My Adorable Lady, *ſaid he,* do you
' think I could entertain a thought that might be
' diſpleaſing to you? Pray be better acquainted
' with my Paſſion and its Motions. I will do you
' Juſtice on that account, *ſaid ſhe,* and 'tis that
' that engages me to make theſe Steps which are
' not very common, I hope you will think your
' ſelf obliged to me for it, and not make the leaſt
' ill uſe of them, my dear *Hypolitus*; and let me
' know all the Circumſtances relating to my Fa-
' ther's Adventures. He gave her an account of it,
and ſhe was ready to give him freſh Proofs of her
Acknowledgment and Love. 'I am indebted to
' you, *ſaid ſhe,* for my Father's Liberty, *continu-*
' *ed ſhe,* nay perhaps for his Life, and therefore
' can't deny you, without Ingratitude, all the Ac-
' knowledgment I am able to give you. Whilſt
they were thus talking together, *Lucilia* interrupting them ſaid, it was near Daybreak, and that
it was more convenient to afford ſome time of reſt
to theſe two Gentlemen under their preſent Circumſtances. *Hypolitus* and *Leander* blamed her
for breaking off their Converſation, which was ſo
precious to them; but *Julia* being willing to follow *Lucilia*'s Advice, conjured her Lover to think
of nothing elſe but of his Cure. ' 'Tis the utmoſt
' of my Wiſh at this time, dear Brother, *ſaid ſhe*
to him, giving him her Hand which he kiſs'd moſt
tenderly,

tenderly, ' and you can't doubt much, without do-
' ing me injuftice, that it concerns me to the high-
' eft degree. She fhew'd abundance of Complaifance to *Leander*, and then returned with *Lucilia*,
to her own Bedchamber. The Earl of *Bedford* had
not flept one Wink all that Night, his Jealoufie
and Inquietude being fuch as would not fuffer him
to take the leaft reft ; all his Thoughts were taken
up in contriving a Defign, fuch a one as he knew
would revenge him fufficiently upon thofe two
Lovers, and the better to fucceed in it, he refolved
to bring it about with all imaginable Secrefy. He
pretended the next day to be very ill of a Fever,
got not out of Bed till pretty late, and then faid
he would go home. *Julia* not daring to contradict
him, went immediately into *Hypolitus*'s Chamber:
' Dear Brother, *faid fhe*, I am obliged to leave
' you, the Earl of *Bedford* is refolved to go away
' immediately. . I once more put you in mind,
' manage Matters with my Father as you think
' fit ; I have no time to tell you any more, but
' pity and love me. I leave *Lucilia* with you,
' till your Wounds are cured. And will you leave
' me, *Julia*, *cry'd he full of Anguifh*, muft that
' Tyrant of my Repofe fnatch you from me. Oh!
' thou too charming Felicity, what makes thee
' turn away from me fo unexpectedly ? And when
' fhall I fee you again, Madam ? Alas! *reply'd fhe*
' *fighing*, that is more than I am able to tell you ;
' I fhall be fufficiently guarded, and fufficiently
' unhappy. *Lucilia* came that Moment to tell her
that every thing was ready, and that her Husband
only ftaid for her coming. Then the Amorous
Hypolitus kiffing her Hands bathed them with his
Tears ; ' Farewel, *faid he*, continue faithful to your
' faithful Lover. *Julia*, without fpeaking one word,
gave him a fine Turquoife fhe drew from her Fin-
ger ;

ger; 'Pray Heavens foon bring the Earl of *War-*
' *wick* into *England*, cry'd he. I wifh it with all
' my Heart, reply'd *Julia*, and you may promife
' your felf every thing from this tender Heart;
.' but act fo, as not to leave the leaft Scruple or
' Nicety to my Vertue, to my Honour, to the
' World, all thefe muft be fully fatisfy'd. She
left him immediately, and taking leave of my
Lady *Nevil*, recommended in very preffing terms
her Brother to her care, and then embracing *Lu-*
cilia feveral times, they parted, with fuch evident marks of trouble in their Countenances, as if
they had had fome forefight of the Misfortunes.
that were likely to befal them.

Julia was no fooner arrived at her own Seat in
Barkfhire, but her Husband privately made all
the neceffary Preparations for the putting in execution his Project of carrying her into *France*.
Three days were fpent before every thing could
be got ready, notwithftanding which, he carry'd
Matters fo clofely, that fhe knew nothing of her
intended Departure, till he ordered her to go into
the Coach; and fhe had enough to do, to get fo
much time as to carry her Jewels along with her.
Is it poffible to exprefs the Anxiety of this Fair
Lady? For being a Perfon of a quick Penetration,
fhe perceived at that very moment, what fhe muft
expect from her Husband; fhe would willingly
have writ to *Hypolitus* and to *Lucilia*, to give them
notice of her Difgrace, to defire their Affiftance,
and even to afford them fome Comfort under that
Affliction fhe forefaw they would lie under; but
was too narrowly watch'd by the Earl of *Bedford*,
to be in a condition to attempt any fuch thing.
Ifabella her Woman was the firft who told her what
fhe had underftood concerning the Refolution her
Husband had taken of carrying her into *France*;
and in fpite of all her Tears and Entreaties, he
L   made

made her go along with him, without any further delay. ' In what is it I have displeased you; *said she,* with an Air so full of Goodness and Sweetness as would have moved a Heart of Stone; ' Ought not you, Sir, to be better satisfy'd
' before you condemn me? 'Twill be always in
' your Power to Punish me; but after you have
' punish'd me, it may be too late to repair the
' wrong you have done me, both in respect to
' the World, and to your self. Enter into your
' own Heart, Madam, *said he in an angry Tone,*
' 'tis that which will justify my Proceeding; and
' if I don't enter with you into a long Debate, 'tis
' not, that I act upon my own Head, or that I am
' not sensible upon what foundation I act, but be-
' cause at this instant it is not a proper time to
' spend our time in trifling Arguments. So he remain'd Deaf to all her Complaints, and all her Tears and Lamentations did not produce the least effect upon him; and without having the least opportunity of advertising *Hypolitus* and *Lucilia* of her Misfortune, she was forced to see her self carry'd to *Dover* by her Jealous Husband, attended only by *Isabella* her Woman. She spoke not one word to him all the while they were upon the Road, but sighed without intermission. They embark'd at *Dover* for *Calais,* whilst *Julia* sent forth her Prayers to Heaven to favour them with a Storm that might force them back into *England,* and that with much more ardour than she would at another time have pray'd for a favourable Wind and Weather. She lay above Deck, her Head resting upon her Hand, her Face covered with a Veil, and her Eyes turn'd toward the *English* Coast, which she left behind with the greatest Anxiety of Mind. ' I am carry'd away by force,
' my dear *Hypolitus,* said she, whilst thou flatter-
' est

' eſt thy ſelf with our good Fortune. See how
' all our hopes are vaniſh'd, all our Projeᵗts over-
' turn'd at one Stroak ! Perhaps we ſhall never ſee
' one another any more: Perhaps I ſhall be ſo
' Unfortunate as to prove the Cauſe of your
' Death, for I am afraid you will not be able to
' ſupport your ſelf againſt ſo fatal a Stroak, as
' that of my Abſence will prove to you. Thus
ſhe paſs'd away her time in anxious Reflecᵗions,
when the Earl of *Bedford* told her, ſhe muſt go
into the Boat, in order to be carried a Shoar. It
being very late before they arrived at *Calais*, they
ſtaid that Night there, and finding her ſelf in her
Chamber with *Iſabella* only, whom ſhe knew ſhe
might confide in, ſhe writ with a Diamond theſe
following Words, in one of the Glaſs Windows.

If Chance ſhould bring you to this place, dear
H——— and your Heart diſcovers to your Eyes
the Charaᵗter and Hand of the Unfortunate J———
let this be an unfeigned Teſtimony of her ever-
laſting Conſtancy to you : Remain Faithful, and do
not Afflicᵗ your ſelf, if you will give me real
Proofs of your Paſſion for me.

Day no ſooner appear'd, but her Husband carry'd her forward to *Paris*, but without affording
her ſo much leiſure as to reſt a few Hours in that
great and fine City, tho' ſhe ſtood much in need
of it, being much tired with her Afflicᵗion, and
the Fatigues of ſo long a Journey. He went
thence towards *Bourbon*, where ſome Years before he had made uſe of the Waters, which are
much in requeſt among the *Engliſh* againſt the
Conſumption, but they muſt be taken upon the
Spot. Before he reach'd *Burbon*, he ſtop'd at a

very

very ancient Abbey of young Ladies, named St. *Menvick*, fituated betwixt *Moulins* and *Bourbon* at a fmall diftance only from the laft of thefe two Towns. Its fituation is fufficiently pleafant, but in a very folitary Ground ; fo that were it not for the Company that reforts thither, at two different Seafons to drink the Waters, it might be ftiled a Defart. The Earl of *Bedford* had formerly contracted an Acquaintance with the Abbefs, being as yet very young and defcended of the noble Family of *Amboife*, one who had a great Value for her felf, and not a very great fhare of Senfe ; fo he doubted not but to prevail with her to take *Julia* into her Cuftody. He thought it no great difficulty to fucceed in his Intentions, for having promifed her a confiderable Yearly Allowance, fhe foon promifed him his Wife fhould be watch'd as narrowly as a Prifoner of State, nor fhould fhe fee or write to any Body, this being all the Earl defired of her : So he delivered up *Julia* to the Abbefs, as likewife her Woman that attended her, and at parting told her with a fcornful Smile ; ' I hope the Fair *Hypoli-*
' *tas* will fcarce venture himfelf fo far for your
' fake ; he will fcarce take fo much Pains again
' to difguife himfelf, in hopes of feeing you,
' and he will fcarce run the hazard of another Im-
' prifonment. She was pierced to the Soul at
thefe Scoffing Expreffions : ' Do not make thefe
' things a Pretence, wherewith to cover the un-
' worthy Treatment I am forced to take at your
' Hands : I had no hand in *Hypolitus*'s Difguife,
' and under this prefent Misfortune, the only
' Comfort I have is, that I have nothing where-
' with to reproach my felf. You treat me with
' the utmoft Injuftice ; but Time will juftify my
' Conduct. He return'd no Anfwer, but left her,
being

being very well fatisfy'd to have fettled this Matter according to his Defire.

Julia was treated not altogether with fo much feverity by the Abbefs, as fhe had promifed her Husband ; but none of all the Religious Ladies, except thofe who were fet to watch all her Motions, were fuffered to fpeak to her; *Ifabella* being the only Perfon in whom fhe could put fome Confidence. This was a young Woman, not unhandfome, very Prudent, and one who bore an extream Love to her Lady; and this made her fet all her Wits to work to find out means to afford her fome Confolation. ' You ought, Madam, ' *faid fhe*, to expect every thing from Time, and ' from *Hypolitus's* Love; your Husband may ' happen to die; my Lord *Warwick* may get your ' Marriage annull'd, as you hope he will, and e- ' ven the greateft Misfortunes have their certain ' Turns. The End of my Life, *faid* Julia *in a* ' *Languifhing Tone*, will be the Period of my Mi- ' feries. I am not fo much as permitted to fue ' for my Liberty; I have a hundred and fifty Jay- ' lors inftead of one, about me: Thus you fee ' me a Prifoner by my Husband's Capricious Tem- ' per; and as to what relates to the annulling of ' my Marriage, that is at too great a diftance to ' make any account upon it; and I don't know ' even whether I fhould be defirous of it, were it ' not that my Honour and Confcience are concern- ' ed in that matter. How am I fure but time may ' make *Hypolitus* alter his Sentiments for me; ' and fuppofing my felf to be at Liberty to leave ' the Earl of *Bedford*, and that *Hypolitus* fhould ' continue faithful, how do you think fhall I get ' out of this Place? No body knows of my be- ' ing here, and I have no opportunity of acquaint- ' ing any of my Friends with it, becaufe all my

'Letters I endeavoured to fend, have been inter-
'cepted; fo that hitherto I have reap'd no other
'benefit from all the endeavours I have made that
'way, but the Shame and Vexation of feeing them
'mifcarry. This was poor *Julia*'s daily Enter-
tianment, and the Nights fhe fpent in Sighs and
Tears; Sleep feldom robb'd her of any time, to
improve her Pain, which at laft prefs'd fo hard
upon her Spirits, that fhe was feized with a moft
violent Diftemper.

Whilft thefe things were tranfacting at St. *Me-
neaw*, let us fee what is become of the Amorous
Hypolitus, who was one of the laft that got intelligence of his beloved Miftreffe's Misfortune. *Lucilia* fent to her Houfe in *Barkfhire*, to know how
fhe did, but my Lord's Servants, according to their
Mafter's Orders, fent word that *Julia* was gone
along with him on a fudden to *London*, upon a
Bufinefs of Confequence. *Lucilia* was not a little
difturbed at fo hafty a Departure, whereof fhe
could not comprehend in the leaft the Caufe, e-
fpecially fince fhe had not given the leaft notice of
it to her; fo that not queftioning but that fome
Myftery of very ill Confequence lay concealed
under this unexpected Journey, to be fully fatisfy'd in the Point, fhe told her Brother, that *Julia*
had fent word fhe defired to fee her; that fhe
would go accordingly, and return in a little time.
This Paffionate Lover conjured her to tell her e-
very thing that could be thought moft tender and
engaging; and that he was ready to die with impatience to fee her again. His and *Leander*'s
Wounds began to have a promifing Afpect, and
neither of them being very dangerous, they hoped for a fpeedy Cure.

Hypolitus

Hypolitus living now in certain hopes of hearing from *Julia*, by his Sister, he appear'd much more satisfy'd than he used to be, and 'twas that that engaged him to say to *Leander*; 'Come, 'dear Friend, *said he*, give me a faithful account 'of the present state of your Heart : What Pro- 'gress have you made with *Lucilia?* I can pro- 'test to you, that to give you the more Leisure 'to entertain her, I often deprive my self of the 'Satisfaction of talking to her about *Julia.* O! 'my dear *Hypolitus*, cry'd he, *Lucilia* acts with 'a great deal of Circumspection : hitherto I have 'not been able to dive into her Sentiments, or 'whether her Heart is capable of Tenderness, or 'not : I have discovered to her my Passion, with that 'Fear which is the constant Attendant of a truly 'Passionate Lover ; she always turn'd it into Jest, 'and whatever I could tell her, it has been im- 'possible for me to engage her into any Serious 'Conversation upon that Point. The first time I 'saw her, I was extreamly delighted with her 'pleasing and diverting Air, but at present it does 'not at all agree with me, and I am under most 'dreadful Apprehensions, least she has no more 'than a general Esteem for me. I have better 'skill in Physiognomy than you, *answered Hy-* 'polirus; besides this, I look upon this Affair 'with somewhat more of cool Blood than you do ; 'and if you will take my word for it, you are not 'indifferent to her. She has spoken to me, con- 'cerning you, with a more than ordinary esteem, 'and in such Terms, as need not the Interpreta- 'tion of a Conjurer to explain them. She ask'd 'me positively, whether I was sure you had lo- 'ved no Lady in *Italy?* And when I told her, you 'did not ; Is it possible, Brother, *added she*, that 'a Person of such extraordinary Deserts should be

'without

' without an Amorous Engagement? For, if one
' may judge by his Looks, he has a Tender Heart.
' 'Tis poffible, *faid I fmiling,* Sifter, that fince he
' has feen you, his Heart may be full of Tender-
' nefs ; and if it fhould be you that has infpired
' thefe Sentiments into him, would you not lend
' me a helping Hand to difcharge the Obligations
' I owe him? Pray, Brother, *faid fhe,* don't en-
' gage me to pay your Debts, your Gratitude will
' be more acceptable than mine, and your Friend,
' I fuppofe, has too nice a Palate to wifh for
' this Exchange. And, dear *Hypolitus,* faid *Le-*
' *ander,* did you difcourfe with her in fuch a
' manner as this? I actually did, *faid he,* as I tell
' you ; and I can affure you, fhe is very well
' pleafed, when we talk concerning you.

Lucilia being by this time got to *Julia's* Houfe,
in *Berkfhire,* had much ado to difcover the real
Truth of what fhe defired to know ; moft of her
Servants were ignorant in the thing, and thofe
few that knew it, durft not tell it ; till at laft fhe
made her application to the Steward: This Man
being much obliged to her, becaufe fhe had, by
her interceffion, procured him this Place in my
Lord's Family, could not forbear to give her an
Account of *Julia's* Journey.

This fad News put her under no fmall Trouble ; her Lamentations and her Tears, were undeniable Proofs of the Tendernefs and Affection
fhe bore to her Sifter. She threw her felf upon
the Bed, and continued there diftracted with
Thoughts, to the higheft degree, for a confiderable time ; and that which proved no fmall addition to her Fear, was, that fhe knew not how to
acquaint her Brother with this Misfortune : She
was afraid leaft his Wounds might grow worfe,
at the recital of fo unexpected an Accident ; and

on the other Hand, lay under as great Apprehenᐧ
fion, that if fhe fhould keep it conceal'd from him,
it might prove prejudicial to her dear *Julia*'s Affairs. Whilſt fhe was under this uncertainty, it
came into her Head, that fhe would confult with
Leander, what courfe fhe had beſt to take in this
Critical Point.

Hypolitus was expecting her return with the utmoſt Impatience; and he was no fooner told fhe
was come, but he fent to defire her to come into
his Chamber : She did all fhe could to difguife
her Grief, notwithſtanding which, he difcovered
fufficiently the Marks thereof in her Eyes and
whole Countenance. ' Don't flatter me, dear Si-
' fter, *faid he*, with a great deal of Confufion and
' Difturbance of Mind, ' fome Accident or other is
' befal'n *Julia*, I find you are inclined to conceal
' it from me ; but this will caufe me at leaſt as
' much pain, as if you difclofed the whole Secret
' to me. 'Tis not my intention, *faid fhe*, to con-
' ceal any thing frﻛm you, *Julia* is fal'n Sick ;
' her Weaknefs fince her laſt Diftemper joyn'd to
' what has happened here, has thrown her into a
' violent Fever. At thefe Words the Tears arofe
in her Eyes, in fpite of all fhe could do to keep
them back. ' O! *Lucilia*, cry'd *Hypolitus*, my Mis-
' fortune is greater than what you tell me of ; 1
' am fure fome very finiſter Accident is happen'd
' to *Julia*, your Tears will fcarce let you fpeak :
' Sifter, *continued he feeing fhe gave him no An-*
' *fwer*, will you fee me expire before your Eyes ?
' I am under fuch an Anguifh of Mind, as is paſt
' all apprehenfion ; tell me what Misfortune has
' befal'n us? For it is certain, that her and my
' Intereſt are infeparable, and that I forebode fuch
' cruel things, that 'tis impoffible for me to aug-
' ment my Pain. *Lucilia* perfiſting in what fhe
had

had told him before; 'You know, *added she,*
' what Tenderneſs I have for *Julia,* and yet you
' are ſurprized to ſee me concern'd at her being
' Ill. You might with much more reaſon won-
' der, if you ſhould ſee me to be otherwiſe. My
' Heart has too quick a foreſight, *reply'd* Hypo-
' litus *fetching a deep Sigh,* Siſter, 'tis not an ea-
' ſie matter to deceive a true Lover : I am reſolved
' to riſe immediately out of Bed, and to go into
' *Barkſhire* ; I will be ſatisfy'd in every thing ;
' I will hazard all, and dive into your Secrets at
' the Expence of my Life, if it muſt be ſo. He
had ſcarce ſpoken theſe Words, but he call'd for
his Gentleman to help him to get out of Bed : he
was but juſt come back from *London,* whither he
had been ſent by *Hypolitus* to the Earl of *Suſſex,*
to acquaint him with every thing that had happened at my Lord *Nevil's* Houſe ; and at the ſame
time, deſired him in his Letter, to inquire whether my Lord *Douglas* had heard any thing of this
Adventure ; and to let him know immediately how
Matters ſtood there, that he might take his Mea-
ſures accordingly.

Lucilia perceiving her Brother reſolved to riſe
out of Bed, in ſpite of his Wounds, ſhe drew as
near as ſhe could to *Leander:* ' Good God, Sir,
' what muſt we do ? *ſaid ſhe to him very ſoftly* ;
' the Unfortunate *Jula* is no more in *Barkſhire,*
' her Husband has carry'd her away into *France* ;
' How ſhall I do to acquaint my Brother with
' this ſad News ? And without it you ſee he will
' certainly go to look after her. *Leander* remain'd
for ſome time under ſuch a Conſternation, that it
could not poſſibly be greater, had this Misfortune
happened to *Lucilia* her ſelf; however recovering
himſelf as ſoon as he could, becauſe he ſaw ſhe
expected his immedia e Anſwer. ' Alas! Madam,
                                 ſaid

' *said he to her*, I don't see how we shall be able
' to conceal it from *Hypolitus* ; h's Distraction is
' such, that it would be a piece of Cruelty to
' leave him longer under such an Uncertainty.

Hypolitus perceiving them to talk softly, drew
nearer to them, being supported by his Gentleman, and then seating himself in an Elbow Chair,
near *Leander's* Bed-fide, with a Countenance, in
which appeared all the Marks of Despair, .' *Lu-*
' *cilia*, *said he*, tells you what has happened, and
' I, who am the only Person concern'd in it, must
' be the only Man from whom she thinks fit to
' conceal it. Brother, *said she*, since you have
' discover'd in my Eyes, that Affliction which
' oppresses my Spirits, I am willing to tell you
' the true cause of it. The Earl of *Bedford* be-
' came jealous and enraged at what happened in
' your Disguise, and has carry'd away *Julia* into
' *France* some days ago ; but we know not where
' or how he intends to dispose of her : he had ta-
' ken care to charge such of his Servants as knew
' of it, to keep the Secret, but the Steward dif-
' closed it to me. This it is that afflicts me, and
' 'tis this I was willing to keep conceal'd from
' you, at least for some days. *Hypolitus* laying
his Arms across, with his Head hanging down upon his Breast, stood like a Statue without saying
one word. ' My dear Friend, *said* Leander, this
' mishap is not past Reprieve, we shall hear where
' this Treacherous Man has carry'd her, we will
' fetch her thence; you will have the Satisfaction
' of being her Deliverer ; and you will see your
' self seconded by the Earl of *Warwick :* You
' know 'tis not justifiable for a Man who takes a
' Chimera into his Head, to treat a Lady of Qua-
' lity at that rate. O ! why will you flatter me
' thus, *cry'd the Disconsolate* Hypolitus, my
' Thoughts

' Thoughts are far different from what you can
' tell me upon this Head ; 'tis I that am the occa-
' sion of *Julia's* Misfortune ; 'tis I, and my impa-
' tient Desires, that have plunged her into this A-
' byss of Troubles ; you have recourse to time to
' allay both our Misfortunes ; But what a slender
' Comfort is this? What is likely to become of
' me, Great God ! What is likely to become of
' me ? Whilst he was thus giving way to his
Affliction, and rendered *Lucilia* and *Leander* almost as inconsolable as himself, word was brought
them, that the Earl of *Suffex* was come, whereat
they were not a little surprized. He came immediately after into the Chamber, and stood almost
amazed to read in all their Faces such lively marks
of Grief. *Hypolitus* embracing him, without being able to arise from his Seat, desired him to sit
down by him ; ' Are you come, dear Friend, *said*
' *he to him*, to bear your share in my Affliction ?
' 'Tis impossible you can imagine any thing that
' could more nearly concern me. I did not know,
' *said he*, of any new cause of Dissatisfaction you
' had ; but I thought I ought not to forget to come
' to give you notice my self, that my Lord *Dou-*
' *glas* having got intelligence of your being here,
' intends to come to Morrow to fetch you from
' hence ; he is most furiously angry with you ;
' so you had best to consider what is to be done
' upon this Occasion : My Advice is, you should
' without losing a Moment's time, tell my Lord
' *Nevil*, that I am sent by him, on purpose to
' fetch you away, and I will take care to conduct
' you to some House in the Country, where we
' may be at leisure to reflect further upon what is
' best to be done according to your own Inclina-
' tions.

Hypolitus,

Hypolitus, inftead of returning an Anfwer to his Friend, cry'd out like a diftracted Man, 'And 'muſt I ſee her no more! That Tyrant has 'ſnatch'd her away from me! I muſt fall under 'this fatal ſtroak! The Earl of *Suſſex*, ſurprized at theſe Words, look'd ſtedfaſt upon *Lucilia*, to make her ſenſible of his Curioſity to know the meaning thereof; ſhe had no ſooner given him an Account of *Julia*'s being carry'd into *France*, but embracing *Hypolitus*, 'This is a new matter of 'Trouble and Vexation, *ſaid he*, but your Cou-'rage muſt ſurmount all theſe Obſtacles, take my 'Word for it; Let us depart hence without de-'lay, it would not do well to meet my Lord *Dou-* '*glas* here; when we are at a greater diſtance and 'in a leſs ſuſpicious place than this is, we have 'nothing elſe to conſider of, but the Deliverance 'of *Julia.*

They were all of the ſame Opinion; 'I am go-'ing to part from you, Lovely *Lucilia*, *ſaid Sig-* '*nior* Leander, *with a low Voice, ſo as to be heard* '*by no Body but her ſelf*, Friendſhip, for once, 'has got the better of Love; but I hope you will 'be obliged to me for this Sacrifice I offer to 'him, it being made in behalf of a Brother 'who, as you have told me, is dearer to you than 'your own Life. I make his Fortune my own, I 'follow him wherever he goes, I leave you be-'hind me, and yet I Adore you. Pray give me 'to underſtand, that you are not inſenſible of 'thoſe Sentiments I have both for you and him; 'that will afford me the greateſt comfort I am ca-'pable of receiving at this Juncture. I ſtand in-'debted to you for every thing, *ſaid* Lucilia *bluſh-* '*ing*, and I am of too great a Soul and Temper, 'to look with indifferency upon that Friendſhip 'you ſhew to my Brother: after this don't urge
'me

‘ me to enlarge my self any farther upon my Sen-
‘ timents for you, but be fatisfy’d I fhall always
‘ do Juftice to your Merits, and that I can’t fee
‘ you leave us without Pain. The Amorous *Leander* feem’d to be overjoy’d to fee himfelf blefs’d
with fo engaging a Farewel.

His Wounds had no lefs impair’d his Strength,
than thofe of *Lypolitus* had done his; notwithftanding which, my Lord and my Lady could not
prevail upon them, with all their Intreaties, to
ftay a little longer, for they were not acquainted
with my Lord *Dougias*’s Intention of coming thither the next day, and how careful they were to
avoid the fight of him : *Hypolitus* and *Leander*
returned their moft hearty Thanks for all the Obligations they had received at their Hands: *Lucilia*
could not part from her Brother without Tears,
who promifed to let her hear from him; and *Leander* defired to give him leave to write to her
what Refolutions fhe fhould take; as fhe, on the
other hand, was very well pleafed to have a plau-
fible Pretence to grant him a Favour fhe was very
defirous to beftow upon him.

The Earl of *Suffex*, mounting on Horfeback,
left his Coach for the two wounded Lords to be
carry’d in, and being provided with a good Quilt,
they went on pretty commodioufly; but that *Hypolitus*, under his prefent Circumftances, took very little care of his Eafe or Health; and Signior
Leander was fo deeply in Love with *Lucilia*, that
her abfence caufed in him all that Pain which a
Lover is capable of feeling upon fuch like occafions. They talk’d very little, and what they faid
ended all in Lamentations.

The Earl of *Suffex* conducted them to a magnificent Seat, about 40 Miles diftant from my Lord
Nevil’s, it belonged to the young Dutchefs of

Northampton, a Lovely young Widow, but then under the severest Affliction, on account of her Husband, who was executed with the Duke of *Northumberland* and *John Dudley*, whom the King had made Earl of *Warwick*; she had chosen this Country Seat for her Retirement, in order to spend the best of her Days there in her doleful Reflections and Melancholy Thoughts. Queen *Mary* had not as yet thought fit to recal her to Court, tho' the Earl of *Suffex*, as well as many other great Lords, used all their Interest with the Queen for that purpose. To be short, the Earl, with all his Indifferency, had not been able to stand it out against the Charms of so Fair a Lady. He had paid her frequent Visits ever since the Misfortune of her Family. Her engaging Temper, her Vertue, her Generosity, all these great Qualifications had made so deep an Impression upon the Earl's Heart, that he soon found those Sentiments of Compassion, (as he thought they were) changed into the most tender Effects of Love.

She received *Hypolitus* and *Leander* with all possible Civility, being taught and disposed by her own Afflictions to compassionate and comfort the Afflicted, and this made her take share with a great deal of Goodness in *Hypolitus*'s Misfortune.

The Earl of *Suffex* knowing her to be a Lady of much Discretion, thought it fit to conceal from her Knowledge his Friend's Passion; and she desired him to assure him, in her behalf, that he might rest assured of her Services, and be welcome to her House as long as he pleased, and even command part of her Estate. Tho' *Hypolitus*, at that time, was scarce sensible of any thing, he could not but be touched with a most profound Sense of this Lady's Generosity; and notwithstanding all the Anxiety of his Mind and his Sadness, he re
turned

turn'd her his hearty Thanks with all imaginable Acknowledgment.

In the mean time my Lord *Douglas* coming to my Lord *Nevil's* House, and finding his Son gone, 'tis almoſt impoſſible to expreſs his Fury and Re-ſentment: He ſpared no pains to find out which way he had taken; but the Earl of *Suſſex* had provided againſt all this, by traveling all Night long, and that in By-Roads ; and no ſooner were they come to my Lady *Northampton's* Houſe, but he took all poſſible Precautions not to be diſcover-ed there. Poor *Lucilia* was forced to ſtand the Brunt alone, and feel the effects of her Father's Fury ; he loaded her with Reproaches, he told her ſhe had conſpired with *Hypolitus* to do every thing they thought would vex him ; and ſo he carry'd her to *London*, without ſhewing the leaſt Concern at the Misfortune of *Lucilia*; the Con-ſiderations of his private Intereſt having ſtifled in his Heart all thoſe Tender Sentiments he ought to have had for this Fair but Unfortunate Lady.

Hypolitus conſulting with his two Friends, they pitch d upon the only way they had left them un-der their preſent Circumſtances. They were all ſenſible that the Earl of *Bedford* having got the ſtart of them for ſeveral days paſt, it would be impoſſible to overtake him, and eſpecially ſince they knew not what way he had taken to go into *France*, it would be in vain to follow, or hope to meet with him before he came to his Journey's end ; ſo it was thought convenient they ſhould ſeparate, and to go to the three Sea Ports for *England* ; and not queſtioning but that they ſhould meet with him in one of thoſe Places upon his return thence, it was agreed betwixt them, that which of them ſhould find him out firſt, ſhould revenge *Julia's* Wrongs with his Sword.

So

So foon as *Hypolitus* and *Leander* found themfelves ftrong enough to travel, they writ to *Lucilia*, defiring my Lady *Northampton* to convey the
Letters to her Hands ; and then returning her all
imaginable Thanks for her Goodnefs, took a moft
tender farewel of one another. ' How much ftand
' I indebted to you, my dear Friends ? *faid* Hypo-
' litus *embracing them*, you efpoufe my Quarrel ;
' and inftead of oppofing your Intentions as I
' ought to do, I conjure you not to negleƈt any
' opportunity of finding out my Enemy. They
told him, he might rely upon them ; and that
they would convince him at the peril of their
Lives, that they loved him above all other things.
Laft of all they came to this farther Agreement ;
That after a Month's ftay in that place where
each of them defign'd for, they fhould return to
London; and meet at the E. of *Suffex's* Houfe, who
went to *Diep* ; *Hypolitus* took the way to *Calais*,
in the Company of his Friend *Leander*, as far as
Dover, where having feen him embark'd for *Calais*, he did the fame in another Ship bound for
the Ifles of *Guernfey* and *Jerfey*, becaufe fometimes Paffengers return that way out of *France*
into *England*.

They happily arrived at their feveral Ports, but
we leave the other two for this time, to follow
Hypolitus to *Calais*. He happening to lodge in
the fame Inn where *Julia* had lodg'd before, the
firft thing he ask'd after was, Whether they had
not feen fuch and fuch a Lady, defcribing to them
her Features and Shape, as well as poffibly he
could, as likewife her Husband. The Woman of
the Houfe told him, fhe had lain there one Night.
Then he ask'd her many more Queftions, fuch as
Lovers are apt to do ; Whether fhe feem'd to be
Melancholy ? Whether fhe Eat heartily ? What

M   fhe

she heard her say? And whatever elſe his Curioſity could prompt him to. At laſt he deſired he might have the ſame Chamber where ſhe had lodged, which he took poſſeſſion of with ſuch an agitation of Mind, as if ſhe had actually been there preſent: He was walking very faſt up and down the Room, ruminating with much Anxiety upon the oddneſs of *Julia's* Adventure, and at laſt caſt his Eyes upon the Glaſs-Window, on which *Julia* had written the beforementioned Words with a Diamond; Good God, how ſurprized was he at the ſight thereof! How he ſtood amazed! And what a Comfort did this prove to him under his preſent Circumſtances! He kiſs'd the Hand-writing, and took out that piece of Glaſs on which it was written, looking upon it as a more precious thing to him, than if it had been the fineſt Oriental Diamond in the World; and as this Demonſtration of his not being forgotten by his beloved Miſtreſs, much encreaſed his Paſſion and Acknowledgment; ſo he took all poſſible Precautions not to miſs the Earl of *Bedford* in his return for *England*, in caſe he ſhould take the way of *Calais*.

He had ſtaid three Weeks, expecting his coming with the utmoſt impatience and eager deſire of revenging *Julia's* Wrongs upon him, when one Night walking near the Sea-ſide, he ſaw him coming towards the Port, where a Boat lay ready to carry him on Board the Veſſel that was to Tranſport him into *England*. *Hypolitus* tranſported with Rage, pull'd him by the Arm; ' Before you ' go into *England*, *ſaid he fiercely to him*, I have ' ſomething to ſay to you. The Earl exaſperated at his haughty Carriage, and ſtill more upon divers other Accounts, followed him immediately: Neither of them ſpoke one Word, but caſt

moſt

moſt furious Looks at one another, their Eyes
ſparkling with Anger like Fire. No ſooner did
they ſee themſelves at a ſufficient diſtance from
the Town, but without any further delay they
drew their Swords, and the one being animated
by Love and Rage, the other by Jealouſie and a
deep Reſentment, they fought with ſo much De-
ſperation, that it was likely this Combat would
ſcarce end but with the loſs of One, if not both their
Lives. They fought with ſo much eagerneſs, that
both of them were ſoon wounded in diverſe places; till at laſt *Hypolitus* enraged to meet with
ſo much reſiſtance from a Man whom he mortally
hated, cloſed and threw him upon the Ground:
He ask'd for Quarter, which *Hypolitus* moſt ge-
neroully promiſed him, on Condition that he
ſhould ſet *Julia* at Liberty; when a Servant of
the Earl of *Bedford's*, who had follow'd his Maſter at a diſtance, and lay concealed behind an old
Boat upon the Sands, near the Sea-ſhoar, ſeeing
his Maſter reduced to this Extremity, came from
behind and ran his Sword into *Hypolitus's* Back,
ſo that he drop'd down for Dead; and the Fellow ſuppoſing no otherwiſe than that he had been
actually ſo, ran preſently to the aſſiſtance of his
Maſter, and ſupporting him with his Arms, carry'd him to a Fiſher's Hutt hard by, where he lay
down upon an old Quilt, till they could get Surgeons to ſearch and dreſs his Wounds. They having no farther Buſineſs at *Calais*, reſolved to get
on Board the Ship that was to carry them into
England, as faſt as they could, which they
did accordingly; and engaged the Surgeon to
go along with them, for fear his Wounds
ſhould open afreſh, by the violent agitation of
the Sea.

In the mean while the too unfortunate *Hypolitus* left deftitute of all help, was wallowing in his own Blood, and that at fo confiderable a diftance from the Town, and pretty late at Night, that theie was but little hopes of his meeting with any feafonable Affiftance in that place. But his Gentleman, who loved him entirely, fearing fome finifter Accident fhould befal him, and not feeing him return by that time it was dark, he took fome along with him with a Flambeaux, who difperfing into feveral parts, enquiied after *Hypolitus*. He having been already three Weeks at *Calais*, began to be pretty well known there, fo they were directed into the Road, which fome Country People had feen him take, in Company of another Perfon. They firft of all efpy'd the Fifher's Hutt, and approaching near it, found fome Blood upon the Ground, (which iffued from the Earl's Wounds as he was carrying thither) and following the Tract, came at laft to the place where *Hypolitus* lay extended upon the Ground, without the leaft fenfe or motion. They cut fome Branches and Twigs of Trees, which they twifted and joyn'd together, and fo carry'd him to his Inn. *Hypolitus*'s Wounds proved fo dangerous, that his Gentleman thought fit to give Advice thereof to my Lord *Douglas*. He was infinitely concerned at this difmal News ; he was his only Son, and a Son of fuch extraordinary Qualifications, as made him beloved even by Strangers ; judge then how much his Family muft be afflicted at this Accident,

My Lord *Douglas*'s Lady and *Lucilia*, went immediately for *Calais*, where they found him almoft at the laft Extremity. Now it was that his Father and Mother, mortally afflicted at this Cafualty, began to repent, but too late, of all the

Seve-

Severities they had laid upon him, to fupprefs a Paffion fo juft and fo innocent as that of *Hypolitus*, who, notwithftanding all the Hardfhips he had endured upon their account, was fo far affect-ed with their Grief, that he conjured them to moderate it, unlefs they intended to encreafe his Misfortune. The Earl of *Suffex* and *Leander*, returning to *London* much about the fame time, heard the News of their Friend's Quarrel and its fatal Confequences, and refolved to go thither immediately to fee him.

Hypolitus at the fight of them, felt within himfelf all that Excefs of Satisfaction, a Man under his Circumftances can be capable of; as they on the contrary, could not but be feized with the utmoft Grief, to fee him fo near his End. Notwithftanding the utmoft Extremity he ftruggled under, he neglected not to prefent *Leander* to my Lord *Douglas*, and to my Lady his Mother; conjuring them to look upon him no otherwife than their own Son ; and praying them, that in cafe it pleafed God to call him out of this World, they fhould adopt him in his ftead : He fpoke thefe words with fo engaging an Air, that they drew Tears from all that heard them. However, at the End of two Months, his Life was judged to be out of danger.

In the mean while Signior *Leander*, who was infinitely in Love with *Lucilia*, had prevail'd upon the Earl of *Suffex*, to fpeak to my Lord *Douglas* in his behalf, and to ask his Confent for a Marriage with his Daughter, that accordingly he might, without lofs of time write to his Father the Senator *Alberti*. The intimate Friendfhip which had been cultivated betwixt my Lord and the Senator *Alberti*, and the Perfonal Merits of *Leander*, fupported by a confiderable Eftate, proved fuch

pow-

powerful Temptations with my Lord *Douglas*, that, confidering he could not eafily beftow his Daughter better than fo, he very favourably received the Propofitions made to him upon that account.

Leander tranfported with Joy, writ to his Father about it, and at the fame time engaged one of his beft Friends to intercede in his behalf with him. Firft of all he beg'd his Pardon for having undertaken fo long a Voyage, under pretence of going only to *Rome*; then told him all the Reafons he thought moft expedient to plead his Excufe; and at laft extoll'd the great Qualifications of *Lucilia* to the Sky, and what Advantages he might expect from my Lord *Douglas*, in cafe he Marry'd her, defiring him to give his Confent to the only thing he moft of all defired in the World, and which would prove the Happinefs of his Life.

The Senator *Alberti* was not a little furprized to underftand his Son was gone to *England*, inftead of going to *Rome* (for hitherto he had managed Matters with fo much dexterity, that his Father actually believed him to be at *Rome*) but confidering that his Son's Welfare depended on this Propofition, he would not fuffer his Anger to get fo far the Afcendant over his Paternal Love, as to obftruct this Match. He knew the Family of the *Douglas*'s, and my Lord Perfonally. He had feen *Hypolitus* and loved him, and gueffing at the Sifter by the Brother, he could not but fuppofe her to be an accomplifh'd young Lady. To be fhort, he readily gave his Confent, and ordered whatever was requifite to make *Leander* appear upon this occafion according to his Quality and Eftate.

Hypolitus

Hypolitus was pretty well recovered when this News was brought to his Friend and Sister ; he was no less sensible of their satisfaction, than if it had been his own, and this contributed not a little towards the advancement of his Cure ; but he was advised by his Physicians and Surgeons to accomplish it by drinking the Waters of *Bourbon:* He was absolutely against it, all his Thoughts being now bent upon Revenge; he could scarcely stand upright when he was contriving already to get into *England*, to find out the Earl of *Bedford*, and either to perish under his Hands, or make him fall by his. But my Lady *Douglas*'s Tears, his Father's Entreaties and Commands, and *Lucila*'s Prayers, at last so far prevailed upon him, that he could not refuse any longer to comply with their Desires. ' Alas ! *said he, when he found himself alone with* ' *them*, what would you have me do for you'? ' You would have me look for proper Remedies, ' and at the same time little consider that I have ' within my Heart a languishing Poison, which ' will never let them take effect, but will soon ' bring me to the Grave : Is it not much better, ' I should bestow that small remainder of Life to ' punish him who thus tyrannizes over *Julia*? But these Arguments were of little weight with his Friends, they opposed others of much more force against them, and so soon as he found himself in a condition to leave his Bed, the Marriage of *Lucilia* with *Leander* was consummated to the mutual Satisfaction of both the young Lovers.

Four Months were now already past since the Earl of *Bedford* and *Hypolitus* fought upon *Calais* Sands, and his Wounds being now compleatly healed up, so as to be able to ride in a Coach, and *Lucilia*'s Equipage got ready, my Lady *Douglas*,

her Mother, refolved to conduct her to *Florence*
My Lord *Douglas* and the Earl of *Suffex* were
for going back to *London* ; and at parting, gave
their Friend all the real Demonſtrations of a tender Friendſhip ; and the Earl, on his part, faithfully promiſed *Hypolitus* to write to him to *Bourbon*, and to give him an account of every thing
that might concern him. ' Let me hear, *ſaid he*,
' how the fair Counteſs of *Northampton* does your
' Sentiments for that Lovely Perſon, and the Ob-
' ligations I owe her in particular, will not per-
' mit me to be indifferent in relation to any thing
' that concerns her ; and if any thing in this World
' was able to allay the Anguiſh of my Heart, and
' make this Life tolerable to me, it would be to
' ſee you both happy together. Signior *Leander*
having alſo contracted a very intimate Friendſhip
with the Earl of *Suffex*, he told him at parting,
in a moſt obliging manner ; ' You take from us,
' that which we look'd upon as moſt amiable a-
' mong us ; but how can a Friend grudge you that
' Happineſs Fortune has put into your Hands ?
' You are ſo worthy of it, that no Body can envy,
' without Injuſtice, your Felicity. *Leander* anſwered him in the moſt obliging Terms in the
World, and ſo they parted.

Hypolitus had by this time got his Equipage in
readineſs to go along with *Leander* and *Lucilia* as
far as *Moulins*, from whence they continued their
Journey to *Lyons*, and ſo to *Florence* ; but he ſtaid
behind at *Moulins*, which is no more than four
Leagues from *Bourbon*.

During their Journey, all the Satisfaction *Hypolitus* obſerved in this new Marry'd Couple, was
not able to make him ſenſible of any ; he continued in the ſame melancholy Humour as before ;
they would ſometimes blame him for it, but he
told

told them with a sad Countenance ; ' Be satisfy'd
' to see me be an Eye-witness of your Happiness,
' without being disturbed at it ; believe me, this
' is the most real proof I can give you of a sin-
' cere Friendship. Alas! can you imagine, but
' that that Felicity you enjoy does recal into my
' Mind the Misfortunes I suffer ? You have not
' met with the least Obstacles in your Passion,
' and *Hymen* has crown'd your Love ; you have
' had no time to fear, to hope, to be jealous, to
' dread your Rivals ; no pain, no sinister Acci-
' dents : But poor I, what have I not been forced
' to undergo ? And how slender a Prospect have I
' at this very time, to see an end of my Suffer-
' ings ? These Reflections cast him sometimes
into such Agonies, as is scarce to be expressed.
They all arrived happily at *Moulins*, which being the place where they were to part Companies,
this Separation proved one of the most tender and
most painful they had seen in a great while before ; for *Lucilia* could not so much as flatter her
self, that she should see her dear Brother again,
unless it were after a great while ; and as for *Leander*, *Lucilia* was the only Person in the World
he loved beyond *Hypolitus*. This Unfortunate Lover had the deepest Sense that could be of the many Obligations he ow'd them ; his Love for *Julia*
proved no diminution to his natural Inclinations,
and his Acknowledgment. He begg'd of them,
not to omit any thing to learn some News of the
Earl of *Warwick*, and to acquaint him with what
they could learn, he having received no News
from him since he left *Marseilles* ; he most earnestly enjoy'd them to send him a Letter to *Venice*,
and make him acquainted with his Daughter's
Misfortune ; he had sometime before got *Leander* to write one to him whilst they were at *Calais*,

and he was much troubled to have received n^o Anfwer to it.

Hypolitus went to *Burbon*, a place but of an indifferent Afpeƈt, the Buildings are very mean, the boyling Water Springs are the only things that makes this Place noted among thofe, who twice in a Year drink them for their Health, and at thofe Seafons you fee a great Concourfe of good Company there; but this was of no ufe to him, he being moſt at eafe, or at leaſt lefs uneafie when he was alone, becaufe he was then at full liberty to give way to his Affliƈtions, a thing he could not do fo conveniently in the Company of others, whofe Prefence put a check upon his Inclinations.

Thus he pafs'd away his time at *Burbon*, without feeking for the leaſt Acquaintance, but fpent his time for the moſt part in Walking, and that in fuch places, as he thought were fartheſt from Company; and if he happened to meet with any in his Walks, there appeared fuch vifible marks of Grief in his whole Countenance, that, tho' according to the Cuſtom of this Place, even Strangers take the freedom to accoſt one another when they meet abroad; and that every Body makes it his Bufinefs to divert themfelves with the variety of Company, yet no Body thought fit to interrupt a Man, whom they faw overwhelm'd in his Melancholy Thoughts.

One Day walking abroad early in the Morning, and taking the firſt Path, he found it was not fo much beaten as the reſt, this brought him infenfibly to a Wildernefs which might be faid to contain all the Beauties of a pleafant Countrey. He ſtop'd on the defcent of a Hill covered by the Branches of fine Trees which afforded a moſt agreeable Shade; he remain'd very penfive for fome
time

time In his Solitude, till at laſt he ingraved, with
a Pen of Steel he had about him, divers Lines on
the Bark of a Tree, under which he had ſeated
himſelf ; they contained in ſubſtance,

That *neither the Meadows, nor Rivulets, nor*
Woods; nor Plains, nor Vales, were able to afford
him the leaſt Delight, unleſs he could ſee them
without thinking on Climene; *whereas ſhe being*
abſent, they ſerved only to augment his Pain.

His whole Mind being taken up with theſe
Thoughts, it was a conſiderable time before he
caſt his Eyes upon a piece of Paper that lay on
the Ground not far from him, and when he ſaw
it, he thought it not worth his while to take it
up, believing it to be a Letter ; and having not
the leaſt Curioſity to be acquainted with its Con-
tents : But it being a pretty windy Day, and ſeeing the Paper often moved by the Wind, a certain
Sentiment of Goodneſs which was natural to him,
for the Perſon unto whom the Letter might belong,
at laſt prevailed with him to take it up, leaſt it
ſhould fall into the Hands of Strangers. He ſoon
perceived there was ſomething wrap'd up in it, and
found it to be a Caſe of Chagreen. He opened it,
but Good God, gueſs at his Surprize, gueſs at his
Joy, when he ſaw it to be the Pourtraiture of *Julia!*
of his dear *Julia*; for at firſt ſight, he thought no
otherwiſe, than that it had been hers; but viewing
it more attentively, found it to be the Counteſs
of *Warwick's* Picture, which he had ſeen frequently in his beloved Miſtreſs's Room: His Eyes were
fix'd with the utmoſt attention on this Piece, which
recalling to his Mind many ſad and ſo many
tender Paſſages, he could not imagine what hazard had put it into his Hands.   It belongs to
          ' *Julia*,

‘ *Julia*, *said he*, ’tis not likely fhe fhould have
‘ parted with it to any Body, perhaps it is ftol’n
‘ from her : I ufed to fee it in a Cafe fet with
‘ Diamonds, and now it is in a Chagreen Cafe ;
‘ but if it be ftol’n, was it ftol’n in *England* or
‘ *France?* However, *said he*, ’tis probable the
‘ Thief is fomewhere in this part of the Country.
Whilft he was ruminating upon the matter, he fees
a Man of an indifferent good Appearance coming
that way, who feeing him hold the Picture in his
Hand, fetch’d a great Cry for Joy ; ‘ I will freely
‘ own to you, Sir, *said he*, *accofting him with Re-*
‘ *fpect*, I was almoft Mad, becaufe I knew not
‘ what I had done with the Picture you have found,
‘ I beg of you, reftore it to me. Pray then do
‘ me firft the Favour, *said* Hypolitus *to him*, to
‘ let me know where you had it. Sir, *said he*, I
‘ am a Picture-drawer ; I come every Year to
‘ *Burbon*, to fell Pictures, becaufe there being a
‘ great Concourfe of People here, I can fell them
‘ eafier and dearer than in any other Place. I of-
‘ ten go to an Abby not above 2 Leagues from
‘ hence, it is called St. *Menoux* ; the Lady Ab-
‘ befs has a very fine Clofet, which fhe intends
‘ to adorn with all manner of Pictures, fhe fhew’d
‘ it me the other day, and ask’d me, whether I
‘ would ftay and work there for fome time?
‘ Whilft I was with her, I faw a certain Lady
‘ come into her Clofet, who by her Accent feem’d
‘ to be a Foreigner ; fhe was handfome to Admi-
‘ ration, notwithftanding fhe look’d fo pale, that
‘ I could guefs no otherwife, but that fhe had been
‘ very ill lately. She ask’d me, whether I could
‘ mend the Drapery of a certain fmall Picture,
‘ upon which, by mifchance, fome Water had
‘ been caft ; fhe call’d for it immediately, and ta-
‘ king it out of a Cafe fet with Diamonds, gave
                                                    it

‘ it into my Hands, and I put it into this Cha-
‘ green Cafe, which I happened to have about
‘ me, and promifed her to go to work upon it
‘ immediately. I did fo accordingly, and was to
‘ carry it to her this very day ; but happening to
‘ fell fome Pictures to a Perfon of Quality, whom
‘ I expected to meet hereabouts. I have, doubtlefs,
‘ pull’d it out of my Pocket, with fome other
‘ things, and fo dropt it.

Hypolitus was fo furpriz’d and overjoy’d at what
he heard the Picture-drawer tell him, that he was
not able to give him the leaft interruption, looking upon it at firft rather like a Dream than a real
Truth. At laft fetching a very deep figh, ‘ If
‘ you would be faithful to me, *faid he to him,*
‘ I will take care you fhall be very well paid for
‘ your Journey. I am a Grateful Man, and have
‘ wherewithal to reward your Fidelity ; but I
‘ muft tell you, I expect you fhould inviolably
‘ keep my Secret. The Picture-drawer imagining
no otherwife, than that he was to draw the Picture
of fome Lady, with whom he was fal’n in Love at
Burbon, told him, That his Fidelity was put to
the Tryal almoft every day, and that hitherto no
Body in the World could fay he had been the
worfe for confiding in him ; that he had fo ftrong
an Idea, that provided he could fee a Perfon but
once, he could draw the Features exactly ; and
that in cafe it was impoffible to come to the fight
of her, he need only defcribe her Features to him,
and that by the ftrength of his own Imagination
he would draw the Picture like her. *Hypolitus*
could not forbear fmiling at the Picture-drawer's
good Opinion of his own Capacity ; ‘ The Point
‘ in queftion, *faid he to him,* is not concerning the
‘ Drawing of a Picture ; but whether you can
‘ contrive a way to introduce me into the Abby
‘ of

‘ of St. *Menoux*, when you go thither? I think
‘ it will not prove very difficult for you fo to do;
‘ I am known by no Body living here; I may ve-
‘ ry well pafs for one of your young Scholars;
‘ and I have learned to defign and make a Draught
‘ of a piece, enough to make me act that part
‘ pretty well. You may fay I am an *Italian*, be-
‘ caufe my Accent is foreign, and undertake the
‘ Work the Abbefs offers to you, at her own
‘ Price, and don’t trouble your felf any further, I
‘ will take care of all the reft. The Picture-
drawer thought he had no reafon to refufe fo advantageous an offer, which would be fo gainful to
him, without running any hazard.

It being refolved to put this Project in Execution the fame Afternoon, *Hypolitus* left all his Servants at *Burbon*, he told the Picture-drawer, his
Name fhould be *Hyacinth*, as long as they ftaid
at St. *Menoux*, and having changed his Cloaths,
they took Coach, (becaufe *Hypolitus* durft not as
yet venture to go on Horfeback) and drove as
hard as they could to St. *Menoux*, for Love is a
fwift Guide, and drives on apace.

When he entred the Abby Gate, he was feized
with fuch a Trembling, as fcarce to be able to
keep himfelf upright, or to walk into the Par-
lour where the Abbefs expected the Picture-
drawer’s coming. She ask’d him immediately,
who he was he had brought along with him? And
that not without much reafon; for tho’ he affected
a more than ordinary Plainnefs both in his Cloaths
and Deportment, yet his Graceful Mien, his Noble Air, his Regular Features; and in fhort, his
whole Perfon had fomething in it fo extraoadina-
ry, that he ftruck with Admiration, all thofe
that faw him. The Picture-drawer told her, he
was an *Italian*, who having an Inclination for
Painting,

Painting, had been his Scholar for fome time:
The Abbefs anfwered, fhe had a mind to have
her Picture drawn, that they fhould begin to morrow, and that fhe had Work enough to employ
them a whole Year.

This was very welcome News to *Hypolitus*, he
got out of Bed before Day-light, and made the
Picture-drawer rife likewife, who was not in the
leaft furprized thereat, being fenfible it was for
weighty Reafons he was fo eager to come to
St.*Menoux* ; and no fooner was the Abbefs awake,
but fhe fent for them to the Abby. *Hypolitus* look'd
every where round him, whether he could not fee
Julia, he was ready to die with impatience to
get fight of her ; his Heart and Mind were in fuch
a Confufion, as is fcarce to be exprefs'd ; but he
was forced to conceal his Paffion, for fear of being
taken notice of, and making himfelf to be fufpected ; neither was he under lefs apprehenfion, in
refpect of his Miftrefs, leaft fhe fhould not be a-
ble to hide her Joy and Surprize at the firft fight
of him, which alone would be enough to ruin
their whole Project.

The Lady Abbefs having feated her felf in a
certain place in her Clofet, where fhe intended to
fit for her Picture : *Hypolitus* to make them believe he was not there for nothing, began to manage and mix the Colours, (under pretence that
they fhould want a confiderable quantity for fo long
a Time as the Abbefs propofed they fhould Work
there) 'tis true, he did it at a very fcurvy rate,
being little acquainted with that Art, but it was
enough for him not to feem Idle. Alas! he was
far from being idle, every Hour was a Year to him
whilft he work'd in continual Expectation of feeing his dear *Julia*.

The

The drawing of a Picture is not to be performed without a Serious Thought; for the Abbess began to be tired, and fearing least it might do a prejudice to her Picture : ' I think I have heard ' say, *said she*, that Picture-drawers have com- ' monly some pleasant Story or other, wherewith ' they divert those that sit for their Pictures; but ' you have not yet told me the least thing that ' may make one Merry, and I am sensible my Face ' will not look long very pleasant, unless you ' find out something that may divert me. Madam, ' *said* Cardini *to her, (this was the Painter's* ' *Name*) I am too much taken up with your Pi- ' cture at present, to discompose my Thoughts; ' and after all, I own I have not Wit enough to ' tell you what may be pleasing or diverting to ' you, but there is *Hyacinth*, whom I commonly ' carry along with me, chiefly to divert the La- ' dies; I assure you, his Conversation is very di- ' verting. Pray then, *said she*; Hyacinth, *casting* ' *a very obliging Look at him*, pray do you tell us ' a Story, because you see *Cardini* enjoyns you so ' to do. *Hypolitus* blush'd for Vexation, being so far from being in a Humour to Talk, that he had much ado to tell them very coldly, he did not know what to say; but my Lady Abbess urging the Matter more and more, he began to fear he might disoblige her, if he persisted in his Refu- sal; and considering it was in her power to ex- clude him from a Place which contain'd the only Object of all his Wishes, he thought it best to o- vercome himself, and then recalling to his Mind a certain Story not unlike one of the old Tales of the Fairesses, he began to speak thus with a most surprizing graceful Air.

' *Ruſſia* is a Country ſo cold, and ſo ſubject to
' Tempeſtuous Weather, that it is a great Karity
' to ſee a fair Day there.   The Hills are for the
' greateſt part of the Year covered with Snow,
' and the Trees are ſo much covered with Ice,that
' when the Sun begins to caſt his Beams upon
' them, you would believe their Branches to be
' one ſolid piece of Chryſtal.   In this Country
' are Foreſts of a moſt prodigious Extent, wherein
' they hunt white Bears, which is ſometimes not
' done without great trouble and danger ; this is
' the moſt noble Exerciſe the *Ruſſians* are acquaint-
' ed with,and which is moſt frequently uſed among
' them.This Nation had once a King named *Adolph*,
' a Prince ſo Beautiful, ſo Polite, and ſo Active
' both in Body and Mind, that it ſeems almoſt
' incredible, that ſo Savage and Unpoliſh'd a
' Country as this is, ſhould produce ſo accom-
' pliſh'd a Perſon.   Before he was full 20 Years
' of Age, he was already engaged in a War a-
' gainſt the *Muſcovites*, wherein he ſhew'd an e-
' qual ſhare of Courage and Intrepedity, and of
' Conduct.   When his Army halted in ſome place
' or other, he was neverthelefs always in Action,
' and often would follow that dangerous Sport of
' Hunting the Bears.   One Day being abroad a
' Hunting, with a numerous Retinue, he follow'd
' the Chace with ſo much eagernefs into a great
' Foreſt thro' different Roads and Paths, that on a
' ſudden he ſaw he had loſt both his way and all
' his Company.   The Night began to draw near,
' he was unacquainted with the Place he was in,
' and ſaw a moſt furious Tempeſt was likely to
' ſurprize him in this Solitude, ſo he thought it
' his beſt way to take, with his Horſe, to the next
' great Road, and there to ſound the Horn ; but
' all this to no purpoſe.   Immediately after, the

N   ſmall

'small Remainder of the Day became more dark
'than the darkeft Night it felf; he could not di-
'fcern the leaft thing, unlefs it were by the Light-
'ning; the noife of the Tunder-claps founded
'moft dreadfully among the vaft Trees and the
'adjacent Mountains, the Winds and Rains en-
'creafed every moment. He endeavoured to
'fhelter himfelf under fome Trees, but by the vi-
'olence of the Rains, the Ground thereabouts
'being foon overflow'd, he was under a neceffity
'of getting out of the Foreft, in hopes to meet
'with fome conveniency or other to fhelter him-
'felf againft the Tempeft. With much ado he
'got at laft out of the Foreft into the open Field;
'but finding himfelf there more expofed to
'the fury of the Rains and Wind, than he
'had been before, he cafting his Eyes about
'him on all fides, and at laft efpying fome
'Light on a high Hill, he turned his Horfe that
'way, and with unfpeakable Difficulty reach'd
'the Foot of an almoft Inacceffible Mountain,
'furrounded with fteep Precipices and craggy
'Rocks. He went forward for two Hours toge-
'ther, fometimes on Foot, fometimes on Horfe-
'back, till he came to a very fpacious Cave, thro'
'the opening of which, he could difcover fome
'Light, (being the fame he had feen before at a
'diftance.) He ftop'd a little before he would en-
'ter into it, believing it to be a Neft of Thieves
'and Robbers, who frequently infeft that Coun-
'try, and who, in all probability, would mur-
'ther him, to commit their Robbery with lefs
'danger. But as moft commonly Princes have
'more noble and more daring Souls than other
'People, he reproach'd himfelf with his fear, and
'going directly to the Entrance of the Cave,
'clap'd his Hand to his Sword, with a Refolution

'to

' to defend his Life, in cafe they fhould affault
' him : At the very Entrance of the Cave, he was
' feized with fuch a violent Shivering, that he
' thought this very moment would be his laft.

' At the noife he made in entring into the
' Cave, an Old Woman, whofe White grev
' Hairs and Wrinkles fufficiently difcovered her
' great Age, came forth from under the craggy
' Rock, and with a feeming Amazement, you
' are the firft of all Mortals, *faid fhe to him*, that
' ever I faw in thefe Regions : Do you know, Sir,
' whofe Dwelling-place this is ? No, *faid* A-
' dolph, Good Woman, I know not where I am.
' This is, *reply'd fhe*, the Seat of *Eolus*, the God
' of the Winds ; this is the place of Retire-
' ment for himfelf and his Children ; I am
' his Mother, and am left alone at home at this
' time, becaufe they are all abroad ; fome to do
' Good, fome to do Mifchief upon Earth. But,
' *continued fhe*, I fee you are wet to the
' Skin by the violent Rains, I will make you
' a Fire, that you may dry your felf ; but, Sir,
' what moft vexes me, is, that your Fare will
' be very hard here ; the Winds live upon light
' Food, but Men want more folid Nourifhment.
' The Prince thank'd her for the kind Reception
' fhe gave him ; he got to the Fire, which was
' lighted in an inftant, becaufe the *Weft* Wind
' juft coming in, blew it up immediately. He
' was no fooner come in when the *North-Eaft*,
' and feveral other Northerly Winds arrived in
' the Cave ; *Eolus* follow'd them in Perfon, at-
' tended by *Boreas, Eaft, Scuth-Weft* and *North*
' Winds ; they were wet all over, and their Hairs
' all clogg'd together ; they were not in the leaft
' civiliz'd, but very rough in their Carriage ; and
' when they began to fpeak to the Prince, he

M 2   ' thought

' thought he fhould have been kill'd by the cold-
' nefs of their Breath. One told them, how he
' had difperfed a whole Fleet of Men of War; a
' fecond, how he had fent feveral Merchants to
' the Bottom of the Sea; a third related, he had
' faved many Veffels from falling into the Hands
' of Pirates; but they all agreed in this, that they
' had torn up a vaft number of Trees by the Roots,
' and overturn'd Walls and Houfes; in fhort, e-
' very one brag'd of what Feats he had done.
' The Old Woman hearkened to them with much
' attention, but on a fudden feeming to be very
' uneafie; What, *faid fhe to them*, did you not
' meet with your Brother *Zephyrus* in your way?
' It is already very late, and he is not come home
' yet, I am uneafie at it: They told her they had
' not feen him, when Prince *Adolph* faw come
' in to the Cave a young Lad, as Fair as they
' paint Love it felf. His Wings were of White
' Feathers, intermix'd with Carnation Colour,
' and fo thin and fine, that they feemed to be in
' a continual motion; his fair Hair curled up into a
' thoufand Buckles hanging down carelefly below
' both his Shoulders; on his Head he had a Gar-
' land of Rofes and Jeffamy, and his whole Air
' was pleafing and agreeable.
    ' Where have vou been fo long, you little Li-
' bertine, *cry'd the Old Woman with a harfh Voice?*
' All the reft of your Brothers have been here a
' good while; you alone take the priviledge of
' indulging your felf, without troubling your
' Head what difturbance you caufe me by your
' long Abfence. Oh! Mother, *faid he*, I was
' very much troubled to come home fo late, be-
' caufe I knew you would take it ill; but I have
' been in the Garden of a Princefs call'd *Felicity*;
' fhe was walking there with all her Nymphs;
                                    fome

' some of them imploy'd themselves in gathering
' Flowers, others lay asleep on the Grass disco-
' vering their Necks, to give me an opportunity
' of drawing near to, and kissing them; some of
' them Danced, others Sang, the Princess her self
' diverted her self in a Walk of Orange Trees; I
' did blow my Breath into her very Face, I play'd
' all round about her, and I now and then gently
' lifted up her Veil: *Zephyrus*, *said she*, how
' pleasant and agreeable art thou? As long as thou
' continuest here, I shall scarce leave this Walk.
' I must confess, that such engaging Words as
' these, coming from the Mouth of so Charming
' a Lady as she was, had such an influence upon
' me, that being no longer Master of my self, I
' could willingly have resolved not to leave her,
' had it not been that I feared to displease you.
' Prince *Adolph* listened to him with so much sa-
' tisfaction, that he was heartily sorry he left off
' speaking so soon. Give me leave, *said he*, love-
' ly *Zephyrus*, to ask you where that Country is,
' over which this Princess has an absolute Sway?
' In the Isle of *Felicity*, *reply'd* Zephyrus; no Bo-
' dy is suffered to come there, tho' every one goes
' in quest of it; for such is the Fate of Mankind,
' that they are not able to find it out: 'Tis true,
' abundance of them go round about it, and some
' flatter themselves to be there, because they are
' cast sometimes into some neighbouring Ports,
' where they enjoy the Fruits of a Calm and Tran-
' quillity: Here most of them would be glad to
' continue, but these Isles, which after all, bear but
' a slender proportion to the Isle of *Felicity* it self,
' are floating Islands, they soon get out of sight;
' and Envy, which will not suffer Mortals to en-
' joy even the Shade of Tranquillity, constantly
' chases them from thence; and I have seen a
' great number of Persons, of uncommon Merits,

' periſh in that attempt. The Prince ask'd him
' many more Queſtions, all which he reſolved
' him with more than ordinary exaƈtneſs and vi-
' vacity of Wit.

' It was now very late, ſo the good Woman
' ordered her Grandchildren to retire each to his
' Hole. *Zephyrus* offered the Prince a place in
' his little Bed, which was very neat, and not
' near ſo cold a corner as the reſt of the Concavi-
' ties of this vaſt Grotto, being covered with
' Herbs and Flowers. *Adolph* lay that Night with
' *Zephyrus*, but ſpent the greateſt part of it in
' talking of the Princeſs of the Iſle of *Felicity.*
' How deſirous ſhould I be to get ſight of her,
' *ſaid the Prince,* and is this a thing impoſſible, as
' not to be attained to, even with your Aſſiſtance?
' *Zephyrus* told him, the Enterprize was full of
' Danger, but that if he had Reſolution enough
' to commit himſelf entirely to his Conduƈt, he
' had thought of a way to accompliſh it; that he
' would take him betwixt his Wings, and thus
' carry him through the vaſt Regions of the Air ;
' I have, *continued he,* a Cloak, which I will
' give you, which, as often as you put it the green
' ſide outwards, you will be Inviſible ; which
' will prove abſolutely neceſſary for the Preſer-
' vation of your Life : For if thoſe that guard
' this Iſle, which are the moſt dreadful Monſters
' you ever heard of, ſhould happen to ſee you,
' you would infallibly be loſt, were you braver
' than *Hercules* himſelf. Prince *Adolph* was ſo
' eager to ſee an End of this Adventure, that not-
' withſtanding all the danger he foreſaw would
' attend it, he embraced his Offer with all ima-
' ginable ſatisfaƈtion. No ſooner began *Aurora*
' to appear in her Chariot, but the Prince full of
' impatience, rouzed *Zephyrus,* who ſlumbered
' a

'a little. I can't let you be at rest, *said he em-*
'*bracing him*; but my most Generous Host, me-
'thinks 'tis time we should be going. Come,
'come, let us go, *said he*, instead of taking it ill,
'I return you Thanks for it; for I can't but own
'to you that I am in Love with a certain Rose,
'which is lively and somewhat mutinous; so
'that perhaps it might occasion a bitter Quarrel
'betwixt us, should I not come to see her as soon
'as it is day; she grows in one of the Gardens of
'the Princess of *Felicity*. He had no sooner spoke
'these words, but he gave the Prince the Cloak.
'he promised him, and was taking him up be-
'twixt his Wings; but finding that way some-
'what incommodious, I will carry you the
'way, *said he*, as I did *Psyche*, by the Command
'of *Love*, when I carry'd her to that Beautiful
'Palace he had caused to be erected for her; so
'he took him under his Arms, and resting a lit-
'tle at the Point of a Rock, to make the Ballance
'equal in his motion, he stretch'd forth his Wings
'and so soared up into the Air. Notwithstand-
'ing all the Prince's Intrepidity, he could not
'forbear to feel some Symptoms of fear, when
'he saw himself carry'd up at so vast a height,
'under the Arms of so young a Lad; so that to
'revive his drooping Spirits, he thought it must
'be a God, knowing that *Love* himself, who
'appears so small, and the most feeble of all the
'rest, is nevertheless the strongest and most terri-
'ble. So leaving himself intirely to his Destiny,
'he began to recollect himself, and to look with
'attention upon all the Places over which he
'passed. Who is able so much as to enumerate
'all these Places, Cities, Kingdoms, Seas, Rivers,
'Plains, Desarts, Forests, unknown Countries,
'and different Nations! He was struck with such

'an

' an Amazement at the fight of all thefe things,
' that having quite loft the ufe of his Tongue,
' *Zephyrus* took care to acquaint him with the
' various Manners and Cuftoms of all the Inhabi-
' tants of the Earth. He flew but gently, and they
' refted a little upon the dreadful Mountains of
' *Caucafus* and *Athos*, and upon feveral others
' that fell in their way. Were I fure, *faid* Ze-
' phyrus, that that fair Rofe I adore, fhould prick
' me with her Thorns, I can't fuffer you to tra-
' verfe fo vaft a Tract of Ground, without allow-
' ing you fome time, to have the fatisfaction of
' contemplating thofe Wonders you fee. Prince
' *Adolph* returned his Thanks for all his Good-
' nefs, but at the fame time told him, he was
' much afraid leaft this *Princefs of Felicity* fhould
' not underftand his Language, and that he fhould
' not be able to fpeak to her. Don't trouble your
' felf on that account, *faid the little God to him,*
' this Princefs has an univerfal Knowledge, and it
' will not be long before you both fpeak the fame
' Language.
  ' At laft they got fight of this defireable Ifland,
' which appeared fo beautiful and delightful to
' the Prince, that he thought no otherwife than
' that he had been in an Enchanted Place. The
' Air was all perfumed, the Dew and Rain fmel-
' led like Rofe and Orange Water, the Spring
' threw out the Water to the very Skies, the Fo-
' refts were full of the rareft Trees that can be
' feen, the Grounds coloured with the moft De-
' licious Flowers ; Rivulets, clearer than the fineft
' Cryftal, gently run through the Plains, making
' an agreeable noife ; the Birds made a moft har-
' monious Melody, exceeding all that the beft
' Mafters of Mufick ever could attain to ; the
' Earth produced her Fruits without any Labour

' or Cultivating, and, with a Wish only, you saw
' your Tables covered and served with all the de-
' licious Meats you could think of. The Palace
' it self far exceeded every thing has been men-
' tioned as yet: The Walls were of Diamonds,
' the Floor and Wainscoting all of Precious Stones;
' Gold was as common there as Stones are with
' us; the Moveables and Furniture, were the
' Workmanship of the *Faries*, and that of the
' most curious Pieces; every thing being so nicely
' done, that it was hard to distinguish, whether
' Magnificence or Contrivance had the greatest
' share in it.

' *Zephyrus* set the Prince down in a pleasant
' Bowling-Green: Sir, *said he*, I have performed
' my Promise; 'tis now your Business to do your
' part, so they Embraced one another. *Adolph*
' return'd him a thousand Thanks, and *Zephyrus*
' impatient to see his Mistress, left him to him-
' self in a very delicious Garden. He took seve-
' ral Turns in divers agreeable Walks, and saw a
' great number of curious Grotto's, so charming
' and beautiful, that it seem'd as if they were
' made on purpose for Delight and Pleasure. In
' one of these he saw a Statue of White Marble,
' representing *Cupid*, a Piece of most excellent
' Workmanship, casting out of his Flambeaux a
' Stream of Water instead of Fire, leaning a-
' gainst an artificial Rock; he saw the following
' Words engraven on a Stone:

He that is ignorant of the Pleasures of Love,
has never tasted any real Happiness; 'tis she alone
that can gratify our Desires, and render this Life
agreeable to us; without her all other Felicities
lose their Charms, and every thing is fading and
fainting.

' *Adolph*

' *Adolph* efpying an Arbour fo clofely covered
' with Greens, that the Sun Beams could not pe-
' netrate into this dark and retired place, feated
' himfelf on the Pedeftal of a Foun:ain, and af-
' ford-d fome Hours reft to his Body, not a lit-
' tle tired by the Fatigues of fo vaft a Jour-
' ney.

' 'Twas almoft Noon, before he awakned, and
' being much vex'd he had loft fo much time in
' vain, to make himfelf amends for it, he made
' all the hafte he could towards the Palace. As
' he drew nearer, he took a full view, and admi-
' red, at his own leifure, all the Beauties there-
' of, with much more attention than he could do
' at a greater diftance ; and it feem'd as if all the
' Artifts in the World had joyn'd their Skill and
' Labour to make it the moft magnificent and
' moft perfect Structure that could be imagined.
' The Prince had all this while kept the Green-
' fide of his Cloak outward, fo that he could fee
' every thing without being feen ; but after all,
' he look'd a long time without being able to fee
' the Entrance into it ; whether the Doors were
' fhut, or whether they were on the oppofite fide,
' before he could find them, he faw a Lovely La-
' dy opening a Window of one entire piece of
' Cryftal, and at the fame time a little Female
' Gardiner running towards the Window ; fhe that
' was at the Window, let down thence a Basket
' of Filligree-Work of Gold, faftned to feveral
' Strings and Knots of curious Ribbons ; fhe bid
' the Gardiner to gather fome Flowers for the
' Princefs, which fhe did in an inftant, and put
' them in the Basket : *Adolph* got upon the Flow-
' ers, and fo was drawn up into the Window by
' the Nymph. You muft imagine, that the fame
' Green Cloak, which had the Vertue of making
' him

' him invifible, muft alfo make him very light,
' for without this Circumftance, it would have
' proved a very hard Task for the Lady to have
' drawn him up to the Window ; through which
' he got into a very fpacious Apartment, and his
' Eyes were furprized with fuch an amazing
' Light, as is paft all imagination. Here he faw
' whole Companies of Nymphs, the eldeft of
' which appear'd not to be above 18 Years of Age,
' and a great many of them much younger ; fome
' were Fair, others Brown, but all of a fine Com-
' plexion, white, frefh colour'd, exactly featur'd,
' with glorious white Teeth ; to be fhort, there
' was not one among all thefe Nymphs but what
' might pafs for a Compleat Beauty. He would
' have fpent the whole Day in admiring their Per-
' fections, and had not the power to ftir out of
' this Charming Apartment, had it not been for
' a moft agreeable Harmony of Mufick, as well
' of Voices, as of the choiceft Mufical Inftru-
' ments, that raifed his Curiofity to fee from
' whence it came; fo drawing near to an adjacent
' Room, he no fooner enter'd it, but heard them
' fing thefe Words.

*Prove Tender, prove Faithful, be conftant to
the laft, 'tis that that will Conquer the Heart of
your Fair One ; Time brings every thing to pafs :
You that are infpired with a mutual Paffion, if
your cruel Deftiny fhortens your happy Moments,
you muft hope for fair Weather, Time brings every
thing to pafs.*

' Whilft the Prince was in the great Apart-
' ment, he thought nothing could have ftood in
' Competition with thofe he faw there ; but he
' foon found himfelf moft agreeably deceived in
' his Opinion ; thefe Female Muficians far fur-
                                          ' paffing

' paffing thofe Nymphs he had feen before in
' Beauty ; and what was almoft prodigious, he
' underftood every thing he heard, tho' he was not
' acquainted with the Language of that Ifle. He
' ftood behind one of the Faireft of thefe Nymphs;
' fhe happened to drop her Veil, and he, without
' confidering that he fhould put her into a fright,
' took it up from the Ground and gave it to her,
' fhe fqueek'd out on a fudden, and I believe this
' to be the firft time they ever knew what fear
' was in thefe happy Manfions : All the reft of
' the Nymps flock'd about her, asking, what was
' the matter with her ? I believe you think me
' to be in a Dream, *faid fhe to them*; but I am
' fure I let my Vail fall to the Ground, and fome-
' thing that is invifible put it into my Hands a-
' gain.   They all fell a Laughing, and fome went
' into the Princefs's Apartment, to divert her with
' this Story.

' Prince *Adolph* followed them by the help of
' his Green Cloak ; he pafs'd through fpacious
' Rooms, Galleries and Chambers without num-
' ber, till at laft he came into the Apartment of
' the Sovereign Lady of the Ifle. She was feat-
' ed on a Throne made out of one intire Carbuncle
' Stone, brighter than the Sun it felf, but the Prin-
' cefs of *Felicity*'s Eyes carry'd ftill a more furpri-
' fing Luftre than the Carbuncle it felf ; fhe was
' fo perfect a Beauty, that fhe appeared more like
' a Favourite of Heaven, than of a Terreftrial Off-
' fpring ; fhe was very Young, and a certain
' Sprightly but Majeftick Air appeared in all her
' Actions, which infpired both Love and Refpect :
' Her Apparel had more of Neatnefs than Magni-
' ficence in it ; her Fair Hairs were adorn-
' ed with Flowers, fhe had a Scarfe on, and
' her Gown was Gauze flower'd with Gold,
                                              She

' She was furrounded with a great many Cupids,
' who danc'd and play'd a thoufand little divert-
' ing Tricks; fome kifs'd her Hands, others climb-
' ing up on both fides of the Throne, put a Crown
' on her Head; the Pleafures were alfo Playing
' and Courting her on all fides; to be fhort, all
' that can be thought or imagined to be Charm-
' ing, is much below what the Prince feafted his
' Eyes with there. He was like one in a Rapture,
' he was fcarce able to bear the Luftre of this Prin-
' cefs's Beauty; and under this Agitation of his
' Heart, all his Thoughts being taken up with that
' Object he already adored, he dropt his Cloak
' and fhe faw him. She had never feen a Man be-
' fore, and therefore was infinitely furprized at
' the fight of him. *Adolph* feeing himfelf thus
' difcovered, threw himfelf at her Feet with the
' utmoft Refpect: Great Princefs, *faid he to her*,
' I have traverfed the Univerfe, to come hither to
' admire your Divine Beauty, I am come to make
' you an Offer of my Heart and all my Defires;
' will you not pleafe to accept of them ? The Prin-
' cefs was a Lady of a fingular Vivacity of Wit,
' notwithftanding which, her Surprize was fuch
' that fhe could not fpeak one word. Hitherto
' fhe had never beheld any thing that appear'd
' more amiable to her Eyes than this Creature, and
' believing him to be the only one of his Kind,
' fhe imagined he muft needs be the fo much cele-
' brated *Phœnix* of the Ancients, but fcarce ever
' feen by any Body; Lovely *Phœnix*, *faid fhe to*
' *him*, (for I judge you are the fame by your Perfe-
' ctions, there being nothing comparable to you
' in this Ifle) I am infinitely pleas'd to fee you
' here; what pity 'tis you fhould be the only one
' of your Kind, many more fuch Birds as you are,
' would make a moft glorious Shew. *Adolph* could
                                   ' not

' not forbear ſmiling at what ſhe told him with a
' moſt graceful Air, full of natural Simplicity ;
' but being unwilling that this Lady for whom he
' felt already a moſt violent Paſſion, ſhould be
' detain'd in Ignorance, in a matter he judged ſhe
' ought to be acquainted with, he took care to
' inſtruct her in every thing of this nature, and ſhe
' proved ſo apt a Scholar, and of ſuch a natural
' Vivacity of Wit, that ſhe even anticipated her
' Maſter in his Leſſons ; ſhe loved him beyond
' her ſelf, and he loved her more than himſelf ;
' all thoſe ſweet Enjoyments Love is able to give,
' all the Beauty and Vivacity of Wit, all the Ten-
' derneſs a Heart is capable of feeling, were cen-
' tred in theſe two tender Lovers ; nothing could
' diſturb their Tranquillity, every thing con-
' curr'd to increaſe their Pleaſures ; they knew
' not what Sickneſs was ; nay, they felt not ſo
' much as the leaſt Inconveniencies or Decay ;
' their Youth was not impair'd by a long Courſe
' of Years, becauſe in this delicious place, they
' drink of the Water of the Fountain of Youth.
' They were unacquainted with Amorous Inquie-
' tudes, with Jealous Surmiſes ; nay, not ſo much
' as with theſe little Wranglings, which common-
' ly end in a happy Accommodation and Renew-
' ing of Love ; I ſay, they knew nothing of all
' theſe things ; they were inebrietated with Plea-
' ſures, and till that day never had any Mortal En-
' joy'd ſo great and ſo conſtant Felicity. But this
' is the Condition of us Mortals, that even that
' Happineſs has its ſad and doleful Conſequences,
' nothing is everlaſting on Earth, but always ſub-
' ject to Change.

' Prince *Adolph* being one day entertaining the
' Princeſs, it came into his Head to ask her, how
' long it was ſince he had enjoy'd the Pleaſure of
'   ' ſeeing

' feeing him? The Time paffes away fo faft
' where you are, *faid he*, that I fcarce ever look'd
' backward, or thought of the Time when I came
' here. I will tell you, *faid fhe*, provided you
' frankly confefs to me beforehand, how long you
' really think it has been. He paufed a while,
' and then faid; When I confult my Heart, and
' think of the fatisfaction I feel within my felf, I
' am almoft apt to believe, I have not been here
' above a Week, my dear Princefs; but when I re-
' cal to my Mind certain things that are paft fome
' time ago, I think it can't be much lefs than
' three Months. She burft out a Laughing; Dear
' *Adolph*, *faid fhe*, *with a very Serious Air*, you
' muft know it is no lefs than three hundred Years.
' Alas! had fhe known how dearly fhe was likely
' to pay for thefe Words, fhe would never have
' fpoken them. Three hundred Years, *cry'd the
' Prince*, how muft the World ftand by this time?
' Who muft be the Univerfal Monarch there? I
' wonder what they are a doing there? When I
' come there again, who will know me? Or
' how fhall I know any Body? My Dominions
' are, doubtlefs, fal'n into the Hands of fome
' ftrange Family? I can't fuppofe there will be
' any left for me; fo that I am likely to be a
' Prince without a Principality; every Body will
' fhun me as if I were a Spectre, and I fhall be
' altogether unacquain'ed with the Manners and
' Cuftoms of thofe among whom I am to live.
' The Princefs beginning to be impatient, *Adolph*,
' *faid fhe interrupting him*, what is it you repine
' at? Don't you fet no more value than fo upon
' all the Favours I have fhewn you, and all the
' Love I bear you? I have given you admiffion
' into my Palace, you are Mafter here, I have
' preferved your Life for three Ages, without the
' leaft

‘ leaſt decay or regret till this moment; whereas,
‘ had it not been for me, where would you have
‘ been by this time? I abhor Ingratitude, Fair
‘ Princeſs, *reply'd he in ſome Confuſion*, I know,
‘ and am ſenſible how much I am indebted to you?
‘ But after all, had I been Dead before this time, I
‘ ſhould perhaps have perform'd ſuch great Acti-
‘ ons as would have render'd my Name famous
‘ for ever to Poſterity ; I can't, without ſhame,
‘ ſee my Courage to lie dormant, and my Name
‘ buried in Oblivion. Such was the brave *Rey-*
‘ *nold* in the Arms of his *Armide*, but Glory
‘ ſnatch'd him thence. So that Glory is likewiſe
‘ to ſnatch you out of my Arms, Barbarous Man,
‘ *cry'd the Princeſs ſhedding a Rivulet of Tears,*
‘ thou haſt a mind to leave me, and therefore art
‘ unworthy of the Pain I feel for thee. She had
‘ no ſooner ſaid theſe Words, but ſhe fell into a
‘ Swoon : The Prince was highly afflicted there-
‘ at, becauſe he loved her extreamly, but at the
‘ ſame time could not forbear upbraiding himſelf
‘ for having ſpent ſo much time with a Miſtreſs,
‘ without any thing that might raiſe his Name
‘ among the Rank of the Great Heroes : In vain
‘ he indeavoured to reſtrain his Sentiments,
‘ or to conceal his Diſſatisfaction, he was ſoon
‘ ſeized with ſuch a Languiſhment, as quite al-
‘ ter'd his whole Diſpoſition ; ſo that whereas hi-
‘ thereto he had miſtaken Months for Ages, he
‘ thought now every Month as long as an Age.
‘ The Princeſs, who perceived it, was afflicted
‘ thereat to the higheſt degree; but notwithſtand-
‘ ing this, would not engage him to ſtay barely
‘ out of Complaiſance; ſo ſhe told him, He ſhould
‘ be Maſter of his own Deſtiny, and might de-
‘ part whenever he thought fit ; but that ſhe much
‘ feared ſome great Misfortune would befal him.
                                          ‘ Theſe

' Thefe laft Words caufed much lefs Diffatisfacti-
' on in him, than he had found Satisfaction in the
' firft ; and tho' the very Thoughts of parting
' from his Princefs, nearly affected his Mind; yet
' hurry'd on by his Deftiny, he bid farewel to her
' he had adored, and by whom he was no lefs
' tenderly beloved; He protefted to her, that
' fo foon as he had performed any Glorious
' Actions to render himfelf more worthy of her
' Favours, he fhould never be at reft till he could
' return and pay his Homage to her, as his Sove-
' reign Lady, and as the only Felicity of his Life.
' His Eloquence, which was natural to him, fup-
' ply'd the defect of his Love ; but the Princefs
' was too clear fighted not to dive into the bottom
' of the Matter, and her Mind prefaged her fhe
' knew not what Misfortune which would rob her
' for ever of the Satisfaction of feeing again
' what was fo dear to her.

' Whatever Violence fhe put upon her own In-
' clinations, fhe was overwhelm'd with Grief paft
' all expreffing : She prefented *Adolph* with a ve-
' ry rich Armour, and with the beft and fineft
' Horfe the World afforded. *Bichar* (that was
' the Horfe's Name) will conduct you, *faid fhe*
' *to him*, thro' all Danger, and make you come
' off with Honour in your Combats ; but have a
' care not to touch the Ground with your Feet,
' before you come into your own Country ; for
' by Vertue of that Spirit of the *Fairies*, the
' Gods have beftow'd upon me, I forefee, that
' if you flight my Advice, *Bichar* will not be in a
' condition to Reprieve you. The Prince promi-
' fed he would follow her good Counfel, and
' kiffing her Hands a thoufand times, went away,
' but in fo much hafte, that he left his Wonder-

O   ful

' ful Cloak behind him. Coming to the Shoar of
' the Isle, *Bichar* swam over Rivers and Seas with
' his Rider, ran over Mountains and thro' Vales,
' thro' Forests and Fields, and that with so much
' swiftness, as if he had been a Wing'd Horse.

' One Evening coming to a small crooked and
' Stone Lane, with Hedges on both sides, he saw
' a Cart overthrown in the middle of the Road,
' which hinder'd his Passage. The Cart was laden
' with Wings of divers shapes and sizes, and un-
' der the Cart lay a very Old Man, who was the
' Carter. His bald Head, his trembling Voice,
' and his Misfortune, moved the Prince to Com-
' passion. *Bichar* was ready to leap over the
' Hedges, when the Old Man call'd to *Adolph* in
' a most pitiful manner ; Pray, Sir, pity my con-
' dition ; unless you will help me, I must perish
' here. The Prince, not able to resist the Entrea-
' ties of the Old Man, and his own Inclinations
' to help him up, alighted from his Horse, and
' reach'd his Hand to him ; but alas ! guess at his
' Surprize, when he saw the Old Man arise with-
' out his Assistance, and that so suddenly, that he
' lay'd hold of him before he was aware of it.
' At last, Prince of *Russia, said he with a dreadful*
' *threatning Voice*, at last I have met with you ;
' my Name is *Time*, I have been in search for you
' these three Ages, I have worn out all these
' Wings wherewith you see this Cart is loaded, to
' fly all over the Universe to find you out; you
' see, that notwithstanding all your care to hide
' your self from me, nothing in this World can
' escape me : At these Words he struck him with
' his Hand upon his Mouth, with so much Vio-
' lence, that he beat the Breath out of his Body,
' and so stifled him upon the Spot.

' *Zephyrus*

'Zephyrus happening to come by juſt at that fa-
' tal Minute, was forced to be an Eye-witneſs, to
' his great regret, of his dear Friend's Misfor-
' tune; and ſo ſoon as the Old Barbarous Fellow
' had left him, he try'd whether he could blow
' freſh Breath into his Body; but finding all his
' Endeavours in vain, he took him under his Arm,
' as he had done before, and weeping bitterly car-
' ry'd him to the Garden of the Palace of *Felicity*;
' there he laid him in a Grotto upon a Rock that
' was flat at top, covering his dead Body with
' Flowers: He erected a Trophy of his Arms,
' and a Column of Jaſper next to it, on which he
' engraved theſe Words.

Time is the Maſter of every thing; Time brings
every thing to paſs; Beauty paſſes away with our
Time; Man frames to himſelf a thouſand new
deſires; and his Mind is diſcompoſed even in the
midſt of his Enjoyments; If he thinks his Pains re-
warded, if he appear contented for ſome time, and
values himſelf upon the Conqueſt he has made; he
will ſoon be convinced by ſome unfortunate Turn of
Affairs, that there is no Love that laſts for ever,
nor any perfect Felicity.

' The diſconſolate Princeſs uſed to come every
' day to this Grotto, ſince the departure of her
' Lover, there to bemoan his Abſence, and to aug-
' ment the Torrents of the Rivulets by a Deluge
' of Tears. Gueſs at her Satisfaction, when ſhe
' found him ſo near her at a time when ſhe thought
' him at a vaſt diſtance; ſhe thought, that being
' much fatigued in his Journey, he had laid him-
' ſelf down to reſt there; ſhe was conſidering
' whether ſhe had beſt to awake him, or not; and

O 2   ' at

‘ at laſt the tender Motions of her Heart over-
‘ ballancing all the reſt, ſhe was opening her
‘ Arms to embrace him ; then it was, that being
‘ made ſenſible of her Misfortune, ſhe cry’d out,
‘ ſhe wept, ſhe made ſuch doleful Moan, as would
‘ have moved even a Stone ; ſhe commanded im-
‘ mediately the Gates of her Palace to be kept ſhut
‘ for ever. Certain ’tis, that ſince that fatal day,
‘ no Body has been able to boaſt, that he has got
‘ ſight of her ; for ſhe ſeldom appears abroad
‘ ſince this Misfortune ; and whenever ſhe does,
‘ Inquietudes and Vexations are her Fore-runners,
‘ and Uneaſineſs and Diſſatisfaction her Follow-
‘ ers. Theſe are her ordinary Attendants. The
‘ whole World is ſufficiently convinced of this
‘ Truth, by woful Experience, and ſince this de-
‘ plorable Adventure, it has been a conſtant Say-
‘ ing ; *That Time brings every thing to paſs,*
‘ *and that there is no Felicity in its full Perfe-*
‘ *ction.*

Hypolitus having finiſh’d his Story, ſhe told
him, ſhe was at this Moment a living Inſtance of
what he had ſaid ; becauſe the fear ſhe was in, of
hearing the pleaſing Relation to be brought to a
period, had not a little diſturbed the Pleaſure ſhe
enjoy’d in hearing it related to her ; ſhe highly
commended his way of repreſenting it with ſo
good a Grace, and was returning her Thanks to
him, when *Julia*’s Waiting Woman came into the
Abbeſs’s Cloſet ; after the firſt Compliment from
her Miſtreſs (who was ſtill in Bed, being troubled
with the Head-ach) ſhe deſired her to lend her
ſome Books, wherewithal to divert her Miſtreſs ;
Iſabella, ſaid the Abbeſs, I have no time at preſent to look for Books ; but I would have you
conduct

conduct *Hyacinth* into her Chamber ; he will divert her much better than all the Books can do ; he has juſt now related to me a very pleaſant Story, and I don't queſtion, but he will have ſo much Complaiſance, as to tell it over again before your Miſtreſs : So ſhe deſired *Hypolitus* to go along with *Iſabella* ; and you may eaſily imagine, he was not very backward to obey the Abbeſs. He took care to hide part of his Face with his Handkerchief, leaſt the Abbeſs might perceive the Alteration this unexpected News produced in his Countenance ; beſides, that it prevented *Iſabella* from being ſurprized at ſo unexpected a ſight, which might have made her to diſcover more of Fear, than was convenient to their preſent purpoſe.

She conducted him to *Julia*'s Chamber, where *Hypolitus* finding himſelf at liberty, kneeled at her Bed-ſide, and being unable to ſpeak one word, took hold of one of her Hands, which he Kiſs'd, with ſuch exceſſive Tranſports of Joy, as is ſcarce to be conceived. The Curtains of her Bed being drawn, and that part of the Room where the Bed ſtood being pretty dark, and her Head laid cloſe within the Pillow, *Julia* could not know him, and therefore did all ſhe could to pull her Hand back. *Hypolitus* putting a wrong Interpretation upon this Coyneſs, which he look'd upon as an effect of her averſion to him, let it go ; but at the ſame time turn'd Pale, a Trembling ſeized him, and he was ready to drop down for Grief : He had ſcarce ſo much ſtrength left, as to tell her with a moſt tender and engaging Air ; ' *Julia* you hate me, you ' hate me ; you lay your Misfortunes at my ' Door, and tho' you know I am only the inno- ' cent Cauſe of them, you have conceived ſuch ' an Antipathy againſt me, that you will not ſo

' much

' much as fuffer me to come near you. Oh!
' what do you fay, my dear *Hypolitus, faid fhe to*
' *him (for fhe knew his Tongue immediately)* how
' little are you acquainted with my true Senti-
' ments! And then embracing him with much Tendernefs, this proved the moft effectual Juftification that could be to *Hypolitus,* who was tranfported with Joy, at fo kind a Reception. They look'd
upon one another for a confiderable time, without
fpeaking one Word; their Eyes being the fole Interpreters of the Agitations of what they felt
within themfelves; they could not forbear to min-
gle their Tears, occafioned partly by Joy, partly by
Sadnefs, their Minds being then divided betwixt
thefe two Paffions; till at laft Joy got the Victory
for that time: Nothing can be imagined more tender or more engaging, than what they told one another, during thofe firft Emotions of their Hearts;
you may be affured they had no time to talk ferioufly of their own Affairs. When People meet
with great Difappointments, if two Perfons Love
to the higheft degree, if they are parted, if they
meet again, the Heart is fo full, their Minds are
quite taken up with their prefent fight, they are
in fuch a confufion, that they are, as if it were,
Tongue-ty'd; and if they utter a few Words,
they are incoherent, or interrupted with Sighs;
and they begin to talk of many things, without
making an end of any one. Every thing puts them
in mind of their prefent Happinefs of being together; and from this Reflection, which adds new
Vigour to their Love, they run upon mutual Affurances of loving one another for ever: and thus
the time paffes away infenfibly; a great many
Hours feem to be no more than a few Minutes.
Thus it happen'd with the Amiable *Julia* and her
Faithful *Hypolitus*; fo that it would be next to

an impoffibility to infert here what they told one another at this firft Interview; but fuch as are of a tender Difpofition, and have felt the effects of this Paffion, may eafily imagine it.

Immediately after the Abbefs's Dinner was over, fhe went attended by *Cardini* to vifit the Fair fick Lady in her Bed-Chamber; fhe ordered her Picture to be brought, to fhew it to *Julia*, and to have her Opinion, Whether the firft Draught thereof was well done. After their Difcourfe had run for fome time upon the Picture; ' I can't ' queftion, Madam, *faid fhe to* Julia, but that ' you are ready to pay me your Acknowledg- ' ment for the care I have taken to fend up *Hya-* ' *cinth* to you. I am fure you can't deny, but ' that he has a great fhare of Wit ; and that he ' can tell a Story, better than the *Fairies* them- ' felves could have done, whereof he has given ' you a Relation. *Julia* underftood not the Ab- ' befs's meaning ; but, at a hazard, told her in ' general Terms, That fhe fhould look upon it as ' an unpardonable thing in her felf, to have neg- ' lected to return her Thanks for this Favour, but ' that fhe had been fo intent upon feeing and hear- ' ing him, that, if fhe thought fit, fhe fhould be ' very well pleafed, to underftand a little of the ' Art of Drawing and Defigning; which, fhe ho- ' ped, might prove a means to divert her Melan- ' choly Thoughts. The Abbefs told her, fhe would not be againft it; and that, whilft *Cardini* was employ'd in Painting for her Clofet, *Hya-cinth* might come to teach her, provided he would now and then fpare time to tell her a Sto-ry. *Hypolitus* was filent, whilft they were talk-ing together; but could not but be infinitely plea-fed, to underftand that he was likely to fee his Miftrefs every Day; and that very moment he would not have changed his Condition with the greateſt Monarch upon Earth.

Matters being thus agreed betwixt them, he fail'd not to viſit his Miſtreſs every Afternoon, and to ſpend, at leaſt, two or three Hours with her. He told her of *Leander*'s Marriage with *Lucilia*; it would be difficult to repreſent the Satisfaction ſhe felt at this good News ; her Tenderneſs for this Friend, had not ſuffered the leaſt Diminution; and ſhe eſteem'd her Spouſe for his extraordinary Merits, and for his being an entire Friend of her dear *Hypolitus*; ſhe told him all that poſſibly ſhe could think on to teſtifie her Joy on this account ; and he laying hold of this Opportunity ; ' If it be ſo, dear Lady, *ſaid he*, that
' you are ſo very ſenſible of *Lucilia*'s good For-
' tune, you ought to endeavour to encreaſe it,
' by ſecuring mine; Go to live with her, you'll
' find every thing ready to obey you there : I will
' follow you thither, and there I may ſee you
' without either trouble or fear : Conſider with
' your ſelf, how ſoon I may be diſcovered here ;
' and with what ill conſequences, to our Affairs,
' this Diſcovery would be attended : Take my
' Advice, Let us make uſe of our preſent good
' Fortune, I will ſafely conduct you thither ; and
' when we are at liberty, we will then conſult
' what is further to be done in our Affairs. My
' Honour, dear *Hypolitus*, my Reputation, *cry'd*
' *ſhe in a melancholy Tone*, what muſt become of
' them? What! would you have me make my E-
' ſcape along with you ? All the Vexations my
' Husband makes me undergo, owe their Origi-
' nal to the Opinion he has conceived, that I love
' you ; this is certainly the Cloak wherewith he
' covers his ill Temper; and to confirm him, and
' the

‘ the World in thefe Surmifes, to juftify his Pro-
‘ ceedings, and to cut out my own Deftruction,
‘ you would have us go away together? Oh! dear
‘ Brother, 'tis impoffible to be done; I had better
‘ die here. How unjuftly you deal with your felf
‘ and me, Madam, *reply'd he in a moft difconfo-*
‘ *late manner*; Can any Body blame you for break-
‘ ing your Chains, for getting out of a Prifon, un-
‘ to which you have been fo undefervedly and un-
‘ worthily confined? If you infift upon my not
‘ going along with you, I will come after you;
‘ and is there any thing in this World more natural
‘ or more common, than to endeavour to regain
‘ one's Liberty after it is loft? My dear *Julia*, if
‘ ever your Inclinations were for me; if my Paf-
‘ fion, if my Conftancy is able to touch your Heart;
‘ grant that to my earneft Prayers, and to my,
‘ Tears, which perhaps you would refufe to your
‘ own Defires. Urge me no more, *Hypolitus, faid*
‘ *fhe to him*, I am reduced almoft to defpair, to fee
‘ my felf neceffitated to refufe what you would
‘ have me to do : It feems to me, that if you lo-
‘ ved me more you would be the fooner inclined
‘ to agree with me in my Sentiments, and fhare my
‘ Pains with me. He continued lying at her Feet
fighing without intermiffion, but return'd no Anfwer for fome time; at laft breaking filence firft,
‘ What then muft become of me, Good God,
‘ *cry'd he?* What muft I do cruel Lady? I am
‘ not capable of convincing you; you delight in
‘ your Troubles; you reject a Remedy which will
‘ infallibly meet with the Approbation of all the
‘ World; Is not this an effect of your Averfion
‘ to me? No, no my dear *Hypolitus, faid fhe with*
‘ *a moft Tender Look, giving him her hand*; no, I
‘ have not the leaft Averfion to you; and I don't
‘ believe you can think fo, for above one Minute:
‘ I

' I am ſtill the ſame *Julia*, who preferʼd your Re-
' poſe to hers, who would not live, but for your
' ſake : but I am alſo the ſame *Julia*, who loves
' Vertue and her Duty beyond you, and beyond
' her ſelf : Do you think me ſo inſenſible of my
' preſent Circumſtances, as not moſt paſſionately
' to wiſh for my Liberty ? And do you think I
' am leſs apprehenſive than you, of the danger of
' your being diſcovered here ? I foreſee all the
' ill Conſequences that would attend it, and the
' very thoughts thereof make me infinitely unea-
' ſie ; but I have an Expedient to offer, which, I
' hope, will put me in a condition to gratify you
' without blame : Let us write to my Father, and
' perſwade him to come hither ; when I am once
' with him, I can then bid defiance to ill Tongues.
Hypolitus repreſented to her, how long a time
this was likely to take up ; and that in the mean
while they might be expoſed to a thouſand ſiniſter unforeſeen Accidents ; but to little purpoſe :
ſhe perſiſted immoveable in her Reſolution ; but
to obey her Commands, and forward as much as
lay in his Power, his own Happineſs, he ſent their
Letters to *Leander*, deſiring they might be di-
ſpatched to the Earl of *Warwick* ; *Julia* writing
concerning her Sufferings, and *Hypolitus* let him
know, by what lucky Chance he had met with
her, when he leaſt of all hoped for any ſuch
thing.

In the mean while the Abbeſs had taken care to
caution *Cardini*, that it was of the utmoſt conſequence, that neither he, nor his Scholar, ſhould
take any of the Fair Strangerʼs Letters, to ſend
them into her own Country : *Cardini* promiſed
upon his Word, he would accept of none ; or if
he did, he would deliver them into her own
Hands.

Hands. He told her, he would be answerable for *Hyacinth*'s Fidelity, which she easily believed; having already conceived a very favourable Opinion of this Stranger, on occasion of his pleasing Relation of the Prince of *Russia*; and she did not in the least question, but that he would prove more obliging to her than to *Julia*. At the same time 'tis impossible to represent to you the high Satisfaction of these two Lovers; they saw one another every day, they pass'd away their time in this delightful Desert with more Pleasure, than if they had lived in the most splendid Court of *Europe*, and had enjoy'd all the Favours of the greatest Monarch on Earth. 'Tis certain, that it is one of Love's Secrets, to cure us of Ambition, and of a thousand other Passions, which tyrannize over those that are incapable of Tenderness. *Hypolitus* related to her every thing that had befal'n him during her Absence; as she, on the other hand, told him all that had happened to her; they would sometimes recal to their Minds, the first beginning of their Passion, with the secret mutual Pleasures that attended it; sometimes they would frame Projects for the time to come, and endeavour to concert measures about future things, which depended on many Uncertainties, so that six Months pass'd away thus insensibly, they thinking all this time as short, as if they had spent it in the *Palace of Felicity*.

Cardini took effectual care (as it had been agreed betwixt *Hypolitus* and him) not to work too fast, and the Abbess took notice of it, because she had agreed with him for the Whole; nay, she judged that the more time he bestowed upon the Work, the better it would be done. All this while *Hypolitus*'s Servants remaining at *Burbon*, without seeing their Master, it was fear'd this might afford

afford fome caufe of fufpicion to fome who love
to dive into other People's Concerns; he ordered
them to go to *Nevers*, and not to tell any Body
that they belonged to him. He received frequently Letters from the Earl of *Suffex* and *Lucilia*,
unto whom he had communicated his prefent
Happinefs; and writ to the Earl of *Douglas*, that
it was the Phyficians Advice, he fhould make ufe
of the Waters during both the Seafons, fo he remain'd undifturbed where he was, and his Friends
urged not his return from *Burbon*.

Among other things, he received with all the
Satisfaction imaginable the News concerning the
Earl of *Warwick*, whofe coming was expected
every day by all his Friends and Relations, who
were all overjoy'd to underftand that he was not
flain, as had been reported, and that *Julia* was his
Daughter; the Earl of *Bedford* was the only
Man who appear'd much difturbed thereat, being under a great uncertainty what courfe he
had beft to take; and *Hypolitus*'s Satisfaction was
foon difturbed with another piece of News, which
came much about the fame time, for the Countefs
of *Douglas*, in her Letter to him, told him, That
if he intended to fee his Father alive, he muft
come quickly, he being fo ill, that his Life was
quite defpaired of. Upon this occafion it was,
that Nature and Reafon got the better of Love
and Tendernefs. *Julia* declared to him, it was
her abfolute Will he fhould go where his Duty
call'd him; and back'd her Counfel with urgent
Reafons, ' Remember, *faid fhe to him*, that this
' will prove a means to bring my Father hither a-
' long with you, at your return; that you will
' reap the Fruits of this Journey, and that I fhall
' have a confiderable fhare in it; and that upon
' that account alfo, it is worth all your Care.

Not

Not that she was much concerned whether she had
a great or small Estate, every thing of that Nature was indifferent to her; for, provided she
could but live with her *Hypolitus*, she had enough
to satisfie both her Love and Ambition; she thought
all the rest not worth her Care and Wishes; but
at the same time she knew he could not be satisfy'd to see her live in a condition below her self,
and that he would stand in need of Moives no
less considerable than these to get him away from
St. *Menoux*; we might rather have said, to snatch
him away: Good God! what a deplorable Condition was he not reduced to? What Pangs, what
Anguish did he not feel within his Soul, at this
doleful parting with *Julia*; nay, what a miserable State were they both entangled in? Such a one,
in effect, as made them ready to expire; whatever can be thought or said, that is Tender and
Passionate, they told one another upon this occasion; and when their Tongues fail'd, the Language of their Eyes, and their Sighs served for
the true Interpreters of the Anxiety of their Hearts,
and of that Grief which had penetrated to their
very Souls. Oh! how, upon such Occasions as
this, we stand in need of all our Vertue and Courage, to counter-ballance the Frailties of our
Heart and Mind; however supported, by hopes,
they flatter'd themselves to meet again before it
was long, and they had very good reason to hope
it.

Cardini promised *Hypolitus* at parting, to take
care *Julia*'s Letters should be dispatch'd safely to
him, and his to *Julia*; and he, to reward his Fidelity and encourage him to continue so for the
future, made him a considerable Present. The
Abbess being told by *Cardini*, that *Hyacinth* was
recall'd by his Father into *Italy*, was very sorry
thereat;

thereat ; but poor *Julia*, notwithstanding she put
all possible violence upon her self to hide part of
her trouble, was not able to overcome it : He
was no sooner got out of sight, but she shut her
self up in her Chamber, and threw her self upon
the Bed, where she remained like one at the last
Gasp ; at last a Torrent of Tears seem'd to ease
her a little in her present Anguish ; she pretended
to be sick, the better to indulge her melancholy
Thoughts, and to avoid being seen : But in some
time after, she began to afflict her self afresh, beyond all measure, because she had not heard the
least News from *Hypolitus*. She writ to the Earl
of *Sussex*, to know whether he were come to
London, and whether her Father was arrived in
England ? He return'd her an Answer, intima-
ting, that they were very uneasie at *London*, at
their not coming, having heard no Tidings of either of them of late ; that my Lord *Douglas* being lately dead, *Hypolitus's* Presence was absolutely necessary there, to settle the Affairs of his
Family. Nothing being more natural, than to
take things as we are apt to conceive them to our
selves, the Unfortunate *Julia* would not be perswaded, but that her Lover was lost at Sea : At
their parting, she imagined that nothing could be
able to encrease her Affliction ; but alas ! She
soon found to her cost, that she was not come, as
yet, to the depth of her Miseries ; and that she
her self was too too ingenious in causing to her
self new Afflictions ; for it was not long, before
she saw her self entangled in more Troubles
than ever.

One day my Lady Abbess coming to see her, happened to drop a Letter, out of Carelessness, in her
Chamber, which she had received that very Morning ; she was no sooner gone out of the Room,
but

but *Isabella* took it up, and gave it to *Julia*; she soon knew it to be the Earl of *Bedford*'s Hand, she opened it trembling, and found in it these Words.

I am obliged, for very urgent Reasons, to leave London *immediately, in order to remove* Julia*; and to put her into a Place, where she may be more secure and private than with you. I have got notice that her Father will soon be at* London*, and that he has got Intelligence of her being at* St. Menoux. *However, Madam, I shall keep the Obligations I owe you, in constant remembrance; and be ready to return them, as I ought to do. I am, Madam, with all possible Respect and Acknowledgment, at your Devotion.*

The Fair *Julia* was quite distracted with Thoughts, at the sight of this Letter; however, after having paused upon it for some time, she judged she ought not to stay any longer in a place where she was likely to be exposed afresh to the violent Treatment of her Husband. Pursuant to this Resolution, she desired *Cardini*, by *Isabella*, to come into her Chamber, under some Pretence or other, which he did; she desired him to go to *Moulins*, to sell some of her Jewels, to buy with some of the Money, a Coach and Horses; charging him to keep the Business secret, and to bring her an ordinary Habit, the better to disguise her self in her Flight, and some Saddle-horses, where-with she intended, in the Night time, to go to *Moulins*. The chief difficulty was, how to get out; but her Chamber looking into the Garden, it was agreed, she was to descend out of the Window, by the help of a Ladder made with Cords, which *Cardini* promis'd to procure her;

and

and as good Fortune would have it, part of the
Wall of the Garden being, a few days before,
tumbled down, they did not queſtion but ſhe might
eaſily get out that way.

Every thing ſucceeded without much difficulty,
juſt as they had laid the deſign betwixt them; for
Cardini having full Liberty to go in and come out
of the Abby, as he pleaſed, he diſcharged his
Truſt with the utmoſt Zeal and Fidelity, and
ſafely conducted her in the Night, with *Iſabella*,
to *Moulins*. *Julia* made no ſtay there, ſhe pre-
ſented the Picture-drawer with a rich Jewel, and
enjoyn'd him to go to *London*, to tell the Earl of
Warwick and *Hypolitus* what had obliged her to
make her Eſcape with ſo much Precipitation;
that ſhe was going to *Florence* to her Siſter *Lucilia*, where ſhe deſired they ſhould let her hear
from them. She did not think fit to commit all
theſe things to a Letter, for fear it ſhould be loſt,
or that by ſome miſchance or other, it might fall
into my Lord *Bedford*'s Hands; for ſhe ſuſpected
he had intercepted ſome of her or *Hypolitus*'s Letters; and that this had occaſioned the Rumour of
her being at St. *Menoux*.

Whilſt ſhe was making the beſt of her way towards *Italy*, ſhe took all poſſible Precautions to
remain *incognito*, and to avoid the ſight of all ſuch
as, prompted by their Curioſity, might be inqui-
ſitive after her Perſon; (for being ſo extreamly
Beautiful, ſhe uſed to meet with as many Ado-
rers as ſhe met with Perſons that ſaw her) but
Cardini having conducted her ſome part of the
way beyond *Moulins*, return'd ſtrait to St. *Menoux*, leaſt he ſhould be ſuſpected of having had
a Hand in *Julia*'s Eſcape. He went to his ordinary Employment, expecting every moment to
hear what noiſe this unexpected Accident would
make

make in the Abbey. It was already pretty late in the Morning, when one of the Religious Ladies belonging to this Abbey, came to tell the Abbefs, that the Door of *Julia*'s Apartment, was not o-pened yet ; that fhe had call'd feveral times *Ifabella*, but that neither the Miftrefs, nor the Woman, had return'd any anfwer to her; and that fhe was afraid there was fomething more than ordinary in the matter. The Abbefs not a little furprized and difturbed at what fhe heard, immediately order'd the Door to be broke open ; but coming into *Julia*'s Chamber, and finding fhe had made her Efcape out of the Window, fhe was almoft diftracted what to do ; fhe fent fome in queft after *Julia*, ordering them to take the Road to *Paris*, not queftioning but that this was the place fhe would have recourfe to ; fhe knew not whom to charge with being acceffory to her Flight, till at laft thinking it could be no Body but the Picture-drawer, fhe had him feiz'd ; they fearch'd him, and put him into a Dungeon, but all in vain, they could not make him tell one word that might tend to the Prejudice of *Julia*. 'The Earl of *Bed-* ' *ford* is expected here every day, *faid the Lady* ' *Abbefs to her Confidents*, he will ask me, what ' is become of his Lady ? What muft I tell him ? ' How will he exclaim againft my Neglect ? ' And not without reafon, fince I have been fo ' carelefs in keeping what he committed to my ' care. She was thus tormenting her felf, when one of her Confidents put her in the Head of an Expedient, which would, at leaft, put a ftop to the Earl's coming, and fecure her againft his Re-proaches, for fome time. ' If you will follow ' my advice, Madam, *faid fhe to her*, I would ' have you write to him immediately, that *Julia* ' being fe'zed with a moft violent Diftemper, ly'd

P   *within*

' within a few days after; that you not only
' took all poffible care of her in her Illnefs, but
' alfo provided for her Funeral Obfequies accord-
' ing to her Quality; that fhe had given all her
' Jewels to her Waiting-Woman, and that there-
' fore you had nothing you could fend to him, of
' what fhe had brought along with her to the Ab-
' by. This Contrivance was very well relifh'd by
the Abbefs, who reflected not much upon the
Confequences thereof; fhe being a Woman of
very good Quality, but Miftrefs of no great fhare
of Senfe, being ruled, in moft things, by this
young Religious Woman, who gave her this Advice. So fhe writ a Letter, the fubftance whereof was according to what they had agreed upon;
but poor *Cardini* was never the better for it; they
kept him a great while fo clofe a Prifoner, that
he had not the leaft opportunity either of juftify-
ing himfelf, or of writing to any Body, to let
them know what a Condition he was in. *Julia*
had the good fortune to get to *Florence*, without
any finifter Accident, but judging it abfolutely
requifite, not to go to *Lucilia*'s Houfe, before fhe
had feen her, and taken fuch meafures with her,
as they fhould think moft fuitable to her prefent
Circumftances, fhe fent a Letter to her, by *Ifabella*. 'Tis impoffible to exprefs the fatisfaction
of *Lucilia*, when fhe underftood that her Sifter
was fo near her, fhe had not patience to ftay one
moment, but immediately went to fee her: They
imbraced one another a thoufand times, they told
one another every thing that can be faid or
thought the moft tender and obliging; and at laft
agreed, *Julia* fhould go for a young Widow, and
a Kinfwoman of *Lucilia*'s, who was to ftay with
her fome time; fhe was to go by the Name of
                                        Howard,

Howard, which being one of the beſt and moſt numerous Families in *England*, it would be a hard matter to find her out by that Name. She got a Mourning Dreſs, ſuch as Widows wear immediately after their Husband's Deceaſe, and ſhe made the Exceſs of her Love, a pretence for her Journey into *Italy*, not being able to ſtay in a place where ſhe had loſt what was ſo dear to her.

But what was the oddeſt Chance of all in this Adventure, was, that at the ſame time ſhe was in Mourning for her pretended deceaſed Husband, he wore his Mourning Apparel for her. The Abbeſs of St. *Menoux*'s Letter came time enough to my Lord *Bedford*'s Hands to ſtop his Journey for that time : He was at firſt much concern'd at the loſs of a Wife, whom once he loved ſo paſſionately ; but her Abſence for ſome time, the cauſe of Complaint he thought he had againſt her, and his inconſtant Temper, ſoon made him forget *Julia*. Her Death was ſoon known all over *London* ; the Counteſs of *Douglas*, and the Earl of *Suſſex*, were moſt ſenſibly afflicted thereat ; and the Earl of *Warwick*, who came into *England* not long after they received this ſad News, was no leſs grieved thereat, than if he had been fully acquainted with all his Daughters Merits, Vertues and Beauty. ' Am I not to be pity'd, *would he* ' *ſay to his Friends*, after ſo long and rigorous a ' Captivity, I have been forced to undergo, after ' ſo long an Abſence from my Native Country, to ' return thither on purpoſe, as it were, to be in- ' form'd of my Daughter's Death ; the only one ' I had in the World, of whom I have heard ſo ' much ſpoken to her Advantage, whom I loved ' ſo tenderly, both for her Mother's and her own ' ſake, whom I had promiſed as a Reward to that ' very Perſon, I owe the higheſt Obligations to

' in

' in the World, and who is ready to die for
' Grief, on account of the ill Treatment she re-
' ceives at her Husband's Hands.

The Earl of *Bedford* sent to desire him to let
him have the Honour of paying him a Visit, but
he would not admit of it, because he retain'd a
very violent Resentment against a Person whom
he look'd upon as the Author of his Daughter's
Misfortune. Thus Matters went in *London* when
Hypolitus arrived there, being stop'd by the way
by an unfortunate Accident : For riding Post from
Paris to *Calais*, he fell with his Horse, and endeavouring to disengage himself out of the Stir-
rop, put his Foot out of Joynt, which proving
extreamly painful, he had much ado to get, by
the assistance of his *Valet de Chambre*, (because he
had sent his other Servants by another way for
England) into the neighbouring Village to
have it put into its right place again; but the
Country Surgeon, proving an ignorant Fellow,
made it rather worse than better ; and the violence of the pain throwing him into a most violent Fever, he was forced to tarry two Months,
before he could continue his Journey.

All this while he did not think it expedient to
write to *Julia*, for fear of affording her fresh
Matter of Grief, tho' what he did for her Repose,
served only to encrease her Inquietudes; his silence almost reduced her to despair ; but alas! it
was now his turn to pay dearly for what he had
made her suffer on that account; for he no sooner
came to *London*, but was inform'd, at the same
time, both of his Father's and his Mistress's
Death. He could not, in the least, call in question the Loss of his *Julia*; my Lady *Douglas*
had got the Abbess of St. *Menoux*'s Letter, which
she sent to her Son, in hopes this might cure him

of

of a Paſſion, which hitherto had cauſed all the
Misfortunes of his Life, at the Expence of all his
Tranquillity, and prevented him from making his
Fortune in the World.

Hypolitus had been long enough at St. *Menoux*, to be well acquainted with the Abbeſs's
Hand-writing; ſo that at the ſight thereof, he
could not doubt any longer of the Death of his
Miſtreſs, and conſequently extinguiſh'd that very
ſpark of hopes that remain'd hitherto in his
Heart. Where ſhall I ſearch for Words capable
to repreſent to you the deſpair the moſt Amorous and moſt Faithful of all Lovers was reduced
to? All that had been ſaid hitherto concerning a
thouſand Accidents of his Life, and his ſucceed-
ing Pains and Grief; the Marriage, the carrying
away, the Abſence of *Julia*; all theſe, I ſay,
bore not the leaſt compariſon to what he felt at
this moſt deplorable Conjuncture ; he would ſee
no Body, nor ſpeak to any Body, but to the Earl
of *Warwick*, and the Earl of *Suſſex*, and they
were forced to have recourſe to my Lady *Douglas*'s Aſſiſtance ; who by her Authority, and moſt
preſſing Inſtances, prevail'd upon him to take
ſome Nouriſhment ; he was ſo far from taking
any reſt, that he ſcarce ever would go to Bed,
and on a ſudden fell into ſuch a Languiſhment,
that every Body thought he would never have o-
vercome it.

One day he communicated to the Earl of *Suſſex* his Reſolution of fighting the Earl of *Bedford* ; this being the only thing which ſeem'd both
to ſupport his Courage and his Life. He deſired
him, to go to the Earl of *Bedford*, and to engage
him to appoint a certain Time and Place where
they might be at liberty once more to meaſure
their Swords, and to put an end to a Quarrel

P 3 which

which could not be decided but with the Lofs of
the Life of one of the two. The Earl did all he
could to put *Hypolitus* in mind, that he ought not
to hazard his Perfon thus, at a time when he was
fcarce in a condition to ftand upright; he told
him again, he was fufficiently fenfible what he
was capable of doing, and that Defpair would
furnifh him with as much ftrength as he fhould
have occafion for; that let things come to the
worft, he could but fall in the Combat, and that
that was not the thing that would frighten him;
and he urged the matter fo home, and with fo much
earneftnefs to the Earl of *Suffex*, that feeing no
means to refufe any longer his Requeft, he went
to the Earl of *Bedford's* : When he faw him, he
found him under no fmall irrefolution, what Anfwer he had beft to give him. It was not very
long fince he was well cured of his Wounds *Hypolitus* gave him at *Calais*; he had made tryal of
his Courage, and knew what violent Motives
induced him to Challenge him. He told the Earl,
that their Majefties had forbid all manner of Du-
els, that he was ready to give him any Satisfaction; but that to make the thing appear in the
Eyes of the World like an accidental Quarrel, he
would decide their Quarrel the firft time *Hypolitus*
and he fhould meet.

No fooner was the Earl of *Suffex* gone to carry
his Anfwer to *Hypolitus*, but the Earl of *Bedford*
got every thing in readinefs, and left *England* under pretence, that he had a mind to go abroad to
Travel. *Hypolitus* did all he could to find him
out, but found too late, that he was gone, to his
infinite diffatisfaction, becaufe he had flatter'd
himfelf with hopes of facrificing him to the Memory of his adorable *Julia*. After this Difappointment, feeing himfelf in a place, where every
thing

thing feem'd to confpire to revive in him his deadly Grief, by recalling to his Mind the remembrance of his fo dearly beloved Miftrefs, he refolved to leave *England*, and to carry his Fortunes
along with him to fome Place or other, where he
hoped he might put an end to them by a Glorious
Death.

The Earl of *Warwick* feeing him abfolutely
refolved to leave his Native Country, offer'd to
take him along with him to *Maltha*, whether he
intended to go along with the *Grand Confervator*
of *Montferrat*, who was not long before come
into *England*; and who, at the interceffion of Cardinal *Pool*, had obtained from her Majefty the
reftitution of all the Revenues belonging to the
Malthefe Knights. *Hypolitus* was very glad to
accept of this Opportunity of fignalizing himfelf,
and to run the fame Fortune with a Man, whom
he loved like his Father, and honoured with a
moft peculiar efteem for his great Qualifications.

The Earl of *Suffex* was alfo inclined to make
this Campaign with them, having fome particular
Reafons to keep for fome time at a diftance from
Court, becaufe the Queen would not hearken to
his Petition, and of feveral other Lords, who earneftly follicited, that the Countefs of *Northampton* might be received again into Favour ; but the
Queen continued to fhew her hatred to the very
Memory of her Unfortunate Spoufe, in the Perfon of this Fair Widow ; and being not ignorant
that the Earl of *Suffex* loved her moft infinitely,
and was very defirous to Marry her, fhe made it
her Bufinefs to crofs this Match ; and told the
Earl, fhe fhould be very well pleafed to fee him
Marry'd to the Daughter of the Vifcount *Monta-
gue*, whom fhe had fent her Ambaffador along with

the

the Bishop of *Ely* to *Rome*. This Lord being upon his Departure, had recommended his Daughter to the Queen, desiring she would see her well Marry'd; and the Queen, who had a great kindness for her, and knew both the Merits, Birth and Estate of the Earl of *Suffex*, thought she could not bestow her better than there; but he resolving not to sacrifice his Passion to his Fortune, chose rather to absent himself for some time, till the Queen might alter her Sentiments, being very well pleasfed to take this opportunity to enter into a stricter Tye of Friendship with him who was his intimate Friend before, and either to acquire Glory, or die together; so they prepared every thing for their Voyage.

Hypolitus was unwilling the Countess of *Douglas* should know any thing of his intended Voyage, being sensible, that the Tenderness of a Mother, would not very well agree with such a design; and that it might prove the occasion of new Vexation to him, not to comply with her Desires; so he kept every thing private, which he might easily do, having his whole Estate in his own Hands. He left *England* in Company of the Earl of *Warwick*, and the Earl of *Suffex*, without letting any Body know whither they intended to go, and *Hypolitus* was reduced to so Languishing and Unfortunate a State, that wherever he went, he expected nothing else but to lead a most deplorable Life. Upon their arrival at *Maltha*, they found things in no small Confusion there, because by a late most dreadful Tempest, some Gailleys, besides several other Ships, were cast away in the Harbour: an Accident which would have moved the greatest Stranger to Compassion, considering the great number of Knights, of other Persons of Note, and of Slaves that lost their Lives upon this Occasion ; however a good number of *Mal-thefe*, whom they call *Bonnevoglies*, becaufe they ferve for very flender Pay at the Oars, offered their Service upon this neceffitous Occafion. Not long after *Francis* of *Lorain*, Grand Prior of *Mal-tha*, came thither with two moft magnificent Gallies, curioufly painted and gilt. This Prince made an appearance, in all refpects, futable to his Illuftrious Extraction, he was (as indeed all the reft of the Houfe of *Lorain* are) very Liberal, ex-treamly Handfom, Gallant, Brave and Magnifi-cent. General *Valette*, upon his Arrival there, refign'd his Command to this Prince; and the Earls of *Warwick* and *Suffex*, and *Hypolitus* meet-ing with a very Friendly Reception from the Great Mafter, he prefented them to the Prince of *Lo-rain*, unto whom they offered their Services, and were received by him aboard the *Capitana*, or Admiral Galley, with all the Marks of diftincti-on they could expect from their Merits, and the Goodnefs of fo difcerning a Prince. He had three Gallies, befides his own, under his Com-mand ; they fail'd to the Coaft of *Barbary*, in queft of *Dragut Rais*; but they met and took a Brigantine of *Tripoli*, commanded by one *Affan Baby*, who informed them, that *Dragut Rais* did not intend to put to Sea this Year, becaufe he was bufied in the Siege of *Tripoli*; upon this News they faw themfelves obliged to alter their Courfe, and to feek for further Opportunities of fignali-zing themfelves elfewhere, which they did ac-cordingly, and thefe three Brave *Englifh* Lords, fhew'd fo much Courage and Conduct in all their Actions, that the Prince being extreamly taken with their Perfons, beftow'd upon them fuch Employments as were worthy their acceptance; and in which they met with frequent Opportuni-ties

ties of expofing their Perfons; which they did upon all Occafions that offer'd, efpecially *Hypolitus,* who at all times was the foremoft, if any dangerous Attempt was to be made; but whilft they are endeavouring to Sacrifice their Lives, let us fee how Matters went in other Places.

The Abbefs of St *Menoux,* perceiving by the Earl of *Bedford's* Anfwer to her laft Letter, that he actually believed his Lady to be dead, and had laid afide his Journey into *France,* thought beft not to keep the Picture-drawer any longer in Prifon, his Imprifonment being fo far from having made him to confefs any thing relating to *Julia's* Efcape, that they found him every day more and more obftinate. His Refolution proved the Occafion of his Liberty; and he had no fooner obtained it, but remembring his Promife made to *Julia,* to go into *England,* he undertook that Journey without delay. Coming to *London,* he made Enquiry after *Hypolitus,* and the Earls of *Warwick* and *Suffex*; but was told, they had not appear'd at Court for fome time paft; and notwithftanding all his Endeavours to find them out, he could not fo much as learn where they were. He then enquired after the Earl of *Bedford*; and was inform'd, that fince *Julia's* Death, he led a very retired Life. *Cardini* was moft fenfibly afflicted at the Death of fo Handfome and Generous a Lady, he imagin'd no otherwife, than that fhe dy'd in her way to *Italy,* overwhelm'd with Grief, and overburthened with the Fatigues of fo long a Journey; fo that finding he could do no further Service at *London,* he went back to *Paris.* Poor *Julia,* at the fame time, lingred in expectation of fome Letters, with the utmoft impatience, without the leaft probability of receiving any; becaufe all thofe, from whom fhe might expect
them

them with any probability, thought her to be before that time in the other World, and never
thought of her, except when they bewailed her
Death.

She lived with her dear *Lucilia*, and pass'd
for a young handsome Widow, who had resolved
to lead a retired Life, without much Conversation in the World; and to speak the Truth, had it
been in her own Choice, she would never have
stirr'd out of her Room, and conversed with no
Body but *Lucilia*. The Inquietudes she laboured
under, as well for her Father, as for her dear
Hypolitus, produced in her Eyes a certain Lan-
guishment, which encreased her Charms. ' Ma-
' dam, *said the Senator* Alberti *to her*, will you
' be always bewailing the Dead? And at the same
' time will you shew no Compassion for those
' you make to die for you? He seconded these
Words, with so passionate an Air and Look, that
she fix'd her Eyes on the Ground to avoid the sight
of him. ' My Lord, *said she in a very Melan-*
' *choly Tone*, I wish you would leave me to the
' Enjoyment of my Troubles, for I take a sort of
' Pleasure in afflicting my self: and in effect, the
Senator's Amorous Addresses furnished her with
fresh matter of Vexation.

He was not so far advanced in Age, as not to
be capable of an Amorous Passion; he had been a
very handsome and gallant Gentleman; he was a
Man resolute and positive in his Opinion, and had
more than once been inclined to Marry again, but
that loving his Son dearly, and knowing he could
not do it, without its proving prejudicial to him,
that consideration had made him not to pursue
that design; but *Julia* appeared to his Eyes so
Handsome, a Lady of so much Sense and Discretion, that from the first Minute he saw her, he

fell

fell moſt paſſionately in Love with her. His Addreſſes were extreamly troubleſome to her, which
made her ſometimes take a Reſolution to treat
him ſo ſcurvily, as to cure his eagerneſs of making his Addreſſes to her : For this purpoſe, ſhe
would ſometimes ridicule thoſe of an advanced
Age, who had Vanity enough to imagine themſelves ſufficiently capable of making a young Woman fall in Love with them: 'What can they
' pretend to, *ſaid ſhe*, but either to meet with a
' Refuſal from a Woman of Honour, or to be
' Jilted by thoſe who are of a contrary Stamp?
' For my part, I muſt own, that were I capable
' of receiving an Amorous Impreſſion, there muſt
' be ſomething of Surprize in the caſe, my Eyes
' muſt be dazled, my Fancy muſt be enchanted
' to ſuch a degree, that my Heart muſt be muti-
' nous againſt my ſelf; and that before I could
' have leiſure ſufficient to reflect ſeriouſly upon
' the matter : Theſe are things which don't be-
' long to thoſe that are in their Decay, and the
' Impreſſions they give, are too weak to turn to
' any conſiderable account to them : 'Tis there-
' fore my Opinion, they can't expect, with reaſon,
' to be belov'd, unleſs it be after a long Acquain-
' tance, and a perfect knowledge of their Me-
' rits : And, after all, I can't conceive how Peo-
' ple ſhould, in cool Blood, expoſe themſelves to
' the greateſt of Dangers for ſuch a like Love to
' be. If we will but never ſo little give ear to
' Reaſon, what monſtrous things does not ſhe ſet
' before our Eyes ? So that it is a kind of Chi-
' mera for a Man who is paſs'd his youthful days,
' to think himſelf capable of raiſing a Paſſion in
' a Woman, who is ſcarce well arrived to an Age
' of Maturity ; but what is much more inſup-
' portable, is when an Old Woman pretends to
' inſpire

' infpire Love Paffion into a young Man ; fhe
' then goes beyond her own Element ; Love,
' which is a wanton Child, loves Pleafures and
' Enjoyments, and a Woman muft be Miftrefs of
' a great fhare of a pleafing and engaging Wit ;
' who, without making her felf ridiculous, can
' pretend, in an advanced Age, to attain to the
' true Character of Love.   An Old Woman who
' laughs heartily in hopes to render her Conver-
' fation more pleafing and agreeable, fhews moft
' commonly a Set of Teeth enough to frighten
' any Body ; nay, fometimes fhe has none at all
' to fhew : and it happens fometimes with a
' doating old Lover, that by a mifchance his Pe-
' ruke drops off, he fhews his Bald Scull, and fo
' loofes all the advantage he had got before by
' his fair and long Wig.   The Senator hearkened
to her Difcourfe with the utmoft Impatience :
' You have fuch an Averfion, *faid he to her*, for
' every thing that has not as much Youth and
' Beauty as your felf, that it is very probable you
' will never be in Love.   Oh ! How is it poffible
' for a Man to hope to pleafe you upon fuch hard
' Terms, efpecially in reference to Beauty ?   But
' Madam, will you give me leave to tell you,
' thefe unhappy Men, in whofe Cafe you make
' your felf both a Party and a Judge, knowing
' how to make their Choice with the moft Dif-
' cretion, are confequently more Refpectful, more
' Conftant, more Difcreet, and more devoted to
' that Object they love?   After having felt the
' Effects of a thoufand trifling Engagements, they
' found unworthy to challenge a place in their
' Hearts, they at this Age make their Choice for
' good and all ; what fatisfaction is there in lo-
' ving and being beloved, if the Flame is of no
' longer continuance than your Wild fires or Me-
' teors,

' teors, which make a great fhew, but never hold,
' and are no fooner feen, but loft again. Thus
they entertain'd one another ; and in fpite of *Julia's* harfh Expreffions (without, however, apply-
ing them to him in particular) in fpite of his Defpair, caufed by her Indifferency, and his fecret
Refentment, it was not in his Power to pull out
of his Heart that fatal Dart that had wounded
him.

Julia, at firft, forefaw not all the danger that
was likely to attend it, and when fhe perceived
it, and would fain have ftop'd the Progrefs of a
Paffion, fhe had given Birth to, fhe found it was
too late, and it was not till then fhe began to be
fenfible of all the danger fhe was likely to be ex-
fed to ; for the Senator, quite tranfported with
his violent Paffion, declared to her, That unlefs
fhe would confent to Marry him, he was refolved and muft die : She did all that lay in her
Power, to reprefent to him the Prejudice fuch a
Marriage would do to *Leander,* what reafons fhe
had to refufe a Match, which muft prove ruin-
ous to her Kinfwoman, and the beft Friend fhe
had ; and that fhe was fully refolved not to change
her Condition as long as fhe lived ; all whatever
fhe could fay, ferved only to afflict, but not to
convince him. He told her at laft, fhe might do
as fhe pleafed, but that he was refolved to difin-
herit his Son ; becaufe it was the Confideration of
his Intereft, that prov'd the Obftacle of his Happinefs ; he back'd his Words with fuch heavy
Threats, and fuch other Extravagancies, as fufficiently fhew'd, that his Paffion was arrived to
the higheft Pitch, and that being unable to keep
himfelf within his due Bounds, *Julia* ought to
fear every thing at his Hands.

He

He was no fooner gone, but fhe went into *Lu-cilia*'s Chamber, her fair Cheeks bathed all over with Tears : 'Oh! dear Sifter, *faid fhe to her,*
' you are not acquainted with all my Misfortunes
' yet. Your Father-in-Law puts me fo clofe to it,
' that I am ready to run diftrafted at it. You
' know you and I ufed now and then to laugh at
' his Paffion ; but, alas! 'Tis no jefting matter,
' he has conceived a Paffion, which, I fear, will
' oblige me to leave you. He would have me
' Marry him ; nay, he pofitively fays, he will ;
' and fpeaks of it to me, with as much Boldnefs
' as a Tyrant would to his Slave. He knows what
' Authority he has here, and I am afraid, I fhall
' be obliged to go from hence, rather than put his
' Violent Temper to a further Tryal. Now judge
' of my Trouble ; I have had not the leaft News
' neither from my Father, nor from *Hypolitus,*
' thefe fourteen Months, fince I have fhelter'd
' my felf here with you ; all that I have been
' able to learn hitherto, amounts only to this ;
' That neither my Father, nor your Brother, are
' at *London* : But, Great God! where can they
' be ! Is it poffible, that after what Intelligence I
' fent them from St. *Menoux* by *Cardini*, I fhould
' be abandon'd by both of them at once? What
' ought I not to fear for them? What ought I
' not to fear from my Husband ? And what
' ought I not to fear at prefent from the Senator?
At thefe Words fhe found her felf fo far opprefs'd
with Grief, that fhe was forced to ftop. ' Don't,
' my dear *Julia*, *faid* Lucilia *to her*, don't give
' way to your Afflictions, beyond what you ought
' to do ; your Misfortunes are, thanks to Hea-
' ven, not paft all Remedy ; I am fatisfy'd, it
' was for weighty Reafons, and fuch as we are
' not able to conceive yet, that the Earl of *War-*
'   *wick,*

‘ *wick* and my Brother left *London*. My Mother,
‘ who is unacquainted, perhaps, with the whole
‘ Matter as yet, will, doubtlefs, find it out,
‘ and give us Advice of it before long: Nay, I
‘ dare almoft be confident, they will come hither
‘ to confummate your Deliverance. As to what
‘ concerns your Spoufe, you need not ftand in fear
‘ of him, as long as you are with me, and for him
‘ who is fo importunate to be your Husband, he
‘ muft be acquainted with what invincible Ob-
‘ ftacles lie in the way, by that means you will
‘ put a ftop to the Carreer of his Paffion. You
‘ are under a miftake, Sifter, *faid* Julia *interrupt-*
‘ *ing her*, the Senator will certainly give not the
‘ leaft Credit to what we can fay upon that Head;
‘ every thing that comes from us, will be fufpect-
‘ ed by him of Falfhood, and be look'd upon as a
‘ cunning Contrivance of ours, to difappoint him
‘ in his Defign ; fo that I am fure, that the re-
‘ vealing of this Secret, which perhaps might
‘ prove a means to be difcovered to the Earl of
‘ *Bedford*, would prove of no effect in refpect of
‘ your Father-in-Law. The beft way to avoid his
‘ Importunities, feems to me to be, to feek for
‘ fhelter for fome time in a Nunnery, and that
‘ with fo much Privacy, that he may not know
‘ whither I am gone.

    This Expedient feeming the beft and eafieft to
Lucilia, they went immediately to a Nunnery,
where fhe had a great Intereft ; but the Amorous
Senator, who dreaded the lofs of his Miftrefs,
and who guefs'd by what fhe had told him, that
fhe might eafily take fuch Meafures as were not
agreeable to his Intentions, failed not to keep a
watchful Eye over all her Actions, and thofe of
Lucilia, and for that purpofe, had, by Prefents,
gain'd one of her Waiting-Women, whom fhe
not

not in the leaft miftrufted, fo that he had immediate notice given him of *Julia*'s defign to retire
within a few days to a Nunnery.

He thought he fhould have been ftruck dead
upon the Spot at this piece of News; he was convinced, by the Refolution fhe had taken, that fhe
had a great Averfion to him, and endeavoured
with all his might, to vanquifh a Paffion which
muft needs put him to unfpeakable Torments;
but in vain did he call his Reafon, his Courage,
nay, even his Refentment to his aid; they ftood
him in no ftead, againft the Tyrannick Power of
the moft cruel and moft violent Paffion that ever
was known : The very Thoughts of lofing *Julia*,
rekindled thofe Flames he intended to extinguifh,
and rekindled them with fo much Violence, that
he refolved to have recourfe to all the moft violent Remedies, fince neither his Conftancy, nor
his fubmiffive Addreffes, had been able to
gain any thing upon her to his Advantage; and
his eagernefs foon furnifh'd him with means to
put it in execution.

Julia's Lodging-Room being below Stairs,
look'd into the Garden, and had a double Glafs-
Door, facing the middle Walk; *Ifabella* ufed to
lie in a large Clofet within her Room, but was
then abfent, being detain'd, on purpofe, by the
fame Woman of *Lucilia*'s, who betray'd all their
Secrets; for *Ifabella* knowing that her Lady loved not to go to Bed, till it was very late, was
not fo forward to be with her at that time. The
Door that look'd into the Garden being fet open
on purpofe to let in the frefh and cool Air, *Julia* fat down to write to her *Hypolitus*; for tho'
fhe knew not whither to fend it, fhe fcarce ever
mifs'd a day without writing one for him; intending to fend them all in one Packet, fo foon as fhe

Q   fhould

ſhould know how to direct to him. She was writing the following Words.

> *At thoſe ſilent Hours, when all the World ſeeks*
> *for reſt, I break mine, my dear* Hypolitus, *to eaſe*
> *my ſelf in telling you my Pains. Alas! they are*
> *exceſſive, and touch me to the Heart. I cannot*
> *learn the leaſt News of you; I know not what is*
> *become of you; and, tho' I can't think your heart*
> *capable of Inconſtancy, I am ſenſible the aſſuran-*
> *ces thou haſt given me of thy Fidelity, are abſo-*
> *lutely neceſſary for the Preſervation of my Life! I*
> *would not take care of this Life, no longer than I*
> *have it to tender to you; this being the only thing*
> *that makes it ſupportable to me; and ſince the Se-*
> *nator* Alberti *has declared his Paſſion to me, I*
>   . . . . .

Here ſhe was ſurprized to ſee come into the
Door, three Men in Masks, who taking her in
their Arms, while a fourth more carefully diſgui-
ſed than all the reſt, ſtopt her Voice, by putting
a Handkerchief into her Mouth, carry'd her away,
in ſpite of all the reſiſtance ſhe was able to make;
they croſs'd the Garden with all imaginable expedition, and it being late and very dark, no Body
in the Houſe perceived any thing of it; *Julia* being put into the Coach, they carry'd her out of
the *Gate of the Croſs*, making the beſt of their
way towards *Siena*; they thought fit to take their
Road thro' the Mountains, which being very
troubleſome and uneven in many Places, the Axel-
tree of the Coach happened to break: The
Nights being very ſhort in the Summer in *Italy*,
Day began to appear, when one of thoſe that
were along with *Julia*, and who ſeem'd to have
an Authority over the reſt, ſeeing the Coach broke
                                                    in

in pieces, ordered them to put her before him, he being on Horseback; she struggled, and kept them off with more Courage and Strength, than could be expected from one of our Sex; ' no, *said she,* ' Barbarous Wretch, thou shalt not make me stir ' from this place, as long as I am alive: Thou ' hast violated the Law of Hospitality. I sought ' for shelter in thy House, as in a Sanctuary; ' and after all this, thou carriest me away by force, ' and art my Persecutor. She had scarce finish'd these Words, pulling away, all this while, her Arms, and struggling with those that were for setting her upon the Horse; and the Respect they bore her, together with her extraordinary Beauty, which scarce any Body living was able to with-stand, inclined them not to use her too roughly, or to make use of all their strength to force her upon the Horse; when they saw eight Men well mounted and arm'd coming in a full Gallop to-wards them; and the first she cast her Eyes upon, was the Senator *Alberti*; they advanced with their Pistols ready cock'd, which was a sufficient warning to those that had carried away *Julia*, to think of standing upon their own defence.

Whilst they were engaged, she took the oppor-tunity of making her Escape; and following a By-Path that led her down from the Mountain into a Vale, she walk'd a good pace, and, as you may imagine, not without a great deal of pain; and even after she was got so far off, as not to hear the noise of their Pistols, and had all the reason to believe, they had now other Work upon their Hands, than to seek after her, yet she was under continual Apprehensions, least some one or other of them might follow and overtake her: ' I must ' fear every thing, *said she to her self,* as well from those that came to my relief, as from those ' that

Q 2

' that carry'd me away ; But who could thefe be ?
' I verily believed it had been the Senator, where-
' as it was he that came to refcue me, and gave
' me this opportunity of making my Efcape. She
had no other Companions, but thefe difmal Reflections, whilft her tender Body being quite tired
out with the Fatigues of the rough and almoft un-
paffable ways, fhe had almoft fpent her Breath;
and as the leaft noife fhe heard, put her into fuch
a Confternation, that without the leaft regard to
her felf fhe ran among the neareft Bufhes and
Bryars, to hide her felf; this poor Lady's Face
was all covered with Blood, her Hairs hung quite
loofe, her Cloaths were miferably torn ; to be
fhort, fhe was an Object worthy the Compaffion
of a Barbarian ; fo that now quite reduced to defpair, without being able to think what to do, fhe
caft her Eyes on all fides, and by good fortune
efpying in the Valley a Shepherd's Hut, fhe made
all the hafte fhe could thither.

In the Hut fhe found a Woman bufie at Work,
who feeing her in fo miferable a condition, ran
towards her, and received her with fuch marks of
Compaffion, as afforded fome Confolation to the
Fair *Julia*, under her prefent Circumftances. If
you will do me a piece of Service, which I will
keep in perpetual Remembrance, *faid fhe to this
good Woman*, find out as foon as poffibly you can,
a place where I may hide my felf, being fenfible
that it will not be long before they will be here,
to take me away by force. The Shepherdefs carry'd her up, without lofing one Minute, into an
old Granary, where they had laid up Provifions
for their Houfe ; and having fhew'd her a dark
hole, where no Body could poffibly find her out,
fhe went down to Work again. Soon after, two
Horfemen came at full fpeed up to the Door of
her

her Hut, and ask'd her abundance of Queſtions concerning *Julia*, whom they deſcribed to her, and would needs tell her, they were ſure ſhe had ſeen her, threatning her, in caſe ſhe did not tell them what was become of her; but, the Shepherdeſs anſwered them with ſo much calmneſs, and an apparent ſimplicity, that they went their way.

So ſoon as they were gone, ſhe went into the Granary to comfort poor *Julia*, almoſt half dead with fear, becauſe ſhe had heard the Senator *Alberti*'s Voice: But being told by the Shepherdeſs, they were quite gone, ſhe gave her ſome Milk and Bread, waſh'd the Blood from off her Face, and attended her with a great deal of Zeal and Charity. *Julia* did not think fit to leave this little Sanctuary, but rather reſolved to tarry there for ſome days, being uncertain what courſe to take ; ſhe dreaded, not a little, the Senator ; but much more that unknown Enemy of hers, who kept his Mask on, even after they carry'd her off ; ſhe judged, not without good reaſon, that ſhe might much eaſier ſtand upon her Guard againſt one ſhe knew, and that ſuch a Misfortune as that, was much the leſſer, in compariſon of ſtanding in fear of all the World ; 'For, *ſaid ſhe* ' *her ſelf*, as long as I don't know the Perſon ' that uſed me with ſo much Violence, I ſhall al- ' ways be in fear of putting my ſelf undeſignedly ' in the Power of thoſe I ought to ſhun.

Theſe different Reflections cauſed ſuch a Confuſion in her Mind, as proved a great addition to her Troubles : The Shepherdeſs's Husband coming home at Night, *Julia* was obliged to give her Conſent to make him a Partaker in the Secret : He was an old Labourer, but of good Natural Parts, and ſoon gueſſing by the Beauty and Ap-

Q 3   parel

patel of his new Gueft, that fhe was a Perfon of
Quality, he was touch'd with Compaffion at her
Affliction. She ask'd him, whether he had feen
any Horfemen abroad ? He told her, he had feen
feveral pafs by, and fome Mask'd and wounded,
riding full fpeed ; that one of them rid, on purpofe, out of his way to ask him, Whether he
had not feen a young Lady all alone; and that
he told them, he had not; fo he went on with
the reft. *Julia* not queftioning but that they
would go in queft of her, had one of the worft
Nights of it that can well be imagined. By good
Chance fhe had her Purfe and fome Jewels about
her, being not as yet undrefs'd when they carry'd
her away ; fo fhe gave fome Money to her Hofts,
to engage them, for their own fakes, to keep her
fecret, and be ferviceable to her. She told them,
crying moft bitterly ; 'You fee what a condition I
' am in, I muft not ftay here, but look out for
' fome place of Security ; but pray advife me,
' what I had beft to do, to keep my felf from
' being known, for I am fo much overburthen'd
' with Grief, that I am not capable of taking any
' Refolution. I would advife you, Madam, *faid*
' *the Shepherdefs*, to put on my Cloaths, and
' under that Difguife, you may be long enough
' without being taken. She approved of her
Counfel, and willing to try what a Figure fhe
was likely to make under that Difguife, fhe dref-
fed her felf like a Shepherdefs, but appear'd fo
handfome, notwithftanding all the care fhe took
to conceal her Air and her Face, that both the Labourer and his Wife, were then of Opinion, that
it was impoffible, under that Drefs, to difguife
her Quality. At laft, after fome furrber confiderations, the good old Man advifed her to difguife her felf under a Man's Habit, and to pafs
for

for a Pilgrim ; for, being very tall, she might pass
for a young Man ; looking upon this as the most
sure and most feasible way, she desired him to go
to *Siena*, and to buy for her what was necessary
for that purpose, and he went accordingly. But
whilst our Shepherd is on his short Journey, let
us see how Matters were carry'd on at *Florence.*

That same Night *Julia* was carried away by
these unknown Persons, the Senator *Alberti* intended to have seized her by force, there by at
least to secure to himself her Person, since he found
it impossible to gain her Heart. *Isabella*, as I told
you before, had staid something longer than ordinary with one of *Lucilia's* Women ; but fearing
her Mistress might be ready to go to Bed, she
went to her Bed-chamber, at the very Minute after
she had been carry'd off ; she found her Veil torn
in pieces, her Table, Candles and Candlesticks
upon the Ground ; and not seeing her Mistress,
immediately suspected something of an ill Accident to have befaln her ; she set up most deplorable Outcries, which alarmed the whole House ;
but especially the Senator, who was then just preparing every thing to put his design in execution.
Coming into the Room, and not seeing *Julia*
there, he was ready to run distracted, not
questioning but that she was carried away ; and
all his Men appointed, for his before mentioned
purpose, being ready at hand, he went without
delay in pursuit of those that had carried her a-
way.

When they came to the *Gate of the Cross*, they
were informed by the Guards, that they had given them some Money to keep it open, under
Pretence, that a Coach with six Horses, was to go
out there that Night, to avoid travelling in the

Q 4   heat

heat of the Day. The Senator *Alberti*, accom-
pany'd by Signior *Leander*, who was got out of
Bed, and attended by thofe that were to be made
ufe of on the fame account, purfued and overtook
them; they fought and foon put them to flight,
being much more in number than they; their
Leader with his Followers made their Efcape
crofs the Mountains, except one, who being mortally wounded, was not likely to go far, nor live
long. *Leander* feeing him drop from his Horfe,
upon the Ground, pulled off his Mask, and did all
he could to make him give him fome infight into
this Adventure. But all he could get out of him
was, that he believed his Mafter being in Love
with *Julia*, had, for a confiderable time, been refolved to carry her away by force; but what had
made him haften to put his defign in execution,
was, that one of the Senator *Alberti*'s Servants,
whom he had debauched by Money to facilitate his
Entrance into the Houfe, had inform'd him, how
the Senator, his Mafter, intended to feize her by
force the felf fame Night. *Leander* ask'd him
the Name of his Mafter; unto which he returned
no Anfwer, but only told him, with a weak and
incoherent Voice; 'Sir, I am at the point of
' Death, pray leave me a few Moments to think
' of my Confcience; and fo he dy'd within a
Quarter of an Hour.

The Senator *Alberti*, upon his return to *Florence*, found himfelf reduced to fuch a degree of
Defpair, as cannot well be expreffed; at laft he
remembred that he had taken up a piece of Paper
not folded up, in *Julia*'s Room, which he thought
was written with her own Hand; he looked for
it and found it in his Pocket; and having perufed
it, was convinced, to his great grief, that fhe loved fome Body elfe, and that it was probable
this

this was the motive that induced her to receive
his Addreſſes with ſo much Scorn. 'I hoped at
' leaſt, *ſay'd be to himſelf*, that ſhe had an indiffe-
' rency for all the World ; and that conſequently
' my Caſe was not worſe than others ; but alas! I
' find my ſelf deceived! This deep melancholy
' that appeared in her Countenance and Actions,
' was occaſioned only by the Abſence of her Lover;
' and all the ſevere and ill Treatment I received
' at her Hands, were as many Sacrifices offered to
' him. He was ruminating a long while, who
this dear *Hypolitus* could be, he ſaw mentioned
in her Letter ; and recalling to his mind *Lucilia*'s
Brother, the ſame *Hypolitus* whom he knew to be
ſo Handſome, ſo full of Wit, made to love and
to be beloved, he began to fear leaſt he ſhould be
his Rival. ' How ought I to treat him, *ſaid he*,
' Good God ! Can't I, at this Age, have the Con-
' fidence to diſpute ſo Fair a Conqueſt with him?
Tranſported with theſe furious Reflections, without heſitating any longer upon the matter, into
Lucilia's Chamber he goes, and accoſting her ;
' Set my Heart at eaſe, dear Daughter, *ſaid he*,
' you have a Brother, whom I have ſeen here,
' pray tell me, Is it he that Loves the Fair *En-*
' *gliſh* Lady that was carry'd away ? I conjure
' you to tell me the Truth without the leaſt diſ-
' guiſe. *Lucilia* pauſed a while upon what Anſwer ſhe was to give him, which making the Senator ſuſpect ſome Myſtery in the thing, he
urged her ſo far home, that ſhe could not refuſe
any longer to give him the whole Relation of *Ju-*
lia's Affairs. He was ſo much ſurprized, as to
be almoſt inconſolable, for having importuned
her with his Paſſion ; 'You would have ſaved me
abundance of Trouble, ſaid he to *Lucilia*, had you
thought me ſooner worthy of being your Confident;

‘ fident ; you were acquainted with the beginning
‘ of my Paffion, as well as with the flender Pro-
‘ grefs I was likely to make, and at the fame time
‘ you have not ftop’d the Current of my Paffion,
‘ which you fee is now upon the point of fwal-
‘ lowing me up into an Abyfs of Mifery. He
loaded her with bitter and fharp Reproaches, and
left her abruptly, fo far overwhelm’d with Love,
Anger, Jealoufie and Pain, that he took his Bed
immediately, being feized with a burning Fever,
which in a few days time put an end to his Life,
being much regretted by his Son and all his
Friends.

Whilft they were bewailing the Senator's Death
at *Florence*, the Unfortunate *Julia*, now difguifed
under a Pilgrim’s Habit, having given a fufficient
Reward to her kind Hofts, and enjoyn’d them to
deliver a Letter to *Lucilia*, wherein fhe gave an
account of her intended Journey, left her Shepherd’s Hut, and took the Road towards *Bologna*,
with an intention to go from thence to *Rome*, and
fo further to *Venice*, in hopes to be fo happy as
to meet there with her Father, or at leaft, with
fome of his Friends; who, upon his account,
would afford her fome fhelter in a Convent, where
fhe might ftay till fhe could appear abroad without danger. All this while the four Horfemen in
Masks, who had feized and carry’d her off by
force, were conftantly in her Thoughts: After a
thoufand Reflections, fhe began to think it might
perhaps be the young Marquefs of *Strotzi* ; he
was defcended of one of the moft Illuftrious Houfes of *Florence*, his Father had fent him abroad a
Travelling, and upon his return, happening to
fee *Julia*, he was ftruck with an Admiration beyond what is commonly obferved in Men, when
they have only a general Inclination for a handfome

fome Woman. He was a Perfon of Merit, he was Brave and Daring; and *Julia* had heard certain Stories told of him, which had fome refemblance to her Adventure; befides, that being a *Florentine*, he needed not fo much fear the ill Confequences of carrying away a Stranger, who being out of her own Country, was not likely to have Friends e-nough there to revenge her Quarrel, So fhe con-cluded, it muft be the Marquefs of *Strotzi*, that was the Author of her prefent Calamities.

She appeared fo very Fair and Handfome, even in this Pilgrim's Habit, that fhe had enough to do to hid her Face from being taken notice of by eve-ry Body that faw her. She had cut her Hairs in the fame way as the Men wear them, hanging carelefly in Locks over her Shoulders, and not in the leaft changed by the heat of the Sun, no more than her Complexion. She made but flen-der days Journeys, becaufe her tender Feet were not able to bear long the Fatigues of a long one on Foot; fhe had already paffed the *Fierofola*, feated on the great Road of the *Appennin* Moun-tains, and was going on towards *Bologna*, when coming into a moft delicious Wood of Orange and Pomegranate Trees, when it was pretty near Sun-fet, much tired with that Days Work, fhe was invited, by the murmuring noife of a moft pleafant Brook, to take a little Reft upon the Green and Sweet-fcented Herbs that grew in great plenty near it; fo laying her Head upon the Root of a Tree, the Branches whereof ferved her in-ftead of an Umbrello, fhe took off her Broad Hat, and her Wearinefs made her infenfibly fall into a found Sleep; but it was not long before fhe was awakened with no fmall Surprize, and much more Pain; for fhe felt a Dart fticking in one of her Legs, and at the fame time heard the
noife

noife of the Horfes, Dogs and Hunters. She made a doleful Outcry, endeavouring at the fame time to pull the painful Dart out of the Wound, when fhe faw coming that way, three Ladies on Horfeback, fo Handfome, of fo goodly an Air, and fo gallantly and nicely drefs'd, that fhe feem'd not to be fenfible of her Pain, for fome time, whilft fhe had the Satisfaction of contemplating them. One among them had a Bow faftned to her Girdle, and a Quiver with Darts upon her Shoulders, fo that one would have taken her for *Diana* amongft her Nymphs. This Charming Lady feeing the Pilgrim's Wound, told him, fhe was much concern'd, and greatly difturbed at his Misfortune, it being, queftionlefs, her that gave it, becaufe fhe knew the Dart. 'What Fatality 'brought you in my way, juft when I only in- ' tended to divert my felf and thefe Ladies, in ' fhewing of them my Dexterity? Certainly we ' are both very unfortunate Perfons; you to feat ' your felf in this Place, and I to wound you thus ' by meer chance. Your Compaffion, Madam, ' *faid* Julia *with a Languifhing Air,* is fufficient ' to allay my trouble on account of the Wound ' you gave me. I can't tell, *reply'd the* Fair Lady, ' whether it may prove a comfort to you, but am ' fenfible I feel a great deal of pity for you, and ' to make, in fome meafure, a reparation for the ' Ill I have done you, pray come and ftay at my ' Houfe till you are fully cured. She then order- ed one of her Attendants, to bind up the Wound as well as he could, to put him in her Charriot and carry him home.

Julia, confidering her prefent Circumftances, judged fhe could not do better, than to accept of her offer; fo fhe returned her Thanks to the La- dy for her Generofity, and the before mentioned

Servant

Servant being with her in the fame Chariot, told
her, his Miſtreſs had been Marry'd but lately ;
that ſhe was of the Family of *Becarello*, well
known at *Bologna*; that ſhe being the only Child
her Father had, and he being unwilling to ſee his
Name extinĉt with his Death, had reſolved to
pitch upon one, who would take both his Name
and his Arms, for his Son-in-Law, and ſettle a conſiderable Eſtate upon them. ' The Lady that gave
' you this Wound, *continued he*, is a Lady of
' Merit and Wit ; her Husband, who at preſent
' is known by the Title and Name of the Mar-
' queſs of *Becarello*, having been abſent for ſome
' time, his Lady uſed to divert her ſelf with
' Hunting, and other ſuch like Diverſions practi-
' ſed among Perſons of her Quality ; and that
' thoſe Ladies, he ſaw with her, were either her
' Kinſwomen or Neighbours. He then asked *Julia*, whither ſhe was going? ' You ſeem, *ſaid
' ſhe to him*, to be ſomething beyond what your
' Habit diſcovers ; I dare be certain, you are of
' Noble Extraĉtion. I ſcarce know what I am,
' *reply'd* Julia *ſighing*; but to ſatisſie your Curi-
' oſity, I am willing to let you know, that my
' Name is *Sylvio*, that I am going to *Loretto* ;
' and that my ill Fortune has reduced me to ſuch
' a Condition, as not any more to fear its Inſults
' hereafter. You tell me all in a few Words,
' *ſaid the other* ; but, according to my Judgment,
' a Perſon ſo Handſome as your ſelf, can ſcarce
' have ſufficient cauſe to appear ſo much afflicted
' as you do. Thus they entertain'd one another till
they came to the Country-Houſe, where this Stranger was lodged in a very handſome Apartment.

The Marchioneſs had a *Valet de Chamber*, who
being a tolerable good Surgeon, dreſs'd *Sylvio's*
Wound, (for ſo we muſt call *Julia*, at leaſt for

some time) the Wound was very deep and painful, but without any danger of Malignant Symptoms. The Marchioness no sooner return'd home,
but she went with the two Gentlewomen that
were a Hunting with her, into the Pilgrim's
Chamber, and the Servant having told her their
Discourse upon the Road, she agreed with him
in Opinion, that there was something so Noble
and Great in his Physiognomy, as made her imagine he must be a Person of Quality. She staid
not long with him at that time ; but she carry'd
away within her Heart, his Idea in so lively a
shape, that under pretence of Hospitality, she
soon came again to see *Sylvio.* ' Are you some-
' what better, *said she, with a very obliging Air*,
' and have you so much Goodness as to pardon
' me for the ill I have done you. Oh! Madam,
' *said he to her*, how little are you acquainted
' with my Temper, if you think I can be con-
' cerned at so insignificant a Wound ? I declare
' to you, I think my self happy to have received
' it by your fair Hands. The Marchioness did as
if she had not understood these last Words; but
these Gallant Expressions touch'd her to the Heart,
imagining she had made as deep an Impression on
her handsome Stranger's Heart, as he had on hers.
She had a young Woman who was both her Companion and Confident, named *Eugenia*; ' Did you
' ever see any thing so Beautiful and Charming
' as this young *Sylvio* ? *said she to her*, Do you
' take notice what Looks he casts at me ? I read
' it in his Eyes ; and the Confusion he has raised
' within my Heart, puts me under so much per-
' plexity, that I am resolved to see him no more.
And she actually so far prevailed over her Inclinations, as not to come into *Sylvio*'s Chamber for
several days after, under pretence, that she was
                                                    not

not very well, for fear her Servants fhould take
notice of it; but tho' fhe did not fee him in Perfon, her Thoughts were always with him.
She became very melancholy, and delighted in
folitary Places only; fo that my Lord *Becarello*,
her Father, who liv'd at *Bologne*, and came frequently to fee her, was not a little furprized and
difturbed to fee fuch an alteration in her. Two
or three days pafs'd, when at laft the Marchionefs
paffing accidentally by *Sylvio's* Chamber, had not
power enough to forbear going in; fhe found
him in Bed, and obferved by his red Eyes and
Voice, that he had been weeping, and believing
no otherwife, than that it was her long ftay that
had caufed his Pain, fhe foon found fhe had gain-
ed but little ground, by not feeing and fpeaking
to him; but that her Heart was loft paft relief, as
foon as fhe found fhe had fo tender a part in his
Remembrance. 'How do you do *Sylvio*, *faid*
'*fhe*, you feem to be overwhelm'd with Sadnefs.
'Madam, *reply'd he*, it is becaufe I am not yet
'accuftomed to my Misfortunes, they feem No-
'velties to me every day: But, *continued fhe*, I
'am afraid, you are too Ingenious in framing
'your own Misfortunes in your Thoughts. No,
'Madam, *reply'd he*, I don't invent any, but what
'I actually am very fenfible of; but I muft alfo
'confefs to you, that on the other hand, I don't
'love to flatter my felf. They remained both very penfive for fome time; the Marchionefs quite
taken up with her Paffion, verily believed *Sylvio* to
be in Love with her; and *Sylvio*, without taking
notice of the Languifhing Looks and Sighs of the
Marchionefs, thought of nothing but her own
Misfortunes and her dear *Hypolitus*.
The Fair Marchionefs returning to her own
Appartment, became more and more fenfible, that
Sylvio

Sylvio was infinitely dear to her ; which put her under no small Perplexity. 'When I reflect up-
' on my prefent Condition, *said she to* Eugenia, I
' find nothing but what muft caufe me the higheft
' of Afflictions : The worft of all is, my Frailty
' of Loving him ; my Frailty, I fay, who being
' now no more my own Miftrefs, can't fo much as
' figh for another Man, but for my Husband,
' without committing a Crime both againft him
' and his Honour ; befides, pray, dear *Eugenia,*
' confider what other difgraces are likely to at-
' tend it. I know not who this *Sylvio* is, he is a
' Stranger whom I met accidentally in a Pilgrim's
' Habit ; he may perhaps, be of mean Birth, and
' altogether undeferving of thofe tender Senti-
' ments I have for him ; but what is moft certain,
' is, that I muft lofe him, and muft lofe him for
' ever. Oh! fatal Dart, *cry'd she*, the Wound
' thou gaveft, will fooner be heal'd, than that
' which this Lovely Stranger has made in my
' Heart.

The Marchionefs forbore, for feveral days, going into *Sylvio's* Appartment ; but fo foon as he
found himfelf in a Condition to ftir a little, he
judged it his Duty to go and pay her his Refpects : He obferved her to colour feveral times,
when he fpoke to her, and imagined fhe was out
of order ; but out of Refpect durft not ask her ;
fhe defired him to fit down by her, and having
look'd upon him for fome time without fpeaking, at laft faid fhe ; '*Sylvio*, you will foon be in
' a condition to leave us ; but before that time
' comes, will you not be fo Complaifant, as to let
' us know the Name of him whom I wounded ;
' and on whofe Account I have been fo much dif-
' compofed ? Madam, *said he*, I am an Unfor-
' tunate Perfon, unworthy your moft obliging
care

' care and curiofity. My Birth and my Fortune
' are both of no great Confideration, you fee me
' in my true Station. I am no more than what I
' appear to you to be. You fay a great deal,
' whilft you fay nothing,*reply'd the Marchionefs*;
' If you are fuch as you appear to me, I fcarce
' know any thing that is above you; and fince, per-
' haps, certain Reafons oblige you not to difco-
' ver your true Quality, pray tell me, at leaft,
' whether you are in Love? I don't ask you this
' Queftion, to engage you in any particular Ac-
' count, any further than you are inclined to give
' it. However, tell me fincerely, whetner you
' have not fome peculiar Confideration for me?
This Queftion reviving in *Sylvio's* Mind his paft
Misfortunes fhe fetch'd a deep Sigh ; ' Yes, Ma-
' dam, *faid he with a Tender Air*, I muft confefs
' I Love, but 'tis without hopes; and am by Fate
' defign'd to be the moft Unfortunate Perfon on
' Earth. The Marchionefs, by thefe words, being confirm'd in her former Opinion, that he loved
her, blufh'd, but would not lift up her Eyes, nor
return an Anfwer. After having paufed a while,
' Then are you to leave us, *Sylvio, faid fhe*, and
' will you fometimes think of me, after you are
' gone? I fhall fooner not remember my felf, *re-*
' *ply'd he*, Madam, believe me, your Goodnefs
' towards me, will never be rafed out of my
' Heart. So, fearing he fhould be troublefome,
he return'd to his own Apartment.

' Alas! I am upon the point of lofing you, Love-
' ly *Silvio*, cry'd fhe, fo foon as fhe faw her felf
' at Liberty to bemoan her Fate ; you are juft
' ready to leave us ; and, after all, I am very
' much deceived, if you don't Love me : But
' why won't you find out fome pretence or other,
' to ftay fomewhat longer in the fame place
' where I am? The reafon is, becaufe you think

R   me

' me not frail enough to Love you ; and you fear
' left you fhould engage too deep in a fruitlefs
' Paffion : Well, avoid the fight of me, charm-
' ing *Sylvio* ; fly from me, I am contented you
' fhould ; your Prefence ferves only to encreafe
' my Misfortune; and, perhaps, when I fee you
' no more, I may ceafe to Love you. She faid no
more, her Tears ftop d her Voice, and detain'd her
in her Clofet for fome time after. *Sylvio* did not
vifit her the next day, nor did meet with any opportunity of fpeaking to her for feveral days after;
but then finding himfelf well enough to continue
his Journey, he paid her a Vifit, to return his
moft humble Thanks to her for all the Favours he
had received at her hands, and to take his leave
of her : He told her, he was not in a Capacity to
return her any effectual Thanks, and fhew his Acknowledgment, but that he would make it his
Bufinefs to make known to the World, in all places wherever he fhould travel, that her Generofity
was not inferiour. to her great Deferts and Beauty. The Marchionefs put an almoft unfpeakable
Conftraint upon her felf, to conceal the Pain fhe
felt within her felf at this cruel feparation : ' Go,
' *Sylvio*, go, *faid fhe to him*, difcharge your Vows ;
' I promife you, 1 will fend up mine to Heaven,
' for the Profperity of your Life. He told her, he
intended to go away to morrow Morning at Day-
break ; and they parted in a few Minutes after.

It being an exceffive hot Night, he threw himfelf upon his Bed, without pulling off his Cloaths,
in hopes of getting a little reft to purfue his next
day's Journey with the more eafe ; the young
Marchionefs, at the fame time, having not refolution enough to let him go away without feeing
him once more, and bidding him farewel, got
out of her Chamber; and it being a bright Moon-
light Night, fhe made no ufe of a Candle ; be-
fides

sides that, being sensible she should be apt to say
something very tender to *Sylvio* at parting, she
should be the less ashamed, when he did not see
her Blush; she also resolved to present him with
her Picture, in hopes that this tender Testimony
of her kind Sentiments, would prevail upon him,
to keep her always in his Remembrance: The
Curtains of *Sylvio*'s Bed being not close drawn, she
saw his Hair spread carelesly over his Shoulders ;
he was fast asleep, and his Beautiful Face put the
Marchioness in mind of that of *Cupid*, when
Psyche came to make him a Visit. ' Oh! *Sylvio*,
' *said she, casting her Amorous Looks at him,*
' were it so, that I had made some Impressions of
' Tendernefs in thy Heart, thou couldst not sleep
' so foundly at a time when thou art just upon
' the point of leaving me! Is it possible, that at
' the same time thy departure is likely to cost me
' so dearly, thou shouldest lie at thy own ease,
' without the least disturbance ? However, wanting Courage to awaken him, she drew nearer, and
by the brightness of the Moon, having a sufficient
opportunity of viewing his Charms, and contemplating all his Perfections, ' What is it can stand
' in Competition with thee in the Universe ? *said*
' *she with a low Voice and full of Admiration* ;
' Who can represent all thy Beauties ? Who is
' able to avoid their force?' Thus she swallow'd
by degrees the Poison which this Fair Stranger's
Charms convey'd insensibly into her Heart. She
put her Picture into his Pocket, flattering her self
that he would be most agreeably surprized, when
he should find there so dear and precious a Present at a time when least of all he expected it: At
last, quite overcome by her Passion, she could not
forbear to put her Mouth to his, and to embrace
him with so much eagernefs, that it seem'd as if
she would never let go her hold again : But Good

God.

God, guefs at her Amazement, when fhe felt her
felf wounded with a Dagger by a Man, whom fhe
foon knew to be the Marquefs *Becarelly,* her Huf-
band, and who no fooner left her, but went towards *Sylvio* to revenge himfelf upon him. Being
throughly awakened at the noife, and not a little
frightned at the approaching danger, he got up as
faft as he could, in order to make his Efcape, but
received a Wound in the Arm, by the fame Hand
that had wounded the Lady. This Man, turn'd
quite furious with Jealoufie, was a going to fecond his Blow, had he not been prevented by two
Gentlemen, who being his Confidents, ftop'd his
Hand, and put him in mind of what Projeƈt had
been concerted betwixt them, which he was not
likely to effeƈt, if he fhould kill this young Stranger; fo they fent *Sylvio* a Prifoner to a ftrong
and dark Tower. The Unfortunate Marchionefs,
in the mean while falling into a Swoon, and
fwimming in her own Blood, her Husband ordered her to be carry'd to her own Apartment, and
to be watch'd clofely like a Prifoner there. You
may judge of the Anxiety of her Heart; and after
all, fhe felt lefs pain at her own Misfortune, than
at what was likely to befal him fhe loved. She
fear'd, not without reafon, leaft her Husband
fhould have facrificed this Innocent Viƈtim to his
Jealoufie; and what was worfe to her than all the
reft, fhe durft not fo much as ask what was
become of him, partly becaufe fhe dreaded fome
fatality, partly becaufe fhe knew not whom to
truft, being fenfible fhe had been betray'd. *Eugenia,* whom fhe had made her Confident, was
indeed the Perfon that had done her Bufinefs; being engaged to watch all her Steps by the Marquefs
Becarelly, before he went on his Journey, a thing
not very difficult to be done, if you joyn great
Promifes to your prefent Liberality. He had enjoyn'd

joyn'd this young Woman to give him an exact account, by Letter, of his Lady's Conduct in his Abfence; and fhe had been fo punctual as to communicate to him every word fhe heard her fay concerning *Sylvio*, and her Paffion for him. The Marquefs enraged at this News, came home with all poffible fpeed, and knowing himfelf concealed for two days, by *Eugenia*'s Affiftance, in his own Houfe, till he fhould have an opportunity of furprizing his Spoufe with her Lover, his Intention was to have her fhut up like a Prifoner, for the reft of her Life, to have all her Eftate adjudged to himfelf, and to proceed againft *Sylvio* as the worft of Criminals; but when he faw her feated upon the Bedfide of this Stranger, he was fo far from being Mafter of his Anger, that during the firft motions of his Jealoufie he wounded them both.

In the mean while *Julia*, under the Difguife of a Pilgrim, and under the Name of *Sylvio*, being fhut up in a dark Tower, remain'd in fo deplorable a Condition, as would have touch'd the worft of her Enemies with Compaffion: She was wounded in the Arm, quite dejected by the long Series of her Misfortunes, difturbed at her hard fate, without any hopes of aid, and in the greateft Perplexity in the World what to do under her prefent difmal Circumftances. She was once inclined to difcover her Sex, as the neareft means to juftifie the Marchionefs, and to obtain her Liberty, and was juft upon the point to fpeak to her Guards to tell the Marquefs *Becarely*, that fhe wanted to fpeak with him; when reflecting more ferioufly upon the matter, fhe began to fear, leaft the Expedient fhe intended to make ufe of, to obtain her releafement, might caufe the lofs of her Life: For confidering, that if her Husband, quite diftracted with Jealoufie and Choler, who had wounded her with a Dagger, fhould be convinced

R 3 of

of her Innocence, and confequently dreading the
effects of her and her Families Refentment, might
fo far tranfgrefs all bounds of Humanity, as to
have her Poifon'd ; to prevent, by this means, the
difcovery of the whole matter; fo that upon fecond Thoughts, fhe judged it more for her fafety,
to let Juftice take its courfe, by which means fhe
fhould free her felf out of her Enemies hands.

She had the worft Night of it that can well be
imagined ; after the Wound given her with the
Dagger was drefs'd, they fearched her, and found
the Marchionefs's Picture in her Pocket; which
they intended to make ufe of as a corroborating
proof againft them both. *Julia* was infinitely
furprized to find this Picture about her, which fhe
had not fo much as ever feen before; neither
could fhe imagine how it came into her Pocket ;
fo they conducted her in a Coach to *Bologna.* It
would prove a very difficult Task to reprefent the
various Troubles this Fair and Unfortunate Lady
laboured under at that time. 'My dear *Hypolitus*,
' *cry'd fhe fighing*, if you were fenfible at this
' very Minute, that your Faithful *Julia* is loaden
' with Irons, under a Man's Difguife, that fhe
' has been carry'd away by force, made her Efcape
' twice, and has twice been wounded, and that
' now fhe is going to a Prifon: Alas ! what would
' you do ? But rather, *continued fhe*, what muft
' I expect from you ? Having not received the
' leaft News from you in fo long a time, what
' reafon have I to imagine, that you fhould
' fo much as remember me ? And is it my hard
' Lot, to have this additional Affliction, to
' think you love me no more ? She cry'd bitterly
all the time fhe was upon the road, tho' her
Tears ftood her in no ftead, but only to expofe
her to the Scorn of thofe that conducted her,
who look'd upon them as an effect of her fear,

ard

and want of Courage. The Marchionefs being
likewife carry'd to *Bologna*, her Husband urged
to have her committed to the Common Prifon,
notwithftanding the Wound fhe had received; but
her Father, who, as well by his Extraction as his
Eftate, made a confiderable Figure in that City,
prevail'd fo far with the Governour, as to have
her confined in the Caftle. So uncommon an Adventure, which had happen'd betwixt Perfons of
the beft Quality, made no fmall noife in thofe
Parts, each Party engaging all the Friends they
could to maintain their Caufe; what ftood the
Marquefs in the greateft ftead, to perfwade the
World that his Accufation was ill grounded, was
the irrefiftible Charms of *Sylvio*; moft of the
Ladies who had the Curiofity to vifit him in Prifon, left their Hearts captivated with him; and
there were but few among them all, but what
felt the fame tender Sentiments for him, as the
Fair Marchionefs had done: But after all this,
tho' moft People thought her not Innocent, yet
her Father's Intereft was fuch, as was thought
would incline the Ballance on his fide, and the
Marquefs had certain intelligence given him, that
the Commiffioners, appointed to try this Caufe,
were for the moft part inclined to acquit the Marchionefs and *Sylvio*. He was under the greateft
Perplexity and Trouble that can well be imagin'd,
for knowing his All lay at ftake, he found himfelf reduced to an abfolute neceffity of maintaining to the utmoft of his Power, what he had
begun with fo much Violence, and fo little Circumfpection. At laft it came into his Head, that
to counterpoize his Wife's Party, he would petition the Governor, that the Commiffioners fhould
not be all *Italians*; but that he being a Foreigner,
one half of them fhould be his Countrymen, according to the Law of that Country, it being a thing

R 4   that

that had frequently, and not without very good reasons, been practis'd in the *Bolognese*. The Count of *Bentivoglio*, Governor of *Bologna*, granted his Requeſt and at the ſame time, both the Father and the Husband of the Fair Marchioneſs, left the choice of them to the Governor's diſpoſal.

The whole Town appear'd at the Caſtle at the day of this Tryal, in expeÐation of the Iſſue thereof, (for the Marchioneſs being all this while detain'd a Priſoner there, the Governor thought this the moſt convenient place for it) there was ſo numerous an Aſſembly of all Degrees and Ages, that the like had not been ſeen in many Years before. The Fair Marchioneſs was brought in clad in Mourning, a Dreſs ſhe judged moſt ſuitable to her preſent Unfortunate Circumſtances; ſhe looked very pale, by reaſon of her Wounds and Troubles; but ſhe appear'd nevertheleſs Charming to all that beheld her: Her Father, a Perſon venerable for his Age and his goodly Mien, conduÐed her by the Hand, follow'd by a good number of Gentlemen belonging to the ſame Family. *Sylvio* was brought in thro' another door, loaden with Irons and Chains; but moſt of thoſe that took a full view of him, thought him (even in this diſmal condition) more qualify'd to make others wear his Chains, than to carry them himſelf. Both theſe pretended Criminals coming before thoſe that were to be their Judges, with Eyes full of Tears, and their Hearts ready to break with Sighs, ' My ' Lords, *ſaid the Marchioneſs*, I implore both ' your Juſtice and Compaſſion; I am Unfortunate ' without being Guilty; Heaven is Witneſs of my ' Innocence, he that proſecutes me at this time ' with ſo much Violence, and with ſo little Re- ' ſpeÐ to my Honour and Reputation, has at the ' moſt, nothing but bare Surmiſes to found his ' Accuſation upon.

Before

Before *Sylvio* could begin to fpeak in his own defence, the Marquefs *Becarelli* ftood up, as did alfo the two Gentlemen, who had feen his Lady in *Sylvio*'s Bed-chamber, and holding the Picture fhe had put into his Pocket, and which they had found upon him, in his Hand ; ' Look here, *faid* ' *he*, an undeniable Evidence of a criminal Cor- ' refpondence betwixt them; no Vertuous Wo- ' man would have beftow'd her Picture upon a ' miferable Pilgrim; and he himfelf can't deny, ' but that it was found in his Pocket. *Sylvio* (whom now we muft call again *Julia*,) *Julia*, I fay, ftruck like as with a Thunderbolt at the found of this Voice, turn'd as pale as Afhes, trem- bled all over her Body and fell into a Swoon. E- very Body there prefent came to her Affiftance, and among the reft, a Foreigner, who was to be of the number of her Judges, who knowing and embracing her with the higheft Tranfports of Joy, that can be conceived, cry'd, ' O *Julia*, O my A- ' dorable *Julia!* Is it you or a Vifion I behold? ' Is it poffible I fhould meet with you again, af- ' ter having bewail'd you fo long, thinking you ' had been in your Grave! There was fcarce any Body there prefent, but what believed the Gen- tleman to have been out of his Wits; however, his Voice had fuch a powerful Influence upon *Julia*, that it foon revived her Spirits; fhe open- ed her Eyes, and the firft Object fhe faw was her dear *Hypolitus* on one fide, and the Earl of *Bed- ford* on the other. At the confufed noife of the Affembly, who often repeated the Name of *Ju- lia*, another of the intended Judges arofe from his Seat, and coming towards her, ' Look here is ' your dear Daughter, *faid* Hypolitus *to him*, my ' Lord, 'tis *Julia*. The Earl of *Warwick* (for it was he) embracing his Daughter, was ready to die for Joy, and fhe throwing her felf at his Feet, bathed

bathed his Hands with Tears, and fuch were their mutual Tranfports at fo unexpected a Meeting, that never any thing was feen comparable to it.

The Earl of *Bedford* acted but a fcurvy part in this Scene; theMarchionefs of *Becarelly*, her Father, the Count *de Bentivoglio*, and in fhort, all that could come near them, furrounded thefe three Friends with their repeated Acclamations, without knowing fully the true caufe thereof. *Julia*, in fpite of her Husband's Prefence, declared in open Court, who fhe was, and finding her felf feconded by a pleafing noife and the clapping of Hands of the Affembly, as foon as fhe thought fhe might be heard, told them, that the Earl of *Bedford*, who was both the Profecutor and Husband of the Marchionefs of *Becarelly*, was likewife hers, and had both thefe Qualifications, and that confequently he had two Wives. The Earl could not deny it to be matter of Fact; fo that whereas he had hitherto profecuted thefe two Ladies, they thought it now their turn to Profecute him; and the Marchionefs's Father, as well as *Julia's* Father, preffing the Count *de Bentivoglio* to have him feized, in order to his Profecution; according to the Laws of the Land, he was committed to Prifon, where he made this voluntary Confeffion.

That confiding in the Abbefs of St. *Menoux's* Integrity, who had given him Advice of *Julia's* Death, in her Letter, he left *England* with an intention to travel; that he had an Inclination to go into *Italy* firft, becaufe he had fome Relations there he was willing to be known to; that my Lord *Becarelly*, being one of them, he went to *Bologna*, where being fal'n defperately in Love with Madam *Becarelly*, he had obtain'd her Father's Confent to Marry her, on Condition, that he fhould take both his Name and Arms. That fome time after coming to *Florence* with his Father-in-Law, and

and one day feeing *Lu ilia* along with *Julia* in a Widow's Apparel at the *Repurata* to hear Mafs there, he thought he fhould have been ftruck into the Ground at fo unexpected a fight; that he thought it not convenient at that time to take any further notice of it, for fear of my Lord *Becarelly*, who was along with him; but refolved to try one of the Senator *Alberti*'s Servants, whether he could engage him in the defign he had laid of carrying away *Julia* by force; that having obtain'd his Confent he came back to *Bologna*, where he ftaid for fome time with the young Marchionefs his Wife; but that he could never be at reft, for fear leaft *Julia* being fo near, might one time or other find out his fecond Marriage, and take that opportunity of revenging her feif for what he had made her fuffer before. That it was upon this confideration, he took care to fecure a Nunnery at *Siena*, where he intended to fhut her up for the remainder of her days, and then return'd to *Florence*. That the fame Servant of the Senator *Alberti*, whom he had made his Confident, came to tell him, that he muft not lofe one moment to put his Defign in execution, becaufe his Mafter had ordered him to keep himfelf in a readinefs, in order to carry her off; that thereupon he and three more putting on Vizard-Masks, carry'd her away; but being foon after purfued and forced to fight thofe that overtook them, he was wounded by a Piftol Ball, and was forced to ftay for fome time at *Siena*, where he ufed frequently to receive Letters from *Eugenia*, the Marchionefs's Confident, who being bribed by him, gave him an account, that his Spoufe was fal'n in Love with a Pilgrim, whom fhe had brought to her Houfe in the Country; that thereupon being almoft diftracted with Jealoufy, he had pufh'd on the matter to that Extremity, they faw his Affairs in at this time.

The

The Earl of *Bedford* quite diſtracted with Rage, Jealouſie and Deſpair, ſoon after found himſelf ſeized with a moſt violent Fever, which at the beginning was judged Mortal; beſides, that the Wound he had receiv'd when he was carrying a-way *Julia*, opening afreſh, put him to the moſt exquiſite Pains; for want of patience to ſee the Cure accompliſh'd before he would ſtir abroad to take Revenge for the ſuppoſed Infidelity of his Wife. So whilſt amongſt the continual Torments of Body and Mind, he lived only in expectation of his Death; *Julia*, the Earl of *Warwick*, and *Hypolitus* taſted all the Sweets of an entire Satis-faction, the higheſt that can poſſibly be conceived upon ſo favourable and ſo long deſired a Conjun-cture. Then it was this Paſſionate Lover, and this Faithful Miſtreſs gave one another account of their mutual Pains, not without a mixture of Tears, becauſe they could ſcarce be fully ſatisfy'd as yet, that that good Fortune they enjoy'd, was either poſſible or real : 'Who is it that is able to expreſs
' my Anguiſh, dear *Julia, ſaid he to her*, when I
' heard the fatal News of your Death; I was
' reſolved not to outlive you long; Death was
' the only thing I wiſh'd for; notwithſtanding
' which, it ſeem'd to me ever ſince, as if Death,
' which I purſued with ſo much Reſolution, and
' courted in the greateſt danger, always expoſing
' my ſelf to the greateſt hazards, was reſolved to
' ſpare me; for I was not ſo much as wounded all
' the time I continued aboard the Galleys of
' *Maltha*; ſo that ſeeing, I was not likely to meet
' that Death, I ſo much deſired, in that Service, and
' finding my Warlike Actions to produce not the
' leaſt effect in diminiſhing my Pain, I reſolved
' to go and ſee my Siſter at *Florence*, with no o-
' ther Intention, than to ſpend all my Time in
' talking continually with her of you. I commu-
' nicated

‘ nicated my Refolution to the Earls of *Warwick*
‘ and *Suffex* ; the firft was very willing to go along
‘ with me, becaufe our Voyage would not take up
‘ much time, being call'd by Honour to Martial
‘ Employments : However, my Lord *Warwick*
‘ having received a Wound in the *Venetian* Ser-
‘ vice, found that a little reft would be neceffary
‘ to perfect his Cure; and as for the Earl of *Suffex*,
‘ he took Shipping for *London*, upon fome agree-
‘ able News he had lately received from the Coun-
‘ tefs of *Northampton*, which gave him hopes of
‘ foon feeing their Deftinies united by the Bands
‘ of Marriage ; and as he had an uncommon Paffi-
‘ on for her, 'tis no wonder if he let flip no time
‘ to be with her as foon as poffibly he could : As
‘ for us two, Madam, *continued he*, after having
‘ ftaid fome time at *Venice*, we began our Journey
‘ for *Florence* ; but the Earl of *Warwick* finding
‘ that Travelling did not fo well agree with him
‘ as yet, (becaufe he grew much worfe) we were
‘ obliged to tarry here fome time : We ufed of-
‘ ten to vifit Count *Bentivoglio*, and the Bufinefs
‘ of the Marchionefs of *Becarelly* making no
‘ fmall noife at this time, he would almoft every
‘ day tell us fome new Story or other concerning
‘ her Husband, or her, or the Pilgrim. Alas ! my
‘ dear Lady, could it ever come into my Head,
‘ that this Pilgrim fhould be my *Julia* ! whofe
‘ Death I bewail'd every Day, and at the fame
‘ time was loaded with Irons in a naufeous Prifon.
‘ At laft the Marquefs *Becarelly*, or to fpeak more
‘ properly, the Earl of *Bedford*, requiring the Go-
‘ vernor to joyn a certain number of *English* Gen-
‘ tlemen, in Commiffion with the *Italians*, to coun-
‘ terpoife the Intereft of his Wife's Family, he de-
‘ fired us to fit with thofe he had pitch'd up-
‘ on before the Bench to try this Caufe. Can there
‘ be a more fad Accident than this ? I was to be

one

' one of your Judges at the Profecution of your
' Husband ; I, I fay, who always refpected you
' as my Sovereign Lady, and who am his Mortal
' Enemy. You are acquainted with all the reft that
' happen'd, except it be the Joy, Tranfports and
' Satisfaction I feel ever fince that happy Day.
Julia return'd in lieu of thefe tender Expreffions,
fuch Affurances as were fufficient to convince *Hypolitus*, that he had not loft the leaft ground in her
Heart, and that fhe knew what value to put upon
a Paffion fo pure and conftant as his. What becomes in the mean while of the Marchionefs of
Becarelly ? 'Twould be a hard Task to reprefent
to you the various Troubles and Perplexities fhe
laboured under when fhe faw *Julia*, and at the
fame time remembred her Paffion for *Sylvio* ; but
what was worfe than all the reft was, that fhe
had not as yet fo much power over her felf as to
ceafe to love *Sylvio* ; fhe retain'd fo lively, an Idea
of him in her Heart, that fhe was a moving Object
of Pity ; 'I am free to confefs to you, *faid fhe to*
' Julia, that I was more fenfibly affiicted at the
' lofs of *Sylvio*, than at all my other Misfortunes ;
' and tho' I had taken a Refolution rather to die
' than endeavour to make him eafe my Pain, it was
' fome fatisfaction to me, to think he was alive,
' and that one time or other Chance might bring
' him again in my way ; but now my Misfortune is
' paft all cure, becaufe I love ftill, and love only a
' Chimera. But my Lovely Marchionefs, *faid* Julia
' *to her*, can't you find out a place for me in your
' Heart, fince mine is much inclined to love you;
' you were much lefs beloved by *Sylvio*, than you
' will be by *Julia*. The Fair *Italian* return'd no
Anfwer, but fhe would often turn her Eyes upon
Julia, and feldom part from her without fhedding
abundance of Tears.
    The two Fathers of thefe two Ladies, had pufh'd

on their Profecution of the E. of *Bedford* with fo
much Vigour, that every Body expeƈted it would
go very hard with the faid Earl, when his Diſtemper encreaſing daily, foon reduced him to the laſt
Extremity. 'Twas at that Conjunƈture, that theſe
two Ladies, being willing to let their Generoſity
take place before their juſt Refentment, got him
removed into the Caſtle, where, inſtead of that
hatred he had fo much deſerved at their Hands,
they ſhew'd their Pity and Duty to him in a moſt
eminent degree, 'till quite overwhelmed with the
remembrance of his Inquietudes, Pains and Misfortunes, Death put an end to his Life, and the Marchioneſs of *Becarelly* immediately after took her
laſt farewel of *Julia*; ' I am going to leave you
' for the remainder of my days, *faiſ ſhe to her*, and
' ſince your Sex is an invincible Obſtacle to all my
' hopes of ever feeing you to be mine, I am refol-
' ved to be no Bodies elſe; I intend to embrace a
' Religious Life, to hide my Frailty and Paſſion
' from all the World. *Julia* left nothing unattemp-
ted to diſſwade her from purſuing this Refolution,
but to no purpoſe; the Marchioneſs was already
gone away, when on a fudden ſhe ſaw her come
back into her Room ; ' Don't refuſe my Requeſt,
' *faid ſhe*, afford me once more the fight of my
' Conqueror in the ſame Dreſs you raiſed my Paſ-
' ſion firſt. *Julia* being then alone, was willing to
comply with her defire, foon put on her Pilgrim's
Habit, and came to the Marchioneſs; but ſhe no
fooner caſt her Eyes upon her, but ſhe was ready
to faint away. ' Alas ! *cry'd ſhe*, I meet with my
' Diſtemper where I thought to have found a Cure.
' *Sylvio*, adorable *Sylvio*, you now keep a place on-
' ly in my Soul, every thing I can conceive of you,
' is a Chimera, which can neither flatter nor cure
' my Pain She aroſe, went out as faſt as ſhe could,
and retired immediately into a Nunnery, to the
great regret of her Father.   *Julia*

Julia took the way to *Florence* with the Earl of *Warwick* and *Hypolitus*, where being informed of the Senator *Alberti*'s Death, they went to Signior *Leander*'s House, whom they found in deep Mourning; but this did not hinder him from difcovering his Satisfaction at the fight of thofe Perfons who were fo dear to him, and *Lucilia* was fcarce able to contain her Joy, becaufe the continual Inquietudes fhe felt on account of her Brother and *Julia*, proved no fmall allay to thofe Enjoyments, and that Tranquillity fhe alfo might have been fenfible of to the utmoft Perfection in a Husband of fuch extraordinary merit. The Earl of *Warwick*, and they being unwilling to fee the accomplifhment of the Happinefs of the Faithful *Hypolitus* and the moft Admirable *Julia* delay'd any longer, the Nuptials were celebrated at one of *Leander*'s Country Houfes; never did the Sun enlighten with her glorious Beams a more pleafing Day than this, never did two Lovers relifh with more Satisfaction and Union what they had purchafed at the expence of fo much care, and of fo many Sighs and Tears; and upon their Return to *England*, never was there a more general Rejoycing feen among all that knew them, on account of their happy Marriage and fafe Arrival in their Native Country. They found the Earl of *Suffex* Marry'd to the Fair Countefs of *Northampton*, and *Hypolitus* took the Title of Earl of *Douglas*, by which he has render'd himfelf Famous to Pofterity, and obtained the Reputation of the moft Polite and moft Couragious of all the greateft Men of his Age.

F I N I S.

The Island of Content

Anonymous

Bibliographical note:

This facsimile has been made from a copy in the British Museum

(12316.cc.30)

THE

Iſland of Content:

OR, A

New PARADISE

Diſcover'd.

In a LETTER from Dr. *Merryman* of the ſame Country, to Dr. *Dullman* of *Great Britain.*

Since Men of Grace, as well as thoſe of Wit,
Place Human Happineſs in mere Conceit,
And pious Saints, of teeming Zeal poſſeſt,
Coin ſtrange Opinions, to deceive the reſt ;
Why not my Muſe Ætherial Worlds invent,
Or Fancy frame new Iſlands of Content ?

By the Author of the Pleaſures of a ſingle Life.

LONDON

Printed : And ſold by *J. Baker*, at the *Black Boy* in *Pater-Noſter-Row.* 1709. Price 6 d.

THE
Island of Content :

Dear Friend,

SINCE my Golden Pills prov'd so acceptable a Present, and you are very importunate to be made acquainted with the State and Condition of our happy *Island of Content*, where such chearful Physick is alone administer'd in all Distempers; pursuant to your Request, I have carefully improv'd some leisure Hours on purpose to oblige you, and have accordingly sent you an exact Account of the Situation of the Place, the Products of the Country, the Constitution of the Government; also the Customs and Manners of the merry Inhabitants of our musical Kingdom, that you may be the better sensible how far the Pleasures of Peace and Dulcitude of Harmony, exceed the noisy Surprizes of uncertain War, and the grinning Malice of domestick Discord. Therefore, that I may not weary out your Patience with a tedious Introduction, I shall treat you as a Friend, and, free of all Partiality to my native Country, let you into the Secret, without farther Preparation, *viz.*

CHAP. I.

Of the Situation and Climate.

WE are happily seated in a very moderate Climate, but suffering no Man to study the

Heathen-

(4)

Heathenish Science of Aſtronomy, I cannot, according to the Rules of Art, pretend to acquaint
you with the Degrees of our Latitude : And the
Reaſons why we think it not ſafe to ſuffer a Star-
gazer among us, are, that they generally dwindle
into Aſtrological Wiſeakers, and by their lying
Propheſies, corrupt the Minds of the People, to the
Diſturbance of the Kingdom ; therefore, when ever
we catch any Perſon writing an Almanack, telling
Fortunes, or pretending to predict what ſhall happen hereafter, we tye his Thumbs behind him with
Coblers Ends, hang a Shoe-maker's Laſt about his
Neck for a Sygil, and then flog him to Death with
a Leathern Strap, without Mercy ; for you muſt
know we dread nothing ſo much as the Subverſion
of our Government, and the Change of our Con-
ſtitution ; for having a due Senſe of our own Happineſs, we are well aſſur'd, from the ſad Experience
of other Countries, that nothing but Miſery would
attend a Revolution. However, as to the comfortable Temperature of our happy Climate, we are
ſuch abſolute Strangers to all manner of Extreams,
that we never need Fire, in Winter, to warm our
Fingers, or Water, in Summer, to cool our Wines,
but enjoy, thro' the Circle of the whole Year, ſuch
a peaceful Serenity in all the Elements, that the
Diſtillations of the Clouds are but gentle Dews,
that give a laſting Fertility to the fragrant Earth,
and only keep the Duſt from riſing, to the Injury
of our Eyes, above its natural Centre ; ſo that we
are neither ſubject to be offended with Dirt, or in-
commoded with Duſt, but always tread upon a
verdent Carpet, freſh as a Bowling-Green after a
ſoft Shower in the Month of April. As we have no
Ice in the coldeſt of our Weather, to make the
Ground deceitful, ſo have we no deſtructive Lightning, or ſurprizing Thunder, in the hotteſt of our
Seaſons, to make our Fears terrible ; nor will the
great ſhaſt of our Hurricanes, either in Spring or Au-
tumn, extinguiſh the Flame of a Farthing-Candle,
the

tho' it be ſtuck lighted, during the whole Storm, upon the Weather-cock of a Steeple.

In ſhort, we are always bleſs'd with ſuch a comfortable Warmth, that a Man may lie ſafely between the Heavens and his Wife, and ſhe between her Husband and the bare Ground, without the Danger of catching Cold, tho' it be in Winter : Nor ſhould we have any Occaſion for Cloths, not ſo much as a Fig-leaſe, did not Decency oblige us to wear Tiffany Apparel. So that from the Exuberance of Nature, and the Moderation of our Climate, ſome of our learned Commentators do prophanely aſſert, that this our Iſland is the very Paradiſe that *Adam* loſt, but was reſtor'd lately to our Great Grand-fathers, as ſome deſerving Branch of the old Gentleman's Family.

Old Paradiſe *is only loſt to ſuch*
Who ſearch too little, or offend too much,
But eaſ'ly ſound by thoſe who can deſcry
The Heav'nly Being with a righteous Eye.

CHAP. II.

Of our Food and Delicacies.

AS to our-Eatables, Nature is here ſo laviſh of her Plenty, that we abound in Variety of Dainties, without human Labour; nor have we any Occaſion to improve our Food by the Art of Cookery, for nothing can be added to make our luſhecus Fruits more wholſome, or more palatable.

As to our Bread, the principal Staff of Life, our fertile Ground is ſo over-run with delicious Potatoes, that we eaſily dig them up where ever we pleaſe, without the Aſſiſtance of any other Spade, than our fore Fingers ; ſo that the only Labour we are at, is, to turn them out of the Ground, ſpread them

them upon the Surface, and there let them lie but half an Hour in the Sun-shine, and they'll be as well bak'd into crusty half-penny Rolls, as if they had been stopp'd up as long in a well-heated Oven; therefore our Poor here have no Occasion to run to Church for the Sake of the Penny Loaves, nor to dissent from it in Hopes of a better Maintenance, for we have no Bakers to plague them with long Tallies, or oppressive Work-houses to keep 'em to hard Fare, as well as hard Labour, for a parcel of rich Knaves to run away with the Profit of their Earnings, that the Saints in Authority over 'em may say long Graces to large Meals, and thank God for what the Devil has given them.

Pleasant Roots and Herbs are our common Food, from the Lord to the Beggar; by which abstemious sort of Living, we hold our Lusts in such an absolute Subjection, that there is not one Great Magistrate among us, that keeps a Harlot under his Lady's Nose, nor one smock-fac'd Flatterer in all our Dominions, that ever made himself a Great Man by committing Adultery; nor do we ever eat Flesh, because we look upon it sinful to destroy one of God's Creatures for the Preservation of another; nor have we any Necessity to prompt us to it, indeed not so much as our own Luxury. As to all forts of Hortelage, every Man has it in his Backfide, as surely as a House of Office; nor can any Inhabitant take a Walk in his Garden, without great Caution, but Clusters of thumping Peaches, and over-grown Nectorals, swinging at the end of stragling Boughs, will be ready at each Step to knock his Teeth down his Throat, as if they were angry with their Owner, that he had not eaten 'em sooner. To be short, we abound with such vast Variety of delicious Products, that our Monkeys and Squirrels feed upon sweet Almonds, and our wild Hogs upon Muskmellons and Pine-apples.

If Brutes, that in our happy Island dwell,
Feed on such dainty Fruits, and live so well;
What Blessings may be found by human Race,
Who thankfully possess so sweet a Place?

CHAP. III.

Of our Wines and potable Juices.

THE outside of every Man's House is here a plentiful Vineyard, for Vines spring up naturally under every Body's Windows, as Mushrooms from the rotten Stump of an old Horse-block, and creep up our Walls over the Eves of our Mansions, as commonly as Ivy grows round an Oak, or Houselick on the top of a Country Bog-house; insomuch that every Inhabitant, when he wants to drink, may squeeze his Grapes with his own Teeth, instead of a Wine-press; however, for Society's Sake, because we cannot be so free in our own Houses, we allow some Taverns, but to prevent Adulteration, we cut down all Apple-trees as fast as they spring up, lest the Purity of our Wines should be debas'd with Cyder; by which Means we keep our Vintners honest, our Juices wholsome, and the People healthful; yet, tho' our Liquors are plenty, and in the highest Perfection, we are a sober Nation, only for want of a large Excise to make it the Interest of our Government to connive at Drunkenness : So that indeed the Cheapness of our Wines, and the due Execution of our Laws against Vice, without the least Help of a Society of Reformation, makes Ebriety a Scandal. Notwithstanding our great Inclinations to Temperance and Chastity, yet the brightest Rainbow can have no Tincture in her mottl'd Diversity, but what we can match with some excellent Liquor of the same Colour, yet we have no Brewers among us; for which
Reason

Reafon our capital Cities are never govern'd by Lord-Mayors and Aldermen. But above all other Potables, I have a certain Cordial Compofition of my own, diftill'd from the Rays of the Sun, *May*-dew, Moon-fhine, and Honey-drops, that I prepare purpofely for the fpeedy Suppreffion of all melancholly Vapours: Which excellent Cordial, I may fay, without Flattery, furpaffes all the Nectar in the Heavens, all the Wines upon Earth, and all the exalted Elements that mix between both to quench the fcorching Drowth of thirfty *Phœbus*. Therefore, fince you inform'd me, in your laft Letter, what a peftilential Stupidity had unhappily over-run that flatulent part of the World wherein you are now refident, I have thought a true Recipe of fo rich a *Noftrum* might be very welcome to a Brother Phyfician of your fingular Pretenfions; but muft ftrictly enjoin you, by all the Bonds of Friendfhip, to lock it faft in your own Bofom, as a valuable Secret. If you happen to find, in your colder Climate, the Ingredients difficult to come by, or too expenfive to turn to Account, then, inftead of *May*-dew, you may ufe Pump-water; for the Rays of the Sun, Leaf-Gold; burnt Silver, in the room of Moon-fhine; and the want of Honey-drops, fupply with common Sugar; tho', whatever you do, be fure you obferve the true Quantities according to my Recipe; for it ought to be a Maxim in Phyfick, *viz. Nulla veritas, nulla virtus*. When you have thus prepar'd it *fecundum Artem*, purfuant to Inftructions, for its fingular Efficacy in all melancholly Diftempers, I would have you call it, *Chear-up*, a Name fo applicable to fo excellent a Cordial, that you cannot find a better in the whole *Nomen Clature*, for one Thimble-full adminifter'd in due Seafon, that is, a little before the Paroxyfm, will certainly cure any dull Fanatick of the Spirit of Contradiction, or the yawning Evil, and make him as merry Company for a whole Afternoon, over a Bottle, as a young Player, or a Mountebank's
Merry-

Merry *Andrew* ; alfo infallibly cures all heavy-heart-
ed Sinners of the Spleen, Hypo, or Night-mare,
Maids of the amorous Sufpiration, Whores of
prick'd Confciences, and Wives of the Vapours ;
and is fo highly in Efteem among the merry Inhabitants of our peaceful Ifland, that it is publickly
fold here, inftead of Brandy, to make the People
laugh.

A cordial Dram, with Moderation us'd,
Revives the Heart, but injures when abus'd.
Enough, that happy Quentum, makes us glad ;
But with too much, we fottifh grow, or mad.

CHAP. IV.

Of our Apparel.

WE abound in Spiders of feveral Sorts and Colours, but all fo very large, that few of 'em
appear lefs than an Ox's Bladder blown to its full
Extenfion, each carrying in his fwelling Bag fo
much tex.able Matter, of a filky Nature, that he
will not only fpin, but weave as much Gaufe in a
Day's Time, as would fill a *Scotch*-man's Pack, every
one's Manufacture differing in Strength, Colour,
and Subftance, according to the Food, Magnitude,
Variation, and Agility of the induftrious Infect that
happens to be the Weaver, which makes their excellent Work fit for fundry Ufes ; fo that when any
Body has a Mind to change their Apparel, it is but
ftepping into their Garden, and they may furnifh
themfelves with a loofe Mantle, (which is the fa-
fhionable Garment here worn) ready fpun and
wove, either futable to their Youth, or agreeable
to their Gravity. Therefore we have no Occafion
here for Mercers and Drapers, to dun and plague
our Quality, that they cannot fit eafy in their

B   own

(10)

own Parlours for fear of some Hawk-nos'd Citizen or other, with a long Bill, fifty Scrapes, and as many humble Beseech ye's, and all to know when he shall come next to go Home without his Money. Neither is any Person here distinguish'd by their Dress, because every Body has the Liberty, without the least Expence, of chusing such Apparel as shall best humour their own Fancy ; for which Reason our very Women here are wholly innocent of Pride, not at all regarding superficial Ornaments, endeavouring only to excel each other in Vertue, Modesty, Eloquence, Musick, and such like Female Graces, that are Ornaments to the Mind, as well as to the Body. We have no Rising by five a Clock of a Sunday Morning, to get to Church by eleven ; no borrowing Jewels upon a Ball-Night, to tempt the Butterflies to attack the Honey-pot ; no costly Dresses for new Intrigues, to the Wife's Scandal and the Husband's Ruin ; no proud lascivious Lady to cry Foh at another, when herself is just going to commit Adultery. In short, our Women of all Degrees, tho' they are commonly beautiful, yet they are very chast, notwithstanding their Garments, as well as those of the Men, are so very transparent, that, were not the principal Covering lin'd with Mulberry-leaves, the Scepter of *Priapus* and the *Mount of Venus* would be almost as visible through our Cobweb-Veils, as any other Indecency, through a pink'd Fan, or a wanton Eye through the Mask of a Harlot. Yet both Sexes deport themselves with such awful Modesty, that we behold each others Beauty with an innocent Admiration, without desiring to unfold the sacred Tiffany, 'till the Laws have granted us a mutual License to enjoy nuptial Felicity.

Bless'd is such Vertue, that can curb Desire,
And, free from Lust, sweet Beauty's Charms admire ;
Yet, when they're licens'd to enjoy the same,
Can say their Love, but never cool their Flame.

CHAP

CHAP. V.

Of the Inhabitants in general, and their Arts, Trades, and Occupations.

OF all Arts and Sciences amongst us, Physick and Musick are held the most venerable, and for these two Reasons : In the first Place, every Body's Life is so extreamly happy, and all that conduces to human Felicity, so easily come by, that all Men are equally unwilling to refign so pleasing a Certainty, for a doubtful Futurity ; so that if a melancholy Fume does but happen to eclipse the natural Chearfulness of any One's Temper, I am presently sent for, to administer some of my Golden Pills, and a Dose or two of my *Chear-up*, which either recovers them presently to their former Spritelinefs, or if the Patient continues but one Hour after in a Fit of the Dumps, we certainly give him over as a dying Victim to the fatal Conqueror. Therefore the Dread of Melancholy, and the Fear of Death, makes them adore their Physicians as their Life's Safe-guard, and so much the more, because they have but three in the whole Island, Dr. *Diet*, Dr. *Quiet*, and Dr. *Merryman* : The first corrects the Patient's Food, and prescribes him Rules to eat by ; the second lulls him to sleep by an emphatical Repetition of some drowsy Poetry of his own writing, which he always uses inftead of Poppy-water ; and when the Patient wakes, then my self administers a Dose of my Golden Pills, and a reviving Thimble-full of my Cordial *Chear-up* ; and if these Methods will not raise his Spirits above the Depression of Melancholy, which is the only Diftemper we are here subject to, then he must even follow the Steps of his Fore-fathers ; for it is not in the Power of human Art to respite him from Eternity.

Secondly,

Secondly, The principal Reaſon why Muſicians
are as much worſhipp'd as Owls among the *Egypti-
ans*, is, that ſince all the Comforts of Life are hand-
ed to us by Nature, without the leaſt Aſſiſtance of
our own Labour, we have nothing elſe to do, beſides Eating, Drinking, and Sleeping, but to fidle
away our Time, ſing, dance, laugh, and be merry:
So that if a Man has but a tunable Nack upon any
Inſtrument, tho' it be but the *Jews-trump*, he ſhall
be as much reſpected and admir'd, if he does not
want Entreaty, as ever *Tubal Cain* was for playing
a Madigral upon his Cockle-ſhells. So that the
only Artiſts that are valuable among us, next to
Phyſicians, are Fidlers, Pipers, Singers, Dancers,
Rimers, and Punſters, tho' the laſt is forc'd to be a
Lacquey to the former, by the Cuſtom of the
Country, and to carry the great Crowd, becauſe
we are all of an Opinion here, that Punning much
better becomes a Fidler's Boy, than it does his Maſter.

We had a Theatre, and a Company of Comedi-
ans for a little Time, but they were always quarrelling about their Miſtreſſes, or who ſhould have
moſt Wages; ſo we furniſh'd 'em with a large Ca-
now, and turn'd 'em out of the Iſland.

We have very few Handicrafts among us, beſides
thoſe who make our Muſical Inſtruments, and they
grow ſuch lazy Rogues, becauſe they live in Clo-
ver, that we are often forc'd to put a Neck and a
Bridge to one of my *Clear-up* Runlets, and ſtring
it up for a Treble Viol, and to make a homely
Shift with a Bow and a Bladder to play our Tho-
rough Baſes on; yet, we are always as well pleas'd
with our Muſick, as you can be with the harmoni-
ous Neighings of your *Italian* Geldings; for whoever here finds the leaſt Fault, or ſhews himſelf diſ-
contented upon any Occaſion, immediately forfeits
his Reſidence, and is baniſh'd the Iſland.

Our Dancing-maſters have more Buſineſs among
our young Ladies, than they can well turn their
Toes

Tees to, tho'they never receive any Reward, above Thanks, for their Labour ; for every thing here is so plenty without Money, that they need as little Pay as they can possibly deserve ; but if any one, by Chance, be catch'd kissing a Scholar, he must patiently suffer his Heels to be par'd, that he may never dance afterwards, or else he must be forc'd in twenty four Hours to depart the Country ; for it is wisely consider'd, that nothing can be a greater Interruption to the Content of Parents, than to have their Daughters debauch'd by those very Miscreants, who have the Confidence to undertake to teach them Breeding ; nay, some are apt to think it carries along with it such a heinous Piece of Treachery, that a Man deserves to be gelt for.

If, in strict Justice, a deceitful Friend
Deserves a Jayl, that tricks me when I lend ;
What must he merit, who his Trust betrays,
Deflow'rs my Child, and robs me of my Ease ?

CHAP. VI.

Of our Laws, and Methods for the Dispatch of Justice.

WE have but one Court of Judicature, no Juries, and but one Judge, who has an absolute Power, without the Circumscription of any Law, to determine all Matters, *Coram Judice*, according to the best of his own Judgment, which he is bound to do upon the first Hearing, without any Delay. *Astrea* like, he is always blindfold when he sits upon the Bench, to prevent Corruption, that he may neither be affected with the Deportment of one Man, or offended with the homely Figure or clownish Behaviour of another, so as to be inclin'd to any manner of Partiality ; nor

does

does he ever hear with more than one Ear at a Time ; for as foon as the Plaintiff begins to fpeak, he always ftops the other, and referves it for the Defendant. Every Perfon here is not only fuffer'd, but under an inevitable Neceffity of pleading his own Caufe, for we have no fuch Things as old mufty Cuftoms, Precedents, or ancient intricate Rules, lock'd up in a barbarous obfolete Language, to puzzle Juftice, delay Judgement, and make Right a Difficulty ; for which Reafon we have no Occafion for thofe nimble-tongu'd Divers into Querks and Quidities, call'd Lawyers : Tho', fome Years fince, our Court admitted of two Orators, one for the Plaintiff, and the other for the Defendant, but in a little Time they had like to have fet the whole Ifland by the Ears ; fo that being found a Nufance, One, who was the greateft Incendiary, was decently tuck'd up upon an o'd Crab-tree, and the other prefently after dy'd for Fear ; fo that ever fince the Inhabitants have been reftor'd to their ancient Content, and every one has the Liberty in plain Words to exhibit his own Cafe, and his Witneffes the Priviledge of fpeaking freely, without being banter'd either out of the Truth, or out of their Senfes ; and that no Man, in any wife, fhould have the Advantage of his Adverfary, we fuffer no Learning above Writing and Reading, to be taught among us ; by which Means we preferve our Peace, prevent the Growth of Blockheads, and defend our ancient Conftitution from all manner of Innovations : Nor indeed is our Court of Judicature troubled with any Matters of Debt, becaufe all Perfons live fo plentifully here, that no Man has Occafion to borrow any thing of his Neighbour : Nor have we any Difputes about Titles of Eftates, becaufe every Man has more than himfelf or his Family knows well what to do with ; fo that moft of our Controverfies are about the Difturbance of our Peace, by warm Words between Neighbours, or accidental Contentions between Man and Wife ;

which,

which, as they happen but seldom, are always punish'd with the utmost Severity, least others should
be corrupted by their evil Example, and the Content of our Island be unhappily impair'd. The Loss
of the Tongue, or perpetual Banishment, are the
usual Sentences pronounc'd by the Judge upon such
Offenders ; which terrible Dooms are never super-
seded upon other Terms than an humble Submission,
an open Penance, a sincere Repentance, and a
publick Recantation : So that notwithstanding
Judgment, if the Convict can find Sureties for his
due Performance of the aforesaid Articles, he is a-
gain restor'd to his former Liberties. From whence
you may observe, that our greatest Severity is not
without Mercy.

He that is truly sad for his Offence,
Merits Compassion by his Penitence ;
And want of Mercy, all good Men agree,
Turns human Justice into Tyranny.

CHAP. VII.

Of our Marriages.

AS we have but little Occasion for either Money or Huswifry, so the only Gifts, Graces,
and Acquirements, that we value in a Woman,
are, Beauty, Modesty, and a charming Excellency
both in Musick and Dancing ; and the higher Perfection she happily enjoys in these amorous Induce-
ments, the greater Fortune we esteem her, and respect her accordingly : And in Regard that Woman was the last most excellent and beautiful Work
that crown'd the whole Creation, we give them
the Precedency in all Cases, excepting Family-Go-
vernment : They chuse first, eat first, drink first,
go to Bed first, and have a peculiar Liberty in dif-
                                                    covering

covering their Affections, without incurring thereby the least Scandal or Reflexion ; for which Reason, Men never addres 'em as in other Countries,
or tire their Ears with impertinent Courtship, but
always leave them to their own Choice : Which extraordinary Priviledge, no Parent has Power to deny any Daughter, when she is fully arriv'd at the
Age of fifteen. And the Method that they use to
signify their Liking to the happy Person that they
honour with their Love, is in Manner following,
viz. The enamour'd Damsel, when she has pitch'd
upon her Man, knits with her pretty Fingers an
artificial Ring of her own Maiden Hair, which she
sends wrap'd up in a white Paper, whereon is in-
scrib'd her own Name very fairly written, and in
what Grove she intends to be walking the next
Day, with some of her Relations. If the Receiver
of the Present be no ways pre-engag'd, and ap-
proves her for his Bride, he keeps the Token, and
tearing out a Mulberry-Leaf from the Lining of
his fore Garment, sends it back to the Lady in a-
nother Piece of Paper, wherein he signifies his kind
Acceptance, and that he will certainly meet her at
the Place appointed ; but if he dislikes the Proposal, he returns the Present by the Bearer, which is
look'd upon here to be the highest Contempt that
can be put upon a Virgin, without he is able to
excuse himself by some substantial Reasons. But
if they happen to meet, the Match is made up upon their first Conference, and the Time is appointed by the young Lady for their Marriage, which is
always thus conditional, viz. That if at any Time
hereafter, for Reasons known to themselves, they
shall both jointly agree upon an absolute Separation, they may both come together, and with one
Accord signify their Consent so to part before the
Parson that marry'd 'em. The same Priest or his
succeeding Incumbent in the same Parish, having
a lawful Power, without farther Contest, to pro-
nounce an utter Separation ; so that either shall have
the

the Freedom of wedding new Spoufes, to their
farther Satisfaction ; and in Cafe of Children, who
are never here thought burthenfome, by Reafon of
our Plenty, the Boys always go with the Man, and
the Girls with the Woman. Without this Liberty, we fhould never be able to preferve the Content of the Publick, which has ever been efteem'd the
higheft Bleffing of our peaceful Ifland ; for nothing
feems more unreafonable here to the wife Confer-
vators of our happy Conftitution, than that Man
and Wife fhould be forc'd by a Law to live together, contrary to their Wills, in perpetual Difcord,
when both might propofe to enjoy afunder undifturb'd Felicity, or to match themfelves fo comfor-
tably a fecond Time, that neither fhould hereafter
find any Caufe of Repentance. Befides, 'tis to this
excellent Cuftom of willing Separation, that we
principally owe the Vertue or our marry'd Women,
and the Continence of their Husbands ; for knowing, that when they are weary of one another,
they may part by Confent, makes the matrimonial
Shackles fit the eafier without galling, and caufes
both Sides to confider, if they fhould bring themfelves under Scandal by any libidinous Practices,
during the firft Marriage-Contract, that if ever
hereafter they fhould fo far difagree, as to be willing to part, no Body would be fo mad to truft
either Man or Woman a fecond Time, who had
fo infamoufly broken their former Covenant ; fo
that we have no marry'd Women that run one
Way with their Gallants, whilft their Husbands
fteal another with their lip-licking Harlots ; no
Courtiers at the Tails of our Citizens Wives and
Daughters, whilft titular Coufins are revenging
the Wrongs done to their finer Ladies. In fhort,
we are a very happy People, not at all addicted to
either Pride, Luft, or Avarice; and tho' any Man
and his Wife may part at Pleafure, if both are
confenting, yet they are generally fuch mutual Lovers of each other, that its feldom put in Practice.

C   Since

Since Love can only make a nuptial Life
Sweet to the Husband, pleasant to the Wife,
When that's declin'd, 'tis hard they should be forc'd
By Law, against their Wills, to live accurs'd.

CHAP. VIII.

Of our Sports and Recreations.

THOSE Sports among us, that are most innocent, are always best belov'd, and account-
ed the most noble ; nor are we at all addicted to
Hunting, Fowling, or Fishing, because we hold
it sinful to make a Pastime of the Life, or to delight in the Blood of any Manner of Creature ;
nay, some are so conscientious, that they will not
venture to play a Game at Push-pin, for fear by
Accident they should prick their Neighbour's Fingers, yet we allow of lawful Sports and Recreations upon the Sabbath-day, but then they are such,
that can no Ways be offensive either to God or
Man, as Consorts of Musick in our Woods and
Groves, floating upon our Rivers in our Canows
and Barges, grave Dancing in our Meadows, without Noise or Disorder, and the like ; and the main
Reason why we grant these Liberties after divine
Service, are, *viz.* That we have no Intriguing to
divert our Quality, few Taverns, and no Coffee-
houses to refresh our Citizens, no Bawdy-houses to
entertain our Youth, no Brandy-Bottles and To-
bacco for our Ladies Closets, neither Sots Holes or
Ale-houses for drunken Porters and Carmen. Therefore we think it but reasonable to tollerate what's
harmless, since our Government gains nothing by
the Sins and Vices of the People. Cards we look
upon to be Witchcraft, and Dice Devilism ; for
which Reason, the Use of both are very strictly
pro-

prohibited, left Gaming fhould fill our Ifland with
that hell-born Retinue which it always draws after it, *viz.* Curfing, Swearing, Cheating, Avarice,
and Contention, fuch diabolical Attendance that
would prove very deftructive to our peaceable Conftitution. We have no Horfes upon our Ifland,
nor indeed Occafion for any ; but inftead thereof,
we have a tame pretty black Animal, with a white
Lift down his Back, that, as to our Pleafure, does
us the fame Service. He is very gentle, yet very
fwift of Foot, about the Bignefs of an Afs, but
rather fnap'd like a Buck, and is fo towardly a Pad,
that we ride him without a Bridle. When we are
once mounted, bid him walk and he'll walk, trot
and he'll trot, run and he'll gallop; and is fo wonderful a Creature of that inherent Docibility, that
we can bring him to fetch and carry, jump over
a Stick, or fwim after a Duck with a Rider upon
his Back, as well as a Spaniel. The common Name
of this Animal, is, an Errandeer, fo call'd, I fuppofe, from his Swiftnefs, and his Shape, being fomewhat like a Stag in Body, and always employ'd
upon fuch Bufinefs, that requires fpeedy Difpatch.
Upon thefe ferviceable Creatures we often take our
Recreation out of our great Cities, among the diftant Villages, founding our Horns and Trumpets
along the Roads as we pafs, with all the chearful
Magnificence that can add Pleafure to our Progrefs. Thus we ramble round the Country, to vifit our Friends and Relations, twice every Year,
and when we have enjoy'd one another in moderate Drinking, Mirth, Mufick, and Dancing, we return Home to our Families, without the Care of
Bufinefs, and by the Charms of our Wives, and
the Sweetnefs of our Children, ftill continue our
Alacrity, and preferve our Content. Our next Enjoyment, is, a familiar Converfation with our a-
micable Neighbours, which we daily renew under
the Shade of our own Vines, and fometimes at the
Tavern, but are always careful of thefe theer Mif-

chiefs,

chiefs, *viz.* Talking to an Uneasiness, Jesting to
Prophaneness, and Drinking to Excess; so that
we have no obscene Discourses, that begin with
Bawdy, run into Blasphemy, and end with Religion; no wrangling about Government, or Disputes upon Matters which none of us understand;
no factious Cabals, to propagate Sedition, or undermine the Church ; no quarrelling about our Sanctity, to give our Adversary, the Devil the better End
of the Staff; no politick Projects, to sell our Country's Welfare to the Avarice of our Superiors; no sinister Inventions, to make nineteen Parts of our Kingdom mere Slaves to the twentieth ; no Party-Divisions, to occasion our Fools to contend about Shadows, whilst we lose our Substance. In short, we
are an amicable People, who, together and apart,
study our King's Ease, the publick Safety, and our
own Happiness. We never privately promote inte-
stine Discords, and consecrate the Subtilty, by openly
recommending Peace, Love, and Unity ; so that
indeed our Sports are innocent, our Recreations delightful, and all our merry Meetings, which are
only upheld for the Advancement of Harmony,
are so well regulated, that nothing passes through-
out our whole Conversation, but what is joyful at
the Present, and sweet in the Reflexion; and the
principal Reasons why we live so secure in this State
of Felicity, are these, *viz.* We are unanimous in
our Devotion, have but little Preaching, and that
orthodox, and are neither plagu'd with either po-
lemick Pamphlets, or deceitful News-Papers.

Where e'ery factious Scribbler is allow'd
To vent his Whimsies, to corrupt the Croud,
And preaching K——s in Alley-Pulpits vend
Their wicked Nonsense. Discords have no End.

C H A P.

CHAP. IX.

Of our Religion and our Clergy.

IN Matters of Faith, we have but one entire O-
pinion, which, without Scruple, is univerſal a-
mong us ; and the nominal Symbol which our
Church bears, is, the Church of Peace, and the
general Appellation by which her Sons are diſtin-
guiſh'd, *viz.* The Brethren of Content. In Affairs Eccleſiaſtical, we are under the Government
but of one Biſhop, and he a true Friend to the
Church, fearing, if we had more, they ſhould diſpute their Seniority, and perplex the Church with
their contentious Wrangles, to the Hurt of her
Community ; ſo that the whole Iſland, it being
but ſmall, is happily reſolv'd into one Biſhoprick :
Nor is any Man choſen into this ſacred Authority,
'till he has given the whole Nation, by his exem-
plary Life, ſufficient Teſtimonials of his extraordinary Wiſdom, ſincere Piety, and unſpotted Integrity ; ſo that whoever is inveſted with this holy
Dignity, is always reverenc'd by the whole People, as a *Moſes* or an *Aaron.* His higheſt Care, is,
to preſerve the Church upon her ancient Foundation, in Love and Unity, and to be watchful and
diligent in ſupplying the Iſland with a peaceable,
knowing, and diſcreet Clergy, ſuch as are qualify'd by their Lives, as well as their Doctrines, to
teach the People their Duty. Nor are they ever
ſuffer'd to adorn their Eloquence with unintelligible Sentences, or abſtruſe Terms, borrow'd from
the Froth of foreign Languages, but are ſtrictly o-
blig'd to be as familiar in their Pulpits, as they are
in their Parlours, all of us agreeing, it is the Buſineſs of our Guides not to puzzle, but inſtruct their
Congregations ; for we are never affected with me-
taphyſical Redomantado's, or apt to admire, like
othe_r

other Nations, what we do not underſtand. Our
Creed and our Worſhip are ſtrictly conſonant to
the Scriptures, and the Preaching of our Clergy
never diſſonant to our Creed. We univerſally approve of divine Muſick in our Churches, as a
ſweet and comfortable Means to elevate ur Souls
in the holy Service of Almighty God; and ſhould
a Man among us but intimate his Averſion to
ſuch heavenly Harmony, he would be lock'd upon as a Brute, without a rational Soul, and unworthy to be admitted into the Houſe of Prayer.
We never enter into the holy Door, but with a
profound Humility, and are all ſo unanimouſly
ſincere in our Devotion, that we think it a Contempt to the divine Majeſty, to ſhew a roving Eye,
or a diſſettl'd Countenance; ſo that none come to
Church, but with a ſincere Intention to perform
their Duty, and in their Looks and Actions to expreſs that Reverence which is highly becoming of
ſo ſolemn an Occaſion. We have no ogling between intriguing Ladies and their amorous Gal-
iants; no ſtudy'd Geſtures, languiſhing Deport-
ments, or bewitching Glances, to excite the Wanton to polute the Temple with adulterous Inclinations; no coming to Church out of Pride, inſtead of Piety, much rather to ſhew the Fineneſs
of their new Apparel, than the Sincerity of their
Devotion; no hiding of female Faces with pink'd
Fans, in the Interim of Prayer, when all the Time
of their pretended Sanctity, they are peeping thro'
the Holes to examine the Faces of the young Gentlemen; no kneeling down with a luſtful Heart,
and an hypocitical Countenance, ſquinting one
Eye at Heaven, and the other at a Lover; no Aſ-
ſignations in the Church-Porch, where to meet
and be wicked after divine Service; nor are we e-
ver troubl'd with tender Conſciences, who are for
ſtripping the Prieſt of his Benefice, as well as his
Surplice, the Church of her Rites and Ceremonies,
the Chancel of its Plate, the Steeple of its Bells,

and

and God's holy Houſe of its Harmony. In ſhort,
we are a People that abominate Pride, love U-
nity, and hate Diſſention, and that ſhew no more
Zeal in our Looks, than what is viſible in our Practices ; we never pray aloud in our Parlours, and
cheat the World in our Shops, heap Calumnies
upon the Innocent, and protect our guilty Brethren, oppreſs our Country, to gratify our Ambition, over-power Truth with notorious Falſities,
or prefer the windy Froth of proud, illiterate Dun-
ces, to the ſound Doctrine of pious, learn'd, and
reverend Inſtructors ; nor do we ſuffer any Man
to aſcend the Pulpit, but ſuch as are truly worthy
of ſo divine an Office, or ever permit the ſacred
Function of the Prieſthood to be mimick'd in Holes
and Corners by Apes, Monkeys, and Baboons, who,
like Quacks and Mountebanks, have no Way to
gain the good Opinion of Fools, but by railing on
their Stages at the true and able Phyſicians ; ſo
that by the extraordinary Care of our Church-Go-
vernors, we are always preſerv'd in ſuch peaceable
Unanimity, that we have not ſo much as one Fanatick among us, to diſturb the Quiet of our
Iſland.

Where one Religion is preſerv'd entire,
It does the Flock with peaceful Minds inſpire;
But where contending Churches are advanc'd,
Deſtructive Feuds by Zeal are countenanc'd.

CHAP. X.

Of our civil Government.

WE eſteem it our great Happineſs, that we are
under the Government of an hereditary Monarchy, which, by the Bleſſing of Providence, has
been long preſerv'd among us, without any Interruption :

ruption : Nor have we any Tradition that gives
us an Account of either Faction, Commotion,
Rebellion, or Revolution, that ever happen'd fince
the firft Settlement of a King over us, who (according to our beft and trueft Hiftories, our old
Ballads, which have been fung down from one Ge-
neration to another) was a good old Gentleman,
who forfook his native Country, with his Children, Friends, and Relations, to fave their Lives
in a Time of Rebellion and Cruelty, when their
Prince was murder'd, the Conftitution torn in
Pieces, Religion made a Mock of, their Eftates fe-
quefter'd into the Hands of Traytors, and the whole
Kingdom painted of a fanguine Complexion, with
the Blood of the Loyal. 'Twas in thefe Times of
Trouble, when there was no other Profpect, but of
Mifery and Deftruction, that our firft King and
Governor, with his whole Family, put themfelves
on board a large Veffel they had bought, and rather chofe to truft themfelves to the Mercy of un-
bridl'd Winds, and the tempeftuous Ocean, than
to the ruder Malice and more ungovernable Rage
of a poyfon'd Rabble, and a fanatick Enemy, who
were made the Inftruments of God's Juftice upon
a finful Nation. When thus embark'd, by the
Help of a Pilot, and fome few Sea-men, they put
out to Sea, where they rov'd for many Weeks under the Protection of Providence, in order to difcover fome uninhabited Country, wherein they
might propofe to live fecure and free from the Tyranny and Oppreffion of fuch inhuman Monfters
as they had left behind them. At length, when
driven to great Hardfhips, thro' the Scarcity of Provifions, good Heaven, in Compaffion to the diftrefs'd Wanderers, fteer'd their Bark in View of
this our fruitful Iſland, who failing round it, and
judging, by the Want of Towns upon the Beech,
it was uninhabited, they ventur'd to caft Anchor
in a commodious Bay, and hoifing out their Boat,
came a-fhore, as it happen'd, in the moft pleafant

Part of the whole Country, where uncultivated
Nature was so very exuberant, that upon their firſt
Entrance, they found every Thing needful for the
Support of Life in a peaceful State of uncontroul-
able Felicity ; for they ſoon perceiv'd, by the Wild-
neſs of the Woods, the Want of paſſable Roads,
and the rude Appearance of every Thing they met
with at their Landing, that they were in no Danger from any prior Inhabitants, except wild Beaſts,
and againſt thoſe they were well arm'd and guarded; ſo that being pleas'd with the Climate, com-
forted by the Products, and delighted with the
Country, they were all highly ſatisfy'd with what
Providence had allotted them, and unanimouſly
reſolv'd to thankfully enjoy the peaceable Poſſeſſion of their new Land of *Canaan* ; and for the
better ſecuring of their farther Happineſs, they
thought it neceſſary to agree upon ſuch a Form of
Government, as might preſerve hereafter their grow-
ing Community from thoſe fatal Troubles and
Diſorders, which had caus'd them to forſake their
native Country. After a ſhort Conſultation of
the wiſeſt Heads among 'em, an abſolute Monarchy, without any Limitation, was determin'd as
the beſt, becauſe they had too lately obſerv'd the
miſerable Confuſions from whence they had withdrawn, were all undiſputably owing to the Pride,
Folly, and Madneſs of a ſtubborn, hot-headed
Senate, who pretended to have Share in the Government. Therefore they were reſolv'd to prevent the like Miſchiefs ariſing in their new Kingdom from the like Cauſes, and thought it much
ſafer to truſt to the Mercy, Wiſdom, and Conduct of one good Man, than to the Heats, Facti-
ons, and Whimſies that might happen to ariſe a-
mong many hundreds. Accordingly the good old
Gentleman, who was the Father of the Family
he had deliver'd out of Slavery, took upon himſelf the ſovereign Authority ; and being anointed
King, under God, by his own Chaplain, aſſum'd

D   the

the Name of *Philodespot*, from his being a true Lover of his injur'd Master. No sooner was he climb'd into his new regal Seat, but he wisely proceeded to settle the Government upon a lasting Foundation, and to order every Thing to the unspeakable Joy and Satisfaction of his Subjects, who were so highly pleas'd with the discreet Management and Princely Conduct of their new King *Philodespot*, that they began to esteem Loyalty as the chiefest Vertue, and greatest Obligation, that ought to be regarded by so happy a People, who found themselves now so absolutely free from all Cruelty and Oppression, and suddenly advanc'd into such a State of Felicity, that they reverenc'd their Royal Patriot as a *Solomon* for his Wisdom, and a *David* for his Goodness, since his only Care and Ambition, were his own just Glory, and his Subjects Happiness. From the sacred Loins of this venerable Prince, descended that wise and peaceable worthy *Philodespot* the IId, who did not only inherit the Throne, but the Vertues of his Father, under whose Government the Content of the Publick still flourish'd above twenty Years, without the least Interruption, 'till, as he had reign'd in Comfort, he expir'd in Peace, and was happily succeeded by his Royal Son, *Philodespot* the IIId, our present Sovereign, a Prince of that matchless Piety, serene Temper, unspeakable Lenity and Goodness to his People, that he would sooner suffer himself to die a Martyr, than to sacrifice the Peace and Welfare of his Subjects, upon any other Terms, than their own Security ; insomuch, that we think our selves, under his excellent Government, the happiest People in the Universe. He has no Flatterers about him, to make their own Markets, by raising and fomenting groundless Fears and Jealousies ; no ambitious Upstarts, to swell their own Fortunes by Fraud, Treachery, and Oppression, but guides the Reins with so much Wisdom and Moderation, and is obey'd in all Things

with

with so much Zeal and Loyalty, that it is impoffible to determine which are the moft happy, the
Prince or the People.

Where the King's juft, and Loyalty prevails,
No Nation of a happy Union fails :
But, where the People from the Prince divide,
They're always curs'd for their rebellious Pride.

CHAP. XI.

Of our Courtiers and our Quality.

NO Perfon is dignify'd or diftinguifh'd here upon any other Account, than for their Wif-
dom, Piety, and Vertue ; and when any of their
Heirs fhall be found wanting of thefe excellent
Gifts and Qualities, their Honour ceafes, and their
Titles are forfeited : Nor are they longer reverenc'd
by the humbler Crowd, than they can fupport their
Merits, not by Art, but by Action, far above the
Level of the common People ; nor are they ever
admitted into publick Authority, 'till they have
given fuch Evidence of their fingular Perfections,
that neither King nor Country have the leaft Reafon, from any vitious Habit, to doubt of their
Integrity ; and if ever they are detected in any e-
vil, Practice between Prince and People, they are
prefently dipt into a Fat of Honey, like a Wick
into Tallow when you make a Candle, then ty'd
in a Wood with their Back to a Tree, that they
may be tickl'd to Death with Bees, Wafps, and
Mufchetoes ; fo that Great Men here, as well as
our Ladies, are wifely careful to be as juft as *Aftrea,*
as vertuous as Nuns, and as pious as Bifhops, and
by the Strictnefs of their Lives, are a great Encouragement to the whole Ifland to follow their Example. If they are proud, covetous, or imperious,
the King defpifes 'em, and the People laugh at

D 2   'em ;

(28)

'em; if they are wanton, vitious, or immoral, we put them into a Pest-house, for fear the wicked Contagion should spread it self thro' the Kingdom, and if they carelesly give the Publick any Testimonies of their Folly, they are divested of their Honour, degraded with a Fool's Cap, a Muckender, and a Slabbering-Bib, and doom'd to be Merry *Andrews* to our travelling Mountebanks. Therefore all our Quality are so very circumspect in their Lives and Practices, and so cautious and exact in the Management of their Posts, and the Execution of Authority, that we never hear of the publick Money being told over a Grid-Iron, or of a crafty Upstart's getting an Estate by cozening our Government, but all Persons here are well content with a bare Sufficiency to support themselves in their Stations, and never seek to improve their own Fortunes, by the Oppression of others : Nor have we any Minions here rais'd above their Merits, for sly Chamber-Practices, officious watching at the Door of Iniquity, or smuggling prohibited Commodities; for our Petticoat Quality are all so wonderful vertuous, that a new-marry'd Lord may go a Progress for twelve Months, and leave his Lady behind him, without the Danger of a Beau-Rival, a spurious Heir, or losing one Jewel out of his Bride's Casket. We have no strong-back'd Sicophants, who set up for Men of Breeding, to play at Cards among our Ladies ; no Sir *Foplin Flutters*, to idolize the Charms of a lascivious Countess, or to sublevate her Fringes to administer Titulation to her itching Honour ; no Curtizans at Court, to riggle their wanton Tails into the Royal Favour of our King, that they may betray the Secrets which they gain by their Levity, to those who better please 'em, by diving farther into their lustful Embraces ; no Stallions at large Stipends, or Concubines in high Keeping ; no Bawds of Title, or fawning Pimps in their own lacquer'd Coaches ; no Junks of Quality to adorn our Churches of a Sunday, that they may

gild

gild their Vices with their hypocritical Sanctity,
and cover their six Days Shame, with their se-
venth Day's Devotion. In short, we have no
promiscuous Venery among our High and Mighty, but every Great Man puts his little bald Stone-
horse into his own Stable, and every Lady takes
Care to shut the Stable-door in her Lord's Absence,
that no intruding Stallion may rival her *Bucephalus*
in his lawful Enjoyments ; so that our Ladies live
without the Fear of Shame, and our Lords without the Danger of Cuckoldom.

In Courts, where Vertue shines among the Great,
It awes the Publick, and adorns the State :
But, where the Guides and Leaders, to their Shame,
Persue their Lusts, the Frape will do the same.

CHAP. XII.

Of our foreign Trade and Commerce.

WE are such great Enemies to superfluous Com-
plements, and unnecessary Ceremonies, that
we are utter Dissenters to all that troublesome
Cringing and Scraping, which the over *Frenchify'd*
Fools of some Nations account the highest Breeding ; therefore, to prevent Foppery, instead of Po-
pery, coming in amongst us, our Government will
permit us to have no Traffick with any Nation but
the *Dutch*, for these two Reasons; first, Because
they are never given to such an Excess of Breeding, as to corrupt our People with over-useful
Manners. And secondly, Because they never pro-
fess any Religion among us ; so that there is no
Danger of their introducing a new Worship, or of
drawing off Communicants from our establish'd
Church ; therefore we have no Cause to fear, that
their nice Examples will turn our Blockheads into
Beaus,

(30)

Beaus, or our Zealots into Schifmaticks. Our Ifland
is by Nature fo well fortify'd, that it is no where ac-
ceffible, but in two Places, and thofe by Art are fo well
fecur'd, that none can furprize us, but by our own Treachery; fo that the firft Time the *Dutch* came to fettle a Trade
with us, we would not fuffer them to fet a Foot upon our
Ifland, 'till they had taken a folemn Oath, that whenever they were on Shore, they fhould keep their Hands in
their Pockets, their Knives in their Mouths, and never
drink a Drop of any ftrong Liquor, 'till they return'd to
their Ships; which Articles are ftrictly obferv'd to
this Day: By this Stratagem, we keep their Fingers
from picking and ftealing, their Tongues from lying
and flandering, the thirfty Brutes from Drunkennefs,
and the Cowards from quarrelling, only he that nego-
ciates, wears his Knife in his Pocket, and has his Mouth
at Liberty; but if ever he be heard to fwear *Tonder* and
Blackfom, he then forfeits his Priviledge. Tho' we always find them a very fubtil People, yet we are as
cunning as they can be; for we never furnifh them with
any of our Commodities, but what we can fpare without impairing our Plenty, and never take any Thing in
Lieu of our Products, but what is ufeful to the Publick.
We are no fuch Fools to expect the beft of our Provifions, 'till we want it our felves, for the Sake of brittle
Dutch Earth, that's bak'd too hard for our Teeth; we
barter not our Bread for a Parcel of *Dutch* Babies, that
our Children may have the one to play with, when
they want the other to eat; we fcorn they fhould grow
rich by our Poverty, proud by our Humility, fat by our
Confumption, thrifty by our Extravagance, wife by our
Folly, and powerful by our Weaknefs. In a Word, we
are very careful that we lofe nothing by 'em, but ufe
them exactly as they would us, and deal with their High
and Mightineffes as they do with every Body, or as we
would with the Devil; fo that in the Main, we only
make 'em our Tallow-Chandlers, our Fifh-mongers,
our Butter-Boxes, our Brandy-Merchants, and the like;
and laftly, our Scavengers to carry our Rubbifh off the
Ifland; for we never fpare 'em any Thing but what
would become a Nufance, if we did not get rid of it.
Yet their Induftry makes all our Superfluities turn to a
good Account, becaufe they carry 'em into thefe foolifh
Nations, who are fo full of Pride and Vanity, that they

barter

barter their own ſtaple Commodities, for any foreign
Fipperies, that will but adorn a jointed Baby, or a Lady's Lap-dog, or give but a new Flavour to a little
warm Water. Thus we keep them at a Bay, tho' we
hold a fair Correſpondence, and never truſt them farther than we are able to manage 'em.

Now I have thus given you a Deſcription of our I-
ſland, and told you what a People we are not, as well
as what we are, I ſhall conclude with a Specimen of our
Lyrick Poetry, that you may ſee how far the Muſes
have honour'd us with their Company; and tho' we
cannot boaſt a learned Retroſpection into the profitable
Labours of old defunct Worthies, who were the Honour and Ornament of paſt Ages; yet, by the Aſſiſtance of the rhiming Goſſips, we are able to conjure
up as flouriſhing a Ballad, as ever you heard ſung at the
Porters Block in *Smithfield,* or purchas'd at *Pye-Corner, viz.*

A SONG.

WHEN fam'd Apollo, *God of Light,*
　　　And Monarch of Wits Throne,
Retires, and leaves old dowdy Night,
　　To wear her Starry Crown;
And when Favonius fans our Iſle
　　With a refreſhing Breeze,
And gently cools the fruitful Soil,
　　And rocks the lofty Trees;

We then with our Mates to our Bowers remove,
　　And with Muſick enliven our Hearts,
Sing innocent Sonnets of Friendſhip and Love,
　　Uncorrupted with flattering Arts.

Whilſt pulpy Grapes on fertile Vines,
　　In juicy Cluſters grow
Above our Heads, and with their Wines
　　Our chearful Cups o'erflow;
When Turtles murmur out their Love,
　　And coo in duſky Shades,
And drooping Boughs, that ſpread above,
　　From Damps defend our Heads;

Then

Then despising all Fraud, we meet with our Friends,
And chat o'er our jolly full Bowls,
But free from Excess, and all sinister Ends,
We chear up and quicken our Souls.

Let foreign Kingdoms wast their Store,
To make their Neighbours yield,
'Till purple Show'rs of wreaking Gore,
Manure the barren Field ;
Let Mothers weep, and Wives lament,
And wring their Hands and rave,
To see their Sons and Husbands sent
To feed the gaping Grave ;

Whilst we unoppress'd, live in Plenty and Peace,
In the Good of the Publick agree,
Have no Wolves in Sheeps Clothing to tear off our Fleece,
But from such Sort of Dangers are free.

We starve no thousands, to enrich
Or gratify a few,
And, to deceive the Publick, stretch
The Wonders that they do :
We humour not the Proud and Great,
To make our selves their Slaves ;
Nor draw in Fools, by Tricks of State,
To be a Prey to Knaves.

We honour our Prince, and take Care of our selves,
Trust none that we know would undo us ;
But wisely steer wide of those Rocks and those Shelves,
Where the Danger is visible to us.

F I N I S.